100 Days of Terror

by Larry Temple

Literary Awards

Suspense & Thriller
Chanticleer Int'l Book Awards
1st Place Winner

Readers' Favorite Book Reviews
5-stars
"100 Days of Terror is a gripping terrorist thriller
with compelling characters, a novel that will,
undoubtedly, put fans of the genre on the edge
of their seats."

100 Days of Terror
is printed by createspace.com

ISBN 978-1-5431-9624-5

100 Days of Terror

I would like to dedicate this
book to my amazing and lovely wife,
Sheryl, who makes life worth living and
to my two wonderful daughters

Special thanks to:
Mark Palony
Brian Wallenfelt
Guido Westenberg
Julie Ann Schmidt
Kara Kuykendall
Andrew Benham
Jim Ducharme
Sandy Vigen
Sara Beeson
Dave Medlin
Jen Leflar
Angela Rogers
Emily Nieters

Email contact:
100daysEmail@gmail.com

Prolog

"The most important failure was one of imagination."

"We do not believe leaders understood the gravity of the threat. The terrorist danger from Bin Ladin and al Qaeda was not a major topic for policy debate among the public, the media, or in the Congress."

"Terrorism was not the overriding national security concern for the U.S. government under either the Clinton or the pre-9/11 Bush administration. The policy challenges were linked to this failure of imagination."

———

"Dammit! We should have figured this out a week ago," he shouts.

"Don't be ridiculous – no one could have figured this out even a day ago," Spencer points out.

"No, you don't get it! They're not just trying to kill us they're trying to destroy us. They've learned we can survive the killings. We're hurt and damaged. We have moments of silence, candlelight vigils, declare never again. We build memorials. We build monuments. We honor our dead, and we move on. Now they get it, the one thing we can't survive – our own destruction," he says remorsefully.

It Begins...

Dow Jones Industrial Average
20,854.78

Nasdaq
5,681.51

19 days earlier...

Noah rolls over and lifts the phone to his ear.

"Reardon," says Spencer.

"Huh..." Reardon says confusedly.

"Reardon! Get up!"

"What?"

"Get up! Are you up?"

"OK, OK, I'm up." He slowly sits up in bed.

"Are you drunk?!"

"No, just hung over. Stop talking so loud," he pleads.

"They found your car."

"OK, so, why are you calling me so early in the morning? In fact, why are you calling me at all? Shouldn't the cops call me?"

"First of all, it's 10:45, second they called the FBI. Your car was torched," she states matter-of-factly.

"Huh? What? Why would the cops call the FBI?"

"They found a note in your car."

"I thought you said my car was torched...," his voice trails off for a moment. "How was there a note?"

"That's the weird part; the note was in a fireproof box in your trunk at the base of a collapsed power line tower in the middle of nowhere," she says trying to make sense of it all herself.

"What!?! I'm so confused," he stammers.

"Me too, all I know is McCullum said to pick you up and drive you there. I'll be at your place in 15 minutes. Meet me down front."

FBI Special Agent Noah Reardon, a sculpted, 6'1" dark haired, blue eyed, former javelin thrower, rolls back into his bed and moans as he hangs up the phone. He has long shooting pains emanating from the base of his skull reaching up over his scalp and pulling back his eyelids. This is not his worst hangover, but it is up there. Reardon's drinking problem has been out of control for over four years now. Once a rising star, now relegated to stakeouts for low level thugs and endless reams of paperwork in the New York office. His former partner, Laura Spencer, is a 5'11" former collegiate swimmer with shoulder length jet black hair always worn in a ponytail. She sat out most of her senior year thanks to a torn ligament in her shoulder. Spencer has been keeping an eye on him ever since he sunk into the bottle, but even by her standards, this is weird. Reardon is trying to collect his thoughts while he is wrapping his mind around what she said. Reardon's car was stolen 10 days ago. He is lying there with Spencer's words dancing through his head. Car ... torched ... note ... power line tower ... his head is pounding like a jackhammer on granite.

Suddenly Reardon is startled awake as he hears the buzzer being pushed repeatedly. He rolls out of bed and walks over to the intercom kicking a beer can along the way. It tings as it hits a wooden chair leg. His apartment is the stereotypical bachelor pad with stains on the furniture and carpet except he is 15 years removed from college. There are beer cans and old take-out containers strewn about the kitchen table and living room.

"What!"
"Get up you moron. I'm here!" she hollers.
"Quit shouting. OK, OK, I'll be down in five," he declares.

Ten minutes later, Reardon pops out the front door of his rundown brownstone. He is disheveled and hasn't shaved for several days. He stinks and his suit hasn't seen a hanger in weeks.

"Wow! You look horrible!"
"Please, stop shouting," he pleads as she gives him the stink eye.
"I'm not yelling," she calmly states.
"OK then, just talk softer," he urges. "So, what's this all about?"
"All I know is McCullum called me into his office, told me they found your car – burnt to a crisp - and it had a note inside."
"What's the note say?"
"I don't know and I didn't ask. McCullum handed me an address and told me to pick you up on the way. He is already en route," she explains.

Reardon and Spencer arrive at the downed power line tower just a few hundred yards from a ramshackle house in the middle of nowhere 40 miles into New Jersey. The shack is a couple miles south of a small community surrounded on three sides by the Wawayanda State Park just a half mile south of the New York state line. There are two police cars, a dark sedan, and a utility truck at the scene. Moments after they arrive, a second utility truck drives up. McCullum is talking to the officer in charge as they walk up. They can't get too close to the car because McCullum has ordered the police and utility trucks to stop and stay back at least 200 feet. The tower is a crumpled heap encasing the car, miraculously leaving it undamaged except for the fact it is now a crispy charred hulk.

McCullum has only been working in the New York office for three years. He doesn't know many details about what happened to Reardon so many years ago or what finally pushed him over the edge. However, he and Reardon have a *special agreement*, albeit a strange one. All McCullum knows is that Reardon spent three brilliant years in Afghanistan working counterterrorism and it had all gotten to him at some point. McCullum is a bull in a China shop and only cares about what his agents can do for him today and the past is a distant memory even for something that just happened a week ago.

"What the hell took you so long?" McCullum barks.
"Umm, traffic was bad," she sputters out.
"Bull! Is he hungover again?" Turning to Reardon, "Are you hung over?" Reardon begins to speak. "Never mind!"

McCullum turns to the officer.

"Get that letter again," McCullum commands, and the officer quickly reaches into the back seat and pulls out a letter in a plastic evidence bag. "Here, read this."

Dear FBI Special Agent Noah Reardon,
New York Office

It's day 10! Rise and shine, I hope this letter finds you in good spirits. Start paying close attention and you might want to start making some phone calls. I have left clues and will leave clues for 10 more days. However, after that you are on your own. But don't worry; I don't think you will need any more clues after Day 20.

Sincerely,
Your good friend

"I don't get it." Spencer says slightly exasperated as the wind whips her ponytail into her face and she hands the letter to Reardon.

"I don't get it either. Why do you think I told you to pick up this sorry excuse for an agent?" McCullum sneers at Reardon. "What does it mean?"

Reardon quickly scans the letter and looks up. "I have no idea. Day 10, yeah, my car was stolen 10 days ago, but who cares," he says earnestly.

"Why does he call you his *good friend*, and what happens after Day 20?" McCullum asks.

"I said I have no idea. What happened?" Reardon asks.

"The power to a city about two miles north of here went out at 12:01 a.m. Someone called into the power company early this morning, and they traced it to here. When they saw the car, they called the police," McCullum explains.

"How did the tower go down?" Spencer asks.

"Blow torches. The power line guys figured those two were cut at the same time and timber." McCullum adds as he points to the carcass of the tower, "I've got a forensics team on the way, so I want everyone to stay back until they check it out. Until then we just stand around here with our dicks in our hands."

McCullum may be a crude and short-tempered bastard as far as all of his agents are concerned, but he knows his stuff and does everything by the book. As McCullum is about to discover over the next several weeks, the book is getting shredded with every passing day. Reardon still remembers McCullum's first day in the office when he called a meeting to convey his warm greetings and words of wisdom to the entire team.

"Hello, I just wanted to get everyone together to introduce myself and set clear expectations. The things I value most are honesty, integrity, and hard work. I have a few simple rules, when you screw up, admit it, fix it, and move on. There aren't enough hours in the day for me to chase any of you around like a little old nursemaid trying to figure out if you screwed up on something. If you've got something to say, say it; you're not going to hurt my feelings and I don't trust people who pussy foot around. You keep all that in mind, and we'll get along swimmingly. Now get back to work."

Short and to the point, that was McCullum. He did not mince words or take bull from anyone. To his credit, McCullum was spot-on with his comments that first day. McCullum defended every agent who was forthright and worked with them to ensure they didn't make the same mistake twice. He was a great teacher and mentor in this regard. Other agents who were not as forthcoming did not last long.

Reardon walks over and slowly slumps down on the bumper of the police cruiser.

McCullum turns to Reardon and demands, "Get your sorry ass up and explain this to me!"

"I'm good here. What do you want me to say? You know as much as I do right now." Reardon explains as he holds his face in his hands.

"Tell me about your car," McCullum glares.

Reardon slowly lifts his head. "Well, some asshole gets me out of bed to ID the charred remains of my car from 200 feet away. That's pretty much the gist of it," he says through clenched teeth.

"Not now you condescending dickweed, tell me about how your car got stolen," McCullum says disgustedly.

"Well, I parked my car just around the corner from my place after getting bent for a while over at Lou's on 5th street ... or was it The Keg on 8th ... or was it..." Reardon says as McCullum interrupts.

"Hey! I don't care about what bar you were drinking at. Did you notice anyone watching you, or did anyone follow you out of the bar?"

"No, I drank until about 11:30, got in my car, and drove home." Reardon continues, "I got up the next morning and went down to drive in, and my car was gone. More accurately, I was thinking *crap* where did I park my car!"

"And..." McCullum prompted.

Reardon's head slumps down again. "Well, I walked every street for 4 blocks in every direction looking for my car. I eventually figured it must've been towed, so I grabbed a taxi and came into the office."

"So, when did you report it stolen?" McCullum presses.

Reardon looks up. "I'm getting there. So, when I got in, I start making some phone calls, but the police have no record of my car being towed." His head drops back down into his hands. "So, I just hung up and figured it wasn't in the system yet. I called back two hours later, and they still don't have it. At this point, I figured I should report it stolen. I was expecting the cops to call me back and tell me the stupid car was 5 blocks from my house."

"What happened next?" McCullum asks.

"Well, nothing. When I got home that night I went for a long walk and found nothing. I figured my car got pinched, no big deal, it *is* New York after all. Although I'm not sure who'd steal my piece of crap car." Reardon lifts his head again. He is ghostly white and feels like a semi could come slamming out the back of his skull at any moment.

"So that's it, nothing for nine days. No notes, no one following you, no strange messages?" McCullum presses.

"Nothing until our dear sweet Agent Laura here calls me and starts babbling about my burnt car, some letter, and us driving out here to God's country."

McCullum tells Spencer to drop Reardon off and meet in the office at 3 o'clock. Reardon is dismissed with a warning to sober up by the afternoon. Reardon slowly stands and walks with the slightest limp as they maneuver around a newly arrived utility truck to Spencer's car. Reardon's knee is finally starting to loosen up. The only days Reardon doesn't notice his knee is when he's hungover and his head is throbbing more than his knee.

Reardon walks into the FBI's New York field office at 3:22 and grabs a coffee. Agents are sitting in the large conference room as he saunters in and sits down. There are two large monitors in the conference room, one displaying a photograph of his scorched car with the collapsed tower and the other showing the note left for Reardon.

"About time you strolled in," McCullum continues as he looks back to the agents sitting at the table, "so whata' we know so far?"

Agent Peterson looks up from his computer. "We just got back a preliminary forensics report and there's not much so far. Some tire tracks and shoe prints. That's it. It appears the site is a hangout for local teenagers to drink, so there are dozens of tire tracks and shoe prints. The team is focusing on prints around the tower. The car was towed to the Jersey field office for analysis."

Peterson is McCullum's go-to guy for anything on a computer. He is a bookish fellow and a bit high strung at times, but he is quick and efficient.

"I want the car here by morning," McCullum demands.

"It'll be a pissing match with the Jersey field office." Peterson adds.

"The note was addressed to our damn agent. They'd better send it over. Put in a formal request, and I can fight that battle in the morning if the car isn't here." McCullum continues, "I don't like the note. I'm going to treat this as an act of terrorism until we decide otherwise. The alternate theory is that Reardon has some deranged psycho ex-girlfriend who's been waiting 20 years to torch his car because he stood her up at prom."

McCullum ponders the term *act of terrorism* just after he says it. He's flashing back to 9/11. Sixteen years ago, this would just be vandalism but now everything is viewed with suspicion. McCullum would not have even given this a second thought except for the note. Something is eating at him, but he can't quite put his finger on it. Someone was going to a lot of trouble for some reason, and he plans to dig until he understands why.

"Reardon, let's start with the note. Who do you think left the note, and why cut down a power line for 500 people in Dickweed, New Jersey?"

"No clue," Reardon replies without looking up.

Spencer interjects, "If we are assuming terrorism, then we should dig into everyone he tracked domestically starting in 2001 and then everyone he worked with in Afghanistan up to 2011."

"That'll be a crap load of names. Good luck tracking them down after all this time," Reardon exclaims.

Reardon was assigned to the domestic counter terrorism unit in 2001 just after 9/11 and worked that until 2008. Eventually he became disgusted with the inter-agency squabbling that was supposed to disappear after 9/11. Eager for a change of pace, he put in for a foreign posting as part of the agency's increasing intelligence gathering function and was posted in Afghanistan. He worked with Joint Special Operations Command (JSOC) as part of a little known and secretive alliance with the FBI. The FBI worked closely with JSOC to locate insurgents and seek out plots using the FBI's expertise in digital tracking. The FBI agents also maintained the chain of evidence for insurgents sent back to the U.S. for trial. He quickly made a name for himself in Afghanistan because of his forthright style and wit. Within a year he became team lead and worked with eight other FBI agents responsible for the region.

"How about the *Day 10* in the note, other clues, and making phone calls?" Asks an agent across the table.

"Again, no idea, I looked through my call history for any unknown numbers. I asked my super if she noticed anyone snooping around and she said there's always someone snooping. I rechecked my mail looking for anything suspicious. Nothing." Reardon retorted.

"Can you remember anyone following you or calling and hanging up?" asks an agent at the end of the table.

"Well! Now that you asked it that way, I just figured it all out!" Reardon says exasperated. "How many times can I say I have no frickin' clue?"

"Back on topic," McCullum snaps. "We get it, we have no clue, so now we need to figure it out. The part about making phone calls is really bugging me. Who the hell are we supposed to call?" McCullum paces back and forth for a few moments assessing the situation. "I want everyone to start calling field offices around the country looking for anything out of the ordinary. Peterson will assign field offices; get on the phones now. I want you to contact them before they close for the day. Start with the east coast. Now everyone get out of here. Except Reardon and Spencer, you two up here and sit!" Only the shortest of moments pass and McCullum becomes instantly impatient. "Why are the rest of you still sitting here – get!"

"Edwards, close the door on your way out." After a couple moments, McCullum sits down, "so I don't know if this is some sort of elaborate practical joke or some psycho has taken a liking to you. The one thing I do know is that I don't like someone singling out one of my agents. I want to cover all the bases. I want you two to start looking into every case you've been involved in for the last six months."

"I haven't done anything worth mentioning for the last six months. I've been on stakeouts eating cold pizza, drinking warm beer, and basically been hammered. Although you should pretend I didn't mention the warm beer and hammered part. When I'm not out there I'm in here doing more mind-numbing paperwork. I haven't testified against anyone in over nine months and no one even knows I'm watching them."

"I don't care, dig into it." McCullum reiterates. "Now get out of here."

Day 11

These things will destroy the human race: politics without principle, progress without compassion, wealth without work, learning without silence, religion without fearlessness, and worship without awareness.
Anthony de Mello

Everyone has reconvened at nine the following morning in the conference room, and McCullum is pacing as he waits for Agent Peterson. Spencer made it a point to pick up Reardon so he wouldn't be late. Reardon and Spencer are sitting near the head of the table. Peterson walks in carrying a pile of papers and sits down.

"Well?" McCullum asks.

"We contacted all 56 field offices and they contacted their resident agencies looking for anything unusual." Peterson pauses.

McCullum spurs on Peterson, "and … this isn't a date, I'm not going to make the next move. Keep talking."

"Well nothing. None of them reported anything unusual. Which doesn't surprise me. If it wasn't for Reardon's car and the note, we would've never been called for something like this. The local cops would've handled it and they would've started looking at disgruntled utility workers trying to make a point or drunken teenagers with access to a welder's torch," Peterson explains.

"Great, so we're nowhere on that front." McCullum turns, "Reardon, any luck with you?"

"We just started looking last night, and we'll need most of today to get through the files," Reardon replies.

"So, we're at square one. Is this an isolated case of some nutball torching your car and messing with you, or are we looking at some terrorist group trying to send a message?" McCullum absentmindedly states as though no one was in the room. He then turns, "Ideas?"

Everyone sits silently for a moment. McCullum hates the uncertainty, he reviewed the preliminary forensics report, but the results were inconclusive. Lots of tire tracks and shoe prints that could belong to any one of a million people. There were some fingerprints on the tower, but they most likely belonged to the teenagers who hang around the tower. The house by the tower has sat abandoned for over a year. The car was torched with gasoline, and no fingerprints on the box or note. Running down all the fingerprints is a nonstarter because if it is terrorists, they wouldn't be dumb enough to leave fingerprints. Again, McCullum thinks, who is dumb enough to cut down a tower so 500 people lose electricity for a few hours? What harm could it do? They'll have a bypass line up in hours and fix the tower within a week. McCullum is tempted to say screw it and let the locals handle it but this goes against his gut. He also sees this as a mystery, finally something he hopes Reardon will sink his teeth into. He plans to keep him involved despite his dreadful attitude. McCullum has his reasons, but he's not holding his breath. He's waited three years and expects to wait three more years if needed.

"OK, I want everyone to call back the field offices and make two points clear. One, I want to know about EVERYTHING that happens in their area. Have'em ask around and start reading the local paper. I don't care how minor, I want to hear about it. Two, if they don't, I will personally come there and rip them a new asshole. Send everything you get to Peterson. Are we clear?" McCullum states with a burning intensity. "Now get out of here. You two stay again." The door closes, and McCullum sits down and leans back as Reardon and Spencer face him. "We're about to get a dump load of useless information – anything from a cat stuck in a damn tree to some drunken teenager who burns down a convenience store while smoking some weed on his break. I need the two of you to get through your six-month backlog as quickly as possible."

"OK, but I'm telling you, we won't find anything, I haven't done dick," Reardon says.

"Well get on it, if you find a lead, I can turn off the spigot of crap that is about to start pouring in from all the field offices."

Day 17

Five days have passed and McCullum has reconvened his team *again* to review the daily list of reports that have been flooding in from the field offices. The new mind-numbing morning routine is already getting to people and they wear expressionless looks on their faces. Reardon is sitting in his chair slumped over with his head on the table. He is clearly hungover and looks like he slept in his clothes again. As predicted, they didn't find anything useful in his files. None of the people he's been watching on stakeouts even know about him. The office is getting 600-800 reports a day from the field offices and every day the team takes turns reading through the list looking for anything that might be a clue. McCullum has hardly paid any attention to Reardon over the last five days, convinced this is still some ridiculous practical joke, without the joke. The key is that he wants him in the office. He's looking for that spark. Additionally, this is clearly a crime and targeted at one of his agents. For that, McCullum gives this situation his full attention.

"OK, everyone pipe down, Peterson, what've we got?" McCullum asks as he has done for the last five days.

"Nothing much, just like yesterday, someone keyed about 100 cars at a car dealership in Nevada, three houses under construction started on fire in the middle of the night in Massachusetts, there was a 50 car pileup near Seattle after a semi jackknifed in the fog, some kids poured green dye in a water reservoir in Idaho, a crane fell over in high winds in Florida, three people died in a construction..."

"Go back..." Reardon interrupts lifting his head.

"The crane?" Peterson asks.

"No, the one before that, the green water, what have you got on that?"

"Give me a sec..." Peterson clicks away at his computer for a few moments and scans the summary report provided by the Idaho field office. "Ahh..." Another fifteen seconds click by as people quietly stare at Peterson. Peterson's head suddenly snaps up, "not much, two days ago the residents of Dillon, a small town in eastern Idaho, woke up and found green water coming out of their faucets. The police concluded some teenagers broke into the underground holding reservoir and dumped in some green dye."

"Why are they so convinced?" Reardon asks.

11

"It doesn't say," Peterson replies.

"Why that one?" McCullum asks.

"It's just strange, and again a small town, barely noticeable."

"Peterson, call them back and get the complete report."

Later in the day, McCullum calls Reardon and Spencer into his office as Peterson is standing next to the desk.

"Sit down, here is the complete report," McCullum is reviewing the file.

"Anything jump out at you?" Reardon asks.

"No, it looks like kids. It looks like they kicked in a rusted door and tagged it on the way out. Nothing special. A couple photos."

McCullum picks up a photo and slides it over to Reardon. He stops it and pulls back his hand to reveal the following letters spray painted on the door, 'NRFBOI.'

"Nurf-bo-eee what's that mean?" McCullum asks turning to Peterson. "Is that a local gang tag?"

"The report makes no mention of gang affiliation." Peterson adds.

"Never mind, I'd be surprised if Dicklick, Idaho, population 10, even has a gang." McCullum realizing he asked a ridiculous question.

"800, sir," Peterson corrects.

"Huh?"

"800, sir, the population is close to 800."

"OK, sorry and pardon me, Dickslice, Idaho, population 800."

They all stand silently looking at the photo on the desk for a moment. Spencer absentmindedly starts to say the letters in her head a few times.

"Wait a second, not, nurf-bo-eee, N-R-F-B-O-I, Noah Reardon, Federal Bureau of Investigation," Spencer suddenly says.

"Give me that!" McCullum quickly commands.

"Holy cow!" says McCullum. "Could it be that easy?"

"Well, the note did say there would be clues," says Reardon.

"It seems a little obvious," interjects Spencer.

"The needle always seems obvious when you are holding it in your hand and we have been looking through a big haystack for 6 days," Reardon says.

"Peterson, call the Idaho field office and have them check for anything else with NRFBOI," McCullum orders.

"Hand me the file," says Reardon as Peterson leaves the office.

Reardon is just sitting quietly as he contemplates the summary page of the report. He starts tapping his finger on the name of the city.

"Well, anything?" Asks McCullum.

"Give me a second ..." he continues tapping his finger "... I know this city for some reason, it seems familiar, Dillon ... Dillon ... Idaho," Reardon continues.

"Have you ever been there or close to there?" Spencer asks.

"No, I've never been to Idaho. Wait a second ... Josh. That's Josh's hometown," Reardon remembers.

"Josh who?" McCullum asks as Spencer looks confusedly at Reardon.

"Sorry, Josh O'Hara, agent Josh O'Hara, he's one of the guys who died in Afghanistan in 2011. I worked with him for three years." Reardon says, pondering the connection.

"This is too much to be a coincidence." McCullum opens his door and screams, "Peterson! Get in here!"

"Where else were they from?" Spencer asks.

"It's been so long." He sits quietly for a moment slowly leaning back in his chair, "Let's see ... ummmm ... Teri Atkinson was from Milwaukee. Jack Harrison was from some small town in northern Iowa. Henry Callahan was from Texas." He pauses for about five seconds as McCullum and Spencer anxiously wait. "And ... I don't remember for the other two," Reardon explains.

Reardon briefly explains what happened in Afghanistan and the circumstances surrounding O'Hara's death. He describes how Josh and five other agents died in an explosion along with four Afghanis in the middle of their secure compound. Reardon was just coming back to the compound and was about a quarter mile from the main gate when an explosion ripped through the compound at 8:10 p.m. Eight soldiers were also killed in the explosion.

"The explosion didn't just kill everyone, the bodies were disintegrated, and the bomb squad said they used three times the explosive they needed to use to get the job done. They figure it was left under the table in the middle of the hooch. This wasn't just a bomb. They were sending a message, letting us know that nowhere was safe. Half the bodies in the hooch were never identified." Reardon explains how they always met in their hooch at eight every night to play cards and discuss their day. He ran late that night because his conversation with an informant went longer than expected.

McCullum told Peterson to look up all the agents who died in the explosion and get their hometowns. After that, Peterson should call the field offices nearest the cities and dispatch agents to talk with local police, and tell them to look for any mysterious events over the last three weeks with NRFBOI spray painted at the scene. This was their first lead in seven days.

"And let me make myself clear, I want the agents to drive over and talk to the local police. I don't care if it's some tiny-ass town half-way to the moon," McCullum commands.

"Got it!" Peterson says as he turns to leave.

Turning to Reardon and Spencer.

"Well there's nothing else we can do tonight – you two go home. We will meet here in the morning – 9 a.m. sharp. Got it Reardon!" McCullum states coldly.

Day 18

Peterson was at the office until ten the night before working with agents from northern California; western Texas; Milwaukee, Wisconsin; northern Iowa; and Atlanta, Georgia. McCullum and Spencer are sitting in his office as Reardon walks in at 9:17. Peterson walks in right after Reardon sits down.

"OK, the only hit we have so far is Milwaukee. An office park had its gas line shut off. Several windows were broken out. By the time security opened up the building at 6 a.m. Monday morning, there was water everywhere. The pipes had frozen and burst. It was below 15 degrees the whole weekend. They estimate the damage at about $700,000. NRFBOI was spray painted on the wall by the gas meter. Police concluded it was some kids," Peterson explained.

"When did this occur?" McCullum asks.

"The security guard does a final sweep of the building on Friday night at 10 p.m. and locks the place up for the weekend. They most likely did this late Friday or early Saturday. I'm going to go out on a limb and say they did it around 12:01 a.m. Saturday morning. If that's true, this is Day 1, it happened nine days before we got the note in Reardon's car." Peterson concludes and then adds, "Agent Teri Johnson grew up just four miles from the office park."

"So, this is providing us a link between you and Afghanistan," McCullum states. "I want to dig into this deeper and track down everyone you worked with in Afghanistan."

"I agree that's a possibility, but it doesn't prove this has to lead back to me in Afghanistan," Reardon points out.

"How so?" McCullum asks.

"It wouldn't take more than five minutes on the internet to figure out the home towns of the agents who died and to track me down," Reardon concludes.

"That may be true, but we haven't got dick to go on right now. So, this is a start, at least, and could lead us somewhere. So that's where were headed," McCullum states unequivocally.

"OK, but it's going to be next to impossible tracking down people from over five years ago in Afghanistan," Reardon reminds them.

McCullum orders Peterson, Spencer, and Reardon to commit their lives to digging up old case files from his time in Afghanistan and reading every single word twice looking for clues.

Day 21

Reardon wakes up exhausted and hungover, they spent two long days in the office reading his old Afghan reports from 2008 to 2011. The two long nights started with a drinking binge. The only tangible thing they have to show for their efforts is a list of nearly 350 names, people he worked with either in passing or long-term. Every name mentioned in any of the Afghan reports was added to a master list. The list is comprised of 227 Afghanis they worked with or tracked as terrorists. The remainder are either Americans or other foreign agents he interacted with while trading intel.

Reardon finally looks at the clock and decides he had better shower. As he stands, he momentarily loses his balance, his leg tightens up and he falls into the nightstand and back onto the bed. His head begins pulsing as he takes his first step towards the bathroom. His head is absolutely throbbing by the time he enters the bathroom three steps later.

Reardon walks into the office at 9:47, and the main conference room is abuzz with activity. The wall mounted TV is muted in the background as Reardon sees footage of a burning tanker truck. Reardon walks over to an agent standing next to the table.

"What happened?"

The agent quickly looks up at Reardon for a moment and then turns to the TV.

"Three tanker trucks exploded on the highway in L.A. last night," he says.

"In an accident?"

"No, three separate locations."

Spencer sees Reardon and hurriedly walks over to him to explain what happened.

"Reardon," she says as she reaches for his elbow from behind, "three tanker trucks were stolen last night and blown up along major highways."

"How many died?"

"No one. It's all on traffic cameras. Just after midnight, the drivers stopped on the highway, turned the trucks widthwise near overpasses, got out, opened up the valves, and tossed a road flare just as they climbed down around to a car waiting for them in the underpass. Each car headed out of the city, and we lost all of them. Each tanker exploded within a minute. It all happened so fast."

"Where did they get the tankers?"

"They were stolen from a tanker depot. They fill the trucks around 9 p.m. and lock up for the night. Drivers normally show up at 4 a.m. to start their daily run."

"Any footage from the depot?"

"Yeah, all three wore hoods and masks. They cut the lock on the key box and just drove off with the tankers. They wore gloves so we won't get any prints. All we can tell is they're somewhere between five-seven and five-eleven, most likely men."

"How about the getaway cars?"

"We were able to read the plates, all out of state and all stolen."

"So, we've got nothin?"

"Not a thing so far. We're starting to look for footage along all the streets leading to the depot hoping to catch a break there. Luckily, people saw the flames and were able to stop short and back up to avoid any injuries."

Just then, McCullum approaches, "Spencer, Reardon, follow me." They exit the main conference room and enter McCullum's office.

"Well, your good friend wasn't too obvious on this one. It's day 21, and this one didn't need a stinking clue," McCullum points out.

"How long will the highways be shut down?" asks Reardon.

"The flames burned so hot they ate right through the road surface and one of the overpasses has pretty extensive damage. It will take at least three days for two highways and likely a week to check the third one and make any repairs. This is a nightmare for L.A. Each one of these highways handles about 180,000 cars per day. Their screwed-up traffic is a bigger nightmare today." McCullum says as he starts pacing.

"What a mess. At least there were no deaths," Spencer adds.

"That's a blessing and a damn conundrum at the same time." McCullum points out. "What are they up to? 21 terrorist acts and no casualties. At least no casualties that we know of because we don't even know if any other places have actually been attacked. So far, we only know about the Day 1 office park, Day 15 green dye, and Day 10 attack with your car."

"Well they're definitely sending a message this time. This is a big escalation," Spencer states as she turns to Reardon.

McCullum turns and stares blankly out the window trying to make something of this, trying to connect the dots. After a few moments a knock at the door interrupts the uneasy silence. McCullum turns and can see it's Peterson through the window slit of his door and motions him in with a slight wave of his hand.

"We just got info on the Day 17 attack."

"Where?" Asks McCullum.

"A small college in west Texas, about fifty miles from the ranch where Agent Henry Callahan grew up."

"Why the hell did it take the Texas office so long to report this?" McCullum blurts out.

"West Texas is a big place and it's a small college town. Local police figured it was just kids and would never have reported it to us unless we called."

"What did they do?" Spencer asks Peterson.

"Three buildings were broken into, and small fires were set. The sprinklers put out the flames, and NRFBOI was spray painted on walls in all three buildings. Classes were cancelled in those buildings for the day so they could clean up the mess and repair some minor damage."

"Well, I don't want to publicize the NRFBOI clues, but it won't take long for this to leak out. The quicker we announce, the quicker we might start seeing a pattern," McCullum states.

"Won't that start a panic?" Spencer says with a concerned look on her face.

"What panic? That they might get their car stolen, lose power, miss a day of school or have a commute from hell? Until today, this was really just

17

annoying for a few groups of people. I think it's time to go public. Now that we have told all the field offices to look for NRFBOI at the crime scenes, it is bound to leak, especially after today," Reardon says as he methodically sits and slumps down in one smooth motion into McCullum's guest chair.

"Get me Edison at the Hoover building. We'll need to clear this with him before we go public. Tell him I want to set up a meeting with the director and that it is related to what happened in L.A."

Two hours later McCullum finishes his call with the director of the FBI and the director is briefing the President's chief of staff. The director's aide has drafted a news release that is going out on the wire service within the hour. McCullum and his team have no idea what to expect. For now, they are keeping Reardon's name out of this and just mentioning the attackers are spray painting a message that includes the letters "FBOI". They don't want to say more than that initially fearing copycat graffiti. They are asking local police to contact their local FBI field office with information on the attacks.

Day 22

Reardon rolls out of bed at 8:27 and turns on the TV. As he sits up two beer cans clink on the floor and come to a rest at his feet. He is still wearing his clothes from the night before. He puts his head down in his hands and breathes out with a slight moan. As he lifts his head he reaches over to the two beer cans sitting on his night table stand and gives them a shake. The first one is empty, and the second one has a little bit sloshing around in the bottom. He tips his head back, drains the warm flat beer into his mouth, and tosses the can into the corner of his room where it finds a home with five other cans and an empty whiskey bottle. At this moment, he keys into what the news reporter is saying. As always, he is listening to Alicia Washburn and newcomer James Newburgh for his morning news. James only started about three months ago, but Reardon has taken a liking to his style.

> Reports are coming in from four cities today, four power substations have been destroyed leaving thousands without power. Substations outside Dodgeville, Wisconsin, west of Madison; Wellington, Kansas, just south of Wichita; Plainview, Texas, just north of Lubbock; and Forsyth, Georgia, just northwest of Macon. All had one power substation destroyed just after midnight local time. The FBI reported yesterday that there is a suspected series of attacks over the last 21 days, and the attackers have been leaving a spray painted "FBOI" at the

scene. So far, federal authorities have only identified four of the initial 20 suspected attacks and are asking local authorities to review all cases over that period which may have initially been viewed as vandalism. Up to this point there are no known injuries resulting from any of these attacks.

Reardon stands up and heads into the bathroom for a long needed hot shower. He can't even remember what time he got home last night. He remembers being in the office until eight and heading to a bar on his way home for a night cap. Reardon walks back into his bedroom with a towel around his waist and a slight limp. The hot water goes a long way to loosening up his leg but he still feels it. As he reaches into the closet for a clean shirt, the news comes back from a commercial and the initial words from Newburgh catch his attention.

A fifth report just came in from Hood River, Oregon, just over 50 miles east of Portland. Residents awoke to no power, and local authorities reported the power substation on the outskirts of town has been destroyed. Initial reports indicate a high explosive was used to knock out the substations. A local station in Dodgeville, Wisconsin, is reporting it will take at least one week to repair the damage. Residents will be without power until the damage is repaired.

Reardon flicks off the TV and begins groping around in a pile of clothes on a chair at the foot of his bed. Forty minutes later and exhausted, he walks into the office to find bedlam. People are racing all over the office. He pauses for a moment to take it all in and is wondering what has caused all the commotion. He walks over to the break area, pours a cup of hot steaming coffee, and leaves about an inch at the top. He then leans over the sink and tops it off with cold water and quickly drinks it down. He refills the cup and begins walking to the conference room. As he stares around, Peterson bumps into him and is taken aback by his appearance. He quickly regains his composure before saying, "Eight more, we have eight more," before quickly walking back to his desk. Reardon thinks, *eight more what?* As he is entering the conference room, Spencer looks over McCullum's head. McCullum notices her glance and spins in his chair.

"Well Reardon, you look like a horse dragged you half way down the street! What took you so long to get in today?" McCullum says unabashedly.
"Ahh…"
"Shut up, I don't even want to hear it!"

"Come up here and sit down a moment. We know of eight more attacks." Spencer says politely. "Since we went public, we've had over 20 calls from the field offices. We were able to confirm eight with the spray painted NRFBOI at the site of the attack., if we can really call them attacks. So far they are really just acts of vandalism."

Reardon sits down and looks at the overhead connected to Spencer's laptop. She has opened a spreadsheet with the first column numbered one to 22. The second column has a total of 14 attacks listed. Days of the week have become a meaningless concept. All they do is think in terms of what day it is now. When people ask when something happened, dates are irrelevant. They now answer Day 7 or Day 15. A new bizarre way of telling time.

Day 1 – 22 Attacks

Day	Attack
1	Office complex flooding, Milwaukee, Wisconsin
2	200 tires slashed at car dealership, Rockville, Maryland
3	
4	120 pigs poisoned, Butte, Montana
5	
6	Sewage treatment center valve closed causing backup into creek, Conway, Arkansas
7	Three power line poles cut down, Moab, Utah
8	
9	Abandoned warehouse burned down, Nashua, New Hampshire
10	Power line tower, Wawayanda State Park, New Jersey
11	
12	Three houses under construction torched, Brookline, Massachusetts
13	Cattle fence cut down, 250 cows end up wandering along highway, El Paso, Texas
14	
15	Green water in reservoir, Dillon, Idaho
16	Grocery store burned down, Clearwater, Florida
17	Three buildings on college campus vandalized, Littlefield, Texas
18	
19	
20	
21	Three tanker truck explosions, Los Angeles, California
22	Five power substations destroyed outside five mid-size cities

McCullum returns to staring at the overhead, and Reardon notices a map is now up on the wall with pins highlighting the location of each attack. Spencer looks up after a moment of contemplating the list.

"This is an escalation, the first time we have attacks in multiple cities." McCullum says, almost in passing as a disinterested bystander making a comment as though no one is listening.

"Have the analysts detected any pattern yet to the attacks?" Spencer asks.

"No, they are still working on it."

Reardon speaks up for the first time. "Are we sure these are all a match?"

"Yes, we have photographic evidence from each crime scene. We had about another dozen reports sent in, but none of those panned out. They all had some sort of graffiti, but none of them were a match." Spencer continues, "it's obvious these are all related to infrastructure, food, water, power, transportation, but none of these is significant. No deaths or even injuries. What's the point? If not for the note in Reardon's car, we wouldn't even be sitting here talking about these attacks because we would not even know about them - much less be viewing them as some grand act of terrorism. The tanker explosions in L.A. would have definitely made the news, and if not for that, it would've taken days to link the power substation explosions. The tanker explosions were a wakeup call so that everyone starts paying attention. It pushed us to go public and get it out there for everyone to see."

About halfway through Spencer's comments, Peterson walks in and leans against the wall near the doorway.

"Any more confirmed attacks?" McCullum asks.

"No sir, a few more calls but none of them match. With the five attacks today and our press release yesterday, perhaps they are looking to start a panic." Peterson states matter-of-factly.

Reardon is looking at the monitor that lists the known attacks. He sees that a fence was cut along a highway releasing about 250 cows in Texas on Day 13, and 120 pigs were poisoned in Montana on Day 4. On Day 6, a valve was closed at a sewage treatment center, and on Day 9 a warehouse was torched in New Hampshire.

"Again, what panic? Some cows wandering the highway and some dead pigs. The avian flu knocks out a few hundred thousand turkeys and chickens every year, and it barely makes the news. A torched warehouse and an overflowing sewage treatment plant is barely news, at least not national news." Reardon reiterates his point from a few days ago.

"Have you thought of anything else after reviewing all your Afghan files?" McCullum asks.

"No."

"What's your theory on all this?"

"I don't have one right now."

McCullum has reviewed the list of names from Reardon's Afghan files but not done anything with the names. As he is contemplating the day's events, he decides to pass the names along to the director with the recommendation that FBI agents in Afghanistan attempt to track down every single Afghani name on the list. Figure out which ones are alive, dead, or untraceable. He is not expecting much since that part of Afghanistan was abandoned by U.S. forces and left to the Taliban and local warlords. At this point, no agent is going to risk his life traipsing around no man's land on a wild goose chase.

People in the office are forming some strange disconnection to what's going on. Attacks are happening, but they are mostly indistinguishable from vandalism. The FBI agents looking for clues are experiencing anxiety because they now sense something is coming. Frustration builds over the lack of clues and witnesses. So far, all the attacks from the first 20 days are isolated and contained. McCullum stands up and starts pacing. After a few moments he pauses and slaps his hand down on the table.

"What the hell are they up to? This is terrorism and not terrorism. The point of terrorism is to destroy, kill, instill fear, and create chaos. For the first 20 days they were just flying under the radar until this sudden escalation. Why now, and where is this heading?"

The incongruities are already starting to eat at McCullum, terrorists carrying out subtle unnoticeable acts of terrorism. That is an oxymoron by any definition. Without the note in Reardon's car, they would not even be involved much less on the leading edge of the investigation. Again, what investigation? They have nothing meaningful. The three tanker trucks in L.A. would likely be chalked up to disgruntled former employees of the gas company or the highway department. The five power substations are clearly something, but local police departments would only be investigating them as local crimes. It would be days, if not weeks, before anyone *might* even begin to link this together.

As Peterson restlessly leans against the doorjamb, an agent walks up to Peterson and hands him a few sheets of paper. He quickly glances at them and speaks.

"We've got another one, 15 cell towers in Glendale, Arizona, just outside Phoenix."

"Blown up?" Spencer asks.

"No, someone cut the lines going up the tower with a bolt cutter and knocked out coverage for about eighteen thousand people."

"When?"

Spencer looks at the calendar on the wall and says, "This would be the Day 5 attack."

"Day 5! What took them so long to get this to us?" McCullum barks.

Peterson takes a few moments to confer with the agent, who just handed him the report, and then turns to address McCullum.

"The NRFBOI was not even part of the original police report. They only painted it on one tower, and that one was already full of graffiti. A passerby actually noticed it for the first time yesterday and called it in to the police, who then called the Phoenix field office. They just sent it to us."

McCullum continues, "This is clearly a game. They've put the game in motion to give us a head start. Why? Without these clues, the first 20 days would have gone unnoticed for weeks if not forever. The last two days would simply be viewed as a coincidence or possibly linked after a few days. But now we're looking, looking for nothing and everything. After 22 days we don't have a single stinking witness or clue other than a note in a burned up car, some video of tanker trucks blowing up, and an explosion from five years ago and half a world away that may or may not be related."

"I bet it's related." Spencer interjects.

"That's what my gut tells me too, but right now we need proof. Reardon, I want you to double check everything. Phone records. Ask people at … at *the places you hang out …*"

"You mean the bars where I drink?"

"Yes, check with people at the bars. See if they've ever seen anyone paying close attention to you."

"The people at the *places I like to hang out* don't like questions like that and aren't generally in the best condition to be making astute observations like that."

McCullum loses his temper and roars, "I don't care! Go check and take Spencer with you."

McCullum continues pacing as Reardon and Spencer head out of the room and they hear him start to bark commands at Peterson. The sound of McCullum's voice drops to a low rumble as they approach the elevators.

The two of them spend the rest of the day canvasing local bars, any bar that Reardon has frequented over the last three months. Spencer is astonished and disappointed with Reardon's knowledge of bars around both the office and his home. Only now is the extent of his drinking problem taking its full effect on her psyche. Eventually Reardon tells Spencer to go home because they come up with nothing. Reardon explains that most of the regulars won't show up until after eight, and they are the least likely to notice anything. Two minutes after Spencer leaves, Reardon is at the bar having a drink and explaining to the bartender who his cute friend is. Reardon explains it is his former partner and the relationship is purely professional. The bartender smiles and says the first drink is on him because he was able to say that with a straight face. Then he turns to serve a guy at the other end of the bar. Reardon finally stumbles home just before midnight and flops across the bed, splaying out like warm butter tossed on smoldering asphalt.

Washington, D.C.

The President's staff discusses these attacks at length but does not feel there is enough for the President to make a statement. The press secretary is grilled for a few moments and simply states the President is monitoring the situation. News agencies are providing some coverage, but it is on the backburner compared to more pressing issues like the ongoing deadlock over the budget and the recent death of a celebrity chef.

May 3, 2001 – New York

Reardon is sitting in the conference room with his team reviewing the electronic surveillance information from over the weekend. Reardon was put in charge of a mafia task force three years ago focused on money laundering. If the mafia could be commended on anything they do, it would be their ability to launder money. They have been making impressive, even revolutionary, strides in hiding and moving around money. So much so, the CIA and NSA now use similar techniques, copied directly from the mafia, to hide and disguise their secret flow of cash around the world. Reardon has never been more intrigued and fully engaged in anything in his life. His task force has managed to *trap* over $43 million in various accounts around the world over the last 12 months. His team is able to leverage international banking laws to freeze assets around the world while his team and local officials investigate the source of the funds. Over half that $43 million has been confiscated and returned to various governments.

Reardon's work has resulted in over 150 arrests in 27 countries. The team's arrest and conviction rate are nearly twice that of any other team doing similar work. His fiancée Sara is continually amazed by what he does when he describes all the new intricate ways the mafia uses to hide and move around their money. She is continually worried about his safety but figures it cannot be too dangerous to sit in an office and watch for mysterious bank transactions. She loved dinner parties where he tried to explain *what he did* to people and everyone just sat there with glazed over eyes. Sara finally convinced him to stop talking about it, explaining that no one understood what he was talking about. She loves his enthusiasm and passion for what he does. Now he simply says he works for the FBI and tries to track down mafia money.

———

Sara met Reardon six months after she moved to New York and it was love at first sight. Sara and her roommate were eating a picnic lunch in Central Park when a Frisbee flew over a hedge of bushes and landed ten feet from them. Sara got up and retrieved it just as a chiseled young man came rushing around the edge of the bushes.

"Sorry about that." Reardon comes to a jolting stop and looks up.
"No problem," she quickly says, his sudden approach caught her off guard for an instant. She stands there glancing at his glistening bare chest for just a moment. She is suddenly self-conscious of the glance and blushes. "Um, here you go."

Reardon reaches for the Frisbee. Sara is a knockout at 5'6" with green eyes and dark brown hair. Her hair is wispy, the type of hair that looks great in the morning as soon as she rolls out of bed. The exact thing her roommate Katie is insanely jealous of and would die for.

"Thanks." Sara refuses to release the Frisbee. "You can let go now."
"Oh, OK." For some reason Reardon lets go at the same moment and it drops to the ground. "Let me get that."
They both reach down simultaneously. "Ow!" They stand up rubbing their heads. "Sorry about that. I shouldn't have let go," says Reardon.

Sara's roommate is looking on in amusement. She can already tell something is going on.

"Um, hi, my name is Noah."

"I'm Sara, and this is my roommate Katie."

Reardon barely glances over, hesitant to take his eyes off Sara. Then from over the bushes, comes a booming voice.

"Hey, numb nuts, did you find the Frisbee yet?"

Reardon turns and shouts to his roommate, "Yeah, I will be there in a minute." Now it's Reardon's turn to blush. He reaches down and picks up the Frisbee. Looking into Sara's deep green eyes, "um, I gotta go." But he doesn't move and holds her gaze. "Would you mind if I called you sometime?" He gives a low bob of his head almost subconsciously tricking her into saying yes. Inside he is shocked he just said that, but it feels right for some reason.

"Um, yeah, that would be fine." She walks over to retrieve her bag, pulls out a pen, and a sheet of paper and quickly scribbles her number on the paper and hands it to him. "Here you go."

"Thanks, I'll call you." He pauses, staring deeply into her eyes for a moment, and then dashes away as quickly as he came.

"Please don't tell me you gave him your real number," Katie says.

"Yeah, I did." She still has a glinting smile on her face.

"Are you crazy? He could be an ax murderer."

"Maybe, but there is only one way to find out."

Reardon knows the three-day rule does not apply in this case and he calls her that night. The next day Katie is relieved when she finds out he is an FBI agent and not an ax murderer.

Sara has lived in her tiny apartment for six months under the watchful eye of Mrs. Brunswick, her 80-something neighbor whose husband passed away just over three years ago. She is a spry old lady with a devilish smile and quick wit.

For some reason, Sara and Katie love their ridiculously small apartment. Mrs. Brunswick immediately hits it off with Sara and Katie. She is always asking questions about their boyfriends to make sure they are good men who treat them right. She sees the loving connection with Sara and Reardon immediately. It warms her to see it because it reminds her of the love she had with her husband.

Reardon proposes nine months after they meet and they agree to a year-long engagement so they can save for the wedding. Mrs. Brunswick was happy to hear they would be moving into her apartment after the wedding because seeing them makes her feel young again.

———

Reardon is sitting around the table with the four other agents on his team. His favorite is Jack, a wiseass of epic proportions. He has never met anyone more politically incorrect. Amy is a wiz at tracking electronic wire transfers and international banking regulations. Dave and Andy seem to have the inside track on how the mafia thinks. Reardon is constantly intrigued at how they are able to think like criminals. They are so alike he refers to them as the twins. Reardon's natural style, enthusiasm for his work, and charisma allow him to coax and push his team to new levels. The team's work over the last three years far outstripped what previous teams accomplished in a decade. Despite his team's eclectic makeup, they gelled perfectly under Reardon's leadership and received several citations for commendable work. Reardon's star was shining bright and everyone wanted to bask in its glow. He was beating people back with a stick, he would get at least two requests a month from people looking to join his team. However, he had exactly the team he wanted, and he wasn't going to do anything to mess with that.

"We tracked a transfer of just over $3 million from Chile to Hong Kong over the weekend," says Amy.

"Are we convinced this is family money?" Reardon asks.

"Yes, it's a payoff from the Ramfini family to a syndicate in Beijing."

"Can we freeze the account?" Reardon asks.

"We tried, but the Hong Kong banker is pushing back. We figure he's on the take, but he's in a tough spot. Since we're shining the spotlight on him and the local authorities are watching him, the money is frozen for all practical purposes."

"How much time do we have?"

"Maybe 48 hours."

"Let's stay on this ... Dave, can you help Amy?"

"Sure," Dave replies.

There is a knock on the door.

"Come in," Reardon says as he waves his arm at the agent looking through the window.

"The director wants to see you."

The director of the New York field office is a surprisingly nice fellow in his mid-fifties. He and Reardon hit it off from the start five years ago and he has been getting great assignments ever since. Urgently getting called into the boss's office isn't unheard of, but it is a bit unusual.

"OK," he turns to his team, "Keep looking through the info, and I'll be back soon."

"Uh oh, someone's getting called into the principal's office. Were you passing notes in class?" Jack asks.

"No, ever since I signed up for the yearbook and prom committee he keeps asking me questions," Reardon says smiling as he exits the room.

About five minutes pass. Reardon quickly bursts through the door.

"Holy crap! You won't believe what just fell in our lap!" Reardon has the glow of a young boy opening the best present ever on Christmas morning.

"What? Just win a lifetime supply of free prostrate exams for the whole team?" Asks Jack.

"No, but close."

"It looks like Jeremy Ramfini is in town."

"You're screwin' with me!" Jack expounds.

"No, turns out his uncle is sick and might be on his death bed."

"There's no way he's that stupid!"

Jeremy Ramfini is a computer wiz and had been trained his entire life to handle money for the family. He fled to Canada about a year ago, when Reardon's team was closing in, and discovered Jeremy was the genius behind many of the new schemes. They received multiple unconfirmed reports that he has been working out of Toronto and Vancouver but never even come close to tracking down his exact location.

"Whoo-hoo! Looks like Christmas came early this year," Jack says excitedly. "How did we catch wind of this?"

"The guy who drove him into the city is trying to get his brother out on early parole and coughed up the information. Suit up. We're going to make a house call. He's at his uncle's house right now."

The team all jumps up and heads down the hall to suit up. Forty-five minutes later they are all sitting in the back of a large delivery truck a half-mile from the uncle's house.

"OK. We go in just after the tactical team. This is a big house, so it might take them a few minutes to clear the place." Reardon's phone rings and he mumbles into the phone twice. "The warrant was just signed." He reaches up to his neck to activate his mic. "Alpha team, report."

"Ready for action," responds a voice from a van one block over.

"Gold team, report."

"Ready to go," responds another voice from a van sitting three blocks away.

"We go in two minutes."

Reardon turns to his team.

"Stay focused. If we get this guy, we cripple a big chunk of their operation. This will set them back at least a year while they try to figure out where he hid all the money."

They nervously sit for another minute until Jack breaks the tension.

"I'm so excited I think my nuts just crawled up into my chest."

"TMI," Amy coldly states as Jack smiles at her.

"OK. Let's go," Reardon says just after activating his mic and bangs on the wall behind the driver. The driver immediately puts the van into drive and pulls away from the curb.

Five minutes later, three trucks pull up simultaneously to the uncle's house. Reardon's van and the Gold team are out front and the Alpha team pulls up at the back along a vacant alley. The two teams come crashing out of their vans and charge toward the doors. The Gold team smashes in the front door. As soon as the front door is open, a loud double knock comes from the driver.

"Let's go," Reardon says.

Dave opens the door, and the team jumps out. As they approach the door, shots ring out. The Gold team is firing up the staircase as Reardon's team crosses the threshold. There is a sudden silence. The Gold team starts moving up the stairs. The Alpha team is securing the main floor. The Alpha leader meets Reardon at the base of the staircase.

"The main floor is secure. We are securing the basement," states the Alpha leader.

Reardon's team flies up the stairs past a body at the top of the stairs. The Gold team has two men in custody down on their knees. Reardon flies into a room at the end of the hall followed by his team. There is an old man in bed hooked up to a heart monitor and IV, an old woman sitting in a chair, and a young woman standing next to the bed, most likely the nurse.

"Where is he?" Reardon asks quickly.

"He's not here," responds the Gold leader.

"Where is he?" He shouts at the young woman. She nervously looks to a book case near the corner of the room. "Crap! The bookcase!" Reardon rushes over, it is slightly ajar from the wall. Reardon pulls on it revealing a hidden passage. "Follow me!"

Reardon leads his team into the dark hidden passage. They fly down a set of stairs. As Reardon approaches the bottom of the stairs, he hears several shots. Reardon comes flying through the opening followed by Amy and Andy. He sees two agents down on the floor writhing in pain. His momentum carries him into a steel cabinet, making a huge racket, and he bounces off it. Jeremy turns to see what is behind him and raises his cobalt blue Ruger just as Amy and Andy expose themselves. The three of them are clumped together. Reardon is off balance and has no time to raise his gun. He uses his momentum, quickly steps forward, and rolls in front of Amy and Andy, wrapping his arms around them to shield them. Two shots in quick succession are fired hitting Reardon in the middle of the back. Reardon is off balance and falls with the impact of the two shots. As soon as Reardon hits the floor, Amy and Andy take aim and fire six shots in less than two seconds. Five hit Jeremy, and he falls to the ground, one just missing him to the right. Dave rushes through the opening as Amy drops to check Reardon. Andy slowly approaches Jeremy with his gun trained on the bleeding man.

"Get his gun!" Amy screams at Andy. Amy reaches up to activate her mic. "Agents down. We need paramedics at the scene!"

After a long moment, Reardon takes in an explosive breath of air as Amy helps pull him into a sitting position on the floor. Dave is feeling Reardon's back.

"Both hit the vest, no blood."

"Thank God!" Amy says instantly with a sigh of relief in her voice.

Four members of the Alpha team fly down the stairs. Andy is kneeling over the body of Jeremy and trying to stop the bleeding. He took a shot to the heart and throat, and there is little Andy can do to stop the bleeding. Andy has his hand pressed against the man's bleeding neck, but he quickly gasps out a last breath and is gone. Dave is attending to an Alpha team member who took a shot through the arm and one to his vest. He is gasping for breath. The other agent took one to the chest and is sitting up with the assistance of his buddies, trying to catch his breath.

"Oh my God that hurts!" Reardon gasps out breathlessly.

"Consider the alternative…" Jack says as he slaps Reardon on the back. Reardon's eyes dart to him as he groans in pain. "Ew, sorry about that. Ready to get up." Reardon nods his head.

"Ohhhhhhh," Reardon blurts out as they hook him under each arm.

"What the hell were you thinking? You could've gotten yourself killed!" Amy blurts out.

"I wasn't thinking," Reardon says through grimaced teeth still in pain.

"Well, good job boss," Jack says as Reardon taps him on the shoulder to indicate he can walk for himself now.

"No problem. You would've done the same."

Amy is hesitant to let go and continues walking closely next to him for several steps. Reardon walks over to the other downed agents, and they quickly exchange a couple words. One is standing and the other is still sitting while his bloody arm is bandaged. Reardon takes a deep breath, then walks over to Dave, and stands over the body, staring down quietly.

"Let's get out of here."

Two hours later, Reardon is released from the hospital, and Amy drives him back to the office.

"Have you called Sara yet?"

"No, not yet, I didn't want to freak her out. I figure it's better to tell her in person."

"Hmm, I guess so."

Reardon drives over to Sara's apartment. He gingerly gets out of the car and goes up to her place. He knocks on the door, and she opens it after a couple moments.

"Hey future husband. 35 days to our wedding!" She has a glowing smile on her face, and she quickly reaches forward and hugs him. He winces. "What?"

"Oh nothing."

"What do you mean, *oh nothing?*"

"Well, first of all, I'm OK."

She immediately pulls back. "Oh my God, what happened?"

He slowly steps into her apartment as she backs up. He carefully removes his jacket, wincing slightly. She reaches forward to help him.

"What happened?"
"Well, again, I'm OK, but I got shot twice today."
"What! What do you mean you got shot twice today! Where?"
"In the back."

She quickly loops behind him and starts to pull up the back of his shirt.

"Ah, slowly, slowly." She suddenly sees two huge black and blue welts in the center of his back.
"Are you OK?"
"Yeah, it just hurts."
"Who else got shot?"
"One agent took a shot to the vest. He's OK, another took a shot to the arm. It went clean through. He'll be fine in a couple of weeks."
"Who was shooting? How is he?"
"Some guy who snuck back from Canada after hiding there for about a year."
"How is he?" She quickly interrupts.
"He's dead – took a few shots to the chest."

She is still staring at the huge bruises.

"Did you…"
"No, I didn't shoot him."
"Did he sneak up behind you?"
"No, I saw him first. He just got me while I was turning. It's no big deal, I'm fine."

Sara quickly hugs him from behind. He winces again.

"Sorry." She moves around in front of him again. "Why didn't you call me?"
"I didn't want to worry you."
"Well, that's going to stop today. We're getting married in 35 days. From now on, I don't care what it is, you call me. Understand?"
"Yeah," he slowly leans in to hug her.
"I'm serious, you call me, I don't care if it's a hangnail, you call me."
"I got it." She glares at him. "Promise."

May 4, 2001 – New York

Reardon pops up out of the subway into a chilly overcast night. The rain is coming down in a drizzle as he crosses the street and enters a bar on the corner. His team is sitting at a table across from the bar. Reardon walks in and pulls up a chair.

"Hey boss. How's the back?" Asks Jack.

"OK," he says as the act of flipping the chair around causes him to wince.

"When are they letting you come back?" prompts Amy.

"Officially, two more days, but I talked to the boss. He said I can come back in the morning if I'm feelin' OK."

"Good, we miss you," said Dave.

"You're a superhero in the office. Getting Jeremy *The Wiz Kid* Ramfini is huge."

Reardon smiles and blushes slightly. "Don't say hero. We were just doing our job."

"Well, you're a super-agent as far as I'm concerned! You stopped two bullets!"

"Ah, I got shot twice, I should have been more careful. Anyone of us could have been killed."

"Yeah, but we didn't," interjects Amy.

The waitress brings a round of beers for everyone. Jack lifts his beer.

"A toast to the best team I've ever worked with."

"Here here," adds Andy.

They all tap their beers together.

"Getting nervous?" asks Dave.

"About what?"

"The wedding."

"I was a couple weeks ago, but after getting shot in the back a couple times … it really helps put things in perspective. So no, I'm not nervous at all right now."

"That'll change, I bet."

"Probably."

Dave, Andy, Amy, and Jack quickly finish off their beers and order two more while Reardon is working through his first beer. Reardon is finally ready to order a second beer.

"Anyone ready for another?"

Everyone nods in agreement. Reardon waves at the waitress to indicate another round for everyone.

"You know why you're a super-agent – it's because you never get smashed, unlike us four assholes. You're always alert and paying attention," comments Jack.

"Speak for yourself," comments Amy.

"Sorry, the wonderful young lady does not like to be referred to as an asshole. Fine, us three assholes. I can already tell that's your last beer. Good ole two-beer Reardon."

"Someone has to keep an eye on you guys."

Amy looks to Jack. "So that's what's keeping you from being a super-agent," Amy sneers.

"Yes, yes, I believe that is exactly it." The beers arrive, and Jack takes a long swig. "Yes, I believe that's exactly what it is..." he slaps Reardon on the back and Reardon winces. "I just don't want to make the boss look bad." He turns from Amy to Reardon. "Though I will admit, I'm getting a little tired of carrying your sorry ass and making you look so good."

"Thanks. I really appreciate that." Reardon raises his glass. "A toast to great friends and the best agents I've ever worked with."

From that day forward, Reardon has the feeling they have passed from being good friends into family. They while away the time for another fifteen minutes. Jack is repeatedly reaching his hand down below the table towards his crotch. Finally, Amy says something.

"Seriously, what's going on down there, got a little jock itch?" Jack suddenly looks up in a slight haze.

"Huh?"

"What's up? I hear they have cream for that."

"No."

"Then what's a matter?"

"I don't know, my penis feels lumpy."

Beer comes flying out of Dave's nose and he begins coughing. Everyone else at the table starts laughing except Jack.

"I'm serious," comments Jack.

"I believe you, but maybe you should check that out when you get home," adds Amy.

After the laughter dies down, Reardon drains the last of his beer and stands.

"Well, thanks guys, I'm outta' here." He reaches for his wallet.

"Hey! Put your money away, we got this," says Jack.

"No, I got this."

"I'm not kidding. Put your wallet away. I'm serious. Or I'm going to show you my lumpy penis."

"OK, thanks."

"Good, besides you're a cheap date. Two beers. Jeez, you and your two-beer limit. Come on, one more beer." He waves his hand encouraging Reardon to sit back down.

"No, I got an early morning, gotta catch the bad guys," he says with a smirk.

"We have nothing in the morning. We got all caught up," says Amy.

"Vincent Difigio."

"Dude, we arrested him two weeks ago."

"Yeah, I know but his arraignment is Friday. I just want to make sure everything is tight. I don't want this guy getting off on a technicality."

"We are tight, we double checked everything last week," says Dave.

"Good, but I want to go over it one more time."

"Look at this guy, you're a frickin' cross between Dick Tracy and J. Edgar," blurts out Jack who is now obviously two sheets to the wind.

"Yeah, but I don't look as good in a dress. Later guys…"

Day 23

Reardon is startled awake by a phone call. It takes three rings before the ringing registers in his fog encased mind. He turns and looks at the clock. It's 8:03 on a dull overcast morning. Reardon just rolls over as the answering machine clicks on and he hears Spencer.

"Reardon! Get up and turn on the news."

Reardon rolls over and picks up the phone. "What?"

"It's the first casualties. Two people died in a bus explosion last night."

"What?" The fog slowly dissipates in his mind as he tries to piece her words into a sentence.

"Well three explosions actually."

"What!"

"Three buses were blown up last night. One of the drivers was taking a nap and was killed in the explosion. Just get up, turn on the news while you are getting ready, and get in here. McCullum wants to talk to you again."

"About what? I don't know anything more than I knew the last time I saw him."

"Just get in here."

At that, Spencer hangs up, and Reardon puts down the phone, picks up the remote, and clicks on the TV to catch Alicia mid-sentence.

...concert buses explode outside the Pinehurst Arena in Lincoln, Nebraska. Concert goers were initially unaware of the explosions. Police on scene called in the bomb squad immediately. So far, there are two confirmed deaths. Paramedics were also called to deal with some minor injuries resulting from the explosions. Let's go to Grant Blickley, who is at the scene and will walk us through last night.

They flash to Grant standing in front of the charred remains of a bus.

Here is what we know so far. At just after midnight, three explosive devices detonated under the three concert buses for the hard rock group Flaming Ambition, currently midway through a nationwide tour. Police just confirmed a second death with seven others suffering minor injuries. It appears the devices were of an incendiary nature and were designed to start a fire rather than to exert a maximum amount of damage. The first death occurred on the lead bus.

The TV suddenly shows the charred remains of two buses from a short distance as the camera pans left to right.

It's believed the bus driver was taking a nap in the back and was likely overcome with smoke and died in the resulting fire. The second bus had five people playing cards and they were able to get off the bus before it was consumed with flames, each suffering minor smoke inhalation along with minor scratches and bruises. The third bus was empty. Two guards were standing near the buses when the devices exploded. The one near the back of bus number three was fatally wounded and died at the hospital within the last hour. The other guard near the lead bus suffered wounds resulting from flying debris coming from under the bus. All three buses were consumed by the flames within minutes. The police chief and mayor were both called at home and the mayor instructed the police chief to call in the SWAT team and set up a secure perimeter before evacuating the stadium fearing secondary attacks. The mayor is a former army ranger and Iraqi veteran and is being commended for his quick thinking. At approximately 12:47, a police captain stepped onto the stage as the music was cut and the lights are turned on. We have a video of the captain stepping onto the stage and the response from the crowd.

The grainy phone video shows the captain beginning to speak into a dead mic. He turns to the side of the stage pointing to the mic, and a moment later the mic turns on with a whine. The captain explains there has been an incident, and everyone needs to evacuate the building. There is a chorus of boos. The officer can't calm down the crowd. Meanwhile the band's manager calls the band over and explains the situation. Suddenly a chorus of people starts screaming "Pig, Pig, Pig." Next thing, the entire stadium is screaming in unison. The lead singer takes the mic and starts to calm the crowd by telling everyone to start leaving. The boos continue. Eventually ushers are encouraging people to leave, and people start to move. The camera returns to Grant.

The stadium of 22,000 people cleared in about 25 minutes. People were noticeably jumpy and nervous, especially the ones passing the charred remains of the three buses surrounded by firetrucks and police. Police have swept the area looking for additional bombs. None have been found, and no other incidences have been reported. Police are continuing to investigate.

McCullum and his team are churning through initial reports with the news on in the background as Reardon enters.

"They're escalating quickly," McCullum points out, "and this is the first day with casualties, one bus driver taking a nap and a security guard. Again, these weren't big blasts, just enough to incinerate the buses and disrupt the lives of 22,000 people. Why?"

Everyone sitting at the table knows this is a rhetorical question. Despite that, Peterson clears his throat and speaks up after lifting his head up from his laptop monitor.

"Sir, I just got a confirmed attack via email. It appears to be the Day 3 attack. A backhoe was used to sever a fiber optic cable along a rural highway just outside Sumter, South Carolina. It was barely noticed because internet traffic was getting rerouted automatically. A tech was running a diagnostic, noticed the connection was down, and started looking into it.

NRFBOI was spray painted on the sign warning to not dig there because of buried fiber optic cable."

"For the love of God, could we make it any easier?!" McCullum blurts out intensely. "All they need to do is read the big signs. Look, dig here to help screw with us. Everyone, what is the common thread in all of this?"

"So far, these are all disruptive and little more. Yes, the killings are an obvious escalation. But they almost seem accidental. The bombs weren't meant to destroy the buses immediately. The bombs were all put at the rear of the buses, and if the driver was closer to the front of the bus, he likely would've survived. The death of the guard was also unfortunate. If he hadn't been leaning against the bus right where the bomb exploded he would've also likely just had injuries." Spencer explains.

"But it still doesn't make sense, even if the deaths were an accident," replies Peterson.

"Let's get back to his question, what's the common theme?" Spencer reiterates. "Death and panic isn't the goal. Destruction doesn't appear to be the goal either. It seems like the goal is disruption, and the destruction is just a necessary by-product to help 'em accomplish their goal. Let's look at last night. 22,000 people had their concert cut short. Why? Now what?"

Everyone sits quietly contemplating the question.

Reardon finally comments, "All these have a ripple effect."

"What do you mean by that?" McCullum asks.

"Take last night. The deaths were almost accidental, again, an unfortunate byproduct. Putting that aside, what happens today? The 22,000 had their lives altered last night and the band is scheduled to play another concert tonight in Omaha. But I saw on the news that they've cancelled that concert and suspended their tour for now. The five power stations have disrupted the lives of over 30,000 people and will likely take at least a week to repair. The tanker trucks will disrupt traffic for at least a few more days until the roads are fully repaired. All the other *attacks* we know about are disruptive and make people second guess things, if even just seemingly minor things."

McCullum stands up and starts pacing. "Interesting."

"So, are these all just random acts or feeding into something greater?" Spencer asks.

Reardon just stares at Spencer as her question lingers in the air. Everyone is just looking at each other not knowing what else to say. They all know there's no discernable pattern right now and no way to anticipate the next attack. Anyone sitting at that table would bet a million dollars there will be an attack that night at 12:01, but not a single one would bet a dollar trying to figure out the next target.

The authorities in L.A. finished analyzing the video from the tanker depot and all the road cameras they could find with the attacker's cars. There isn't a single frame of footage that helps them ID the attackers.

Washington, D.C.

The tone of the president's staff has altered dramatically from just 24 hours ago. The president and his staff now feel compelled to have the president address the nation immediately. Only one staffer feels that is a mistake. She points out that the attackers clearly have an agenda, granted a mysterious agenda, but they are controlling the situation and trying to lead us somewhere with all these attacks. Having the president speak before we know anything would just play into their hands. The news agencies are certainly following along like rabid dogs. Every news report starts with the attack, and they are now methodically stepping through all known attacks over the last 23 days. Just a day earlier they only made passing reference to the attacks. This has turned into *real* news with the first reported deaths. She recommends they simply issue a statement and let the press secretary address questions. Ultimately the president agrees and they work the rest of the day to get ahead of the story. They don't want to just react. They are hoping to have enough leads for a quick arrest. The president can lead with information on how quickly they apprehended the terrorists.

The president returns to the Oval Office to resume his *normal* day job and receives multiple reports throughout the day. He becomes frustrated when a few initial leads hit a dead end. Multiple eyewitnesses in the area describe people they saw near the time of the explosions. No descriptions match. Finally, with no leads and his staff expressing concern that he may appear out of touch, the president steps into the press room at just after 8 p.m. to answer questions. His comments make the late news and are replayed in the morning. He provides no meaningful information in 20 minutes at the podium. Finally, he stops the questions and retires from the room, throwing hand written notes onto the floor in angry frustration as soon as the door to the press room closes behind him. The looming uncertainty is starting to have subtle side effects. The one thing Wall Street hates is uncertainty. As a result, the markets have dipped slightly over the last three days.

June 8, 2001– New York

Reardon wakes up in a cold sweat after tossing and turning most of the night. He lies there for another ten minutes before deciding to get up and walks into his small cramped bathroom. He stops and stares into the mirror for a moment before a glowing smile comes over his face. It's his wedding day. He and Sara have been waiting nearly a year since he proposed. Just at that moment, his roommate and best man, Ben comes into the bathroom and drops his boxers as he sits on the toilet. Ben and Reardon met in their second year at NYU and have been best friends and roommates ever since.

"Dude! Seriously, today? It's my wedding day."

"I gotta take a dump. Besides you're not doing anything. You're just staring at your pretty smile in the mirror from what I can tell. Just keep lookin' at that."

"I would but you sorta' ruined the moment." Suddenly Reardon starts to wave his hand. "You stink, did you stick a dead squirrel up your butt last week to ferment? That's just not right. There is something wrong with you."

"Blah blah blah, don't you have a wedding to get ready for?"

The smile returns to Reardon's face. He decides to step out of the bathroom.

"Call me when you're done. I wanna' shower."

"Yeah, I'll be a while – why don't you go get yourself some breakfast," he pauses and says, "Hey, I'll miss you."

Reardon turns. "I'll miss you too," he says sincerely.

"Oh my God, I was kidding, don't be such a pussy!"

Reardon just smiles and walks away.

Four hours later Ben, Reardon, and his two other groomsmen are all primping and making sure their bow-ties are straight. Ben steps in front of Reardon, reaches for his bow tie, and turns it 90 degrees so it is suddenly pushing into his neck at an angle.

"There, perfect."

"Ha, ha." Reardon turns to the mirror and straightens his bow tie.

"Nervous?"

"Not really."

"Good." He pauses for a moment and picks a piece of lint off Reardon's shoulder. "Seriously," he stares him directly in the eye, "if you start crying during the ceremony, I'm going to punch you in the Jimmy and drop you like a sack of tators. We clear?"

"Yeah, we're clear."

Ben gives him a crushing hug.

"I love you man. It's not too late to run. Just say the word, I'll have a taxi here in ten minutes, and we are outta' here."

"Thanks, but I'm good."

"Man, who'd a thought an hour in the park and a Frisbee would lead to you getting hitched. I'd drag your ass out of here right now if I wasn't convinced you were head over heels in love with her."

"What can I say? I'm all in."

Ben smiles at Reardon and slaps him on the shoulder, "Let's go do this."

———

Reardon and Sara arrive home two weeks later after an incredible honeymoon in Barbados. They kicked out her roommate and moved all his stuff into her apartment a couple weeks before the wedding. Reardon is just standing next to the door with his bags.

"You can open it, use your key," she says.

"I'm not sure where my key is right now."

"Leave it to a man to lose his key." She pulls her keys from her pocket and unlocks the door and just as she opens it a crack Reardon suddenly speaks.

"Wait, stop right there."

"What?" She says slightly alarmed. He smiles. "What?"

"Put down your bag?"

"Why?"

"Just do it."

As soon as she does Reardon lowers his bags and as he stands he sweeps her off her feet.

"I want to make sure we do this right."

"Oh my gosh, really? What is this? The 1940s…"

Reardon pushes open the door with his foot and slowly enters the apartment careful not to hit her head. The apartment is a mess. Most of Reardon's stuff is still in boxes stacked in the far corner of the cramped living room. His bike is leaning against the back of the sofa. There is an extra chair stacked on one of her chairs. She tried to convince him to leave it, but it's his *favorite* chair. Sara is suddenly wondering how there was ever room for two in this apartment. Reardon puts her down and reaches into the hall to pull in the bags. He closes the door and stares at her for a moment.

"I have a surprise for you…"
"What?"
"It's in the bedroom," he smirks at her.
"Really? We just got home. I want to take a quick shower first. I stink."
"No, it's not that."
Reardon leads her back to the bedroom. "Close your eyes."
"Should I be scared?"
"No, just close your eyes." She closes her eyes and Reardon leads her to the foot of the bed.
"OK, open your eyes."

She just stares for a minute. Reardon is taken back by her silence, another few moments pass. Suddenly she turns and has a tear in her eye.

"What's a matter? We can move it if you want?"
"No, it's perfect."

Reardon was being honest when he said he didn't know where his key was. He gave his key to his roommate Ben so he could deliver a late wedding gift. Hanging above the bed encased in a frame behind glass is a Frisbee, a clump of grass, and four leaves. Reardon had such a good feeling about Sara after talking to her on the phone that first time he got up the next morning and went to the exact place where they first met. He grabbed several clumps of grass and four leaves that had fallen where they were standing and put them in a cardboard box for safe keeping.

"The grass and leaves are from the exact place we were standing when we first met."
"And that's the Frisbee?"
"Yes."
"Wow, Ben must really love you to give that up."
"Technically, it's on loan. He said, *I get it back if, you know, things don't work out.*" Sara jabs him in the ribs.
"That's not funny."
"His words, not mine." She now has a tear running from her other eye.
"I think that's the best present anyone has ever given me." She gets on her tippy toes and kisses him. She decides the shower can wait after all.

August 15, 2001– New York

Reardon is at home getting dressed in his best suit for a morning ceremony at the New York field office. A week ago he was informed that he was being awarded the Medal of Valor by no one other than the Director of the FBI himself for his selfless act of heroism. From the get-go Reardon tried to downplay what he did back in May. He knew anyone on his team would have put themselves in the line of fire to protect him. But it wasn't anyone else, it was him. So, he was willing to accept it, but he viewed it as a team award. The way he saw it, he nearly got himself or someone on his team killed. If Jack or Amy were the first one down the stairs, he knows they would have turned to protect him and he'd be honored to be attending their award ceremony. Sara walks out of the bathroom and turns her back to him.

"Zip me up."

Reardon dutifully starts zipping her up as she pulls her hair up and out of the way. "You look gorgeous. I'm glad you were able to take the day off."

"Mrs. Noah Reardon would never miss anything like this. I still love the sound of that. Mrs. Noah Reardon."

"I love the sound of that too." He wraps his arms around her from behind and cups her left breast. "I love the feel of you. Promise to leave this on until tonight so I can help you out of it too?"

"I think I can arrange that. Now let me finish getting ready."

Reardon releases her and Sara walks into the bathroom. She comes out three minutes later with an emerald green broach necklace and matching earrings.

"Wow! You are a stunner." Reardon closes the gap and wraps his arms around her. "I love you so much."

"Oh baby, I love you too and I'm so proud of you. But if you ever do anything like this again, I swear I will kill you myself. Remember, you're a married man now."

"You know I can't promise that."

"I know, all part of why I love you. But if I ever lose you, I'll be lost. Lost forever." Her head drops with a forlorn look on her face.

He uses his finger to lift her chin. "Me too. I promise I'll do everything I can to come home every night safe and sound. Is that good enough?"

"No, but it'll do."

After weeks of downplaying what he did back in May, Reardon is awarded the FBI's Medal of Valor. It's small ceremony on the 15th floor of the New York office overlooking the World Trade Center towers. Reardon's entire team is there along with his boss, the director of the New York field office, the Director of the FBI, and about 20 other agents. During his short thank you speech he selflessly thanks his team for all their dedicated work and ends with a simple and humble statement.

"I view this as a team award. Anyone of us would have done the same."

There is a short round of applause. Reardon turns to Sara and gives her a big hug. A moment later his boss interrupts.

"Sara, if it's not too much trouble, I would like to steal your husband for a few minutes."
"Certainly," she looks at Reardon. "Hurry back."
"As soon as I can."

They walk over to his office and close the door.

"Have a seat," he motions to a chair and they sit. "I just wanted to take a moment and tell you a couple things."
"Sure."
"First of all, congratulations, you're one of the best agents I've ever worked with."
"Thanks."
"Second, I want you to take on a larger role."
"But…"
"Don't worry, I'm not going to take away your team."
"OK … good."
"I want your team to keep doing what it does best, but I want them to start training the other teams to do what you do. I want you to take on a larger leadership role. People respect you and follow your lead. I think you could really help build out these other teams."
"If I'm good, it's only because my team is good."
"Noah, while I appreciate your modesty, it's more than just your team. I think I could have assigned you four baboons and they would be getting more done than half the teams around here."
"Thanks, I appreciate your confidence in me."

"It's well deserved. Anyways, I want you to take the rest of the day off. And when you get in tomorrow, we'll discuss this further. Sound good?" He stands and extends his hand to Reardon.

"Yeah. Thanks."

"Good, see you in the morning."

Reardon leaves the office and sneaks up next to Sara who is talking with Reardon's team. He puts his hand on her elbow and she turns.

"Good news."

"What?"

"I've got the rest of the day off. Let's get out of here and grab some lunch. Let's find a fancy place since we are dressed for it." Reardon turns to his team. "Sorry, guys, looks like I'm outta' here. Boss gave me the rest of the day off."

They grumble for a moment and wish him well. As they start to walk away, he leans in.

"I've got some other good news too."

"What?"

"Sort of a promotion…"

"What's that mean?"

"I'm not really sure, my team will be training in other teams and they want me to take the lead on that."

"That's great baby," she turns and hugs him, "so what does that really mean?"

"I don't know, we're meeting in the morning to talk over the details."

Reardon and Sara went out for a great lunch and headed back to their apartment. As it turns out, Sara didn't need to keep the dress on until the evening after all.

Day 28

Dow Jones Industrial Average
20,054.78
Total decline: 2.0%
Total loss: $103 Billion

Nasdaq
5,547.98
Total decline: 2.4%
Total loss: $200 Billion

The day draws to a close with Reardon watching the news, a bottle in one hand and the remote in the other. As the newscaster is recounting the events of the week.

Police and government agencies continue to scramble looking for clues and witnesses to the attacks over the last five days. Local and federal authorities now link each of these events with an unknown terrorist organization. The loading docks of a food distribution center near Orlando, Florida, were destroyed on what authorities are referring to as Day 24. The following day, residents awoke to discover thousands of dead fish floating on the surface of Kilowatt Lake in Memphis, Tennessee. Three water towers were destroyed in Ames, Iowa, leaving over 10,000 residents without water. Two days ago, three Civil War monuments were damaged in Gettysburg, and early this morning a truck bomb was parked against a wall of a state correctional facility and then detonated in Chateaugay, New York. No prisoners escaped when the facility was rocked by the explosion at 12:01 a.m. None of the attacks over the last five days resulted in any casualties. Officials are still perplexed by the seemingly random nature of the attacks with no apparent intent to inflict bodily harm. Current estimates put the damage at over $10 million for the last five days and well over $50 million since the spree of attacks purportedly began 28 days ago. Federal officials have now linked attacks to 27 of the last 28 days, and federal officials are working closely with local officials to identify the remaining undiscovered attack.

The list of attacks is scrolling across the screen as Reardon takes another long draw from the bottle. Authorities are still trying to identify the attack from Day 8.

Day 1 – 28 Attacks

Day	Attack
1	Office complex flooding, Milwaukee, Wisconsin
2	200 tires slashed at car dealership, Rockville, Maryland
3	Backhoe severs buried fiber optic cable, Sumter, South Carolina
4	120 pigs poisoned, Butte, Montana
5	15 cell towers damaged, Glendale, Arizona
6	Sewage treatment center valve closed causing backup into creek, Conway, Arkansas
7	Three power line poles cut down, Moab, Utah

8	
9	Abandoned warehouse burned down, Nashua, New Hampshire
10	Power line tower, Haskell, New Jersey
11	Pennies wedged near wheels of a train so it can't move, Dover, Delaware
12	Three houses under construction torched, Brookline, Massachusetts
13	Cattle fence cut down, 250 cows end up wandering along highway, El Paso, Texas
14	20 windshields smashed at car dealership, Grand Island, Nebraska
15	Green water in reservoir, Dillon, Idaho
16	Grocery store burned down, Clearwater, Florida
17	Three buildings on college campus vandalized, Littlefield, Texas
18	Engine car for Mt. Washington Cog Railway vandalized, New Hampshire
19	Windows broken in historic Dodge City, Kansas
20	Two houses under construction burned down, Spokane, Washington
21	Three tanker truck explosions, Los Angeles, California
22	Five power substations destroyed outside five mid-size cities
23	Tour buses destroyed outside Pinehurst Arena in Lincoln, Nebraska
24	Food distribution warehouse, Orlando, Florida
25	Fish poisoned in Kilowatt Lake, Memphis, Tennessee
26	Water towers destroyed, Ames, Iowa
27	Civil war monuments destroyed, Gettysburg, Virginia
28	Correctional facility explosion, Chateaugay, New York

As Reardon sits there half-awake, the coverage continues. Congresspeople are clamoring for airtime on all the major networks to express their deep-seated concern. Never one to let a good crisis go to waste, most newscasters are focusing on the heavy hitters. However, one senator is rising to the top among the junior senators and has finagled more news time than even the senate majority leader and speaker of the souse on several days. Sen. Eidelmen is a brash young senator just starting his second term. He managed to land a seat on the Energy Committee thanks to an incumbent senator getting unexpectedly beaten in a hotly contested race in the south.

Sen. Eidelmen continues his fiery rhetoric directed at the president late yesterday. The senator continues to call the president's response weak, claiming intelligence agencies are spending billions of dollars a year to protect our country and that we can't track down a small band of terrorists exacting their revenge on America. Calling the President and his advisors asleep at the wheel.

Reardon turns off the television, finishes the bottle, and leans his head back on the sofa. As he begins to doze off an image of his wife flashes into his mind and a tear runs down his face.

September 8, 2001– New York

Reardon is excitedly rushing home from work for his three-month wedding anniversary. They still haven't completely settled into Sara's apartment. There are still a few boxes in the corner holding up his bike, and his favorite chair is awkwardly blocking the path to the kitchen.

Reardon is standing at the door with his bag and a bouquet of roses. He puts down his bag and gingerly balances the roses on top of it. Then he takes off his suit coat and tie, folding them neatly and balancing them on his bag as well. Next comes his shirt and just as he almost has his pants off Mrs. Brunswick opens her door and steps into the hallway. As she turns to lock her door she sees him standing in his socks and boxer shorts. This is a new one to her.

"Oh!" suddenly surprised. "You kids," she says and smiles.
"Hello, Mrs. Brunswick. How are you today?"
Starting to fiddle with her keys, "I'm fine."
Reardon quickly raps on the door three times. Reaching down to grab all his clothes in one hand and the flowers and his bag in the other, he quickly says, "Honey, open the door, my hands are full."
A shocked look comes over her face as she opens the door. "What are you doing?" She quickly pokes her head out looking left and then right only to see Mrs. Brunswick walking towards them. "Oh my gosh, I'm so sorry."
"It's OK dear, I wish I was still so lucky," a wry smile lighting up her face.

She pulls on his arm to get him in the apartment before anyone else sees him.

"Happy three-month anniversary my dear."
"What are you doing?"

"It's not so much what I'm doing but more what I would like to be doing." He puts down his clothes, bag, and flowers on the table and embraces her. "I'm feelin' lucky."

She pulls back momentarily, smiling, then goes up on her tippy toes and starts kissing him.

Washington, D.C.

The president's staff is confounded by what is happening across the nation. The president is getting twice-a-day briefings from the FBI, CIA, NSA, TSA, and a dozen other agencies as authorities scramble to find clues or identify a pattern to the attacks. Leading Democrats and Republicans are hitting every news show demanding answers and already pointing at the other side for being weak on terrorism. However, with one exception, all the statements are relatively subdued because of the stunning lack of real information. Each person fearing a statement today will come back and haunt them tomorrow.

The lack of mass casualties is keeping this below the level of the November 2015 attacks in Paris in which 130 people were killed by armed gunmen in three different locations or the June 2016 attack where a lone gunman killed nearly 50 people at an Orlando nightclub. There are three distinct differences; one is the near lack of casualties; two is the anonymity of the attackers, and three is the consistency. The president's staff is trying to form a strategy that can be outlined in the daily press briefings. The intensity of the briefings is reaching a fevered pitch with more calls for the president to address the nation once again. For the last five days, the press secretary is simply dodging the question saying that the president is working closely with his staff and the directors of the intelligence agencies to identify the perpetrators of these terrorist attacks. The truth is the president's staff is deadlocked, unlike anything they have experienced since dealing with North Korea over a year ago. No one on his staff agrees with anything as the next logical step forward. In the meantime, the attacks continue along with the cost and confusion. The uncertainty in the stock markets causes another slight dip.

Day 29

Dow Jones Industrial Average
19,247.71
Total decline: 4.5%
Total loss: $234 Billion

Nasdaq
5,503.58
Total decline: 3.1%
Total loss: $266 Billion

He who can destroy a thing, controls a thing.
Frank Herbert

Reardon is dead asleep as a pounding noise slowly enters into his dream. His mind is trying to wrap itself around the sound. He is methodically drawn towards consciousness as the pounding continues. He slowly opens his eyes and moans as the morning light slices through his curtains now aware of his surroundings. After a moment, he realizes the noise is coming from the front door.

"Reardon! Reardon! Get Up!" Spencer is pounding on the door. Reardon limps over to the door and opens it. "Holy Hell! What took you so long?"

"Arrg. Holy Hell yourself, what time is it?"

"It's early. Have you seen the news yet?" Spencer presses.

"No, do I look like I've seen the news?" Reardon turns to look at his clock, "Criminy, it's 5:27! What is it this morning, did they bomb an outhouse or a fast food joint?"

"No, just turn on the TV," she says with palpable anxiety in her voice.

Reardon knows this is serious; he sits on the sofa and flips on the TV to catch the newscaster mid-sentence.

...scramble for suspects. This type of attack will be devastating to the cities for years. Authorities are still trying to understand how the terrorists coordinated such an attack unnoticed. For those just joining us, 22 bridges were destroyed last night on the Mississippi River severing the connections between the Twin Cities of Minneapolis and St. Paul. The bombs were detonated at 12:01 a.m. in a coordinated attack. Authorities have no idea if there are any casualties as police scramble to put boats in the water and search for victims in the middle of the night. Police are now reviewing traffic cameras to see if any cars may have gone in the water after the bridges collapsed.

"Holy shit!" Reardon blurts out and he starts pacing with his characteristic limp still wearing his clothes from the night before.

"Yeah, holy shit and then some," Spencer adds. "Get dressed, or should I say, shower and get some clean clothes on. McCullum is probably already waiting for us."

Reardon has his head down as he slowly paces back and forth contemplating what he has just heard.

"Dammit! We should have figured this out a week ago," he shouts.

"Don't be ridiculous – no one could have figured this out even a day ago." Spencer points out.

"No, you don't get it! They're not just trying to kill us they're trying to destroy us. They've learned we can survive the killings. We're hurt and damaged. We have moments of silence, candlelight vigils, declare *never again*. We build memorials. We build monuments. We honor our dead, and we move on. Now they get it, the one thing we can't survive – our own destruction," he says remorsefully.

Reardon and Spencer enter the office at 6:24 and the office is already a buzz with heart-throbbing raw adrenaline. Reardon assumes all FBI and police agencies have been notified and are going on high alert across the country. This was a major escalation for his *good friend*. Spencer briefs McCullum on what they discussed in the car while they drove to the office.

"Why these targets?" McCullum asks.

"They are disrupting our daily lives, our daily comforts, our daily routines. That's the source of our safety, the belief that everything will be OK today, in this moment," Reardon replies. "They are pulling back the veneer of our daily lives."

"I want to know everything about your time in Afghanistan."

May 12, 2009 – Afghanistan

Threats are everywhere, even at home. The prescription for endless war poses a far greater danger to Americans than perceived enemies do, for reasons the terrorist organizations understand very well.
Noam Chomsky

Reardon and Abdul are driving back to the compound after a four-and-a-half-hour drive over hot sweaty uneven terrain. Their escort Humvee is trailing close behind with four soldiers serving as their protective detail. Reardon met Abdul on his first day in Afghanistan just after arriving at the hooch. They have enjoyed many long-winded philosophical discussions over the last year. On this particular day, the mission was a bust, nine hours of driving for nothing. The informant scared off for any number of reasons or possibly even killed by his own people if they discovered he was planning to talk with the Americans.

"That was a waste of a full day."

"Ahh, my good friend, anything to get me out of the compound is a good day," Abdul replied.

They sit quietly for a few more minutes until Reardon speaks.

"So, let's get back to what we were talking about before we got rerouted. What will I never understand?"

"True despair, no matter how bad things get here, you still have the dream and vision of home. A place where everything is OK, and you can crawl into your bed and forget the world."

"And..."

"And here, there is no dream, before you came, these people had only the basic necessities. A few villages were lucky enough to have running water and electricity. These villages waited decades for what you consider givens. In America, you never give even the slightest thought to these. Your great worry is that the line at Starbucks isn't too long. You come and bomb the insurgents you think are hiding in these villages. And they are. But your bombings have no real affect other than destruction. This is their home and family, and you leave them with nothing. The dream of their home is a pile of rubble, and they bury their dead. When you are done, you can just walk away. You must first lose everything, including hope. Until then you will never understand true despair."

"I think I do understand. I see it in the faces of people as we drive through villages. It's as obvious as the nose on their faces."

"Yes, seeing is one thing. Understanding is another."

They sit quietly for another ten minutes. Reardon has been working with Abdul for nearly a year, at this point in time and they have become good friends. Reardon has grown to appreciate their open and candid conversations.

"Do you think we're having an impact here?"

"What do you mean?"

"Making things better?"

"Your goal is to eliminate terrorism through terrorism, that is how you are viewed here. You are not a liberating force. You are an invading army that people want to defeat. While many hate the extremists in this country, they will always hate you more because you are outsiders. This is not a philosophical discussion where you can convince people you are in the right and here to help them. This is instinctual. Generations of Afghanis have learned to distrust outsiders. It's in our bones and in our faces, and you just don't recognize it."

"Wow, no really, tell me what you think ... don't sugar coat it." Abdul stares at him quizzically. "It's a joke. I just wasn't expecting such a blunt answer."

"American humor is still very strange to me."

"Sometimes it's strange to me too." Reardon pauses and just looks forward for a few moments. "I'm curious, do you trust me?"

"Up to a point."

"What *is* that point?"

"The point is where you start to believe you can actually make a difference here. Once you hit that point, you are useless to me."

"Useless?" Reardon is baffled by his comment.

"Yes, because from that point on everything, you do will be rooted in a lie. For now, we must continue to play our game. You keep pretending you can make a difference, and I will keep finding bad people doing bad things, or good people doing good things, for you to kill. It really does all depend on your perspective, doesn't it?" Reardon knows it's a rhetorical question. "It all depends on which side you're on. That is really what it comes down to doesn't it? Look at your own founding fathers. You call them heroes and King George called them traitors. Today they would be called terrorists by any measure. If they had the means at the time, they would have crossed the ocean and blown up Buckingham Palace if that is what it would take. To us, the Twin Towers represent your Buckingham Palace and all the decadence that resides there."

"But they killed innocent people."

"And you kill innocent people here with your airstrikes. How is it different? Your government does so much more. Your government kills people who tell inconvenient truths. Your government supports horrible and vicious dictators, Idi Armin, Hosni Mubarak, Sadaam Hussain, and Manuel Noriega. All these leaders needed to say was that they led a wonderful democratic nation in order to stave off the communist domination of the world. That is all it took for your leaders to look the other way as they kidnapped and tortured their own people. Your own CIA kills foreign leaders and manipulates election results in other countries to suit their own needs. Surely you know all this. You can't be blind to these facts. Instead you say, that's not me, that's not what we're doing this time. America doesn't care about the people. You care about yourselves and the money and power that comes from that. Afghanistan has no strategic importance to America. There is no reason for you to be here. You are here today because of what 19 men did in 2001. 19 men! Your government simply needs to keep up the appearance that you are doing something. You will simply be here until someone decides you can leave. Anyone who attempts to contradict or interfere with America's drive for money and power is a terrorist in your mind by definition."

Reardon sits silently for a few moments, stunned by his comments. Not that he is wrong, but instead, by the clarity of what he has said. Finally, Reardon speaks, "I can't argue with you."

"Good. Let's just continue to play the game and hope we both survive."

From that day forward Reardon viewed the war in a whole new light. Deep down he had realized everything Abdul had just clearly stated months ago but kept it buried. Abdul just brought it all to the surface so he could face it more openly and honestly. He was here to do a job, so he should just get on with it and do it.

———

Reardon is now sitting across the table from McCullum as agents hover and buzz around like flies.

"Think disruption, not destruction."

"What does that even mean? Why the hell aren't they trying to kill people?"

"Abdul and I"

McCullum interrupts, "Who the hell is Abdul?"

"Abdul was my Afghan liaison officer; his body was never identified after the explosion. We worked together for three years and used to talk about this. How the bombings and fighting were horrifying, but the aftermath was worse. No food, water, communications. Everything gone, knowing it could be years before things returned to *normal*. Worse yet, the war may never end and therefore things never go back to normal. Geopolitics meant nothing to the villagers. Despair was the real enemy for the innocent civilians who survived our bombings."

Within minutes, Peterson has brought up pictures of everyone who died in the February, 2011 explosion. As Peterson steps through each of the ten photos, Reardon gives a quick bio on the six agents and four Afghani liaison officers. Reardon starts to well up seeing the pictures of his friends once again. McCullum wants to know which one is most likely the bomber.

Reardon passionately defends each one of them. He still believes none of them could have done it. He convinces McCullum it had to be someone else who either worked at the camp or managed to sneak in undetected. To this day, there are still no official suspects and no one has claimed responsibility.

McCullum orders everyone to clear the room except for Reardon and Spencer. Over the last three weeks, McCullum has asked plenty of questions about Afghanistan, but the questions were just dancing around the edges of what he did there. This time McCullum wants to know everything, he asks probing questions one after another.

McCullum has scanned all of Reardon's files, but the stuff he asks about now is stuff you can't find in any file, the kind of stuff that *never* makes it into a file.

Reardon spends the next two hours describing everything he can about Afghanistan to McCullum as Spencer quietly listens in. He discusses the long days, the stress in trying to turn chatter into actionable intel, calling in the attacks, and then the heart wrenching news of innocent deaths. The cold calculating arithmetic of death is brutally difficult. If he wants to kill two people in a group of twenty, many of them innocents, is it worth it if it could save a hundred or even a thousand?

This is war, the answer is *yes* … his targets would not hesitate for moment. Initially, Reardon just accepts this as part of the job but the deaths of children are particularly distressing. He would always wait if he knew children were present. He explains how the death count just keeps building and how people quietly question if what they are doing is really making things better or worse. The second guessing is both infuriating and all-consuming, requiring an exhaustive amount of mental effort to suppress it so he can do his job.

Over the years, Spencer has tried to get him to open up and talk about what he did there, but he always changed the subject. She was sad that their relationship had deteriorated over the years, but once Reardon lost his wife and daughter, he changed. He turned inward and sank into the bottle. This is the first time she has ever heard all the horrifying details of what went on there and how death was simply part of life. She could barely imagine the stress Reardon went through during those years. She had an urge to just reach out and hug him, something she now realizes she should have done after he lost his family. In the end, he estimates he is responsible for killing well over 250 people while in Afghanistan, unfortunately, many of them innocent bystanders.

McCullum asks Spencer to leave the room, and she shuts the door on the way out.

"Reardon, I want you to stay on top of this, I want you in the office every day. So far you are the closest thing we have to an actual link."

"Why? I'm not sure how I can help."

"Because you might notice something we miss."

"What about only giving me nightmare assignments?"

"The deal is you work on what I assign you. You understand? I want you in here even if you are just a fly on the wall. Got it?"

"Yeah."

McCullum is still hoping to see a spark, that *spark* that finally hit him so many years ago. He spends the next thirty minutes picking Reardon's brain about Afghanistan. McCullum desperately wants a direct link between Reardon and his time overseas so they can focus the investigation in one place.

"Have you heard back on the list of names I gave you last week?"

"No not yet. I asked the director's aide about it yesterday and he said it was on the back burner until we could find a stronger link. After this, today, I don't think they are going to be worried about waiting for a stronger link."

Just to make sure, McCullum calls the director's aide again and leaves a message. It would be easy for the list to get lost in the shuffle after today's attack.

As the morning slowly draws to a close and more accurate information comes in, they learn 19 bridges collapsed and three others are severely damaged and unusable, with severe cracks in the foundation. Newscasters report the Highway 35W bridge collapsed in the explosions. Minnesotans are now forced to relive the horror of the previous bridge's collapse in 2007, resulting in 13 dead and 145 injured as the bridge collapsed during rush hour traffic. Newscasters remember when the world rushed in to pay condolences.

The only saving grace is that the bridge was destroyed at midnight with only four cars falling into the river. Search boats are in the water along the Mississippi and a section of Minnesota River looking for victims near the 19 collapsed bridges. Traffic cameras revealed 83 vehicles ended up going down with the bridges. 74 vehicles dropped with the bridges, and nine additional cars fell either unaware of the collapse or unable to stop in time.

So far rescue crews have recovered 14 bodies from 11 cars. Sixty-seven people were rescued, many with severe injuries, their cars sitting at odd angles just out of the water on collapsed decking. Many cars are still missing. The governor of Minnesota declares a state of emergency ordering people to simply remain at home rather than go out into the utter chaos that has already developed for commuters during early morning rush hour. Highways turned into parking lots for hours as cars slowly exit and work their way back home on side streets while listening to the radio in order to understand the calamity that befell the Twin Cities. Emergency crews and police are working to construct barriers and redirect all traffic away from the bridges.

The President calls the governor to discuss the situation and promises emergency federal funds. Broadcasters and pundits are already discussing if Congress should declare war, but against whom? None of the attacks have been linked to any specific group. Federal agencies are scouring all Islamic websites looking for any group taking credit, but none do. All are reveling in the attacks making broad claims about the downfall of America and death to Americans. All federal agencies monitoring communications are operating at a fever pitch and searching for any chatter about the attacks or upcoming attacks. They find nothing. All the communications they discover are simply congratulatory messages to anyone who might be responsible.

McCullum's office is in bedlam as news reports keep coming in. Congresspeople dominate the airwaves demanding answers and trying to understand where our intelligence broke down. Reardon is just sitting there soaking in the cacophony of sound emanating from the entire floor. The President is expected to address the nation later today. This pushes the timetable of the President's address up three days. Although they still had not agreed on the content, they did choose a deadline just to keep the reporters and congress at bay. The Dow opens with a huge drop and slowly recovers, ending down about 4% for the day.

"Holy hell! Why didn't we get wind of this?" McCullum asks.
"Wind of what? We could've never anticipated this. We can't guard everything everywhere all the time," Reardon responds.
"At least we are seeing a clear pattern of them going after our infrastructure," Spencer adds.
"That's our biggest problem then. It's tough enough to guard big targets, but trying to guard everything is impossible," McCullum concludes.

Later in the day the conference room is still abuzz with activity. Suddenly McCullum glances over at the TV and sees a banner across the TV that reads "MSP Airport Shuts Down".

McCullum screams, "Everyone SHUTUP!", as he reaches for the remote and unmutes the TV.

The FAA released a statement approximately 15 minutes ago that it is shutting down the Minneapolis-St. Paul International Airport. The statement from the FAA reads, and I quote, *we have decided to shut down the airport because we are unable to safely execute flight operations*, end quote. The statement goes on to explain that air traffic, ground crews, and other operational crews are simply exhausted and pushed to their breaking point. All incoming flights have been diverted. Because of the traffic deadlock with the loss of the bridges, half the people who would normally be at work by now are physically unable to get to work. The other half are simply unable to get to work because of the absolute chaos on all roads around the Twin Cities. All the highways are parking lots.

The FAA did not specify a date for reopening the airport. Let's step back and take a look at what this means to the Twin Cities by the numbers. The 22 bridges normally handle over 1.2 million vehicle crossings per day. Approximately, 250,000 workers are unable to drive to their place of employment because of the destroyed bridges. Another estimated 100,000 people are unable to perform their jobs. This includes delivery vehicles, truckers delivering food and other products, and postal workers. Countless others are simply unable to get on with their daily lives. The Twin Cities metropolitan area is home to over 3 million people, and the loss of the bridges has literally split them in half. This loss will be devastating to the area for years. It will take months to rebuild even the smallest bridge. After the 35W bridge collapse in 2007, it took nine months to rebuild the bridge. Let's take a look at what bridges they do have left.

Newscaster Alicia Washburn steps over to a large screen TV showing the Twin Cities highway system and points to a green line that shows a highway connection between downtown Minneapolis and St. Paul.

Yesterday, the shortest route was 11 miles taking Interstate Highway 94 across the Mississippi River.

She then touches the screen and 22 red X's appear over the bridge locations with two alternate routes appearing in green, one showing a route heading north and another heading south.

> Now, as you can see with the loss of the bridges, the shortest route from downtown Minneapolis to downtown St. Paul traveling north is 57 miles. You need to travel north about 25 miles before you hit the next river crossing. Here to the south the shortest route is 52 miles, you need to travel south about 22 miles before you can cross the river. Each of these two bridge crossings highlighted with green circles typically handles about 40,000 vehicles per day.

> For all practical purposes, it will be next to impossible for people to cross the river for months. Hundreds of thousands of people will simply be unable to get to work or perform their normal job. Anyone attempting to take these highlighted routes will be stuck in traffic for hours. We should also note that hundreds of fiber optic cables, power lines, natural gas lines, and other utility lines were also severed when the bridges went down leading to havoc for residents all over the Twin Cities who have also lost power, gas, internet, and telephone. An estimated 800,000 homes have been affected.

> Earlier today, shortly after the governor declared a state of emergency, the University of Minnesota also shut down. Only a fraction of professors and support staff were able to get to the university because the bridge connecting the east and west banks of the university was destroyed.

A graphic is up showing how the Mississippi River literally bisects the university. Everyone is silently sitting around the conference table as the enormity of the loss hits them. What a stunning loss this is to the entire midwest region. Moments later a reporter informs everyone the President is about to address the nation. The podium in the press room at the White House is now visible as the president approaches and everyone pauses to listen.

> My fellow Americans, today is the most horrendous day America has experienced since the unfathomable terrorist attacks on 9/11. Fortunately, the loss of life is minimal; however, the loss of one life is too many. My heart goes out to the families who have lost loved ones. I can assure you that all Federal Agencies are on high alert and will work non-stop until the perpetrators of these heinous acts are found and brought to justice. These acts of terrorism will not be tolerated. I have

spoken with the governor of Minnesota and I have promised emergency federal funds and ordered the Army Corps of Engineers to seek immediate solutions in order to restore order to the cities of St. Paul and Minneapolis. That is all I have to say right now. We will reconvene tomorrow for questions.

The moment the president steps away from the podium, pandemonium breaks out from the press corp. Fifty questions fly at the President all at once as he steps through the door exiting the press room. The door closes, and the room falls silent. Everyone in the conference room sits quietly for several moments. They know the president didn't say more because he couldn't say more. All the *Federal Agencies* are working non-stop, but so far, they have nothing and there is certainly no way the President could dance around that question.

The conversation turns to attempting to identify the source of the explosives. Early reports, based on the blast patterns, indicate the likely use of C-4 explosives and detonating cord (detcord) from mining operations. Experts, including a former assistant director of the ATF, drone on for hours all afternoon discussing and reiterating the possible source of the explosives and what measures federal authorities will use to identify the explosives and then the source. They are discussing all the possible sources and how law enforcement will look for recent thefts involving high explosives.

Reardon is thinking how the discussion is exhausting to watch, with each expert rehashing the same list of unknowns. Reporters awkwardly try to keep the discussion going. Asking the same questions *over and over again* in slightly different ways to fill the time. During commercial breaks, the stations are trying to sell you antacids and the latest prescription drug that will solve all your problems if the list of side effects doesn't kill you first. McCullum finally orders everyone to go home at 9:30 knowing there is nothing more they can do tonight.

The long day finally concludes with Spencer dropping off Reardon at his place at just before ten.

"I don't know why you're even dropping me off. In two more hours, something horrendous is about to happen."

"Yes, but unfortunately, sleeping in the office isn't going to help with anything right now."

The long 14 hours in the office with no break remind him of his days in Afghanistan when they were working with a hot bit of intel. Trying to locate a specific terrorist and call in an air strike before they moved locations and disappeared into the mist again, sometimes for months at a time. The intensity was beyond insane, with the long hours and the pressure to confirm the intel and avoid civilian casualties where possible. That is really what ate at him; he knew no matter how careful they were, innocents would get killed. Getting reports of small children was particularly distressing because it made him think of his own beautiful girl.

As soon as he entered his brownstone, he unscrewed the cap on a fifth of gin and took a long swig then coughing only to take in more. His drinking over the last couple of weeks had taken on a new intensity. It was different, and after today he knew there was more to come, he knew they were going to escalate, and just keep piling on the destruction like he helped do in Afghanistan.

It always started off so innocently. They were just looking for one person, the last bad guy. If they could get this one person they could all go home. It was never just one person. Finding that person would lead to more intel, which led to more names, more hideouts, more air strikes, and ground attacks. Cities and towns, just shanties compared to small American towns, were slowly eaten away until only piles of rubble were left in dozens of locations. It was an unyielding reign of terror. People who've lived on the edge of oblivion for decades were pushed even closer to the precipice. The American government was unable to admit that they were creating terrorists at a greater rate than they were killing them. Reardon and the other agents knew this at an instinctual level, but always kept it just below the surface. Facing up to that fact meant they could no longer do their job in good conscience, so it remained just below the surface. By 11:30, Reardon was once again passed out on his sofa from sheer exhaustion, the half empty bottle having fallen out of his limp hand.

Washington, D.C.

The president and his staff are in for a sleepless night. The President is in a live conference with the heads of all the intelligence agencies.

"Please tell me someone has got something to go on right now."

The conference is dead still with silence.

"I swear to God if any of you are sitting on something right now, trying to hide it from the others, I will fire every last one of you. This is no time for any sort of interagency pissing match. If you've got something, I want it now!"

Simultaneously, multiple people mumble out responses indicating they have no intel at this time. The President would still not be surprised if someone was keeping their cards close to their chest. One thing he can't stand is spooks. They are the most paranoid group of lunatics he has ever met. But then again, they get paid to be paranoid lunatics. It's when that paranoia interferes with making forward progress that he gets pissed. The president ends the conference with a final warning to get him some actionable intel.

He and his chief of staff return to the conference room where his staff is waiting. As soon as he walks in, he asks for options. The deafening silence is uninspiring.

"Come on people, I need options. What is a reasonable response to this?"

Ironically, that is exactly what they were discussing while he was out. They discussed a litany of options all coming back to the same unanswered question. Who? Without a *who* they've got nothing. In a typical scenario, the president orders a measured response against the group responsible for the attack. Groups typically take credit immediately and provide the *who*. The *what* is discussed, planned, and executed within a few weeks. Airstrikes and targeted killings typically quell the righteous indignation of the American public without producing any meaningful results. This tit for tat mentality continues to result in a stalemate. An endless war is a rallying cry for terrorist groups looking to boost their membership and lash out with renewed vigor.

His staff briefly discusses the economic impact both to Minnesota and nationally. That morning the Dow Jones dropped 1200 points in early trading and rebounds to close down 302 points. This is the first attack that has long-term tangible consequences. There are 17 Fortune 500 companies headquartered in Minnesota including General Mills and Target. Each one is impacted by the loss of the bridges. The president asks his Secretary of Commerce to prepare a report outlining the economic impact to both Minnesota and the midwest. He asks for projections on job losses and how long it will take to recover those jobs.

The president steps out for a while, and instructs his chief of staff to develop a recommendation. Ninety minutes later, the president returns expecting to hear a recommendation.

"So, what is a reasonable path forward right now?" Asks the president.

"Well Mr. President, we feel we have three options right now," begins his chief of staff. "The first option is to focus on finding a pattern to the attacks and guarding those locations."

But guard where? The attacks are seemingly random. Even though the governor has declared a state of emergency in Minnesota, it is unlikely that Minnesota is the target for the next attack because, up to this point, they have never attacked the same place twice.

"Are we close to finding a pattern?"

"Frankly, no, Mr. President."

"Then let's move on," instructs the president.

"The second option is to essentially wait for more information and clues that will lead to an arrest."

This is not a purely passive response. The chief of staff continues.

"We will re-double our efforts to analyze as much information as we can from each attack site so far. Go through everything with a fine-toothed comb looking for something we have missed so far."

"That's a fine suggestion, but it seems like a normal course of action. I would expect every agency to re-examine everything they have. What's next?"

"The third option is declaring a nationwide state of emergency."

"Doesn't that seem a little extreme at this point in time?"

The President is right and continues his thought.

"Imagine if I sent in federal troops to Orlando after the night club shooting to restore order? Or to Ft. Lauderdale after the airport shooting. There is simply no legal basis."

Declaring a state of emergency in a city or state is reserved for catastrophic events. This is typically used for ensuring the restoration of order after a hurricane or large city-wide riots. The situation simply does not currently warrant such a call to action. Even if the president did consider this a viable option, the logistics behind this are mind boggling.

"Mr. President, while I agree under normal circumstances, this is true," interjects the Secretary of Defense. "This is a national emergency."

"Yes, it is, but I don't see how that will help. I need another option."

"With all due respect Mr. President, we need to take action now," continues the Secretary.

"The role of the National Guard is to maintain order and not act as a police force actively searching out criminals. They are not equipped to handle law enforcement activities."

The secretary presses again, "we need to take an active position."

"Are you suggesting we invoke the Insurrection Act?"

The room falls silent with such a suggestion.

The mere mention of the Insurrection Act would have been unheard of a mere 10 days ago. The President prompts the room by asking again.

"Are you suggesting we invoke the Insurrection Act?" Everyone sits in continued silence. The president presses on, "Suspend the Posse Comitatus Act and declare Martial Law?"

"No sir," quickly responds the secretary.

"Then I don't see how merely declaring a state of emergency could possibly help."

The Insurrection Act is an extreme measure and would only be seriously considered for a time of war or national upheaval. Even if he suspends Posse Comitatus and begins stationing the U.S. military around the country, there is not enough to cover the entire country. The moral and legal considerations of suspending civil liberties would also be enormous, having never been considered at a national level. The president finally dismisses his staff just after eleven, realizing they are making no progress, and even losing ground, as tempers flare.

Day 30

Dow Jones Industrial Average
18,944.99
Total decline: 6.0%
Total loss: $312 Billion

Nasdaq
5,357.84
Total decline: 5.7%
Total loss: $484 Billion

Cities are made for enemies to destroy.
Will Oldham

Reardon awakes to his door buzzer and slowly walks over to his intercom.

Reardon is barely able to utter a slurred "whaaattt" into the intercom.
"Let me in!" Spencer demands.

Reardon hits the button to let her in and opens his door a crack.

"Get dressed."
"What was it this time? Are we going to do this every stinking morning?"
"Eleven airports this morning."
"What do you mean eleven airports?"
"They blew highway overpasses, blocking the highways leading into the airports."
"Crap! How many killed?"
"Nine confirmed dead."
"How did they do it this time?"
"Truck bombs, they parked them at the base of the overpass columns and set them off remotely. That's all they are reporting right now."
"Which airports?"
"Big ones, Atlanta, San Francisco, Chicago, New York. We need to get in so we can find out more details."
"How will that help?"
"Get dressed, I'm taking you in."
"The hell you are, I need more sleep. I'm still plastered. I can't go into the office like this, and me sitting in the office isn't going to make the news come in any faster."
"FINE!" Spencer turns in frustration clenching her fists. "I will go in for a while, come back, and get you around 10."
"I don't need a ride from you. I can get myself to work. Just let me sleep."
"OK, but if you're not in by noon, I'm coming back for you."
"Fine," Reardon begrudgingly agrees. Anything to get her out so he can sleep.

Reardon turns on the TV as he flops down on the sofa. As he sits there, he can imagine everyone sitting around the large conference table. Agents just staring at the screen watching as newscasters show photo after photo of overpasses now in shambles as traffic is backed up for miles. The newscasters alternate between scenes in San Francisco, Phoenix, Miami, Atlanta, Orlando, Chicago, Charlotte, Denver, New York, Las Vegas, Dallas, and the Twin Cities. Twelve of the sixteen largest airports in the nation are now in turmoil. Tens of millions are now affected by the bombings in two days. The Minneapolis-St. Paul airport remains closed as flight crews and airport personnel are unable to get to the airport along with any type of supplies, including jet fuel.

All the airports are cancelling flights because of the same issues faced by people in Minnesota as people are unable to get into the airports in any reasonable manner.

In Minnesota, they are interviewing government officials and discussing the devastating effects of the 22 lost bridges. They are, once again, explaining how commuters are now forced to drive north and south of the cities to bridges designed for only a fraction of the traffic they have been experiencing over the last 24 hours. The governor of Minnesota is once again asking people to stay at home and stay off the roads. Hundreds of thousands comply with the order, but enough people still want to get from one side of the cities to the other, causing misery on the roads. The governor does not want to compound the agony by ordering any bridge closures. Police are along the highways leading to these bridges trying to maintain some semblance of order. The bridges are a necessity for hundreds of thousands of people to get to work every day. Newscasters are asking how many days the governor can keep ordering a state of emergency before the economy is devastated. Even if commuters are given the go ahead, drives that used to take 20 minutes will now take at least 4-6 hours if not longer. It will take at least a year before all the bridges are rebuilt, and the ones along the major highways may take even longer to rebuild. The newscasters switch back to discussing the other eleven cities. Once again, Reardon imagines McCullum quietly sitting at the conference table with his team, sitting helpless. Then he imagines a similar scene at nearly every Federal Agency across the country because it has just gotten that bad. The newscaster continues with her report.

The explosions all happened simultaneously at 4 a.m. Eastern time. The San Francisco airport is surrounded by water on three sides, and Highway 101 passes along the west edge of the airport. The terrorists blew up three highway overpasses at the northwest and southwest corners of the airport, cutting off nearly all traffic in and out of the airport except for a couple of small service roads, effectively cutting off all traffic. The two service roads are completely congested with traffic as tempers flare. The one and only road leading into the Denver International Airport is an overpass on E470, running north and south, was destroyed, again cutting off traffic. In Chicago, the Highway 190 overpass was destroyed blocking most of the incoming traffic to Chicago's O'Hare Airport.

As the newscaster continues, image after image of destruction flashes across the screen.

In Orlando, along highway 426, two overpasses, just to the north and south were destroyed, cutting off most traffic into the airport. Federal officials are currently estimating 42 people were killed in the explosions and nearly 80 more injured, many with life threatening injuries. It will take days to get an exact count. The FAA estimates over 12,000 flights will be cancelled today because flight crews will be unable to get to their airplanes along with support personnel. The overpasses near the airports are also major highways in most cities and causing nightmarish driving conditions. The loss of the overpasses is devastating, but not nearly as devastating as the loss of the bridges in Minneapolis. Crews are already waiting to clear rubble from all the overpass sites. However, they will need to work in conjunction with federal authorities as they try to collect evidence in order to track down the terrorists.

The president has put the nation on high alert and declared a state of emergency in all the cities affected by the bombings. Local authorities are reviewing camera footage from last night looking at the license plates of the trucks used in the bombings along with the cars that picked up the driver from each truck and drove off just before each explosion. Currently, we have no additional information as Federal Authorities are refusing to release any of the footage from the traffic cameras.

Reardon has made his way into the office and is sitting in the corner of the conference room slumped in a chair. The TV goes to a commercial and McCullum mutes the TV in the conference room.

McCullum summarizes the situation with one succinct word, "Dammit!"

Everyone in the room slowly turns to face McCullum.

"OK, at least we have some footage of these bastards this time. Peterson, call all the field offices and get us that footage. I want it within an hour."

Peterson quickly hustles out of the room. McCullum is pacing back and forth thinking back to 9/11 and how that left everyone shocked and speechless. While that was still the most horrific day in his life, this one has an enormous sinking feeling. He's trying to understand the rationale behind the attacks. Again, loss of life was not the primary goal. He remembers how all air traffic was stopped for three days after 9/11 and then the following day things went back to normal. The new normal, where no hijacking would ever be viewed as a hijacking ever again. In our new world, every hijacking was a potential suicide mission. This was different, they didn't touch a single plane but the effect is nearly the same. Twelve of the largest airports in the nation are now crippled, and the ripple effect crosses the entire nation and the world. It will take weeks before ANY major airport will resume normal operations. The Minneapolis airport may be shut down for months as officials try to figure out how to get people in and out of the airport. Just having half the airport workers stuck on the other side of the river is a logistical nightmare. How do you run an airport with only half your normal staff? Not to mention the 3 million people whose lives have been turned into utter chaos with the loss of a mere 22 bridges.

McCullum is bordering on delirium between the stress and lack of sleep over the last 11 days. He is realizing he is not equipped to handle these types of situations. All the scenarios they ran over the last five years have all dealt with massive loss of life and catastrophic losses, but not bridges and overpasses. On the other hand, these were exactly the type of attacks Reardon was expecting. He saw the devastating effects of these types of attacks in Afghanistan where people are accustomed to agonizing hardships. When America first attacked Afghanistan all those years ago, the first thing the Army did was blow up all the bridges they weren't planning to use for themselves. He knew these types of attacks would be even more effective and devastating to Americans who were accustomed to comfort and convenience.

By the end of the day, the FAA shutdown all eleven airports for the same reason. Flight crews, airport personnel, and passengers are unable to get in and out of the airports in any reasonable amount of time. The few remaining service roads are all completely congested along with the highways surrounding the airports. Officials currently have no plans and report the airports will shut down for at least three days while they develop a plan to bring the airports back online and reposition the planes that have been diverted. Nearly every large airport across the nation is already feeling the impact as overnight flights are diverted and connecting flights are cancelled. Logjams are forming at the airports taking the diverted aircraft. These airports are running out of gates for passengers to disembark. Planes sit for hours as flight crews figure out the best way to safely get people off the planes. In many cases, the planes are parked and passengers get off and walk across the tarmac to get to the terminal. Thousands upon thousands end up at least a hundred miles from their intended destination. International carriers are also quickly adjusting as these 11 airports handle hundreds of international flights every day. This has now become a global problem.

By the end of the day, McCullum has reviewed the camera footage from every attack. A car and truck pull over at each underpass, the truck driver slides out the passenger seat door away from passing traffic. The driver ducks down as he moves forward to get in the awaiting car. The car speeds away and the truck bombs explode ten minutes later. All the license plates are stolen, and the cars disappeared onto side roads outside of the city. All the drivers wore hoods, masks, and gloves so they have no way to identify anyone involved in the bombings. McCullum lowers his head after the last video thinking this was handled flawlessly. No one even gives a second thought to a truck sitting along a highway. Why would they? McCullum is at his wits end. He's wondering how can they defend against this. They are still at square one after thirty days.

McCullum wants to learn more about what they can do with video surveillance, so he calls Peterson into his office and assigns him a new task.

Washington, D.C.

The president has been in the situation room since 5:07 a.m. after being awakened at 4:23 and informed of the attacks on the airports. He now considers the attacks an open declaration of war and puts the Pentagon on high alert. The Chairman of the Joint Chiefs of Staff has been by the president's side since 5:53. The president has been discussing military options and attempting to determine the best way to strike back. As the discussions continue, one sticking point is a thorn in their side. Attack who?

"I suggest we identify all groups capable of launching this type of coordinated attack and bomb them back to kingdom come," coldly states the Secretary of Defense. "We have the locations of 39 training camps throughout the Middle East, North Africa, and Afghanistan."

The secretary does not even realize he is caught in his own lie. If they believed any group was capable of launching such a coordinated attack then the U.S. would have made a preemptive strike.

"Name the group?" asks the chief of staff.

The Secretary now realizing his mistake, "Well, there are a few key groups we could target."

"Yes, but we don't believe any of them are even close to doing this. Isn't that right?"

"Yes," the Secretary demurs.

"I admire your conviction, but how is blowing the hell out of 39 foreign camps going to help right now?" asks the president.

This shotgun approach is briefly discussed, ultimately deemed too expansive, and the outcome is too unpredictable. Besides, they can't even verify if the attackers are from the Middle East or North Africa. They also don't feel an attack on a specific target will have any direct impact on the attacks in the U.S. So far, they can't find any link that leads them to believe the attacks are orchestrated overseas.

It appears the attacks are all planned and executed from within the United States. Is this a case of purely domestic terrorism?

At the opening bell the Dow, NYSE, and Nasdaq all plunge. They consider suspending trading but decide against it. By the end of the day, the Dow has dropped nearly 3000 points. Nasdaq and the NYSE are both down over 13%. People have lost over $2 trillion in just hours. The President is informed of the catastrophic historic drop but ignores it. People losing trillions of dollars needs to be pushed to the back burner so he can focus on the task at hand.

The President discusses activating all National Guard units across the entire country. This is a step just short of declaring a state of emergency. However, there is no consensus on where to place them. The initial thought is to guard bridges and overpasses near important locations. The immediate issue with such a strategy is that the attacks are never consistent, in fact, every attack is unique. Theoretically, the bridges and overpasses are probably the safest locations right now and need no protection. The key is to predict the next set of potential targets and protect those locations. The President's staff is making wild guesses about what is next. Anything from football stadiums to grocery stores to factories. No matter how outlandish they would have seemed a month ago, they all sound plausible now.

At noon, the President meets with congressional leaders to discuss a declaration of war. The leaders are in favor of declaring war, but again it comes back to *who*. For all practical purposes, we are still at war with Iraq and Afghanistan, and there is no sense in declaring war with them again. There is no link to any other country, so declaring war against Iran, Syria,

Malaysia, or even Easter Island is equally preposterous. The leaders are pressing the President to take action, but they can see the anguish on his face. And as they have been informed time and time again, there are no suspects or even persons of interest. They all realize this is the ultimate form of guerrilla warfare, and unlike previous wars, carpet bombing the enemy is not a viable option. The President nearly collapses from dehydration at 4 p.m., and his Chief of Staff convinces him to get some rest and eat something before he passes out.

August 12, 2009 – Afghanistan

Conscience is the most dangerous thing you possess. If you wake it up, it may destroy you. To live a life of total moral rigor is not necessarily the way to go. It's the path for very few people. Most people need to come up with some kind of middle ground that satisfies their practical, moral, and philosophical esthetic needs.
John Patrick Shanley

Reardon and Abdul approach the main gate and tell the guard on duty that they are going for a walk. The guard cocks his head in surprise. The guard is thinking these guys are nuts and he logs their departure and opens the gate. Minutes earlier, Reardon eyed Abdul with some trepidation when Abdul asked him to go on a walk, especially on a hot sweltering night like tonight, just before 7 o'clock and still nearly 100 degrees. In the year they have worked together, Abdul never asked him to go for a walk. He did not fear any sort of trap. It was just unusual, in fact completely out of the ordinary. He pauses for a few moments and stares into Abdul's eyes before saying yes. Out of habit, he reaches for his pistol and holster but then puts it back thinking screw it. He was just going for a walk, like a normal person in an abnormal world. They don't say another word until they are 100 yards from the gate.

"So, what's up? This is unusual," asks Reardon.
"Nothing for now, let's just walk, as friends, and pretend all is right with the world."

And with that, they just walked for nearly 20 minutes before Abdul says another word.

"I miss normal," Abdul states unabashedly.

"What?"

"I miss normal, granted Afghan normal is much different than American normal."

"I don't think so, I think normal is normal the world around."

"I'm surprised you can say that with a straight face after being here for so long."

"What?"

"For us, normal is just long hot dry days, hard work, and if you are lucky enough to have electricity, hope it stays on all day."

"OK, you got me there. Americans have gone soft."

They walk about another five minutes, and Abdul motions to turn around. They head back to their hooch for their nightly 8 o'clock pow wow. Just after they turn, Abdul begins speaking.

"Something has been bothering me," he pauses. "We are friends, so I feel comfortable asking you these questions."

"Go on."

"America has been here for years, and you claim you are only here for the terrorists. But you're really attacking everyone. You may not be dropping bombs on everyone, but what you do is just as damaging. Villages are destroyed, roads and bridges destroyed. The average person has nowhere to go. Many of these people have never been more than 10 miles from where they were born. The terrorists have money, resources, and trucks. You come in and destroy cities and villages, and before you can blink, the terrorists are gone and the people left behind try to rebuild what little they had."

"I can't disagree with you. That is the end result. It's unfortunate."

"Yes, that is easy for you to say, but doesn't help. I know you can't help. You are here to do a specific job, and I'm here to help you do that specific job." They walk for a few more minutes. "How do you think Americans would deal with this?"

"Honestly, one thing has really caught me off guard. Since 9/11 there have been no attacks linked to Al Qaeda on American soil. Why? If anything, you would think our presence here would provoke them even more. Sure, we may have likely foiled some attacks, but certainly not all attacks. They will of course never tell the American public what attacks they have stopped, only that *thanks to our ongoing efforts against terrorism threats on American soil have been stopped.* Is it that they're thinking too big?"

"How do you mean?"

"If they are planning attacks, they are going after big glamorous targets in big cities. Targets that are well protected with people watching all the time for anything out of the ordinary. If you want to really hurt Americans, you hurt their wallet and disrupt their daily lives. That's what they should focus on."

"What would disrupt their lives?"

"An endless number of small things. People just want their daily coffee, a smooth drive to work, and a care free day once they get home. People get pissed…"

"What is pissed?" Abdul interrupts.

"Mad. They get mad if they can't have their coffee fix or if there is an accident on the highway and it takes them an extra hour to get home. Add to that high gas prices and long lines at the grocery store, and people get irate."

"Surely it can't be that simple."

"You'd be surprised. Americans are creatures of habit and like their daily comforts. While we're accustomed to dealing with natural disasters like hurricanes, earthquakes, and floods, they come and then they're gone. People rebuild. The national news pays close attention for the next few days and then moves on. You don't hear about it again until the one, five, or ten-year anniversary of these tragic events, including 9/11. We just don't want to deal with tragedy, much less inconvenience, on a daily basis."

"You have a low regard for your fellow Americans."

"It's not a low regard. It's simply the truth, and I'm no different than anyone else."

"You seem to be dealing with your time here pretty well. I've seen others get here and been crawling out of their skin dealing with how they must live here."

"Despite the horrible job we must do, the death and destruction, I find a certain kind of peace with the simplicity of how we live here. Ultimately, I'm here trying to keep America safe."

And with that, Reardon quietly considered what he just said knowing the truth of that was the only thing that justified the time away from his wife and little girl. Just then they approached the front gate, checked back in with the guard, and headed to the hooch for their nightly bull session. They solved no problems, but it was good to just talk on a peaceful walk in the countryside.

Day 31

Dow Jones Industrial Average
15,894.91
Total decline: 21.1%
Total loss: $1.09 Trillion

Nasdaq
4,631.23
Total decline: 18.5%
Total loss: $1.57 Trillion

Reardon wakes up to a ringing phone next to his ear as he lies sprawled out on his bed. He slowly reaches up, missing the phone twice before his heavy forearm finally hits the receiver and it drops to the floor. He hears Spencer saying his name as he reaches for the receiver and finally puts it to his ear as he looks at the clock and moans.

"Yeah, yeah, I'm here. What?"
Spencer quickly blurts out, "Jet fuel pump stations. Get to the office as soon as you can."
"OK, pump stations. Got it," and Reardon rolls onto his back while still not comprehending.

Two hours later, Reardon awakes thinking only a few moments have passed. He looks at the clock and realizes he fell back asleep. The phone call comes back to him. Pump stations. What does pump stations mean? He hesitates, looking at the remote and thinking about what horrible news he is about to hear, but pump stations has piqued his curiosity. He catches the newscaster mid-sentence.

…four jet fuel pump stations have been destroyed. The most significant pump station is the one near the Mississippi Alabama border. This pump station moves jet fuel from the Houston, Texas, refinery and delivers it to all the major airports in Alabama, Georgia, Tennessee, North and South Carolina, Virginia, and finally up to New Jersey and New York. The Northeast corridor has multiple pipelines, but the loss will still have an effect. Three other pump stations in Missouri were also destroyed, disrupting the jet fuel supply in several Midwest states. As with the Northeast, there are many redundant pipelines in the central Midwest, but this is going to have an impact.

Nearly all airports handling commercial air traffic have their jet fuel delivered through an extensive system of pipelines that span the country. The Texas mainline is 40 inches wide. The fuel travels 3 to 5 miles per hour, and it takes an average of 18 and a half days to travel from Houston to New York harbor. That is a flow of about 5.5 million gallons per hour. 15 tank farms along the way store 1.2 billion gallons of fuel in order to provide a 45 day supply so there is no immediate danger of a jet fuel shortage, however, the damage is done. Airports will need to dip into these reserves.

At that moment, Reardon decides to get up. He painfully gets to an upright position with a stellar throb echoing through his head. At the same moment, a shooting pain is simultaneously coming from his leg as he slowly edges towards the bathroom. He heads into the shower but changes his mind and returns to the edge of his bed. Just then his focus returns to the TV.

The University of Minnesota has cancelled all classes once again, and 8 other colleges in the Twin Cities located in close proximity to the river have also cancelled classes for the same reasons. Approximately half of the staff and students who live off campus are physically unable to get to school. The impact has been immediate across the entire Twin Cities. Hospitals are short staffed. Paramedic units are understaffed along with police and fire departments. The hospitals are already coordinating their efforts to share staff. Critical medication supplies are running low. Doctors, nurses, and other hospital staff who are now separated from their hospital are beginning to work at hospitals closer to home. While this is reducing the staffing shortage, it is still chaos as doctors and nurses must start working together under strenuous circumstances and learning how their new hospitals operate. The governor is asking people to stay at home for a third straight day in order to leave the roads open for emergency vehicles and supply vehicles.

Food shortages are becoming a concern. The main food distribution center for the Twin Cities is on the west side of the river, and several grocery stores, especially on the east side of the river, are running out of food as people flock to the grocery stores to store up on food.

The implications of this are enormous. Even when the governor gives the go ahead for people to return to work, there will still be hundreds of thousands of people unable to get to work for all practical purposes. The Army Corps of engineers is investigating the use of temporary bridges. If they can be used, they will only handle a fraction of the daily traffic. The three bridges to survive the attack have been deemed structurally unsound. Although they did not completely collapse the bridge decking did drop six to twenty-four inches with the columns being severely cracked. Two are also listing. The Governor has ordered all three bridges to be destroyed so the rebuilding process can start as soon as possible. Prior to the loss of the 22 bridges, the closest bridges to the north and south handled about 40,000 vehicles each per day. They would need to handle an additional 1.2 million crossings, which is simply not practical. The Minneapolis-St. Paul airport remains closed.

Across the country, highway crews continue clearing debris from the highway overpasses blocking access to eleven other airports across the nation. The FAA has reported that the airports will remain closed for at least two more days resulting in thousands of cancelled flights across the country. The effect extends well beyond the adjacent airports because planes and crews are out of position, many being stranded due to cancellations from yesterday. International flights are also being cancelled by the hundreds.

Local authorities are quickly coming up with plans to replace the overpasses as soon as the debris is cleared. It will take a minimum of three weeks to reconstruct the overpasses and return normal traffic flow. In the meantime, commuters are dealing with huge delays as traffic is rerouted in each city.

The image on the television switches to Sen. Eidelmen standing on the steps of the Capitol. He seizes an opportunity to be bold and make a name for himself with this crisis.

The response from the President on these acts of terrorism has been beyond weak. He is showing the world our soft underbelly and showing how we are impotent against a small band of terrorists roaming our nation inflicting damage. The President should immediately...

Reardon shuts off the TV and stands up, setting the empty can on the table. He limps towards the kitchen for his morning meal. He is out of eggs, so he settles for a stale bagel and some OJ. Finally, his leg has loosened up, and he's walking with a slight gate. He walks into his room and gets dressed. He finally decides there is no reason to even go into the office. He calls Spencer and explains there is nothing he can do. Spencer is perturbed, but she agrees there is nothing he can do. Reardon lazily flops down onto the sofa with a six-pack recently retrieved from the fridge and cracks open a can just after flipping on the TV. He catches the last 10 seconds of an ad for men's briefs. He just pauses for a moment thinking this is great. The world is collapsing around us but, let's make sure we are wearing comfortable briefs. The world must go on. His attention snaps back to the TV as James Newburgh's first words catch him off guard.

The Mall of America in Minnesota just issued a statement declaring its intention to shut down at noon today and remain closed indefinitely. This is another blow to the Minnesota economy. Let's hand it over to Suzanne Davis who has the statement and a few quick facts about the Mall of America.

The camera pans over to a young woman dressed in a loose fitting rose colored dress with immaculate long black hair sweeping down across one eye. She quickly brushes the hair from her left eye and begins to summarize the statement.

The Mall of America is located less than one mile south of the Minneapolis-St. Paul airport and just west of the Minnesota River, where two nearby bridges were destroyed two days ago. The statement reads that the mall is shutting down for the same reasons as the airport. Only a fraction of the employees and customers are able to get to the mall. In addition to the request from the Governor that people remain in their homes and only travel when needed. The mall is also citing their desire to close down for security reasons to ensure no attacks are instigated at the Mall of America. Let's take a look at a few facts obtained from the Mall of America's website.

Suzanne steps over to a large monitor and starts reading the facts and figures from the screen.

The Mall of America is 5.6 million square feet with 520 stores - large enough to hold 32 Boeing 747s. 40% of all visitors are tourists and there are over 40 million visitors per year. The Mall of America generates about $2 billion of economic activity for the state of Minnesota each year. With its closing, that will put 11,000 year-around employees out of a job temporarily, costing the mall about $5.5 million per day. In the statement, they point out they will work to open as quickly as possible. However, with such ongoing chaos in the Twin Cities, there is really no good guess on when the mall will re-open. The mall is not the only business that will need to shut down as a result of the lost bridges. The true economic impact will begin to unfold over the next several weeks as Minnesotans and everyone across the Midwest begin to feel the impact.

Reardon finally showers and opens his closet to find freshly laundered shirts. His landlady was nice enough to do his laundry. This is not the first time she has done this. She did it several times after he lost his family. She was tired of him looking so ratty and disheveled heading to work. This is the first time she has done it for nearly a year. He puts on a freshly laundered shirt and feels like a new man for a few moments before walking back into the bathroom and realizing he still looks horrible. He touches up a couple places he missed shaving and combs his hair. He realizes he is long overdue for a haircut. He stares at himself for a few moments in the mirror and decides to go into the office since he really has nothing else to do. Within an hour he is back at the office and walks directly to the conference room that is quietly subdued. Everyone looks like someone just ran over their dog or cat. McCullum is irate and slowly pacing. If this were a cartoon, smoke would be streaming from his ears.

"I want to renew our efforts at trying to find the source of the explosives. Where the hell are they getting all these explosives? The stuff they're using is military grade. We must track all this stuff pretty closely."

"We do. I was researching this last night and found some pretty disturbing facts." Peterson interjects. "I found out explosives still go missing all the time. Heck, we can't even keep track of all our nukes."

"What the hell are you talking about?" McCullum asks.

"Well between 1950 and 1968, we *lost* nine nuclear bombs, mainly in lost aircraft over water. One actually rolled off the deck of a carrier into the ocean 80 miles off the coast of Japan. A diver recently just found one of the nine, lost for 50 years, just off the coast of Georgia. The Soviets have also lost their fair share."

"That was a long time ago." Spencer quips.

"Well..." Peterson takes a long pause, "in 2007 the Air Force misplaced six cruise missiles with nuclear warheads for 36 hours. They *thought* the warheads had been removed and stored before loading the missiles onto a plane. The plane was just sitting at the air force base unprotected, from a *holy crap* these are nuclear bombs so we better keep a close eye on them perspective." Peterson snorts out a little laugh. No one else is amused. "Needless to say, a lot of people got in trouble for that. Several commanders were relieved of duty and brought up on charges."

"Enough about nukes, tell me about the C-4 and detcord." McCullum presses.

"Well, I found a recently released GAO report from 1989, the most current report I could find. Anything newer is still classified. Anyways, the report indicates about 50 pounds was lost and about 300 pounds was stolen from 1985 to 89." Peterson pauses as McCullum scrunches his face in disbelief. "Not much has changed since then."

"How so?" McCullum states as he starts to pace back and forth.

"Nowadays, according to the ATF approximately 200 pounds of C-4 is lost or stolen each year. The government also sells it to licensed companies who use it for various reasons. Based on the explosions so far, experts estimate the terrorists have used approximately 170 pounds of C-4 so far plus the detcord. We of course have no idea if they have more."

"So, for all we know, they have another 100 pounds of this stuff sitting around. This is a frickin' nightmare. We might as well just be handing it out like candy at a parade!" McCullum says in an exasperated voice.

"They might have a lot more. The largest recovery in the last 15 years was back in 2005. A tip led to recovering 150 pounds of C-4, 2,500 blasting caps, and 20,000 feet of detcord from a chop-shop in New Mexico. But this one is the most interesting. In 2013, about the same time as the Boston Marathon bombings, emulsion explosives, cast boosters, detcord, *and* 559 pounds of C-4 were stolen from a federal bunker near Billings, Montana. This robbery might be the source of what we are dealing with now."

"Jesus Christ Peterson! Why didn't you start with that? I don't need all the foreplay." McCullum blurts out. "If they have access to that many explosives, we are looking at a fire storm coming our way."

"That's the problem. We have no idea who they are or what they have access to," Reardon states flatly. "You're also focused on *what* they are trying to destroy. We should focus on *why* they are trying to destroy it and what it means."

McCullum looks a Reardon for a moment to soak in his comment. Others just stare at Reardon for a moment, not sure what to make of his comment. Suddenly, a new agent asks about emulsion explosives and everyone listens as Peterson provides a quick overview. McCullum continues to pace quietly.

"Emulsion explosives are an ammonium nitrate based explosive mixed with fuel oil. It's easy to use and highly stable. It's just as powerful as C-4 and typically used in mining operations. It's pellet based and easy to pump into bore holes and detonate. Ironically, when ammonium nitrate was first developed they did not fully understand its properties and considered it quite safe. So much so, that it was stored outside in the early 1920s. One of the biggest mishaps was in Oppau, Germany, back in 1921. The rain caused it to cake into one giant heap and they wanted to move it, so they placed a few sticks of dynamite in the heap to break it up. The explosion was so great that it left a giant crater that is now a lake and there is a plaque commemorating the obliterated town. The worst accident in the U.S. was back in 1947 when 2,300 tons exploded at a port in Texas, nearly 600 died. It was one of the largest non-nuclear explosions in history."

"Alright, alright! That's enough of a history lesson for now. Everyone out. I need time to think. Reardon, you stay."

Everyone files out of the room and McCullum grabs a chair across from Reardon.

"What do you mean *why* they are trying to destroy it?"

"The *what* is easy. We already figured that out. They are going after infrastructure. Now we need to consider the *why*. What is the result of their actions? Not death. That is a byproduct of attacks. They are after something. They have a goal."

"What do you think that is?"

"They are trying to cause us to second guess everything, to be afraid of everything, and instill a feeling of despair. That is far worse than just blowing everything up. They are just pecking away at us, and it's clear we have no plan or appropriate response for this. We won't stop this unless we get lucky or they decide to stop."

April 3, 2011 – New York

Reardon awakes with a start in a cold sweat. His sudden movement wakes his wife Sara. Reardon rolls over and Sara can tell it's another bad night for him. Sara is at a loss for what to do. She has tried to talk to him about it several times. When he first got back from Afghanistan in February, she noticed him getting up in the night a couple times a week. He said he was still just unwinding and getting over the stress. She accepted this and did not think much of it. Over the last two weeks the restlessness has increased, and the nightmares have started to intensify. A couple weeks ago, it was just mumbling in his sleep, but now the violent spasms that wake him are starting to scare her. She says nothing and does her best to fall asleep. She wakes up just after dawn breaks. As she looks over, the bed is empty. She quietly gets up and looks around the corner into the kitchen. She sees an empty beer can in front of Reardon just as he is cracking open a second can. She retreats back into the bedroom. She knows something has to change.

After Reardon leaves for the office, she calls Spencer. Spencer is surprised by all of this and says he's been just fine at the office. They talk for a few minutes, and Sara hangs up. Later in the morning, Spencer and Reardon are out for lunch.

"Sara called me this morning."

"Huh? Why?"

"She said you have been having trouble sleeping."

"Yeah, a couple nights. I'm fine."

"Typical man answer, *I'm fine.* She said it's been building over a couple of months since you got back and getting worse by the week."

"So, yeah, maybe more than a couple times."

"You should go see Dr. Miller. I hear she's good."

"I'm not going to see a shrink. I'm fine."

"Well, I told Sara about Dr. Miller."

"Crap! Why did you do that?"

"Because I care."

"Can you figure out a different way to care?"

Later that night, Reardon arrives home a little tipsy. This is the last straw for Sara. She explodes, and they have a huge fight. After nearly 30 minutes, Reardon agrees to see the psychiatrist. He promises to call Dr. Miller the next morning.

April 8, 2011 – New York

Reardon arrives at Dr. Miller's office. It's an unassuming office. She has no secretary - just a note on the door:

Please come in and have a seat.
I will be with you in a few minutes.

Dr. Miller is one of the FBI's in-house psychiatrists specially trained to deal with the types of issues agents deal with as part of the job. She is 52 with greying auburn hair and an imposing woman even at five feet tall. She has a kind and knowing smile and a piercing glare. Most of her time is spent dealing with domestic agents, especially ones that do a lot of undercover work and the stress that comes with leading two lives. Over the past five years, she has been seeing more and more agents returning from Iraq and Afghanistan. PTSD is becoming a growing issue within the ranks of the FBI. While she will certainly never understand what they go through there, she knows the right questions to ask. She can help them deal with what they saw, and more importantly, what they did. Reardon has been sitting for just over a minute and finally decides to pick up a magazine. Just at that moment, the secondary door opens leading to Dr. Miller's office.

"Agent Reardon?"
"Yes"

Reardon puts down the magazine as he stands.

"Please come in, may I call you Noah?"
"Yes"
"Good, please call me Liz."
"OK, Liz."
"You can either have a seat or lie down," as she motions her hand.
"OK, I think I'll sit."
"So, what brings you here today?"
"My wife says I have been having nightmares, and they are getting worse."
"Do you agree with that? You said your wife has noticed. Have you noticed?"
"Yeah, I guess so. I haven't been sleeping well for a couple weeks now."
"I read your file and see you have been back for almost two months now. Were you having troubles sleeping before you got back?"
"Yeah."
"How far back can you remember having trouble sleeping?"
"I'm a little uncomfortable talking about this right now."
"OK, would you like to talk about something else? Or, we can end the session and pick it up next week. More to the point, I would like to see you next week. Would that be OK?"
"OK, I guess I want to be done for the day."
"OK."

Dr. Miller stands up and thanks Reardon for coming as she opens the door.

"Can you be here next week at this time?"
"Sure."

That evening, Sara asks how his session went and with his usual curt remarks, he explained it was fine. They just talked about his sleep, and they are meeting again next week. Sara let it drop for the night, just glad he is seeing someone.

Day 32

Reardon awakes to silence and looks at the clock, 10:27. He then looks at the answering machine and sees he has no calls. At this moment, he is wondering what's going on. He was fully expecting a frantic call from Spencer imploring him to come into the office. He flips on the TV and hears the news for the day with a scrolling banner across the bottom of the TV reading *Three plants damaged overnight in Georgia, Vermont, and Pennsylvania*. Just after reading the banner, his ears click into the sound coming out of the TV, and the newscaster explains that three truck bombs were detonated last night. One was outside a toilet paper factory near Atlanta, Georgia. The other two truck bombs detonated outside detergent factories just after midnight in Harrisburg, Pennsylvania, and Montpelier, Vermont. So far, authorities have no suspects and are canvasing the area for witnesses and clues. All three factories are located in relative isolation in rural areas. Reardon sits on the edge of his bed for a couple of minutes, decides to go into the office, and arrives just over an hour later.

As Reardon enters the office, he can hear McCullum bellowing from the conference room. Just as he enters the conference room, McCullum is pacing.

"This is beyond ridiculous. What the hell are they up to? They have created total chaos by blowing up 22 bridges and a crapload of overpasses. One day it's shutting down our entire airline system, and the next day it's toilet paper and laundry detergent. What are they trying to do? Keep us at home and keep us from crappin' and doing our clothes?"

McCullum continues to slowly pace as everyone quietly watches.

In the meantime, the muted TV reporters are delving into details around all the ensuing chaos. In the Twin Cities, food shortages are becoming an alarming concern as food distributor Super Valu, located in a western suburb of Minneapolis, is unable to reach any grocery stores located on the east side of the rivers. Delivery trucks are struggling to make any deliveries due to the congested traffic and being cut off from half their customers. Fuel shortages are also starting as gas stations run out of gas and are unable to get resupplied. The governor of Minnesota is imploring people to only make trips that are vital and to conserve fuel. People who had their power and natural gas lines cut as part of the bridges going down are also struggling to stay warm as temperatures are dropping into the low 30s overnight. People are fighting over the dwindling supplies at grocery stores and gas stations. Simply put, this is a disaster of epic proportions with no end in sight and no way to return to normal.

Members of congress are hitting all the news stations demanding answers and looking to law enforcement to quickly capture these terrorists and bring them to justice. They are explaining that this is clearly a breakdown in our intelligence services and demanding that heads will roll. The reality is that law enforcement is no closer to finding any suspects than they were when Reardon's car was first discovered.

As images continue to splash on the muted screen, reporters continue to discuss the Twin Cities stating that 23 deaths are now linked to the disaster because emergency personnel are simply unable to get to people's homes in time to provide emergency care. Hospitals are also continuously understaffed and continue to figure out how to shift people around in order to satisfy staffing requirements. Medical supplies are dwindling. Critical operations are delayed or cancelled due to insufficient hospital staff. Important drugs that are typically flown in a day or two before treatment are now delayed causing patients to miss important treatments for life-threatening ailments.

The TV goes to a commercial break, and when the news returns, images continue to flash across the screen as agents frantically scurry in and out of the room. There are images of heavy machinery working at the site of the San Francisco airport. All debris has been cleared, and highway workers are starting to put in place vertical columns and support beams that will support the new roadbed. Statistics start flashing on the screen for the Atlanta airport (the busiest airport in the world).

Average flights per day: 2603
Total passengers per day: 260,000
Cargo per day (metric tons): 1795
Employs: 63,000 people
Nonstop service to 60+ international destinations in 45+ countries

San Francisco airport:
Average flights per day: 1166
Total passengers per day: 134,000
Cargo per day (metric tons): 1183

Chicago O'Hare airport:
Average flights per day: 2300
Total passengers per day: 204,000
Cargo per day (metric tons): 4644

Officially, all twelve affected airports remain closed for passenger traffic. Military flight operations continue along with a trickle of cargo flights that try to ensure that vital cargo reaches its final destination where possible. The economic impact of the delays in cargo alone is estimated at $200 million per day. Nearly every large airport in the nation has cancelled flights due to lack of planes or flight personnel. International flight schedules are also in disarray as tens of thousands are now unable to either fly into or out of the U.S. The FAA is working with foreign airlines and is attempting to figure out how to get their passengers home. Airlines are repositioning airplanes and flight crews so they can be put to a better use than just sitting at the closed airports. Newscasters are discussing the staggering economic impact and how the travel plans for millions are now disrupted. People planning to fly home are now stranded in these cities and will be for an indefinite period of time. Hotels are filling up, and rental car agencies are running out of cars as people desperate to get home are renting cars and driving them half-way across the country. Greyhound and Amtrak ridership is booming.

McCullum turns to the window and idly stares out for a few moments. Six agents, including Spencer and Peterson, are frantically typing away on their keyboards.

"I want everyone out except for Reardon, Spencer, and Peterson." McCullum flatly states as he turns to the conference table.

Not needing to be told twice, the four other agents gather their belongings and depart. The last agent out closes the door.

"Reardon, come up here. It's time to talk again."

Reardon slowly rises and walks over, gingerly favoring his bad knee. McCullum turns to Peterson, who is quietly sitting in front of his computer.

"Peterson, do you have those numbers for me?"
"Yes, sir. The U.S. handles about 87,000 flights per day. That includes about 28,000 passenger flights and over 2,100 air cargo flights, like FedEx and UPS. The rest are either private or military. The twelve airports that are now shut down handle about 42% of all passenger traffic in the country. These twelve airports alone cancelled over 11,000 commercial flights again today – this is huge. Plus, each of these airports is a gigantic hub. Hundreds of airports are either sending or receiving airplanes from these airports every day. So, it is leading to thousands of additional cancelations. In reality,

every airport in the nation is impacted to some degree. International flights are also taking a big hit. Atlanta alone has direct flights to over 45 countries every day."

"Reardon, what do you make of this?"

"What specifically?"

"The targets they have chosen."

"Standard operating procedure for what we did in Afghanistan. Disrupt people's lives. However, in their case, it was much more basic stuff, bridges and the water supply. Electricity in the few areas that had it. We wanted to flush out the Taliban and keep them moving, keep them out in the open and vulnerable. The irony is that it had little effect. They were already mainly living on the outskirts of town and in caves. But when they did come into town, we wanted them to find nothing. We didn't do this indiscriminately, but where we did it, it was horrible and complete. We left the people with nothing."

"What's still eating at me is that we have no definite link between you and the attacks beyond that stinking letter from three weeks ago. And for that matter, not a single clue of any type that is moving us any closer to finding these bastards and shutting down their attacks."

"I'll say it again. Their goal isn't destruction. It's disruption. They don't need to kill us to hurt us."

"Again, why are you so certain?"

"Simple, because I saw what it did in Afghanistan. The effects are immediate and complete with people that had nothing. If this keeps up, America will spin out of control for no other reason than mass hysteria as people lose their jobs and the stock market continues to drop wiping out billions every day. Peterson, how much has the Dow dropped since this started?"

"Over 4,000 points."

"See, that's in just 12 days, and this will continue. The automated trading programs have been shut down for over a week to slow the decline, and they've reduced trading hours. I bet they'll start closing the exchange if the drops become too significant. After 9/11, they did not re-open the New York Stock Exchange and Nasdaq until September 17th in order to avoid panic selling. Even then the Dow dropped nearly 700 points."

"It sounds like you have really thought this through." McCullum adds.

"Not really. Heard it on CNN last night. They said in 2001, the exchanges lost nearly $1.4 trillion in just five days. The markets are turning into a powder keg, and it won't take much to set them off. They were talking about how the drop could be worse than '29, '87, and 9/11 combined."

McCullum turns back to the window and momentarily gazes out. He crosses his arms and his shoulders droop slightly.

"Peterson, anything else?" McCullum asks with no emotion in his voice.

"The President has ordered the National Guard to patrol every single bridge, ramp, and overpass leading into all major airports around the clock."

"What's the point?" Reardon says with a slight mocking laugh. "They'll never attack the same thing twice. Why bother? It's how they keep us off guard."

"We have to try something." Spencer interjects.

"Well, let's try something else," replies Reardon.

"OK, enough. Anything else?" Asks McCullum.

"Yes sir, I have that info on surveillance cameras you wanted."

"Good, let's hear it. How can we use the cameras to catch these guys?"

"Well, I don't have any good news. Every day in the U.S. we record well over a million hours of surveillance footage. Most of it's stored for less than 48 hours. Only 5% is stored longer, maybe up to 30 days. It's rare for anything to be kept longer than that. Many of the cameras are outdated. The images are too grainy, and some places still likely record on VHS tapes and just record over and over on the same tapes. The main reason most footage is kept less than 48 hours is because of cost. It's simply too much data, and we rarely go back and look at it. So why spend the money? Anyways, there's no shortage of video to look at. In fact, there's too much. Most of it's stored locally, and there's no way to collect all of it. Even if we could, there's no database in the world that could hold that much information. Then, even if we could collect it all, there is no way we could process and cross reference it fast enough. The average American is recorded 75 times a day. The cameras are everywhere - ATMs, stores, gas pumps, the gym, and restaurants. This is compounded by the fact that when you don't know what you're looking for, then everything is a match and nothing is a match. Some places have more cameras than you can imagine. Times Square has over 6000 cameras. So far, every shot we have is with them wearing masks and dark glasses."

"Can we get some basic facial characteristics through the masks?"

"No, they would need to be skin tight. Even if we could do some basic comparison, it would be a comparison against what? It goes back to collecting all that footage. Besides, cameras are recording over a billion facial images a day, and we don't know who we're looking for at this point in time. We probably have every one of them on tape 100 times just like every one of us is on tape 100 times. Imagine if I told you to find a specific person from Idaho without telling you anything else to go on. The person could fly in tomorrow, and you could pass them on the street ten times a day for the next week and have no clue. We've got them on camera. I'm convinced of that. The problem is we have *everyone* on camera."

"It can't be that hard to find people." Spencer interjects.

"Look at our 10 Most Wanted List. People are on that for years sometimes and we can't track'em down *and* we have a photo for every one of them," adds Peterson.

The room falls quiet.

"Hell's fury is going to come down on us if we don't come up with something soon … All of you get out of here. I need to think." McCullum says as he slowly turns to look out the window.

Washington, D.C.

The president is living in his situation room and has rarely stepped out for the last four days. Tempers flare as one outlandish theory is discussed and shot down after another. The intelligence agencies are finding no useful chatter whatsoever. The NSA has been working around the clock tracking money transfers into the country from anywhere over the last six months. They are reviewing all phone calls over the past six months that raised red flags. They are increasing electronic surveillance everywhere. They are closely guarding their super-secret, and illegal, tracking activities that continue in the post-Snowden era. Snowden was a public embarrassment but did little to slow their covert tracking. The NSA, CIA, TSA, and FBI all come up emptyhanded. They have concluded these are sleeper cells in deep cover operating independently and in unison to coordinate attacks. They have no idea if this is domestic terrorism or not. Every organization expands their search parameters and starts looking back one year. If that fails, they will look back two years.

The INS is starting to meticulously search through all its immigration records looking for anything they have missed on anyone arriving in the country over the last six months. The initial focus is people arriving from Middle Eastern countries and Afghanistan. The president asks the INS to formally coordinate a nationwide Watch List across all agencies. Anyone who raises a red flag is added to the list. The president wants a single list so ten different agencies don't try to track down one person repeatedly. Initial concerns are raised over privacy and the legality of passing information between agencies. The NSA and CIA hate the idea fearing it will divulge too much of their internal workings and expose highly secretive programs. In a meeting with all key agencies, the president makes it clear that they will figure out the legality of it later. Despite his clear orders, people lower down still drag their feet fearing they will be prosecuted for breaking the law. He then has a separate private meeting with the directors of the NSA and CIA. He already knows they will not comply.

The INS will collect the names and then pass out lists of names to the TSA, FBI, and other domestic agencies so they can work with local police to track down people. There is no protocol for anything like this. It leads to chaos. Despite the chaos, people get to work.

The president returns to a meeting with his staff as the conversation shifts and they contradict themselves and start all over repeating their circular logic. The only glaringly obvious thing they know is that they have learned nothing over the last four days. The president returns to the Oval office so his staff can continue to explore options in peace and quiet.

An hour later, the president meets with the director of the NSA. He becomes frustrated within minutes. He knows the director is not telling him everything and doesn't even try to hide that fact. He knows they are still doing secret work that he's never supposed to hear about.

"I need to know everything you're doing," states the president.
"Mr. President, with all due respect, *need to know* prevents me from telling you everything."
"That's bullshit!"
"Perhaps, but I can assure you that our computers are churning through all available data."

This much is true, all the computers in the bowels of the NSA are churning through all available data. The director is implying all *legally available* data. The President knows when he says *all available data* that he really means *all data*.

The NSA has learned the following lesson over the years: when you give people the freedom to do anything – they will. And the NSA wants to know about it, all of it. On the other hand, they don't want anyone to know what they are doing. In fact, the NSA director is the only government official authorized to submit a bill for goods purchased with no explanation. The chief judge of the Foreign Intelligence Surveillance Court of Review, which attempts to regulate the NSA, admits they are incapable of investigating reports alleging that the NSA breaks its own secret rules.

The president does not press, so he can maintain the usual plausible deniability. The director brushes over the details of the telephone calls, financial transactions, and emails. The president is still bothered by the NSA's ongoing intrusion into the life of every American and their complete disregard for privacy and civil rights. However, today his righteous indignation is overridden with a sense of relief knowing they are looking at everything and everyone.

Other agencies continue looking for a pattern in the attacks, attempting to identify the next target. All attempts to find a pattern are failing miserably. The president is demanding answers while simultaneously seeing all the information flowing in knowing there are no answers – only more questions with each successive day. All he can think is how we are spending billions of dollars a day on intelligence and coming up with nothing.

The press corps is bordering on near psychosis with the lack of information flowing from the White House. Daily briefings with the press secretary are bordering on the ridiculous as she repeats the same information with each briefing. The reporters complain, *yes, we know the president is working with his staff. Yes, we know he is getting daily briefings from all the key agencies. Yes, we know he will come and talk to us when he has breaking news.* The briefings have turned into some perverted Faustian play. Each reporter would sell their soul for just a tidbit of new information.

April 15, 2011 – New York

Reardon arrives at Dr. Miller's office for this second appointment. Ironically, she comes out just after Reardon picks up a magazine. If this happens a third time he will be convinced she has a camera watching him. That thought caught him off guard. *Third time*, it already sounds like he has accepted the fact that he will be coming here for a while. At least until he starts sleeping through the night.

"Good morning, Noah. Please come in."

Reardon follows her in and sits in the chair again.

"How have you been sleeping since last week?"
"About the same. I've slept on the sofa a couple nights so Sara, ah, my wife, can get a good night's sleep."
"Good. How has that worked out?"
"It's OK."

"Well I'm glad you came back. Many don't. So, now that you're here, let me explain how I work. Basically, I'm here to listen. I want to hear what types of things you dealt with while you were in Afghanistan. The biggest thing with most people is just opening up and discussing what they did. I'm in no hurry. This will take as long as it needs to take. Any questions?"

"Yeah, what's the end result?"

"I would like to say peace, but for many that never comes. I think of it more in terms of acceptance. Whatever happened, happened. I am here to help you find a path forward and deal with it. I'd like to say *cure you*, but that's not how it works."

"OK, so let's get started."

For the rest of the hour, Reardon explains his day-to-day activities for those three years. He keeps everything high level and superficial. At the end of the hour, Liz thanks him and asks again if he can make the same time next week. Reardon leaves, feeling both a little relieved and apprehensive at the same time. An uneasy feeling to say the least since he doesn't yet know what to make of the fair doctor. He wasn't sure how to explain it to her, how to put it into words. The constant terror, constantly on edge, that's what ate at him, knowing it might never stop. Now that it has stopped, on some level, he misses the rush and anticipation that came with every day. It was a perverse feeling and inexplicable at the same time.

Washington, D.C.

The discussions inside the situation room are becoming stranger and more bizarre with every passing hour. The NSA and other agencies are finding thousands of leads when reviewing record after record. They have no specific criteria because all these people got through the system; anything from typos to missing information now raises a red flag. There is no shortage of information and data, and that's the problem, it's too much data. They just need to figure out the right data to search for in the ocean of confusion. Most leads are quickly dismissed, but the pressure to not screw up is intense. Given the frenzy of concern no one is beyond suspicion. Each person knows any clue they miss will lead to dead Americans.

Agents are sent out to track down and interview anyone who still raises eyebrows. The list is already thousands of names long and growing. The logistics of tracking down so many people on a rolling Watch List so quickly is daunting, but everyone understands the urgency. The President receives updates multiple times throughout the day, each one as bleak as the last. Hundreds are interviewed every day and they find people just living out their lives, which is good, but not what they are looking for.

The chief of staff assigns all his people a simple task. Get in a room and start talking through possible solutions. It does not take long for ideas to come spilling out. Each person is frantically taking notes and blurting out suggestions hoping to come up with something inspirational.

"What if we declare martial law in a few large cities and enforce a curfew?"
"But which cities?"

People start listing off all the obvious candidates, New York, Chicago, Miami, and Los Angeles.

"What if we simply posted a guard at all the bridges, tunnels, and water towers?"
"That's just a subset of what we need to protect. What else would we need to guard?" Asks another.

A chorus of answers start to fly through the air.

"Refineries."
"Reservoirs."
"Factories and shopping malls."
"Sewage treatment centers."
"High voltage power line towers."

The chorus of ideas continues for another twenty seconds.

"How many places are we talking about in total?" Someone else asks. Everyone sits in silence as people start running numbers through their head.
"Probably a million," someone quietly states and then says with more authority, "If we guarded everything 24 hours a day that would be a few million people on guard."

Even a million is a wild estimate. The reality is that nobody really knows. The conversation slowly dies of natural causes. The chief of staff enters to check on their progress. So far, he is unimpressed and leaves so they can continue their work.

"What if we try a nationwide bed check where everyone would need to call in and verify they are home at midnight?"

The list of outlandish suggestions never stops, and the chief of staff puts an end to it after four hours. He collects the list of *reasonable* suggestions and reviews it before presenting it to the President just after dinner. The President becomes frustrated by the lack of direction and progress. However, he knows he has no better suggestions, so he quietly ponders each suggestion on the list praying something will jump out at him and provide something insightful. In reality, no one is even coming close to insightful. He would settle for quasi-realistic at this point in time.

The nation is in growing turmoil as the realization hits that millions of lives are disrupted, and the world is now looking to the United States for answers. Nearly half a million foreign travelers are stranded in the United States and nearly three-quarters of a million Americans are stranded overseas. People are frantically trying to rebook flights. The President is also dealing with financial markets that are on the verge of total collapse. The ripple effect is now global as world leaders are demanding the President work out a plan to stabilize the financial markets and return their citizens home. The calls for immediate action are resonating on every news channel. Many people view the president and his staff as completely inept, which could not be further from the truth. It is simply a complete case of sensory overload. Imagine being told to find a specific grain of sand on a beach somewhere between the Jersey shoreline and Miami Beach, you are given five minutes, and all you know is the grain is small and round. That is the volume of information all the government agencies are sorting through.

July 14, 2013 – New York

McCullum is in his office finishing some paperwork for the day. An expected knock draws his attention away from his paperwork. It's 6 o'clock. McCullum waves in Reardon, who comes in and sits in the guest chair. McCullum has been in the New York field office for just over three months, and his office still has a sterile feel to it.

"Sorry about the late hour. It's tough to squeeze in these one-on-ones during the day." McCullum has been slowly meeting with everyone in the office to get to know them a little better. "This shouldn't take too long."

"No problem. I didn't have anything better to do."

McCullum pulls a file from his top desk drawer. "I've been taking a close look at your file. There's some great work in here. Great work in Afghanistan."

"Thanks," said in an almost apathetic way.

"There's something specific I want to address before we go any further. I know you like to hit the bottle pretty hard." McCullum looks for a response and gets none. "You do a pretty good job of covering it up."

"Thanks – I guess," is his only response.

"You were a great agent and I want to get you back to that."

"Thanks…"

"Do you still enjoy being an agent?"

"Yeah."

"Do you want to keep doing it?"

"Yeah."

"Hmm," he stares directly into Reardon's eyes and can tell deep down he is telling the truth. "I'm going to tell you something, something that stays between you and me. Deal?"

"Sure."

"I'm an alcoholic. Took my last drink December 24, 1991."

"Why are you telling me this?"

"I've got a deal for you."

"OK, shoot." The wheels are turning in Reardon's head – *where's he going with this?*

"Well, let me start with why I became an alcoholic. I was a young agent, full of piss and vinegar. I graduated from the academy in '82 and immediately filed for an overseas assignment. I ended up in the Middle East in early '83. It was a great assignment, got to see a lot and learned a lot. It was fun until October 23rd when the suicide bombers blew up the Beirut Marine barracks. Two days after the attack, I was one of the agents sent in to investigate. We were there for the whole thing trying to piece together the evidence. What's burned into my memory is the bodies, not even bodies, limbs, torsos, heads. Sometimes pieces no bigger than a marble."

McCullum stands, starts pacing, and then stares out the window.

"I thought I was the toughest son of a bitch the world ever saw, but not for this. It was horrible. That's not what pushed me over the edge, over the next two years I saw so much. Stuff they can't train you for. It started slow, just a drink to calm my nerves, then a drink to help me sleep. Then I needed two drinks. You know exactly what I'm talking about don't you?"

"Yeah." Reardon barely makes eye contact as McCullum turns.

"About six months after I got back it was getting a little too out of control. I was bringing it into the office. Finally, I was called into the office, like you here today. I was working out of the Kansas City field office. Richard Lincoln was the agent in charge. Best damn agent I ever worked with and a recovering alcoholic. He confronted me and made me a deal. The same deal I'm going to make with you today. If you want it. I have two choices. I can ship you off to some God forsaken field office and let them deal with you, or I can offer you a shot to make it here."

"What are the conditions?"

"Simple, I'm going to give you shit work to do, worse than what you have been doing the last year. But your drinking is affecting your work. I'll put you on stuff I don't really care about. Stuff no one really cares about, places I just need a warm body."

"Sounds great so far."

"In return, you just try to hold it all together. I'm never going to ask you to stop drinking or go to an AA meeting. No time limit. That's the deal. I know you've been seeing Dr. Miller. She's good. I would like you to keep seeing her."

"Why won't you ever ask me to stop drinking?"

"Would it help?" McCullum asks, knowing it's a rhetorical question.

"Good point. What's the catch?"

"No catch. Just do the work I assign you and let me know when you've been dry for three months. When you tell me that, we put you back on real work and see how it goes."

"How long did this Richard guy wait for you?"

"Six years. I did some pretty unbelievable stuff during that time. I can't believe he stuck with me. I'll be honest, I was struggling with this decision, but Spencer's gone to bat for you so many times over the last three months I've decided to give you a shot. I've only done this twice before."

"How did those work out?"

"One went well and the other quit and disappeared, probably dead by now."

"I don't get it. Why do you do it?"

"Let's just say I'm repaying a favor I can never repay. Without Richard's faith in me I'd either be dead or still swimming around in the bottom of a bottle."

"Fair enough."

"In the meantime, this conversation never happened. Starting Monday, you're on my hit list as far as anyone knows getting assignments that are the worst of the worst. If you want to come in and talk sometime, fine. But I don't need that – or want that. This is all about you. You're a good agent, and we want you back. Do we have a deal?"

Reardon leans back in his chair and just stares at McCullum for a long while. They never break eye contact. "Deal."

"Good. Now get the hell out of here. I've got work to do."

Reardon is walking out thinking his Guardian Angel just saved his skin – again. He knows Spencer has defended him on several occasions and in numerous different ways. He has a lot to thank her for, but he just doesn't know how to say it.

Day 34

Reardon rolls out of bed at 10:37 and flips on the TV. Spencer finally sees the futility of waking him each morning because he is just a cranky little bastard and it doesn't get him into the office any sooner. His good friend still hasn't contacted him since the initial note, so there is no urgency in him being in the office. He knows he is a pure hindrance at this point and only keeps going in for McCullum. As he's watching the news, he is caught off guard. There is no breaking news. The newscasters are discussing how no reports are coming in relating to any terrorist attack.

> Authorities are perplexed and grateful by the seeming lack of an attack this morning. We are continuing to monitor all news feeds awaiting news of a potential attack, but nothing yet. People are already speculating that last night's attack was thwarted and federal authorities are refusing to disclose the details. In the meantime, let us update you on the aftermath of the attacks over the last several days. The pharmaceutical plant near Richmond, Virginia, that makes Viagra and anti-depressants, remains closed today as crews continue to clean up the manufacturing plant after yesterday's attack. The Army Corps of Engineers is working with the Minnesota Department of Transportation on plans to install temporary floating bridges at several locations to help ease the impact of the lost bridges. Due to the high bluffs in multiple locations, the Army reports temporary bridges reaching street level are not realistic and will need a more thought out long-term solution. Senator Eidelmen is renewing calls for a congressional hearing on the CIA and how…

Reardon shuts off the TV and leans forward to pick up a warm beer that has been calling to him since last night. He kills the can and prepares to stand up as his phone buzzes on his dust covered table. He looks at the text message on his phone. All it says is "Hello" from an unknown number. He ignores the message, placing the phone back on the table and knocking a can onto the floor as he stands. At the same moment it pings off the floor, his phone buzzes again and he leans over it looking down at the message.

"Got a minute?"

Reardon picks up his phone, presses his finger to the reader, goes to the message, and stares more closely at the number. After a moment, he decides to type in "Who is this?"

"Guess"

"Santa Claus"

"Not quite, my good friend"

Reardon sits back down reeling from what he is seeing on his phone.

"I don't have long, I am sure your people are already trying to trace this."

"Why are you texting me?"

"I just wanted to let you know we are not taking a break today. The check is in the mail as they say. Talk to you later." Ten seconds later another text comes in. "Patience with Day 8."

Reardon is still shocked by the text. He just sits on the sofa for a few minutes, and then his phone rings.

"Rear…"

Spencer immediately interrupts, "We see you got a text."

"I know I got a text. How do you know I got a text? You're tapping my phone!"

Reardon hears McCullum bark out in the background, "Give me the phone!" Spencer hands the phone to McCullum. "Reardon, I want your ass in the office in 30 minutes – got it?"

"Who the hell said…", as Reardon pulls back the phone he sees the call ended.

Reardon paces back and forth for a moment deciding what to do. At this point, there is only one thing he can do. He cracks open another warm beer on the counter, slams it down before dropping the can on an overflowing garbage can, and walks away as the can rolls off the top and clanks down next to an array of other garbage on the floor. Reardon returns from the bathroom after a long warm shower and slowly opens the fridge. The first thing he grabs is a bottle of Advil that he always keeps in the fridge for easy access. He pours four pills into his hand and pops them in his mouth as he returns the bottle to the shelf and grabs a cold beer this time. He opens the beer and takes a long swig to wash down the Advil. Reardon is starting to wonder why his *good friend* contacted him now, but his throbbing headache wins out.

Giving into hunger, Reardon grabs some left over Chinese food in the fridge and starts eating it cold directly from the soy sauce stained box. It has been nearly 40 minutes since Spencer called and was expecting a knock on the door any minute offering to drive him in, but the knock never comes. Ten minutes later, Reardon steps off his sidewalk and hails a cab. He knows he is still hammered from last night and the two extra beers didn't help. Reardon limps into the office just over an hour after his pleasant conversation with McCullum. Reardon walks into the conference room just as agent Peterson is reporting what they have found out about the phone.

"We know it's a burn phone and know it was manufactured over two years ago. We are starting to trace who sold it and when. The texts came in from a cell tower on the outskirts of a small town in south eastern Pennsylvania. The texter picked a good place, only one cell tower picked up the phone so there is no way to triangulate a position. The tower has a reach of over 20 miles. The phone was likely powered on," he glances at Reardon. "You got the texts, and then powered off or most likely destroyed. There's a million small roads all over the countryside, so trying to find the location to collect any physical evidence is useless," Peterson concludes.

"Damn! This is our first lead in over three weeks. No ransom demand, no ultimatum, no nothing," McCullum utters as he paces back and forth.

"At least we have a clue. The check is in the mail, and that they aren't taking a day off," Spencer adds.

McCullum finally acknowledges Reardon's presence. "Reardon, any clue what any of that means?"

"No."

"Why did he mention Day 8? What are we waiting for?"

"No idea."

"Let's forget about that for now," McCullum quickly interjects, "what about the check in the mail?"

"Referencing the mail or a check could mean the next attack might be directed at a bank or the postal service," says Peterson.

"Yeah, but the check is in the mail is usually referring to something we are literally expecting in the mail or some sort of delay tactic. Maybe their plan for today fell through and they are trying to cover for it." Spencer suggests.

Reardon is just sitting back in the chair with his eyes closed. His head is throbbing as people continue to throw around theories. People are suddenly talking in small groups amongst themselves as McCullum continues to pace back and forth. The group's early morning hopes that the attack was stopped or the attacks will now stop altogether are now dashed with this new clue. Reardon has come to terms with the fact that they are monitoring his phone. Between the pulsating throbs, he knew he would do the same thing to a fellow agent. It was just procedure, and McCullum was by the book. He was just pissed they never told him. But he thought, why would they, he's a mess. Rarely shows up to the office on time, and when he does, he's either hungover or drunk. The attacks have pushed his drinking to a level he never thought he would achieve and he's been working at this for years.

Peterson finally spoke up drowning the chorus of voices. "WAIT! What if the letter isn't really a letter, and the mail isn't really the mail. What if there is some sort of alternate meaning?"

The room looks on in stunned silence as they consider his comment and people start to mumble in small groups again.

"Oh my God!" as Reardon raises his head. "And what if the comment *taking a break* doesn't really mean *taking a break*! There is no reason to sit around guessing."

"Clear the room! Reardon, Spencer, up here," McCullum barks.

After everyone clears the room, Reardon and Spencer sit down as McCullum stares out the window for a moment and then turns.

"Who is the text from?"
"I don't know."
"Guess."
"Abdul was the only one who called me his good friend but he's gone, besides everyone in the compound there knew that. We worked with dozens of Afghan liaisons over the three years and any one of them heard it multiple times."
"OK, let's start at square one. I would say the text we received goes a long way to confirm there is a link between you and your work in Afghanistan, but we still don't know that for certain. This could still be a ruse to throw us off the real trail. Second, six agents and four Afghan liaisons, including Abdul were killed in the 2011 explosion. Third, we still have no idea who planted the explosives. We concluded it was not an inside job. Rather, someone snuck into the compound and left without leaving a trace. Is that all true?" McCullum finally asks.
"...and they were never able to conclusively identify all the victims," Reardon adds.
"So, there is a chance this was an inside job. It could have been a suicide mission," McCullum asked.
"Yes, but I didn't see it then and I don't see it now. Every one of them wanted us there and wanted a better life for their family and friends. They hated al Qaeda and the Taliban more than we did."

"OK, but it's not an impossible theory that it could be an inside job, or even that they planted the bomb and snuck out of the compound after the chaos of the explosion."

"Yeah, that is technically correct."

"OK, so what if Abdul is the one who planted the bomb and snuck out."

"No way. No how." Reardon insisted.

"How are you so sure?"

"Abdul's wife and son were killed by the Taliban, that's what pushed him to help us. He told me he contemplated suicide for weeks but finally decided he wanted to fight. He would do anything to make Afghanistan a better place. Besides, you can't live with a man in close quarters for three years and not get to know him."

"OK, but can we just assume the person who sent the text could be one of the Afghans we thought died in the explosion?" Spencer suggested.

"Fine," Reardon said with exasperation.

"And while we're at it, let's assume it was Abdul, just for argument's sake," continued McCullum.

"Fine," Reardon said rolling his eyes and leaning back in his chair, "But I can promise you Abdul did not survive the explosion."

"Again, for arguments sake," Spencer reiterated.

"Fine. If this is really Abdul, then we should take him pretty literally. If something is in the mail, that's it. All we can do is wait."

McCullum asks, "Is the texter sending you something?"

"Hell if I know, and I doubt he's sending it Federal Express or we'd already have it by now. All we can do is wait for now."

McCullum dismisses them and immediately calls the Director to discuss the text messages. They discuss his theory about it being one of the four Afghanis. The knee-jerk reaction is to put the photos out and begin a nationwide search. The downside is that they have no confirmed actual link to the Middle East or Afghanistan. They fear putting out an alert for people of Middle Eastern descent will start a backlash that will sweep across the nation. They have already been getting occasional reports of attacks on Muslims and vandalism at various Mosques relating to what is already going on. Putting out the photos of four individuals who are dead will throw gasoline on the fire. They may still be dealing with domestic terrorists and do not want to start a panic based on misguided assumptions. The agency made that mistake after Timothy McVeigh bombed the Murrah building back in 1995.

The Director hangs up and immediately heads to the White House so he can meet with the President face to face.

As the day drones on, and TV reporters keep theorizing about why there was no attack, the team keeps trying to collect more information about the phone. All they know is that it was purchased about two years ago and bought from a convenience store in the Los Angeles area. At this point, the phone was a dead end. No one would remember some guy who bought a phone two years ago, and any video surveillance is long gone. The text messages have not been reported to the public.

The President and his cabinet are briefed along with the heads of the CIA, TSA, NSA, and a dozen other agencies. It is only a matter of time before the information leaks. Up to this point, Reardon's name and involvement have remained a closely guarded secret, and McCullum warned that he would rip everyone a new orifice if word got out.

Since the initial note, it was an easy secret to keep because there was no confirmed involvement or link between Reardon and the note left in the car. However, with the text, the chances for Reardon really knowing the attacker went up a hundred-fold, and Reardon's link to the terrorists won't remain a secret for long no matter how many threats McCullum makes.

"This bothers me. If this guy is using a phone he bought two years ago then this has been in the planning for at least that long."

"For cryin' in the night Spencer! I didn't need to know the guy is using a phone from two years ago to know this is pretty well thought out. The bigger question is when we'll get a break so we can catch this bastard," McCullum roars.

McCullum is especially pissed because a turf war is growing over the case. Everyone wants lead on the case because catching the bastards will make their career. On the other hand, with no clues or leads since the initial note, people are hesitant to step up because everyone is just chasing their tail at this point. Worse than that, they really aren't chasing anything. Information is flowing in at an incredible rate. There are no clues or leads in anything they receive. People finally go to bed exhausted only to turn on the news and hear what happened the night before. That is the most frustrating part so far, the feeling of complete helplessness. With the text messages this morning, McCullum knows the case is his whether he likes it or not. The problem is his link to the terrorist is a stinking drunk and washed up agent. Nonetheless, McCullum calls the director's aide again to see if they have made any progress on the list of names McCullum provided nearly two weeks ago. The aide said the list is on the director's desk and he will review it as soon as he has a chance. This isn't good enough. McCullum insists on a meeting with the director again. The director finally agrees to give this high priority since the text messages from today are the only real breadcrumbs they have to follow.

Washington, D.C.

The president's staff is frantically scrambling and has nothing in their playbook to even consider a response to these kinds of attacks. They have closely studied the November, 2015, Paris attacks where eight people attacked three locations simultaneously and shut down the boarders of an entire country for three days after one night and no immediate follow up attacks. The police had dead bodies, video, physical evidence, and a trail to follow. This case has none of that. The attackers are ghosts and leave no trail.

The agents tracking down people on the rolling Watch List are quickly hitting a major obstacle – they can't find about ten percent of the people. The addresses listed on their immigration forms are either wrong or out of date. People are constantly moving around the country, and just because they can't find them doesn't imply they are a terrorist. However, given the current circumstances, *every* missing person is a potential terrorist. On the other hand, moving or not being found is not a crime. Despite that, ABPs are put out for each missing person and they move from the Watch List to the Persons of Interest List. People are now assumed guilty until proven innocent. The Persons of Interest List quickly grows into the hundreds and increases in length every hour.

The cabinet is discussing everything from shutting down the borders to detaining and questioning anyone who has entered the country in the last six months. Both options equally preposterous and unrealistic. They are also looking at all domestic groups, anyone from the Michigan Militia to fringe church groups. Anyone who might be looking to destroy the United States is now suspect. This list is also endless. They have raised the threat level at all Federal installations, nuclear sites, and anything else deemed significant. They quickly also realize this is a useless step because all the attacks are against low value targets. Top analysts at every agency are running through simulations and trying to detect a pattern to the attacks. So far, no one has even come up with a plausible, much less a realistic, theory.

Day 40

Dow Jones Industrial Average
13,897.32
Total decline: 31.0%
Total loss: $1.61 Trillion

Nasdaq
4,012.38
Total decline: 29.4%
Total loss: $2.49 Trillion

Reardon suddenly awakes at 4:27 a.m., and after 30 minutes of rolling around, finally decides to get up. He can tell he is still drunk but can't fall asleep for some reason. Exasperated, he gets up for a tall glass of water and then melts into his sofa like hot wax on cloth. After a couple sips, he turns on the TV as the anchor woman is summarizing the overnight attacks on Dallas.

> Emergency response teams have been onsite for just over four hours. So far there are nine confirmed deaths and 14 injuries. Emergency crews are still looking to ensure there are no cars under the four collapsed overpasses. The Texas State Highway Spur 366 tunnel collapse is much more devastating. Emergency crews have no idea how many cars are trapped or how many are injured. The Texas Department of Transportation has reviewed traffic cameras and confirmed that eight cars were in the tunnel at the time of the explosion. Here you can see a white van that is believed to be carrying the explosives. The explosion occurred just after midnight local time. Authorities have no idea how many of the eight cars were directly impacted by the blast and how many were caught in the falling debris.

Reardon just leans forward, puts down the glass of water, and slumps to the side as he starts weeping.

June 22, 2010 - Afghanistan

> Radical Islamic extremists surely hope that an attack on Iraq will kill many people and destroy much of the country, providing recruits for terrorist actions.
> Noam Chomsky

Reardon and Abdul are sitting next to a dusty outcropping just before dawn waiting for an informant. They awoke at 4 o'clock and drove nearly two hours to get here before dawn. Their support Humvee is just over two miles away and checking in frequently. It's like having an overly protective big brother. Their orders are to never be more than a quarter mile from Reardon, but he insisted fearing they would spook the informant. This informant is probably the most cautious informant they work with, always before dawn and always an isolated location.

"So, what do you miss the most about home besides your wife and young daughter? I only ask because you seem more sullen lately." Abdul asks while glancing slightly to his right trying to avoid Reardon's gaze.

Abdul knows this is not the issue but he is just trying to start a conversation to pass the time.

"You don't hide your intentions very well. You know everything I miss about home."
"Yes, I know, so what is it? I've seen it building for over a week now. I figured you would've brought it up by now, you always do, so I know this is different."
"I don't know how to describe it. I can barely even wrap my mind around it."

They sit quietly for about two more minutes before Reardon clears his throat.

"I've been having nightmares for one thing. That's never happened before."
"Describe them."
"That's the problem, I wake up breathing heavily and have these flashes for a moment or two before my mind goes blank."
"Images of what?"
"Destruction."
"Of what."
"Lives. Not just death, but shattered lives. The desperation that I can see that you say I'll never understand. I don't know what to make of it."

———

Reardon awakes as the phone rings, and he reaches for the receiver.
"Have you heard about Dallas?"

"Yes, I woke up early this morning. Couldn't sleep."

"I already talked to McCullum. He said you haven't had any more texts."

"Thanks, but you could've just asked me that."

"I didn't ask him. He just mentioned it. Are you planning to come into the office today?"

"What's the point? But yeah, I'll be in later. These were suicide bombers this time, weren't they?"

"Just in the tunnel. All the rest got away again. Same MO, parks the truck and a buddy drives them away. McCullum is worried because this is another escalation when you consider they are now willing to kill themselves."

"This shouldn't be a surprise, it was bound to happen when they are this devoted to destruction."

Spencer's voice is listless and distant. "Yeah ... I'll talk to you when you get in."

Reardon picks up his glass of water and flips on the TV.

...authorities still have no clues, but let's re-cap the last seven days. Day 33, the pharmaceutical plant is still shut down as crews continue to make repairs. The Day 34 attack, initially believed to have been disrupted, is now believed to be complete. Authorities have now confirmed approximately 1000 letters were mailed to district court houses, state representatives, and libraries across the country. So far, there are no reported illnesses or deaths associated with the letters. Up to this point, all the letters tested have contained only flour or powdered sugar. The letters started a panic as they started showing up all across the country forcing people to relive the 2001 anthrax attacks that killed 5 and infected 17 others. Authorities are still trying to trace the origin of each letter estimating they were sent from at least 40 locations.

The water pipes leading to three California agricultural areas have been repaired from the Day 35 attack. The Day 36 attack on the Powell/Hyde trolley car wheelhouse in San Francisco will take months to repair due to the lack of replacement parts. Many parts will need to be custom cast.

The ten small roadside cafes destroyed by bombs throughout the south are all a complete loss after the ensuing fires destroyed the buildings on Day 37. The small dam damaged outside Alma, Nebraska, on Day 38 caused no immediate water damage. However, they want to ensure it is repaired before the next major rainfall to avoid any flooding. The three concrete mixing plants on Day 39 near Macon, Georgia are thought to be a complete loss.

And now on Day 40, the destruction of four highway overpasses and one tunnel in Dallas. Residents of the Dallas/Fort Worth area are asked to stay home in order to keep the roads clear and travel only if absolutely necessary while authorities assess the damage. An estimated 250,000 vehicles traverse the overpasses and tunnel on an average day. The effects will be similar to those felt in Minneapolis-St. Paul, but on a much smaller scale. The Twin Cities remain in utter chaos with food and gasoline shortages running rampant.

The National Guard from Minnesota and Wisconsin has been activated to assist with delivering MREs and bottled water. The National Guard has also set up temporary food distribution centers attempting to re-supply grocery stores as semi-trailers do their best to make it into the cities. Every single business in the Twin Cities has been impacted in some way. The governor has asked the legislature to set up a fund for companies so they can get short-term, interest-free loans to ensure they can meet their payroll obligations before a wave of companies start going out of business, leading to a tidal wave that would only further devastate the mid-western economy.

The eleven airports impacted by the Day 30 attacks are still trying to return to normal operation, and only a small fraction of flights are coming and going. Buses now transport passengers in and out of the airports along service roads with passengers trying to get home given highest priority. There are still an estimated 300,000 people stranded in remote cities, many choosing to rent a car and drive home when one becomes available. The impact of freight shipments is also leading to major headaches for distributors, and inventory is piling up across the nation. FedEx and UPS deliveries are crippled. Restaurants across the country that once depended on daily deliveries of fresh seafood or fresh produce are reeling to adapt. The U.S. Postal ...

Reardon switches off the television, leans back, and closes his eyes. This is already becoming a bigger mess than he could have ever imagined. He knows there is more to come, and there is nothing anyone can do to stop it. America is getting a taste of its own medicine. He wakes up about an hour later and limps to the shower.

Reardon walks into the office about noon and heads to the conference room. Peterson is sitting at his computer as Spencer is watching the TV with the latest reports and hearing the usual. No suspects in custody. Driver picked up and left the city. Untraceable stolen license plates. Reardon slumps down into the chair next to Spencer.

"Anything new? Any clues?"

"No, nothing. They are still clearing the tunnel and hoping to find survivors. However, they doubt that is likely, if the flames did not kill people, the heat and lack of oxygen certainly did. The governor has put the Texas National Guard on high alert and raised the threat level across the state. However, as we know, there is no real need for that because it's unlikely there will be any more attacks today and no way to predict the attack tomorrow."

"How is McCullum doing?"

"I'll tell you how the hell McCullum is doing!" McCullum barks as he walks into the conference room. "I'm pissed to the hilt. At least it sounds like one of those bastards is dead. Cowardly suicide bombers. No way to defend against them."

McCullum walks up to the TV and listens for a few moments before he tells Spencer to turn it off.

"What do we know?" McCullum looks at Peterson as he asks.

"Same MO. The truck is parked next to the overpass column, a trailing car picks up the driver, and they are off, heading out of the city and disappearing into the …"

"I guessed all that, dammit. Tell me something I don't know. What about the truck exploding in the tunnel?"

"Well we don't really know anything. We have video of the truck entering the tunnel and then boom. They counted six cars that went in that did not come out. Two cars near the truck are surely destroyed. All the cameras in the tunnel were knocked out by the explosion. They are shoring up the tunnel on both sides so they can safely start to remove debris and start looking for survivors. The tunnel will be shut down for weeks and may need to be totally redone based on the extent of the damage. It is simply too early to know."

"Dammit!" reiterates McCullum.

McCullum taps his toe into the wall for a moment.

"More overpasses. Peterson did you put together those numbers I wanted yet?"

"Yeah, I just finished about fifteen minutes ago."

"OK, let's hear it."

"Well, there are over 600,000 bridges in the U.S. and I couldn't even find an estimate on the number of overpasses, probably well over two million. There are about 60 road tunnels of 1000 meters or more and a countless number of shorter tunnels. There are about 205,000 cell phone towers, 185,000 high voltage power line towers, 75,000 water towers, 160,000 miles of pipelines carrying hazardous liquids like jet fuel…"

"OK, I get it." McCullum says as he cuts him off. "So, what I'm hearing is we are screwed until we catch these guys!"

Everyone in the office spends short periods of time watching news reports and seeing updates on Dallas, the Twin Cities, and what the FAA is doing to handle the chaos among the airlines. Agents spend their days looking through reams of information that are constantly flowing in. The phones are ringing off the hooks with one false lead after another. Every stalled car on the road is a potential car bomb. Bomb squads are working around the clock investigating everything from stalled cars to mysterious boxes sitting anywhere and everywhere. Four airports have reopened with crews working around the clock to replace the overpasses in order to return the flow of traffic. It will take several more days for them to return to full capacity. Three other airports are expecting to open within the next two days. The Minneapolis-St. Paul airport is still completely shut down except for military and cargo flights delivering supplies.

The only consistency with all the attacks is that they have nothing to go on. Not a single actionable piece of evidence. Congresspeople are calling for blood and action, but against who? And more importantly, where? There is no one to retaliate against. No foreign group or country has claimed any responsibility whatsoever. The President once again spoke to the nation proclaiming his shock and horror with the ongoing attacks and that law enforcement is taking immediate action working to find the terrorists. He says this as everyone in the office is idly sitting around the table in stunned silence. The same stunned silence since the bridges were destroyed in Minneapolis. They know, more than anyone, the president's promises are hollow and wistful dreams at this point in time. In the twenty days since L.A., with twenty attacks at dozens of locations, they have nothing to go on.

When there's a lack of real information, any conspiracy theory will do. Theories are coming out of the woodwork and spreading on the internet like wildfire. A few groups think the American government is behind the attacks. Others are convinced it is radical Islamists. There have been an increasing number of attacks on Muslims, and local news agencies are reminding the public that they have no clues and no suspects. A few groups blame North Korea. The leading contender is Russia, with people believing they are attempting to undermine the U.S. government so they can take over the Ukraine while the U.S. is distracted with its own problems. Those all seem rational and plausible compared to the more outlandish theories. One extremely vocal group is blaming extraterrestrials, concluding only aliens could get in and out without leaving any trace and explaining why we can't catch them. Those are all fine and good. Reardon's favorite theory is that the government is testing a new nerve agent on the U.S. population and that none of these attacks have really happened. People only *believe* they have happened. That one is so stupid it made him laugh.

McCullum is receiving daily updates from agents in Afghanistan on Reardon's list of names. So far, agents have tracked down twenty-nine of the 227 names on the list. Twenty-five of them are terrorists, fourteen are reported dead. The eleven others are still actively pursued by U.S. forces. The remaining four worked with the U.S. but are believed dead. Most of this information is based on reports filed soon after Reardon left Afghanistan. McCullum is at best disappointed but not surprised. Since Reardon's team and U.S. forces pulled out of the region in February of 2011 it has returned to the Wild West. There is no FBI presence in the region. The only time we enter the region is with Special Ops there to perform a specific mission and to get out as soon as the mission completes. The agents are attempting to contact the former liaisons listed in the files, the ones the U.S. worked with so closely over the years but are coming up short. This is not a surprise, most of them cut off all ties with the Americans in order to protect their lives. Many likely assumed false identities and moved as an additional precaution. The current set of FBI agents was not in Afghanistan back in 2011 and so have no personal relationships to build on. This fact coupled with the long time period that has elapsed is making it almost impossible to track down people on the list.

Washington, D.C.

The president's staff is briefing the president on the situation in Dallas. While the situation in Dallas is devastating, the real impact is the ongoing catastrophe in Minnesota, the near collapse of the airline system, and the historic losses in the stock market. The damage is done to the airline industry. They have lost billions. With the airports re-opening, there is renewed confidence that some semblance of normal will return, but not in any meaningful way so long as the attacks persist. There is nothing he can realistically do about the stock markets. The stock market is all about consumer confidence and profits. Both are in the toilet right now. All he can do is hope the markets hang on and the economy doesn't completely collapse.

The president is stacking some papers on his desk as his eye catches the report he received nine days ago.

The confidential report conveyed the following information:
    87,000 – Approximate number of flights per day
    28,500 – Commercial flights (Delta, Southwest, American, etc)
    27,000 – General aviation (private flights)
    24,500 – Air taxi flights (hired planes)
    5,200 – Military flights
    2,100 – Air cargo flights (FexEx, UPS, etc)

He crumples the sheet of paper and drops it in his waste basket knowing they are slowly moving past this hurdle but he still has a knot in his stomach wondering what is next.

One ongoing discussion over the last three days revolves around Russian involvement. This makes the president extremely uneasy. Three days ago, a credible theory was presented to the president. A wonk in the bowels of the NSA developed the theory a week ago. The theory explains how the Russians could have activated some Cold War agents who have been living here for decades and also sent in new agents to help carry out the attacks. At the core of the theory is Russian imperialism. The Russians want to rebuild their empire and need the Americans out of the way. Their ability to retake the Crimea from Ukraine in 2015 has emboldened the Russians. If the Americans are distracted, the Russians could use this opportunity to retake the Ukraine, the Baltics, and other former members of the U.S.S.R. with impunity. The Russians definitely have the resources to put such a plan in motion. But could they keep it a secret?

The theory did not hold much credibility until U.S. agents deep inside the Kremlin discovered secret talks underway discussing how to take advantage of America's current *situation*. The biggest issue is deciding which came first, the chicken or the egg. Are the Russians discussing this because it is all part of their master plan, or are they discussing it because the U.S. is under attack and they see an opportunity? If the former, this is clearly an act of war and could lead to World War III. The latter simply makes sense; of course they would be having discussions like this. Most analysts do not feel the Russians would be this bold and dismiss the theory. However, until they have proof one way or the other, they need to consider all options. They also still discuss the likelihood of North Korea or even Venezuela orchestrating the attacks. Nothing is off the table at this point in time. All these discussions just muddy the waters.

The president is fully aware of the *Reardon Connection*, as it is now called, and the text messages. This remains a closely guarded secret. The U.S. knows Russian spies were operating continuously in Afghanistan throughout the U.S. occupation. Could the texts to Reardon just be a simplistic ploy to distract them? Could the Russians have gotten wind of the discussions between Reardon and his liaison? This is just as preposterous as assuming one of the dead liaison officers has risen from the dead and is behind the attacks.

The president is tired of hearing one outlandish theory after another with no end in sight. What keeps him up at night is that one of the outlandish theories is spot on. One theory is not preposterous. Was Reardon's liaison officer a Russian spy? Did Abdul feed all this information to the Russians? If so, it would be the perfect ploy. If the Russians are ultimately behind the attacks and there is no way to connect them to it, then it is the perfect crime. Authorities still have no idea who is committing the attacks, it could be Afghanis, Russians, or even Samoans. The president needs proof, something solid. The NSA and CIA are pouring over all Russian communiques looking for a smoking gun. After three days of frantic searching, they find nothing. All communication is after the fact. They are just communicating what has happened and nothing about what will happen next. Every discussion leads back to square one – *who*? The situation is beyond infuriating.

Another ongoing frustration for the president is that all the armchair quarterbacks are spouting off with myth and innuendo. The president knows this is the case because all he is dealing with is myth and innuendo. A particularly annoying voice in the chorus is that piss-ant junior senator. Eidelmen just won't shut up. His name has come up multiple times during his meetings with congressional leadership. The senate majority leader expresses his frustration to the president because they can't get him under control.

The president has another late-night briefing with his chief of staff, the speaker, and the senate majority leader in the oval office. The president turns from staring out the window and sits in his chair behind the desk. He motions for the speaker and senator to sit down. His chief of staff is standing next to the desk. Publicly, they have all been doing the dance and attacking each other. The president criticizes Congress for not funding the advanced intelligence activities and for personally holding the Speaker and senate majority leader responsible. Specifically naming the Committees on Homeland Security and Defense. They also play their part attacking the president for being asleep at the wheel and not doing enough to push the CIA and NSA. If you didn't know any better, you'd think they would get in a fist fight the moment they are left alone in a room together. Behind closed doors, they remain adversarial, but only to a point. During the first two weeks after L.A., they were really fighting and pushing each other's buttons expecting a quick resolution. The tone has changed since the 1000 letters laced with flour and powdered sugar started showing up across the nation. They are still jockeying for position so they can ultimately take advantage of the situation to advance their own agenda. Until then, they realize they need to work together to just save their careers right now.

"This is unbelievable! We've still got nothing." The president says while staring at them intently. "All these billions of dollars for nothing. I can tell you what's going on right now in nearly every embassy around the world, and we can crack the codes of nearly every country in the world. But we can't track down some bastards traipsing around the countryside blowing everything up. How is this possible?"

The speaker and senator are used to these kinds of conversations with the president. They have learned to simply sit and listen. He just needs to talk things through for about ten minutes. They both sit quietly as the president continues to speak. Finally, they hear what they have been waiting for.

"So, what do you think?" The president finally asks. This is their cue to speak.

"Well, Mr. President, right now, we're screwed," states the senator.

"I know we're screwed."

"Well, I think we're all on the same page when it comes to intel," injects the senator. "How the NSA, FBI, and CIA can't find a single clue is beyond me. I assume the NSA has every phone conversation I've ever made recorded and stored in their basement. Hell, they're probably listening to us right now. The FBI probably knows every woman I've screwed in the last twenty years. God help me if my wife ever sees the list. This is an embarrassment, and it's going to cost every one of us re-election if we don't figure it out soon," continues the senator. "I'm getting tired of being grilled by the press."

"You, Jesus Christ, you have no idea. I feel like I'm sending the press secretary down to get crucified every day."

"Well, in the meantime, we just need to ride out the storm. I'll keep my people under control," says the senator.

"And what about Eidelmen? How can we shut that little prick up? That asshole is pissing me off," says the president.

"Well, I've had a couple conversations with him, and well, frankly, he's ignoring me."

"Figure out a way to slap him down and get him back in line. What have we got on him?"

"That's just it, nothing good. We know of a few illegal campaign contributions, but in this town who doesn't? So, we aren't going to open that box."

"He's got to have a skeleton in his closet we can use."

"We're looking."

"What's he want?"

"A seat on the Finance or Defense Committee."

The president laughs out loud. "Are you kidding me?"

"No."

"Like you're just going to put him on one of those because he's got a big mouth. Get something on him so we can shut that little bastard up." The president pauses for a moment, "We're all up shit creek right now. This is the biggest nightmare I've ever seen."

"My aid is thinking about sending a few hookers his way and getting some photos. He won't want that getting out." The senator says this as though it is as simple as inviting someone over for tea.

"Do you think he's that stupid?" asks the president.

"He'll follow his pecker for the right woman. It might take a few tries but we'll get him if we need to." The speaker nods with approval.

Finally, the Speaker comments. "Back to the terrorists. What can we do?"

This catches the president off guard, "Huh?"

"What can we do? We need to do something that shows we're still in control. Unless we do something soon, re-election won't matter because the markets are going to collapse and send us back to the stone age. The world is already a powder keg, and if we lose face, Russia is going to start walking all over eastern Europe again. Every two-bit dictator is going to know they can do whatever they want because we are too busy tracking down some terrorists in our backyard. If this continues, we're screwed six ways to Sunday."

"Stop for a sec. I need time to think." There is a short pause and the president waves his hand. This is their signal to leave and they both stand.

"Thank you, Mr. President," they recite in unison.

The president and his chief of staff have been gearing up for his re-election campaign for over six months, and this distraction is not helping. Election Day is a mere 18 months away. The president already knows his leading contender is the senator walking out the door right now. The speaker is a member of his party, so he knows he doesn't need to worry about him, for now. The chief of staff sits across from the president.

"I don't like this one bit."

"Which part?" the President asks.

"I think there's more going on with Eidelmen."

"Me too. I think the senator is a little piss-ant liar. I think he's putting Eidelmen up to this. I bet he already has the photos of that little prick with a hooker or two."

"That would make sense. If he can undermine you, then that only strengthens his position. Pretty smart when you think about it. If things continue, he will be a thorn in your side, and the senator can start to back Eidelmen. If things go bad, he just cuts him loose. It's a win-win for him."

"That's how I am looking at it too. We need to keep a close eye on this. We have to protect my numbers. My approval rating has dropped 10 points since last month. We need to get ahead of this. If my numbers drop any lower the self-righteous Speaker might start becoming a problem if he decides to run." The president stands up and faces out the window. "Holy hell!" He turns. "What are my options?"

"You're not going to like hearing this. I don't have any right now."

The president stares at him in disbelief. "Then what am I paying you for?"

"Don't worry, I'll come up with something. The biggest thing we need to do is draw the attention away from you." The chief of staff shifts his weight in the chair and uncrosses his legs as he leans forward. "I have my staff looking at the voting records of all the senior congresspeople. We need to find the ones who voted against appropriations to fight terrorism and start pointing the blame towards them."

"How will that work?"

"I haven't figured that out yet. But it's the best I've got right now."

"I don't see how that'll be enough if this continues."

"Don't worry…"

The president cuts him off, "Don't tell me to not worry!"

"Yes, sir," he says as he tilts his head down.

"Get everyone on this. We need to figure out how to protect my numbers. I can't have low numbers when people start announcing their candidacy."

"Don't…" he cuts himself off. "I'm on this. We'll have something for you in the morning. I also think we should start watching the majority leader more closely. I need to know if he's having any closed-door meetings with Eidelmen."

"Yeah, do that. If he can't shut up Eidelmen within the week, I'm going to assume they have some photos of him screwing the family dog, and they're putting him up to this." He turns looking out the window. "I'm going to bed. Let's pick this up in the morning."

"Yes, sir."

Day 42

Reardon rolls out of bed at 9:53 and showers. He does not even bother to turn on the TV. He strolls into the office at just after 11 o'clock with a wrinkled suit smelling of old sweat. He is well overdue for a haircut, and it is sticking up in the back. He walks into the conference room and is surprised to find Peterson and Spencer quietly working at their computers, and the TVs are even off. In fact, the whole office is quiet and subdued. It looks like just another boring day at the office, circa two months ago. Reardon pulls out a chair next to Spencer that has one of the arms caught under the table. This is enough to jiggle the table and breaks their concentration as they both look up. Peterson immediately returns to his work.

"What is it today?" Reardon inquires.

"Ten big shopping malls, ten of the 15 largest in the country. They used drones this time," Spencer replies.

"What do you mean by that?" He leans in to see what Spencer has on her monitor.

"Oh God! You smell."

"Huh?"

"You stink. In fact, you need to just lean back."

Reardon leans back.

"OK, now roll back a couple of feet. Did you sleep in those clothes?"

"No. I haven't made it to the drycleaner for a while."

"Please, do that tonight. You reek."

Spencer's glance returns to her screen and a moment passes before she nonchalantly asks, "Are you living with a raccoon?"

"Huh?" Reardon says with a dull oafish look on his face.

"Are you living with a raccoon?" She asks again.

"No," he replies confusedly. "Why would you ask that?"

"Because your hair looks like a raccoon was humping your head all night," she smiles, never looking at Reardon.

Reardon self-consciously reaches up and starts to pat down his hair. "Ha, ha, very funny."

She turns with a huge grin. "It was just a comment, didn't mean to offend."

"OK, OK, anyways, what is the damage to the malls?"

Spencer waves her hand in front of her face a couple of times. "Most of the malls have huge glass ceilings. Drones were used to place multiple explosives on the glass. The biggest blast was at The Galleria in Houston. Nearly an acre of glass came crashing down. After the initial explosions, several drones at each mall flew down the hallways and then detonated. All hell broke loose at that point. The explosions started fires causing the sprinklers to go off, causing additional water damage. There were two casualties, a night cleaning crew at the King of Prussia Mall in Pennsylvania. All the malls are shut down. The news report says that over 3,000 stores have shut down, and over 32,000 people can't go to work today."

"Holy cow! Any clues?"

"No, nothing. Of course. They are trying to identify where the people were stationed when they put the drones in the air. So far, nothing. They are, of course, pulling the feeds from all the traffic cameras in the area."

"What is the range of a drone?"

"These days, a really good one, about a mile." Peterson interjects.

"Wow, that is a big area to search." Reardon pauses to contemplate that for moment, "Any update on yesterday?"

"They confirmed it was C-4 explosives. All seven rollercoasters are shut down, and it will take weeks to repair. Five of the seven parks re-opened today. The other two decided to remain closed for security reasons."

"I doubt many people are going to go to the parks that did re-open. People will be too freaked out."

Reardon and Spencer just sit quietly for a few moments.

"This is just horrible. When I joined this team back in 2002, I thought I would make a difference. Look at us. We're just sitting here waiting for the next attack, grasping at straws. How is it that we haven't come close to catching even one of these guys?" Reardon says.

"Don't say you haven't made a difference. You have."

"How?"

"Well, well…"

"Exactly, we're just sitting here." Reardon motions over his shoulder. "Look around. People are turning numb to it all. We're all just sitting here like it's a normal day at the office. Everyone is devoting every waking moment to this, and we're making no headway."

"Don't focus on that. Think of all the good work we did back then and all the attacks we disrupted."

"That was then. This is now."

"Don't worry, we'll catch a break."

Reardon goes out for lunch and comes back into the office at just after one. He gets off the elevator, slowly strolls into the conference room, and sits. Fifteen minutes pass as Reardon continues sitting there unobtrusively. He is reading an email when suddenly his phone vibrates and a text comes in from an unknown number.

"Got a minute?" The text reads.

"Yes." Reardon quickly replies. Reardon speaks up, "I've got something here."

Spencer walks over quickly seeing Reardon typing into his phone.

"What is it?"

"Another text from an unknown number."

"McCullum, we've got another text." Spencer yells.

"Everyone out of here! Peterson, start a trace."

By now everyone understands that means everyone but Reardon, Spencer, and Peterson. Peterson just got the notification of the incoming text on his computer as Reardon is reading it. They are monitoring every text coming into his phone.

"I'm on it."

Reardon is typing a response to "How are you today?"

"I'm fine. Thanks. Who is this?"

"A friend," comes the reply.

"My friends don't do things like this."

"Some friends do."

McCullum is standing over Peterson, he can see the texts flashing on Peterson's screen.

"Reardon, keep him talking. I mean texting! Ahh! You know what I mean."

Peterson looks up, "Holy cow they are close."

"How close?" McCullum asks.

"In the city. Triangulating now…"

Reardon keeps the conversation going.

"Who is this?"
"A friend."
"Why are you doing this?"
"All part of the plan my good friend."
"Can we meet?"
"Yes, eventually, but now is not the time. Think old wood for Day 8. Good bye."

Spencer looks up.

"He just signed off."
"The signal is still live," Peterson says excitedly. "The signal is still live. Got it, 508 East 5th Street. That's about two miles from here."

Twenty-five minutes later a SWAT team is surrounding the five-story apartment building.

"Do we still have the signal?" McCullum asks the tech in the mobile command van."
"This seems too easy," Spencer comments.
"They had to screw up sometime and get lazy or stupid." McCullum retorts. "Tell all units to move in."

The FBI is moving through the apartment building with scanners that give off a rapid pinging sound as they get closer to the phone. The ping goes constant when they are within 15 feet. Eventually two groups of agents converge in the middle of a hallway. They signal McCullum they are outside a corner apartment. McCullum gives the signal to drop the door and go in. One agent kicks in the door and they throw in a percussion grenade. The explosion is ear piercing. They barge into the apartment and find no one. Once the smoke clears a tech crew comes up to start looking through the apartment. The apartment is in shambles, broken glass and paper litters the floor. McCullum is standing in the middle of the living room. A tech approaches from the wall with the now shattered TV. He is holding a small white box with a couple wires hanging off, inside is a cell phone.

"This is what we detected."
"What the hell is this?" McCullum grabs it from the tech.
"It's a cell phone in a box."
"I can see that, why is it behind the TV?"

"Don't know, just a convenient way to hide it. I'm guessing the cell phone is set up to forward all incoming texts."

"All right."

Just at that moment, a decrepit, short, old man appears in the doorway escorted by an agent. The old man is wearing dark glasses and uses a cane.

"Agent McCullum, this man says he lives here."

"Everyone out! I need a minute. Don't go far. Just go out to the hallway and wait. Bring him in," McCullum says to the agent.

McCullum spends the next ten minutes talking to the old man. He has a tough time getting anything out of the old man because he keeps asking about what he did wrong and who will fix his door. McCullum's assurances are not working. He finally calms down the old man enough to get some details. The old man explains that about two months ago, a nice young man comes to the door saying they have been receiving reports of problems with the cable boxes. He says everything is fine, but the young man insists and says that if he checks now, it will save him a trip later. So, the old man lets him come in and fix things. McCullum asks for a description and quickly realizes the man is nearly blind. All the old man can see is light and shapes. The old man can't even see the mess in the apartment. He says the guy was probably taller than him and thinks he was wearing a ball cap. He quickly recants, not even sure about the hat. McCullum quickly realizes they have been played. He thanks the old man and calls everyone back in. As he leaves, he makes it clear to the lead of the tech team to fix the door and clean up. Thirty minutes later, McCullum is back in the conference room.

"Peterson, have you been able to trace the phone that was the source of the texts."

"Yes. But I'm sure he's long gone by now. We lost nearly two hours on this wild goose chase."

"Dammit! Now they're taunting us," McCullum exclaims.

"Where did the signal come from?" Spencer asks.

"Upstate New York. Pretty isolated."

"What about the old wood on Day 8 clue?"

"Nothing. I did a web search and found nothing specific. It could mean a million things."

"OK, keep looking into it – it's got to mean something."

McCullum turns and looks out the window a few seconds. The moment he glances at his watch his whole body tenses.

"Villainous little bastards! I want this guy. ... Everyone, go home. We're done for the day. We just need to sit back and wait for what happens next. I hate this." McCullum is now pacing along the window. "You heard me. Go home!"

Peterson suddenly speaks up, "I have an idea. I thought of this about a week ago, but it wouldn't have helped until now." His sudden comment breaks the tension. "What if we look for all the phones bought over a year ago that have either never been activated or activated in the last two months?"

"How will that help?" Spencer asks.

"Bear with me. After the first text message, we assumed the phone was turned on, used, and destroyed immediately. A burn phone, that's what it's used for – untraceable from our perspective. But the one planted a few blocks from here was on for weeks."

"Yeah," Spencer says prompting him to continue.

"So, what if we get that list of numbers and start searching for them. We might find some of those phones planted here and there. Even if it just gives us a couple extra minutes to track incoming texts, that will help."

"I like this." McCullum is interested. "How can we get the list of numbers?"

"We'd need a court order, but I don't think that will be a problem."

"Yeah, and how many numbers are we talking about?"

"I really have no idea, it could be anywhere from a few hundred to a few thousand. I doubt it would be more than 10,000 after all this time."

"OK, get on it," McCullum absentmindedly comments because his mind starts to race with ideas.

Peterson stands up and walks out with his laptop.

McCullum turns to Spencer and Reardon. "OK, so what else can we do like this?"

"If we can find a phone that is already planted we might be able to access its call history and see if they used it for any calls or texts as part of a test run," Reardon says.

"Good! What else?" McCullum asks.

"If they have any cell phones attached to explosives, we might be able to get to them and disarm them before they get a chance to blow," Reardon adds. "That would be out of character for them right now, but they might try that."

"Good."

They spend the next thirty minutes bantering back and forth with ideas. Many of the ideas are rehashed from weeks ago, but it doesn't matter. They are talking and thinking outside the box. After a while, the harsh reality kicks in that they are back to grasping at straws. Unless Peterson's list of numbers garners results, they are still at square one.

Reardon and Spencer slowly file out of the room. Spencer offers Reardon a ride, but he says he'll walk. Spencer knows this is just a euphemism for going to a bar on the way home, but she is too tired to argue. Not tonight, she thinks. She is thinking how much she misses the old Reardon and what they had together. She misses when he would razz her like a big brother. The long stakeouts were horrible, but now she would give a million bucks to get that back even if just for a day.

April 12, 2002 – Quantico

Everyone is still reeling from the 9/11 attacks. Everyone was in stunned confusion for weeks after the attack. *How could this happen? Why didn't we see it coming?* President Bush has been working closely with his cabinet and the heads of the FBI, CIA, and NSA. There are all kinds of rumors about how teams are going to get moved around and restructured. The rumors come to an end when the director of the New York office has a team meeting and announces the changes.

Reardon's team is disbanded and assigned to various groups. Counter terrorism is now the number one priority. Reardon was put in charge of a domestic counter terrorism unit in January, three months ago. The New York team is tasked with identifying individuals associated with Middle Eastern terrorism groups living in the U.S. and recruiting new members. The goal is to head off attacks and round up those responsible. He immediately discovers his new team is woefully understaffed and requests five additional agents. Three months later, he is approved for two new agents.

One agent is a transfer from the Midwest. For the other recruit, he is given permission to look through the files of soon-to-be graduates from Quantico. He doesn't want to look through 100 files, so he asks for the top five from the class. After reviewing the files, he selects two and flies to Quantico the next day for interviews. The first agent he interviews is brilliant, according to his test scores. He is from a small town 50 miles east of Dallas. The interview lasts about an hour, but they never really click. He concludes this guy will do in a pinch. Reardon takes an hour-long lunch break and comes back to the interview room about 10 minutes before the second interview starts so he can prepare. As he opens the door a young woman is already sitting at the table. Reardon pauses to verify he is in the correct room. He takes a half step back and then sees his jacket and bag slung over the chair. He knows he's in the right room.

"Sorry, I thought I was in the wrong room. I wasn't expecting anyone to be in here."

"It's OK, I am habitually early. My mother said it all started when I was born three weeks premature. I just couldn't wait to get going."

"OK." Reardon says with a slight head nod, not knowing how to really respond. After an awkward pause, he extends his hand. "Noah Reardon."

"Laura Spencer, nice to meet you."

"Yes." Reardon shakes her hand and moves around behind the table and sits. "So..."

"So..."

Reardon is surprised that her early arrival has thrown him off his game so easily. He quickly regains his composure.

"So."

"Yes, I believe you already said that."

"Yes, I did." Reardon already likes her.

Reardon pulls out a half used yellow notepad from his bag, flips to the next page, and pulls a pen from his pocket.

"So." He pauses a moment and grins. "Yes, I've already said that, three times now." Spencer smiles. "So, tell me about yourself."

"Well, I grew up just outside Canton, Ohio, and I have a degree in criminology from Georgetown University and ..."

"Yes, sorry, I know that," Reardon interrupts. "I read your file. Please tell me something not in your file."

"Like what?"

"Like surprise me."

"Well, I was a tomboy growing up and loved working on old cars with my dad. Is that the sort of thing you want to know?"

"Yeah, what else?"

"I never met a piece of chocolate I didn't like."

"Really? There is some pretty bad chocolate out there."

"True, but I just view it as getting me one step closer to a good piece."

"OK. What else..."

With that they banter back and forth for about ten minutes. Eventually Reardon starts asking her about why she got into criminology and what brought her to the FBI. He likes her answers. They feel honest and not the canned answers he usually gets when interviewing. She asks about his team and the work she will do. With five minutes left in the hour, Reardon comes to the point.

"I think you'll be a good fit. I'll give you the night to think it over and let me know in the morning."

"Yes."

"Yes, you'll let me know in the morning?"

"No. Yes, I'm in. I don't need the night to think about it."

Day 45

Reardon is shocked awake from a loud noise coming from the street. It's 6:43 a.m. He is tempted to turn on the TV, but his head is throbbing. He rolls over and goes back to sleep. Two hours later, Reardon awakes to a phone call and slowly rolls over.

"Yeah."

"Do you have water?" Spencer quickly asks.

"Ah, yeah, I guess so."

"No. Does your water work?"

"What? What do you mean?"

"Are you up?"

"Not yet."

"Get up and see if your water works."

"Ah, OK, why?"

"Just do it!"

Reardon rolls out of bed and slowly limps towards the kitchen sink. He turns on his water, and it seems to work just fine.

"Yeah, my water works. Why?"

"They blew up one of the water tunnels and damaged another one. The city is reporting that people may experience water loss throughout the day. It was just reported about 30 minutes ago. They don't know how bad it is right now."

"What do you mean blew up?"

"They collapsed one of the tunnels for the Catskill Aqueduct and damaged one of the shafts for the Delaware Aqueduct near where they are digging the new bypass tunnel."

"What bypass tunnel?"

"It's a long story. Just get in here as soon as you can."

Spencer hangs up. Reardon limps back over to his bed and flicks on the TV. The initial shot is from a helicopter showing a large area with water gurgling out of the ground and flooding surrounding fields. The newscaster is just starting to speak.

Reports are still coming in, and this is a developing situation. What we know so far is that part of the Catskill Aqueduct collapsed, and thousands of gallons of water are currently pouring into fields just north of Philipstown, New York. Locals report hearing a loud noise at approximately 8 a.m. Eastern Standard Time. Authorities are convinced this is an act of terrorism with the confirmation of an explosion in shaft 6 of the Delaware Aqueduct. The Catskill Aqueduct is one of three that supplies approximately 1.2 billion gallons of water to New York City every day. The Delaware and Catskill Aqueducts account for nearly 90% of that supply.

A graphic suddenly appears showing a cross-section of the Catskill aqueduct.

The Catskill Aqueduct is 163 miles long, and 55 miles of that is referred to as cut and cover. The collapse occurred along a stretch of the cut and cover tunnel. The damaged tunnel is 17 feet 6 inches at the base and 17 feet in height. The tunnel is composed of 12-inch thick concrete at the top and covered by 3 feet of dirt at the apex. Authorities now believe high explosives were set along a 30-foot stretch, collapsing a section approximately 15 by 30 feet and dropping several tons of concrete and dirt into the tunnel. The tunnel carries approximately 400 million gallons of water to New York City on an average day.

While water is still flowing authorities are trying to ascertain how much is spilling out and how all the fallen debris will affect the system downstream. Although the system is primarily fed by gravity, engineers are examining what will happen if debris hits the intake valves for any of the several pumps that bring the water back up to street level. It may take several days to determine the impact. In the meantime, authorities are planning to reduce the flow in the Catskill Aqueduct to 25% in an attempt to drop the water level low enough to stop the water from overflowing.

There is no news on the damage to shaft 6 of the Delaware Aqueduct because of the flooding caused by the explosion. This aqueduct provides New York City with half of the city's water. Authorities are not sure if the aqueduct itself is damaged or if the damage is to access pipes leading to the aqueduct. Either is particularly concerning because shaft 6 is the terminus for the 2.5 mile bypass currently under construction. The bypass tunnel running beneath the Hudson River from Newburgh to Wappinger, New York, is part of a $1.2 billion project to circumvent a leak that began in the 1990s and releases approximately 35 million gallons of water per day. The project is expected to complete in 2021. Until the damage in shaft 6 is understood, we will have no idea how this will impact the project. Residents of New York are urged to conserve water. The city will provide additional guidance at a press conference scheduled for noon.

Reardon just sits there with a stunned look on his face thinking how this is getting out of hand. How could a small group of people do so much damage? More importantly, he is thinking about how fragile the infrastructure is all over the nation. If New York City were to run out of water there will suddenly be 8.3 million people who need to get out of the city and the ensuing mayhem associated with such an exodus.

Reardon gets up, hobbles over to the kitchen, pours himself a double, and then downs another before heading into the bathroom. After he showers, he catches a taxi to the office. As Reardon walks into the office, he heads for the main conference room where McCullum and Spencer are sitting with four other agents watching the television. Reardon walks in and sits down just after 11. Everyone is still just sitting there in stunned silence. After a few minutes, McCullum stands up, starts pacing, and stares out the window for a few moments. He grabs the remote for the TV and mutes it.

"Peterson, let me know as soon as the agents get to Philipstown."
"Will do. They should be there within two hours."
"Spencer, look into what type of video monitoring they have along the aqueduct. I want video, all the video from one end to the other on all three of the aqueducts. Got it! Why 8 a.m.?" McCullum mumbles.
"Huh?" Spencer asks.
"Why 8 a.m.? Why the change? They are getting later. Are they just trying to keep us off guard or giving us a chance to get a good night sleep?"
"I don't know."
"Forget about it for now. Get me that video."

Just as Spencer is about to get up and walk out of the room, she looks up to see breaking coverage from California splashing across the screen.

"What's this?" Spencer asks while pointing to the TV.

McCullum extends his folded arm and unmutes the TV.

"...now reports part of the San Francisco aqueduct has been damaged. A section known as the Kirkwood penstock, a vertical drop of exposed water pipe leading to the Kirkwood powerhouse, has just been destroyed. We have crews heading to the area right now. This is part of the Hetch Hetchy Power system that provides both power and water to the city of San Francisco. The water supply runs from Yosemite National Park to San Francisco. We are still working to collect more information on this breaking story and ..."

McCullum mutes the TV again.

"Screw me! Now they're going after our water supply!" McCullum quickly paces back and forth a moment before Spencer interrupts.
"Should we contact the San Francisco office to get more info?"
"No, not right now, they can handle it, and we need to wrap our arms around our own problem!"

McCullum has Peterson constantly working on a list of probable targets in New York and New Jersey that he started three weeks ago. At first, the list was too high-level, so he sent Peterson back to the drawing board for a more detailed list. The problem is the detailed list has over 15,000 items and is growing every day. Peterson just started doing internet searches that included *bridge, overpass, tunnel, electric, water main, building, dam,* and *historic.* Peterson had not gotten around to aqueduct yet. However, McCullum knows the aqueduct has been under surveillance since Day 30 after the Twin Cities were attacked. He wants to know more details so he can understand how this happened.

Washington, D.C.

Hours pass as more information flows in. The White House is in crisis mode as the president is meeting with his staff looking at possible options. The reality is that there are no options. They still have no idea who is orchestrating the attacks or why. The pressure is building to find information on upcoming attacks; however, the CIA and NSA are still finding no electronic chatter. The overseas terrorist organizations are still relishing the chaos, but none are claiming responsibility. The situation is beyond maddening for all involved. They are also trying to understand if any domestic groups are organized well enough to pull off an orchestrated set of attacks like this – so far, the answer is a resounding *no*. The president's staff is once again putting together a brief outlining the damage and impact of the damage. The president is also planning to address the nation once again as they attempt to make sense out of what is happening and assuring the American public that they are doing everything they can do in order to stop the attacks.

The president receives a summary two hours after the explosion in San Francisco.

> San Francisco has recovered from the rolling blackouts of early morning as utility companies draw more power from other sources. The concern is that these circuits will become overloaded, plunging the city into darkness. The mayor is asking citizens to reduce their use of electricity and unplug anything they are not using. The larger concern is that the city is losing over 20% of its water supply. The mayor is mandating water conservation measures to ensure that the city can maintain adequate water levels.

The president quietly enters the cabinet room and sits down. As soon as the president is seated, everyone follows. The president sits quietly for about 20 seconds. The awkward silence hangs in the air.

"I think it's time to have a serious conversation about the Insurrection Act."

A few are stunned by this revelation, but others feel it is a logical next step. He asked a staffer to start carefully reviewing the Insurrection Act and the Posse Comitatus Act two days ago. He read a summary just before he went to bed last night. He knew the general details but had never given it any serious thought because he knew he would never need to use it. He is even uncomfortable talking about it because it means they have hit a critical point in his presidency. Moreover, a critical point in the nation's history.

The Insurrection Act, originally passed in 1807, is designed to give the President specific, and more importantly limited, power to put down insurrections, conspiracies, and rebellions in order to protect the nation. It was renamed the *Enforcement of the Laws to Restore Public Order* Act in 2006 after changes were made to deal with a post-9/11 world. The changes grant the president greater authority to deploy troops and explicitly mention terrorist attacks, serious public health emergencies, and *other condition.*

The last clause is subject to great public debate among legal scholars and conspiracy theorists. The current situation clearly falls between terrorist attacks and *other condition*. The Posse Comitatus Act was the result of ongoing military occupation in the South after the Civil War during Reconstruction. The act, passed in 1878, prevents the president from using the U.S. military within the United States except in conjunction with the Insurrection Act. Maintaining order among the civilian population is left to the police and FBI.

In order to ensure the meeting is productive, the president invites Admiral Beede, Chairman of the Joint Chiefs of Staff, to provide military advice. He also invites his presidential legal counsel to discuss the intricacies of the law and the grey areas. The act is riddled with grey areas, especially, when discussing how to use it nationwide. The restrictions are in place for a specific reason: to prevent the President from using the military to take over the country and install himself as dictator. With the act comes the ability to suspend civil liberties and habeas corpus. People can be taken into custody without reason and held indefinitely without due process. In other words, *anyone* deemed a threat can get dropped in a deep hole and never heard from again. This includes reporters, publishers, and anyone questioning the president. For this reason, there is a strict time limit on certain aspects of the law. A malicious president could quickly use the authority to start making congresspeople disappear and leave those left behind hesitant to speak up. A quick path to dictatorship.

Everyone in the room understands this, and the discussion is deadly serious. The best intentions can quickly spiral out of control. Initially, the discussion revolves around the mechanics of the operation. In order to hunt down the terrorists and cover the entire United States, all National Guard units would be activated. All active service members in the U.S. would also go on active deployment within the country. However, neither of these is permissible without invoking the Insurrection Act. Even then, the manpower would still not be enough to have a meaningful impact considering the random nature of the attacks and pursuing unknown perpetrators. Next, the discussion turns to bringing home overseas units from Japan, Germany, the Philippines, South Korea, and a dozen other countries. That would make us vulnerable to attack overseas. North Korea might use this as an opportunity to overrun South Korea. Russia could view this as a weakness and increase its aggressive behavior. The risks are high. Even with *all* the troops, there is still concern that it would not be enough to be effective. The discussion naturally turns to how the troops would be used. To be effective, they would need to perform searches and seizures, hoping to catch people carrying anything that could be used to carry out terrorist attacks. They also have the authority to confiscate guns, as was done in New Orleans after Katrina struck. Authorities in New Orleans wanted to ensure they could maintain order and peace. How would they define the rules of engagement for the military personnel? How should they react if someone refuses to have either their vehicle or person searched? Minor conflicts could quickly escalate into violent conflicts.

Since they have no idea who they are looking for, everyone becomes a suspect. Do they use racial profiling? The president's staff begins discussing various scenarios, such as, mandatory vehicle inspections and checkpoints at state borders. They discuss random inspection sites because if people know of the checkpoints, they will systematically avoid them, undermining the effectiveness.

They discuss random home inspections and how to handle situations where they find illegal goods or weapons. The sole purpose of the inspections is to root out terrorists, not to find meth labs. They get sidetracked constantly chasing down one rat hole after another. They spend a great deal of time discussing unintended consequences. What if the military gets out of control or groups feel threatened? It could spur a rebellion among militias. Militias have been warning for years that the government has been looking for an excuse to take over, and this is a first step. The terrorists are likely hiding in the same types of places that militias call home for their weekend-warrior escapades. Snooping around in the wrong place could quickly lead to open war with militias or any group. This is an extremely real possibility. Unleashing the U.S. military on the country could quickly turn this into a self-fulfilling prophecy, spurring insurrections and rebellion.

After many tense hours, they discuss the legality of various scenarios. The act was clearly intended for terrorist attacks, but people argue the act could not have anticipated this type of attack. Tempers begin to flare. After three hours, the president tells everyone to take a break and go to lunch. They will pick up the discussion after lunch and reconvene at 1:30. Normally, the president would not be involved in these endless discussions. Instead he would send them off to figure out a solution and present two or three options for him to choose from. However, there is nothing normal about this, and he wants to be involved in every aspect of the discussion. Dozens of staffers are working on these scenarios 24 hours a day and providing updated summaries to their bosses over lunch.

After lunch, with new options in hand, they discuss more scenarios for several hours. The sticking point with the Insurrection Act is the phase highlighted in the president's brief:

SEC. 1076. Sec. 333 (A) (i) domestic violence has occurred to such an extent that the constituted authority of the State or possession are incapable of maintaining public order

His staff argues that technically this has not happened. Therefore, the Insurrection Act is not a viable option for the president at this time. Some argue that they were not thinking about this situation when they wrote it. They even discuss a situation where the president invokes the Insurrection Act; the ACLU files a lawsuit and a Federal Court judge puts an injunction in place to stop the president until it can undergo a judicial review. Then what?

Admiral Beede does a lot of talking after a brief discussion with the other chiefs. They express grave concerns over recalling troops on short notice, especially from South Korea. It could lead to open season on the small regiment of troops that are left behind in hostile regions around the world. Then he discusses how most troops are simply not trained for this type of duty. Training would be a key component, and time is the one thing they don't have. The staff then returns to rat hole after rat hole. The complexity of this is staggering at both a macro and micro level. The president dismisses his staff just after 6 p.m., goes back to the Oval Office, and slumps in his chair. He is overwhelmed. He is not dealing with an insurrection or rebellion, either would be easy in comparison. He needs to search the entire country from top to bottom in order to find a couple dozen people without violating the rights of every single American. He needs to solve one problem without creating five more. In a country of laws, how do you deal with situations that don't fit the standard model?

This is exactly what they mean when they discuss the weight of the presidency.

Day 46

Dow Jones Industrial Average
13,439.49
Total decline: 33.3%
Total loss: $1.73 Trillion

Nasdaq
3,719.94
Total decline: 34.5%
Total loss: $2.93 Trillion

Reardon makes a special effort to get into the office and sets his alarm for 7 o'clock. It doesn't work. He finally rolls over at 9:43 and turns on the TV. All he can see is image after image of tall office buildings and fire crews. After about three seconds, the newscaster starts talking.

Five cities were simultaneously rocked by explosions at 3 a.m. Eastern Standard Time in Pittsburgh, Nashville, Jacksonville, Kansas City, and Portland, Oregon last night. The attacks were exactly the same at each building. An initial explosion blew an opening in front of the building, shattering glass and allowing another drone to fly into the main elevator bank of each building. A larger, secondary explosion destroyed or severely damaged the elevator doors, setting off the sprinkler systems and causing additional damage. There is no report of casualties at this time. The results of the explosions effectively shut down the buildings because people are unable to safely enter and use the elevators. The buildings range in height from 30 to 62 floors. Each of these buildings has been shut down until further notice while they are inspected and searched for any additional explosives. We estimate at least 100,000 people are affected because of the 15 buildings shutting down. It will take weeks to clean up, repair, and re-open these buildings. In the meantime, the economic impact will be felt throughout each of these cities.

The station goes to a break. Reardon rolls out of bed and limps towards the shower with a splitting headache. As he returns from the shower the news coverage has shifted back to the aqueducts in New York and California.

In New York the Catskill Aqueduct continues to operate at 25% capacity in an effort to stop the overflow and assess the damage. The governor has confirmed the breach is the result of an explosion, leaving a hole approximately 15 feet by 36 feet. Heavy machinery is being brought in to retrieve the larger chunks of concrete to help improve the flow.

The city is still assessing any potential damage that will be caused by soil and smaller chunks of concrete that are currently making their way along the aqueduct. They have no way to assess the damage in shaft 6 of the Delaware Aqueduct located just south of the Hudson River due to flooding in the shaft. The flow of water remains at full capacity to offset the reduced flow in the Catskill Aqueduct. In the meantime, the mayor has put water restrictions in place to ensure that no one loses water completely.

City engineers are working out plans on how to proceed with repairs after they have more information on each breach. At some point in time, they will need to completely shut down and drain the Delaware Aqueduct to assess the damage. This will be a catastrophic event for New York City.

In California, the Kirkwood power plant is now offline, and the water flowing through the Kirkwood penstock has been completely shut off. There are no immediate water or power outage concerns for San Francisco. San Francisco consumes approximately 235 million gallons of water per day. The water comes from Yosemite through a series of three underground aqueducts, and the power generated by that water is transmitted over high-voltage power lines. The breach in the Kirkwood penstock will cut about 20% of the water flowing into San Francisco within days as reservoirs are drained.

Reardon decides to go into the office against his better judgement, but he goes knowing McCullum wants him there. As he catches the tail end of the news, he swigs down two cans of beer and some whiskey before heading out his front door to hail a cab. He is wondering what could be next. They have obviously done their homework and knocked out low security targets and are slowly building just as he discussed with Abdul. Reardon wonders if Abdul could have shared their conversations with someone even in passing not realizing the effect or who may have overheard.

Reardon walks into the conference room strumming with activity. He grabs a chair just inside the door to observe. Spencer catches him out of the corner of her eye while talking to Peterson near the front of the room. Reardon sits there quietly for over five minutes, staring at the images on the muted TV. They switch from one newscaster to another with emergency crews filing around in the background. Just as they flash to Pittsburgh, McCullum walks in to the room with his commanding presence. He does not even notice Reardon sitting near the door, given how intent he is to get the meeting going.

"Everyone, sit down. Someone turn off that TV. I want Peterson to share a report with everyone. Peterson."

"Our agents and police spent all yesterday scouring the aqueducts for clues. Jackson," he motions to an agent in the room, "talked with a farmer yesterday. The man's house is just over a half mile from the Catskill explosion. He reported that he saw a work crew there digging about a month ago. He could not recall the exact date. He didn't give it a second thought at the time, seeing work crews performing repairs is not out of the ordinary. It appears they were using an entrenching tool. Based on his description, we are speculating that the work crew packed plastic explosives and detcord into plastic tubing and used the entrencher to bury the tubing packed with explosives. Being buried like this helped maximize the force of the explosion. Quite clever actually."

Peterson looks at McCullum. He is not amused by the observation, and Peterson continues. At least McCullum understands why nothing out of the ordinary was reported by anyone over the last couple of days. They were thinking ahead and planted the explosives around Day 16 when no one cared what some work crew was doing in the middle of a field.

"Anyways, we don't know if the charge was set off with a timer or set off remotely. Either way, the result was the same. Boom."

"Why didn't he take the time to call the utility company to make sure they should be there?" asked an agent sitting halfway down the table, out of direct line of sight from McCullum. McCullum leans forward and bellows.

"REALLY! There are work crews everywhere. If I took the time to call in every time I saw a work crew, I'd spend the rest of my life on hold to hear *yeah, they're just repairing something."*

McCullum stands up and motions with his finger out to their main office area.

"There could be a work crew out there cutting a hole in the floor right now, ready to put in a fire pole, and we wouldn't ask a single question. We would just figure they're supposed to be there. Work crews are everywhere, and we look right past them. We all have too much crap going on in our lives to worry about what some work crew is doing. Peterson, keep going."

"That's all I have sir."

"Oh," McCullum is caught off guard, "Fine then."

"They are certainly thinking ahead," Spencer observes. "Given this, we should assume they have other explosives in place. At least that gives us something to go on."

"Great! Now we need to look under every rock and in every nook and cranny hoping we find some C-4 and hoping it's not booby-trapped. This nightmare just keeps going. Our agents and the police are going to have to start looking everywhere, hoping they get lucky and find a bomb before it goes off. Peterson, get this to the director and put out a nationwide alert to all the field offices with what we've learned. Tell them it's time to start playing hide-and-seek. If we get lucky, we'll find some before it's too late."

McCullum feels slightly better because this is a lead, however it does little in reality to relieve their tenuous position. As he continues to talk, the TV is silently scrolling the full list of attacks.

Day 1 – 46 Attacks

Day	Attack
1	Office complex flooding, Milwaukee, Wisconsin
2	200 tires slashed at car dealership, Rockville, Maryland
3	Backhoe severs buried fiber optic cable, Sumter, South Carolina
4	120 pigs poisoned, Butte, Montana
5	15 cell towers damaged, Glendale, Arizona
6	Sewage treatment center valve closed causing backup into creek, Conway, Arkansas
7	Three power line poles cut down, Moab, Utah
8	
9	Abandoned warehouse burned down, Nashua, New Hampshire
10	Power line tower, Haskell, New Jersey
11	Pennies under the wheels of a train so it can't move, Dover, Delaware
12	Three houses under construction torched, Brookline, Massachusetts
13	Cattle fence cut down, 250 cows end up wandering along highway, El Paso, Texas

14	20 windshields smashed at car dealership, Grand Island, Nebraska
15	Green water in reservoir, Dillon, Idaho
16	Grocery store burned down, Clearwater, Florida
17	Three buildings on college campus vandalized, Littlefield, Texas
18	Engine car for Mt. Washington Cog Railway vandalized, New Hampshire
19	Windows broken in historic Dodge City, Kansas
20	Two houses under construction burned down, Spokane, Washington
21	Three tanker truck explosions, Los Angeles, California
22	Five power substations destroyed outside five mid-size cities
23	Tour buses destroyed outside Pinehurst Arena in Lincoln, Nebraska
24	Food distribution warehouse, Orlando, Florida
25	Fish poisoned in Kilowatt Lake, Memphis, Tennessee
26	Water towers destroyed, Ames, Iowa
27	Civil war monuments destroyed, Gettysburg, Virginia
28	Correctional Facility explosion, Chateaugay, New York
29	Bridges destroyed, Twin Cities, Minnesota
30	Airport highway overpasses destroyed, SFO, CLT, PHX, MIA, ATL, MCO, ORD, DEN, JFK, LAS, DFW
31	Jet fuel pipelines, Georgia and Missouri
32	Toilet paper and detergent plants destroyed, Penn, Vermont, and Georgia
33	Pharmaceutical plant, makes Viagra and anti-depressants, near Richmond, Virginia
34	1000 letters with powdery substances sent to mayors, city council members, federal judges, across country
35	Water pipes going to central California farms destroyed
36	Wheel house for cable cars destroyed in San Francisco, California
37	10 bombs destroy small roadside cafes across country
38	Small dam damaged outside Alma, Nebraska
39	Three concrete mixing plants destroyed, Macon, Georgia
40	Highway overpasses and tunnel destroyed, Dallas, Texas
41	7 roller coasters damaged at amusement parks
42	Bombs destroy glass ceilings at 10 large malls
43	5 sewer treatment plants damaged, Kansas City, Kansas
44	Famous trees destroyed, The Survivor Tree, Oklahoma City, Oklahoma; The Big Tree, Rockport, Texas; The Dueling Oak,

	New Orleans, Louisiana; The Angel Oak Tree, Johns Island, South Carolina
45	New York City aqueduct damaged
46	Large buildings damaged, Pittsburgh, Pennsylvania, Nashville, Tennessee, Portland, Oregon, Kansas City, Kansas, Jacksonville, Florida

Washington, D.C.

Over lunch, the president and his chief of staff discuss Eidelmen extensively. Eidelmen is continuing to hit the airwaves hard, getting time on CNN and MSNBC. His chief of staff confirmed that the senate majority leader met with Eidelmen twice. The president is now convinced Eidelmen is just being used as a pawn to strengthen the senator's position as he prepares to run for president.

"I think we need to forget about Eidelmen and shift our attention to the majority leader," says the chief of staff flatly.

"Since we can't shut up Eidelmen, I don't think we have a choice. We need to figure out a way to cut him off at the knees."

Lunch ends, and the president reconvenes with his staff. The goal of the meeting is to figure out a path forward with the Insurrection Act. He is hoping there will be a fresh perspective after people slept on it. He decides to start at the beginning. They review the wording of the Insurrection Act once again.

From the start, there is no agreement over whether these attacks warrant invoking the act. There is clearly domestic violence; however, local authorities are still in control. The last time the act was invoked on a large scale was in 2005 after hurricane Katrina struck. The Bush administration wanted Gov. Blanco to turn over control of the National Guard to the president. She refused, leading to a pissing match. Bush could have still sent in federal troops but decided not to. Federal, state, and local authorities bickered on the next steps, and in the meantime, conditions deteriorated, leading to a hellish humanitarian disaster in New Orleans.

In the current situation, there is no clear place to start with deployments. The president's staff would need to quickly come up with a proposal that would satisfy the governor of each state. Without a quick unilateral agreement, all the negotiations would quickly stall and become untenable. His staff argues for over an hour on what to do next. Finally, the president dismisses his staff. Frustrated, he meets privately with his chief of staff and

Admiral Beede. They conclude this is truly uncharted territory with no clear path forward.

"Give me something to go on…" The president is desperate for any viable options.

"Well, Mr. President, the Insurrection Act is not a half measure," Admiral Beede pauses for a moment. "If we do this half-ass, it will be a complete waste of time. We need to commit. The problem is that I'm not sure if the act is a viable option."

"I would recommend we quietly start bringing troops home to prepare."

"It won't stay a secret for more than five seconds," adds Beede.

"Admiral, I want you to write up a recommendation for bringing home troops. Make it clear how many you would need and where they would come from."

"Yes, sir."

The president waves his hand as a signal for them to leave. This is a step. Only time will tell if it's the right direction. In the meantime, the attacks continue and the response from the federal government is neutered.

An hour later, the President receives a devastating economic report outlining the impact to the economy. The main thrust of the report is the impact on the airline industry. It's slowly limping back to some semblance of order. Air cargo is still sitting in piles all around the United States. The ongoing chaos in the Twin Cities garners its own separate page. The inability of the MSP airport to handle any commercial passenger traffic is still a pressing issue. Hundreds of companies have simply shut down, putting thousands out of work. There are no accurate numbers on how many Minnesotans are now out of work. However, the greater issue is dealing with the food and fuel shortages. Plane rides and jobs will need to wait. The president slumps in his chair after he reads the page. The report includes an overall dollar estimate surpassing $100 billion, but he ignores it because he knows the number is just some economist's best guess. If they had asked another person for the number, it would be drastically different.

The next section of the report discusses the collapsing financial markets. To many, this is their largest concern. Money has a way of focusing people's attention. Every single American with a pension, 401(k) plan, or even just a penny stock is losing money hand over fist. Trillions of dollars have gone up in smoke. The value of the dollar is destabilizing the world economy in hundreds of subtle ways. The president knows the markets typically recover within a few months after an attack. A single attack. This unrelenting series of attacks continues to push the markets down every single day. The New

York Stock Exchange is shutting down on a frequent basis to give people time to cool off and stem the tide of a total sell off. The only thing keeping the markets alive at all is the persistent promise that *tomorrow* will be the last day of attacks. So, far tomorrow never comes. The president completes the report and lazily drops it on his desk. He pushes back from his desk and rubs his palms into his eyes. He becomes teary eyed as he rises from the chair and begins the long walk to his bed from the Oval Office. The Secret Service devotedly falls in behind him and quietly follows him down the hall. The nation is on the precipice of collapse, and he feels alone in a crowd.

One unmistakable trend is that the pace of cyber-attacks has picked up dramatically. Intelligence agencies can't tell if this is a clue or a distraction. If the Russians are behind the terrorist attacks, then this is a clue. If the Russians are simply exploiting an opportunity, then this is a massive distraction. The problem is that no one knows which it is at this point in time, and everyone is desperately attempting to answer that question. Working against an enemy attacking from without and within is overwhelming every agency's ability to find answers.

June 24, 2010 – Afghanistan

Abdul is quietly sitting next to Reardon on a deserted road in the middle of nowhere. The escort vehicle is just a quarter mile away parked next to an outcropping of rock and hidden from sight. It's been over an hour, and they were expecting a no show before they even arrived. This is a new informant they are trying to cultivate. The odds of a new informant showing up are about 20:1 the first time, especially if they see a big Humvee sitting there.

"So, the other day you were telling me of your nightmares. You were talking about shattered lives. Do they continue?"
"Yes, three more last night. I still can't remember any details."
"Perhaps that is for the best."
"Maybe."
"It doesn't take much to shatter a life here does it?"
"No. But it would be easy to do in America."
"I don't believe you. You have so much. It would take weeks to deprive Americans of even their most basic comforts."
"Not so, the more intricate the machine the easier it is to break."
"What is intricate?"
"Complex or complicated."
"Explain."

"Please don't be insulted, but here people live simple lives, out of necessity."

"No insult at all. This is just a fact."

"Well, in America, everything depends on everything else. Start with water and electricity. These are just givens. Sure, after big storms people lose their homes to flooding and hurricanes. The news crews descend in droves and talk about all the human tragedy. Then, lose interest after a day or two, maybe a week if it's really tragic but then they move onto the next tragedy of the week. The 24-hour news cycle must move on to keep up its ratings. They don't really care what they report, just that people keep tuning in. They are always looking for an angle, a human interest story, a way to exploit the truth, or lies, in order to build the sensationalism of it all. Imagine a news story that won't stop."

"How do you mean?"

"Like here. Imagine if every day something new happens that is related to the day before, a slowly building tragedy. If you want to hurt Americans, you don't need to kill them, you just need to deprive them. One day you take away their water, the next day their coffee. The day after that, you make them afraid to go to the shopping mall."

"Why would this matter?"

"Terrorism is really about fear, not death. Fear of the unknown is a much more dangerous weapon. You just keep pecking, day after day at those little things we all depend on but don't give a second thought to. The news media would go insane. Congresspeople would be asking for heads to roll. Forget about high value targets. Go after the small stuff. We can't possibly guard everything or have a camera looking at everything every second of the day. The president would be deploring the terrorists and riding the NSA and CIA until they break. Creating chaos would be a simple task."

"I still don't believe it."

"It would be simple. All you would need to do is plant people a couple years in advance and have them just wait. They stay low, and you just keep in touch with them through snail mail."

"What is snail mail?"

"Regular mail, envelopes and paper. We are so busy looking for electronic chatter that they would never even notice letters being sent around the country. Then one day you just start. People wouldn't even notice in the beginning. You might even need to leave them a note just so they don't miss it. Then just keep building, one thing after another, always small things. Hardly anyone would need to die."

"How do you mean, it would just start?"

"You would just plant about 10 teams of three or four people around the country. They would do small things to get prepared. Steal license plates. Buy old cars for cash in small towns and never register them. You would send them supplies via FedEx. They would buy fertilizer one bag at a time and stockpile it for later. Always low key. Then you give them the go ahead a couple months in advance, and they move out and live on the road for a month or so. After that, it is all scripted. Each team has its assignments. Start small. One day a team burns down an old warehouse. The day after that, another team cuts down some powerlines in the middle of nowhere. No one would even notice at first. Without some clues, no one could even piece it all together. Kids are doing all kinds of crap every day. A dozen old warehouses probably burn down every day. Some kids prank a rancher they hate by cutting down a fence and let out a couple hundred head of cattle onto the highway. There is no end to what you could do."

"It seems like you have put some thought into this."

"Well, I have an abundance of time these days to just think. Too much time to think. About why we are here and how it is helping. If this keeps up, more soldiers are going to die here and in Iraq than people died on 9/11. I see what we're doing to people who mean us no harm, and that gets me thinking about how people could hurt Americans who are doing them no harm. At home, we watch TV and see people burning flags and screaming death to America. What they really mean is death to the American government. Death to the policymakers. Before 9/11, people didn't care about what was going on here any more than people here cared about what the average American is doing."

"What you say is true, but the radicals don't differentiate. They just see evil America and believe that if the Americans really cared, they would stop the government. Instead they see the American people as complicit."

"True, but complicit isn't the right word. Indifferent would be a better word."

"Well, I recommend we never speak of this conversation again to anyone. This is a dangerous topic."

"Agreed."

Day 47

Reardon drags his butt into the conference room just after 11 o'clock and plops down next to Peterson. He is being overly gregarious as he starts talking to Peterson, making it more obvious with each slurred word that he's drunk.

"Get him the hell out of here and put him in a room to sleep it off," McCullum barks.

Spencer and Peterson are the only other two in the room, so they get the message loud and clear. They each grab an arm and head him back to a bunk room so he can get some sleep.

"Hey, where're we going?"
"You look tired. Let's head back to the bunk room so you can take a nap."

Reardon initially resists their efforts but they turn him.

"I did all this."
"This isn't your fault."
"But I told Abdul how to do all this. This is so horrible, I want them to stop."
"We want them to stop, too."
"They won't stop. Even if I beg them, they won't stop."

Spencer and Peterson continue to slowly walk him as tears start to roll down his cheeks.

"It's all my fault."
"You just need to sleep," Spencer says soothingly.

Spencer and Peterson walk back into the conference room as McCullum continues to pace.

"Reardon has really gone off the deep end since this all started," states McCullum
"I think this is causing all the memories from Afghanistan to come flooding back," Spencer says unabashedly defending Reardon.

Spencer's anger is building as Reardon is sleeping it off. Four hours later Reardon slowly walks back into the conference room with a warm coffee in his hand. Spencer and Peterson are the only two in the room and are closely staring at Peterson's laptop.

"See anything interesting? Finding any clues?"
Spencer is livid. "To hell with you Reardon! You have a lot of nerve coming in straight up drunk. We're trying to get some actual work done. We're trying to catch the bad guys. You act like you don't even give a damn," shouts Spencer.
"Well, I will ask again. Finding any clues?"

"No, not a single clue!"

"So, I would say I'm not missing much."

Reardon turns and starts to walk out of the conference room.

"Wait!" Spencer quickly walks up to him. "I'm sorry, this is just so horrible."

"I think you're spending too much time with McCullum."

"I swore before we started working for McCullum."

"Yeah, but now you swear like a longshoreman. But don't worry, it's pretty hot."

With that comment, Spencer gives Reardon a pretty severe jab to his side causing him to spill a third of his coffee. Reardon smiles.

"How is that for hot?"

"Pretty good. I'm sorry you're so frustrated, but you're not going to find a clue until they want you to find another clue."

"Why are you so confident when you say that?"

"It's what I would do, it's what you would do. It's a big country and easy to stay low and stay out of sight."

"We would still find you."

"Yes, you would find me, but you're not looking for me. That's the point. You have no idea who you are looking for. There's got to be at least a couple dozen guys, maybe even thirty or forty. If they had all faxed in a photo with a bio before this all started, then we would have nabbed many of them by now. But that's not what they did. You're looking for a group of thirty or forty in 330 million. That's a big haystack. This isn't Russia in the good old days where the Kremlin could tell you the whereabouts of nearly anyone on any given day. There are at least a half-million people moving around the U.S. on any given day, and many of them don't want to be found."

"Yeah, but we'll catch a break."

"Maybe, but like Peterson said, it can take years to find people on the FBI's 10 Most Wanted List. It usually takes a big break, a lucky break, to just find one of them, *and* we have a photo and a rap sheet on every one of them. We're looking for ghosts."

"We're going to do it. We have to do it. Go home. You're a mess."

"OK," resolved to the fact that he would just be a hindrance.

"Can you promise me you won't drink, just for this one night?"

"No, I'm not going to make that promise, and if I did, we'd both know it was a lie."

"Yeah, but it's a lie I could live with for tonight."

Just at that moment, McCullum comes storming into the room.

"Stinkin' drones! I knew these things would be nothing but trouble the first time I saw one."

McCullum walks to the head of the table, grabs a folder and leaves as quickly as he came. Unexpectedly, Spencer turns and asks Reardon to sit down. He walks up near the front and sits down. Spencer and Reardon just gingerly lean back and slowly bounce in their chairs. Peterson suddenly looks up.

"I was doing some reading last night. Mostly on Iraq. Not sure why. Anyways, did you know Iraq was created back in 1920? The borders were defined by the League of Nations after the fall of the Ottoman Empire and placed under British rule. From what I can tell, the British just drew lines around their oil fields and decided to call it a country. They even named it Iraq. The problem is they did not pay any attention to the ethnic groups living in the region. The Shia, Suni, and Kurds all have long standing conflicts with each other. Seems like a real recipe for success. I'm joking." Reardon and Spencer nod when Peterson looks up, smiling like he just cracked the best joke of the year. "I guess the British thought they would rule forever so they didn't really think about it that much. Instead, it was a powder keg from day one."

Spencer and Reardon just smile at each other and keep rocking in their chairs as Peterson continues.

"The main reason they cared so much was their new dependence on oil after Churchill switched the Royal Navy from coal to oil. He did it when he was Lord of the Admiralty between 1915 and 1918. This move formally cemented the strategic importance of the Middle East from that day forward. The British Empire had to ensure it always had an ample and ready supply of oil. The Middle East has been a highly strategic mess ever since. During World War II, it was a real chess match working against the Nazis and the Axis powers to ensure they maintained control of the oil supply and the Suez Canal."

They listen to Peterson wax poetic about the Middle East for about another two minutes before McCullum comes back in the room.

"Peterson, have they retrieved the body of the suicide bomber in the Dallas tunnel attack yet?"

"No, and they don't think they ever will. The fire burned so hot it turned everything into ash. They're not even sure if they will get a VIN off the truck, not that it matters."

"Dammit! One dead end after another."

"They have cleared the tunnel and put in temporary supports. There are structural engineers looking," at that moment McCullum leaves the room mid-sentence, "into the extent of the damage." Peterson shrugs his shoulders. "Hmm, I guess he's pretty busy."

June 10, 2002 – New York

Reardon is sitting at his desk and glances up to see Laura Spencer coming off the elevators at the far edge of the office with an escort. It's her first day and she's early, as he expected. The escort brings her right to Reardon's desk.

"Thank you for showing her in, Ms. Hanson."

"No problem," she says while turning to walk away.

"So…"

"So." Spencer replies.

Reardon quickly scans the bank of conference rooms along the edge of the office and sees two that are open.

"Let's grab a conference room."

"OK."

"Welcome to New York." He says as he walks her towards the conference room. "Have any trouble finding the place?"

"No, I took a taxi from my new apartment. I'll figure out the subway in a couple of days."

"Good. Have a seat. So, welcome to the team."

"Thanks."

"I'll set up a meet-n-greet with the team on Tuesday. For today you can just get settled in. It'll give the IT geeks time to get you set up on your system. Your desk will be just down from mine."

They both sit and relax. Reardon spends the next hour getting her up to speed on their current assignments. The biggest thing he points out is that all the agencies are stumbling over each other right now. Nine months removed from 9/11, and all the agencies are beefing up their anti-terrorism teams and trying to find their footing in the new world order. It is not going well. There have been three separate occasions already where undercover agents from the FBI have arrested undercover cops posing as recruiters for terrorist groups. It's just short of the Keystone Cops and would be funny if not for the circumstances that started us down this road. The good news is that everyone is working more closely together. The bad news is that there are too many cooks in the kitchen. He explains that fears within the intelligence community are plateauing. Initially, they feared quick retaliatory attacks on U.S. soil after launching Afghanistan's Operation Enduring Freedom in October, 2001. They are now more concerned that radicals within the U.S. are actively recruiting more members and will stage attacks on a recurring basis.

"Our job is to find out who is recruiting, who they're recruiting, and what they plan to do with the recruits once they have them. Any questions?"

"Yeah, so based on what you've said, it doesn't sound like we're going to arrest people as soon as we find them."

"Correct, we're gathering intelligence and trying to understand their structure. If we can identify an imminent attack, then we'll take action to neutralize the threat immediately."

"Does that make sense?"

"Yeah, for now."

"Why *for now*."

"Well it just seems like if we spend a lot of time watching then they will build up their organization as we watch. From what I've read, there are no organized groups right now inside the U.S. and no real threat."

"That is true, as far as we know, and you make a good point. But that's what we plan to find out. This is our directive, and if that's what they do, then we will be in at the ground floor with our undercover agents."

"OK."

After they finish, Reardon swings by his desk and extracts a laptop from his desk drawer with a post-it note containing a login name and a password. He leads her down to her desk and hands her the laptop.

"Get logged in and start getting things set up. There's a number on the bottom if you need any IT help. Other than that, swing by at noon and we will go out for lunch. My treat."

———

After Peterson gets done with his history lesson, Reardon decides to pick up some Chinese food on his way home. He plops down in front of the TV with his food and a couple cold beers. He catches the evening news just as they are coming back from a commercial for Depends undergarments.

Residents of Dallas are still dealing with the devastating loss of four main highways and a tunnel into Dallas on Day 40. Texas authorities report it will take months to repair the damage, and they are still assessing the structural damage on road segments adjacent to the fallen sections of roadway.

The five Kansas City sewage treatment facilities that were damaged three days ago, on Day 43, are still undergoing repairs. 182,000 residents are still prohibited from using water in their homes because there is simply no way to treat the waste. The city is continuing to set up temporary public restrooms in the affected neighborhoods and asking as many residents as possible to move in with relatives or friends outside the impacted area. It's estimated it will take at least three weeks to get the treatment centers back online. The two treatment centers with the most severe damage may take up to six months to repair, and authorities are looking into options on how to reroute sewer lines in order to bypass the most heavily damaged treatment centers. Authorities are now estimating the damage at well over $1.5 million, plus the expense of setting up hundreds of public restrooms. Kansas City has requests out to neighboring states requesting additional port-o-potties in order to accommodate 182,000 people.

The Pennsylvania toilet paper factory that had a wall destroyed on Day 32 of the attacks is expecting to restart its operations in two days. The ensuing electrical fire destroyed 20% of the building before it was contained, and the plant supervisor stated it will only be operating at 50% capacity for the next several months until the building is fully repaired. The two detergent plants, in Vermont and Georgia, that were also rocked by explosions will remain closed for at least two weeks while undergoing repairs.

The Day 33 attack on the pharmaceutical plant in Virginia responsible for making 70% of all anti-depressants and 50% of erectile dysfunction drugs in the United States is in ruins after the highly volatile chemicals used for making the drugs led to multiple explosions. Politicians and government authorities are still struggling to discover either a motive or a pattern for the attacks. Federal authorities also have no leads or suspects at this time. While terrorist groups continue to celebrate the ongoing destruction caused by the attacks, none are claiming responsibility. We will continue...

Reardon shuts off the TV and leans back on the sofa, closing his eyes to block out the world. After about 10 minutes of quiet contemplation, he opens his eyes and leans forward to finish his meal in silence before grabbing the bottle of whiskey he also bought on the way home. This bottle inaugurates a five-day bender.

July 6, 2010 – Afghanistan

Abdul and Reardon are waiting for an informant just over 20 miles from camp. This is about as close as it gets and is a pleasant change of pace for Reardon. The long drives were once soothing, but now they are a constant source of danger as Taliban forces are slowly becoming bolder. All the official reports indicate the Army is still in full control of the region, but returning troops are telling a different story. The effectiveness of U.S. troops is becoming a bigger policy debate. Boots on the ground becomes the new mantra for the administration in Washington. The secretary of defense is lobbying to increase funding and do a final push to crush the Taliban. Abdul and Reardon have been sitting quietly, looking at the ridge lines fearing a sniper attack. The eyes in the sky report the coast is clear.

"I would like to talk about what we discussed a couple weeks ago. I have many questions. I just don't see how it could work."

"You mean the daily attacks?"

"Yes."

"As I said, you would need to plan ahead and do it slowly. Thirty or forty guys buying fertilizer, just one bag a week, never at the same place, always pay cash. Never buy anything in bulk – too easy to raise a red flag. It will take a couple years to stockpile enough for car bombs. Go on hikes and bike rides just looking for stuff, powerlines, gas lines, fiber optic cable. We put up signs. It's not hard to find. The tough part would be getting high explosives, enough to take out bridges. You can only do so much with car bombs. Getting C-4 and detcord is tough, but not impossible. Do you get the idea now?"

"Yes. Isn't using the mail pretty slow?"

"Yes, but it's safe. I would not even use the phone."

"Do they track all calls?"

"They say no, but I don't believe them. I bet they have computers crunching through every call looking for patterns, so why risk it?"

"Wouldn't they start putting up roadblocks and searching everyone?"

"It's not like here. Millions of people are on the roads every single day. Millions traveling state to state. There's just no way they could check everyone. Besides, even if they tried, the civil libertarians would start filing so many lawsuits it would become a joke."

"Even if they are just trying to stop terrorists?"

"I really have no idea how the Government would react. But if you are always on the move and never hit the same place twice, I have no idea how they could defend against it."

"I still find this hard to believe."

"That's fine, but I'm telling you it would work."

"This is a very dangerous idea you discuss."

"Yeah," Reardon smirks as he nods his head. "It is."

Abdul and Reardon quietly sit and reflect while they continue to wait.

Day 51

After five days of drinking, Reardon is finally tired of his apartment. He decides to take a break from drinking at his place and gets a little rowdy at a new bar about two miles from his place and ends up in the drunk tank. Unwilling to stay there overnight, he decides to call Spencer to drag his ass out of jail and back to his place. As soon as he hangs up, he second guesses himself, wondering if a night in the tank would've been easier. When she arrives, she doesn't say a thing and doesn't even ask. She just drives him home, helps him get in the house, says good night, and leaves him flopped on his bed. He awakes the next morning and turns on the television just as the news is coming back from a commercial about hemorrhoid cream. Despite all the horrible things going on all over the nation, people still need to take care of their hemorrhoids he thought. His favorite news duo of James Newburgh and Alicia Washburn are relaying the bad news of the day.

For those of you just joining us, let's recap last night's 11 p.m. attack. In Cleveland the Parma, Brecksville, Seven Hills Tower Farm was severely damaged. Every TV station in the Cleveland area and most of the AM and FM stations in Cleveland broadcast from this area.

A map of the greater Cleveland area is displayed in the upper left corner of the screen as James continues to discuss the latest attack in the Midwest. Alicia then takes over.

Two other attacks occurred in Boise, Idaho and Memphis, Tennessee. In Boise, three towers were destroyed knocking out 19 AM and FM radio stations. In Memphis, two towers were destroyed knocking out

14 AM and FM stations. There are currently no estimates on how long it will take to repair the damage and restore the transmitters. The damage is estimated at $10 million. These attacks also severely cripple the Emergency Broadcast System.

At that moment, the camera flashes over to James who smoothly transitions to recounting the previous day's events and an update from Washington.

Officials in Washington, D.C., continue to scramble for answers. The president's assurances that the attackers will soon be caught are wearing thin. The directors of the FBI, NSA, and CIA are holding daily briefings with the president's staff and are attempting to identify the attackers or discover a pattern to the attacks. So far, both have been equally unsuccessful. Rumors continue to abound regarding involvement from the Middle East, Russia, and North Korea.

In the absence of real information, any information will do and the list of theories continues to spiral out of control. Suddenly a map of the United States flashes on the screen with red dots representing the location of each attack over the last fifty-one days. There are over 80 dots on the map in a seemingly random pattern.

As you can see, there is no rhyme or reason to the pattern of dots. The government has put out an open call to any citizen who can identify a pattern. Everyone, from kids in high school to some of the greatest think-tanks in the world is taking on the challenge. So far, nothing. Most people in the know do not believe there is a pattern; however, they are desperate for any clues at this moment.

Let's review the attacks and repair efforts taking place from the last seven days. New York City has put in place severe water restrictions after the Day 45 attack to ensure that the city does not run out of water. Chunks of concrete are partially blocking intake valves at the downstream pump stations, and engineers are working on the best way to remove the debris without shutting off the flow of water. The 15 buildings attacked on Day 46 are slowly being repaired. Offices on the lower floors are reopened for people willing to walk the stairs. It is still expected to take at least a week before the elevator doors are repaired and they pass safety inspections.

As James talks, images of the damage are slowly displayed. Then there are short clips of people negotiating around work areas and climbing steps.

The natural gas compressor stations destroyed on Day 47 in southern Idaho, southern Maine, and northern Georgia are still offline. The resulting large explosions and disruption of natural gas is shutting down businesses, impacting power plants, and affecting nearly three million people. The pipeline in southern Maine is the only source of natural gas for the state. The destruction of the station in southern Idaho severs the flow of natural gas between Colorado and the northwest. The northwest is supplied through multiple pipelines, so the impact is minimal. There are also many redundant gas pipelines so the disruption in Georgia is also minimal. That does not change the fact that this is another blow to America's infrastructure. The initial estimates are that it will take at least one week to put in a bypass line and several weeks to repair each compressor station, if not months. The United States uses approximately 26.7 trillion cubic feet per year. 31% of the natural gas is used for electric power generation and 29% is for industrial use. The nation's dependence on natural gas has been consistently increasing over the last decade. The greatest increase in electrical generation comes from natural gas, an increase of over 400 billion kWh since 2004. A severe disruption in the natural gas lines would have a ripple effect across the entire nation if gas was cut to a significant number of electric power stations. We will take a break and continue with our coverage.

Reardon slowly pushes himself upright from his filthy sofa and slowly heads into the kitchen for a glass of water and two beers. A few moments later, Reardon falls back into the sofa and cracks open a beer. The newscast comes back showing James and Alicia turning to face the camera. The camera cuts to Alicia who continues.

The Meadowlands attack on Day 48 continues to delay traffic as New Jersey officials attempt to bring the Adaptive Signal System for Traffic Reduction back on line. The system controls traffic signals over a 40 square mile area in the New Jersey Meadowlands, serving more than 400,000 cars per day. The area includes Jersey City, Lyndhurst, Rutherford, East Rutherford, and Ridgefield Park. The synchronized system has been offline for three days since the Lyndhurst Administration building was severely damaged by multiple explosions. The purpose of the system is to continuously monitor and streamline traffic flow to reduce delays. Without the system, the average commute time has increased at least 50% for most commuters.

James takes over to discuss the Day 49 attack in Boston.

Rescue crews in Boston are still hoping to find survivors after the Day 49 attack. The truck bombings in the I-90 Ted Williams tunnel running below Boston harbor have put the entire city on edge. Authorities have confirmed 8 deaths with an estimated 47 people still missing. Crews in Boston are dealing with tons of fallen debris and water slowly seeping in from the harbor above. There were initial fears that the entire tunnel would collapse, and the tunnel would flood with water. So far, the flooding is limited. The Governor has put the state on high alert. This is only the second attack utilizing suicide bombers. Officials are racing to find clues hidden in the debris.

The only thing we know about the attackers or the trucks is that the license plates were stolen. They are not expecting to find any physical evidence due to the extreme heat generated by the explosion and subsequent fire. Within an hour of the attack, New York City closed down the Holland and Lincoln tunnels as a precautionary measure. A combined total of nearly 160,000 vehicles pass through these tunnels each day. The last three days have led to nightmarish road conditions. New York City has not yet announced when they plan to re-open the tunnels. The Day 50 attack continues to leave hundreds of thousands of people without power. The high-voltage power lines leaving the Columbia Generating Station in south central Washington state and the Wolf Creek Generating Station in eastern Kansas were destroyed. The power lines for these nuclear power plants were destroyed about 15 miles from the power plants in isolated locations. The Columbia plant damage is particularly concerning because the plant generates about 10% of the state's electricity. Crews are expecting to set up temporary towers and reestablish the flow of electricity within three days while the towers are re-built.

Alicia continues and is about to provide additional coverage of today's attack just as Reardon shuts off the TV. He lets out a long moan as he pushes his head back into the sofa, pushing his hands into the wall above his head as he stretches. After a moment, he slowly stands up and heads in for a long overdue shower. He stands in the tub for over 15 minutes just letting the water leach out the stress in his muscles. This is painful to watch again because he saw the recurring damage of the unrelenting attacks in Afghanistan.

Peterson's idea to track down unused pre-paid burn phones has worked in spades as far as volume is concerned. In the week since Peterson's warrant was issued, he has collected over 6000 phone numbers meeting his criteria. Apparently, these phones are easily lost or put away for a rainy day.

Nonetheless, every single phone is now on a tracking list. So far, not a single meaningful hit. There were a few dozen activated within the last two months, but they all appear to have been used and thrown away. Authorities will continue to monitor the list of numbers.

September 14, 2010 – Afghanistan

Just days after watching the nine-year anniversary of the 9/11 attacks, Reardon awakes in a hot sweat. He starts to wipe his eyes as he realizes he was crying in his sleep. This has never happened before. He wipes his eyes as he rolls out of bed. He always credited himself as being one of the toughest guys he'd ever met. But then again, he was never expecting to go through what he has gone through the last two and a half years. Seeing the constant struggle for life, just to gather the bare essentials like food and water, is a constant struggle for the people here.

In their compound, they wanted for practically nothing, always an ample supply of food and water. Before he came he'd been warned about the psychological effects of seeing people living hand to mouth. Aid workers dealing with starving children will start to eat less and make themselves sick. Seeing people suffering day after day, children with bloated bellies, and suffering from malnutrition is mentally draining. The aid workers need to push past that and ensure they stay healthy. If they can't help themselves, then they can't help anyone else either. Reardon quickly understood this when he arrived back in March of 2008. If that was the extent of it, he still thinks he would be OK. But that was not the extent of it. It was complex. They were there to protect American lives while taking lives, all too frequently innocent lives. Collateral damage being the kind euphemism to keep your mind distracted from the truth. Killing to save lives. Destruction to maintain order. Attempting to win the hearts of the indigenous people while destroying their lives. On paper, it all makes sense. Better to fight them over here than at home. But fight who? This was the Vietnam of our generation. All of these things raced through Reardon's mind as he sat on the edge of his bunk drying his eyes.

After a few moments, a call came from outside and a knock on the door.

"My good friend, are you nearly ready?" Abdul asks.
"No, but come on in." As Reardon quickly stands up, his knee in a brace.
"How is your knee?"
"It hurts like a son of a gun."

Just ten days earlier, they were meeting with local officials in a small city just 60 miles away. They had heard that Taliban fighters had been through the day before and wanted to see what the locals could tell them. They planned to show the tribal elders some photos to see if anyone important had been through the village. The elders did identify a high-priority target. It was good to learn this. What they did not know was the visit to the village was a ruse to draw them in. Apaches had flown cover to ensure that there were no vehicles along the route waiting to ambush them. What the Apaches couldn't see was that they left behind a single fighter just outside the village the night before. He had been lying in wait overnight. The fighter slowly moved through the village and took up a position at a distance and watched. The soldiers in the escort Humvee were positioned around their vehicle on high alert. However, after nearly 30 minutes of waiting for Reardon and Abdul, the tenor of their attention had dropped slightly. Just as Reardon exited the building, the fighter came running down the village road with a kack, kack, kack, reverberating off the walls of the enclosed space. The fighter was in a dead all-out run. Bullets dinging off the walls and vehicles. Abdul, who was just passing the threshold of the door, saw Reardon take a shot to the leg. He dove, pushing Reardon behind their Humvee. Abdul hit the ground with a thud and knocked the wind out of Reardon as he went down. Reardon was suddenly gasping for breath while writhing in pain. Abdul happened to push him down and onto the leg that had just been hit, driving his knee cap into the cobblestone road. One of the soldiers in the Humvee took three direct shots and went down. Two hit his flak jacket and one through his upper arm. With Reardon and Abdul down and out of the way, the remaining soldiers immediately opened fire and laid out the charging fighter. They then hunched down, looking in all directions for the next attack. It never came. After a few minutes, one of the soldiers slowly approached the dead fighter and checked for a pulse. He was dead, taking three shots to the upper torso and four more shots to various parts of his body. The soldier called the all-clear, and in the meantime, the medic was already attending to Reardon. The shot went clean through his calf. The medic applied a pressure bandage and helped Reardon to a sitting position. Reardon looked up to see Abdul sitting on the bumper with a rivulet of blood running down the side of his face and a blood soaked sleeve.

"You're hit," Reardon said as he points to Abdul drawing the medic's attention to Abdul.
"I hit my head on the cobblestone as I toppled over you. I'm OK."
"Your arm is bleeding."
"The bullet just grazed me, it looks worse than it is."

The medic pulled out a gauze pad, pressed it to Abdul's head, and then lifted Abdul's hand on his good arm to hold it in place. He then pulled out a scissors and cut back his shirt, revealing a half inch wide streak of raw flesh just over an inch long.

"This is going to hurt."

Just then, the medic sprayed on foam that burned like hell, applied a bandage, and wrapped gauze around his arm three times to hold it in place. He then attended to Abdul's head. A small cut just above the hairline was bleeding like a stuck pig. Once he taped the bandage in place, he wiped clean the blood dripping from Abdul's brow and the rivulet down the side of his face. In the meantime, another soldier patched up the arm of the downed soldier and called in a helicopter to evacuate the three injured. Thirty minutes later, Reardon and Abdul were in the air with the injured soldier. Reardon is lucky, nothing but muscle and clean through. The surgeons stitched up his muscle tissue around the wound on each side of his calf and then put in eight stitches on each side to seal the skin. They x-ray his knee and see a hairline fracture in his kneecap and what looks like some damaged cartilage. It will heal they assure him.

Abdul and Reardon stay at the med station for eight days before Reardon went out of his mind and requested to get back to his post. He turns down the offer to go stateside to recuperate. He knows his wife would never let him go back into harm's way if he went home. By staying here and maintaining the distance, he could explain it away as a small wound that would keep him off his leg for a couple weeks. The quicker he got out of the hospital, the more plausible his story would become.

Abdul steps closer to Reardon's hospital bed and offers to help Reardon stand, but he waves him off.

"I'm OK. My knee is more stiff than anything." Reardon suddenly stares Abdul straight in the eye. "I don't feel like I have said it enough…"
"Think nothing of it," Abdul interrupts. "You would have done the same for me. Let's never speak of this again, my good friend."

The matter drops, and Reardon gets dressed for the day. They slowly walk to breakfast. They are flown back to their compound just after lunch and return to their work.

December 21, 2002 – New York

Reardon and Spencer are sitting in a car just west of 67th street on Garfield Ave in the Bronx. It was a bone chilling night by New York standards. They've been waiting in the car for over an hour and the inside windows are frosted over. They finally crack a window to let some of the moisture out. There are six agents from his team within two miles of their position. They got a tip that a local hookah shop is being used as a recruiting center. They've had three agents go in undercover over the last four months. For the first three months nothing happened, but now one agent in particular has made a good impression with his frequent complaints about how it is difficult to get a good paying job and how he is treated as a Muslim. Finally, the manager of the store says there is someone he wants the guy to meet. They first met a week ago. Tonight is the second meeting. The agents are there purely as backup. They couldn't risk the agent wearing a wire.

After some idle chit chat over the last hour, they have been sitting quietly for about 15 minutes. One thing Reardon really appreciates is Spencer's ability to sit quietly and not let the silence feel like a huge awkward chasm between them. As a result, he always chooses her anytime he thinks he will be stuck on a stakeout for a long time. Reardon finally breaks the silence.

"It's been about six months. So, what do you think of the work so far?"

"Which part? The long hours, stale coffee, or greasy, fatty, takeout food on stakeouts? I love it all. Oh, and then let's not forget all the paperwork."

"Seriously, what do you think?"

"It's different than I thought. I guess I watched too much TV growing up, I was expecting car chases and running down people in alleys."

"Yeah, that's not uncommon. I was expecting about the same when I started. Turns out it's about 99% grunt work. Not quite as glamorous huh?"

"No. But all in all, I enjoy it. I feel it has more purpose than a lot of other work I could do. That's what I was looking for."

"You're not an idealist, are you?"

"God no, it's just the only job I could get with a criminology degree. It was either FBI agent or cocktail waitress at Hooters. I think I made the right call. My ass would look terrible in those short-shorts."

Reardon laughs. Spencer is the first partner he has ever enjoyed spending time with on long stakeouts. The fact that she is hilarious helps a lot too. Spencer has been getting some crap in the office because she is always working with Reardon so closely. A couple female agents hint something else might be going on. She ignores their comments. As a tall, good-looking woman, she is accustomed to getting hit on, but she is good at diverting the conversation. Reardon has never even come close to hitting on her. She quickly realized it would never be a concern. She can see it in Reardon's eyes when he talks about Sara. Sara is Reardon's world. Reardon lights up when he talks about her, even when he is venting about some crazy argument they are having at home.

Day 52

Dow Jones Industrial Average
11,354.43
Total decline: 43.7%
Total loss: $2.27 Trillion

Nasdaq
3,204.94
Total decline: 43.6%
Total loss: $3.71 Trillion

Reardon awakes to a loud noise emanating from the street in front of his brownstone. He slowly rolls over and stares at the clock. It's 9:38. He hears more noise from out front but ignores it. After ten more minutes of persistent noise, he decides to get up and take a look. The city has chosen this lovely morning to start digging up the road two houses down. He drops his hand from the drape, and it gently falls back into place. He walks to the bathroom for a long overdue shave and hot shower. The thought finally crosses his mind to head back into the office and see what's going on.

Just over an hour and a half later, he quietly strolls into the office and heads for the conference room.

"Well! Look what the cat dragged in! Nice of you to grace us with your presence," barks McCullum.

Most people can't fathom why McCullum takes so much crap from Reardon, but between his promise and Spencer's reassurances, McCullum is true to his word.

Reardon is the best man Spencer ever met besides her father. Reardon is kind, caring, and was a devoted family man, just like her father. Reardon helped her through the roughest time in her life when her father died unexpectedly and she is forever loyal to him. Reardon is the brother she never had. He looked out for her and now she's glad to look out for him. Now and forever more.

Spencer looks up from her computer and quickly walks over to Reardon.

"The attack was in Seattle this time. The loading docks of a food warehouse were destroyed. They ran a stretch of detcord from one end to the other. The explosion was not big enough to blow a hole in the doors, but it was powerful enough to bend them and pop them off their tracks. Enough damage so they won't open," Spencer quickly explains.

"Anyone hurt?"

"Thankfully no. Bomb squad came in, of course, and didn't find anything else. No surprise there."

"That's good."

"The distro center is in the process of ripping all the doors off their tracks so they can load the semis as they come in. However, police have not cleared the scene, and they're shut down completely for right now."

"Another annoying attack without any meaningful destruction. Nothing compared to what I have seen on the TV for the last five days. How are they doing with the Boston tunnels?"

"It's a mess. They can't stop the flooding in the tunnel. The pumps are able to keep up, but they can't run them indefinitely. The crews are clearing debris as quickly and carefully as they can. They found two survivors alive last night, but most of the people they find are dead. So far, 29 confirmed deaths. It's a mess."

"Reardon!"

Reardon turns and looks at McCullum.

"Everyone, clear the room. Spencer, you too. Reardon, up here."

Everyone files out of the room, and Reardon slowly moves towards the head of the table. Just as Reardon approaches the front chair, McCullum sits down and motions for Reardon to do the same. This is unusual for McCullum, he is a pacer so Spencer already knows something weird is up.

"Let's have a heart to heart."

"OK."

"First of all, you're trying my patience, but God knows I did the same thing. I can't count the number of times I showed up to the office totally plastered. I thought I was hiding it really well. I never fooled Richard; I could see it in his eye every time. You still have my word I will see you through this. I'm not going to dishonor Richard's memory – I'm going to get you through this." He pauses and just stares into Reardon's face. "Are you still seeing Dr. Miller every month?"

"Yeah, we talk every month."

"OK, good." McCullum leans back in his chair as though waiting for Reardon to answer some unspoken question. Reardon casually stares back at McCullum. McCullum finally breaks the silence. "What the hell's going on here?"

"How do you mean?"

"I mean, I think there's more here than meets the eye, and I think you know something you're not saying."

"I know a lot that I'm not saying."

"Like what?"

"Like they are peeling back the veil exposing our vulnerabilities."

"What does that even mean?"

"Like what do you think they are trying to accomplish?" Reardon asks with slight annoyance.

"Hell, what are any terrorists trying to do?"

"Exactly, what are they trying to do? What is their goal?"

"I don't know, nobody knows, except you. I think you know."

"I do. We went over there to stop terrorism, kill the bad guys, and come home. We failed miserably. We created more terrorists than we killed. Our presence was the best recruiting poster they could have hoped for. Every innocent we killed. Every bridge, or road, or village we destroyed was another stroke of paint on their recruiting poster. What we did for the ones left behind was worse than killing them. We took people who were on the edge of survival and pushed them closer. Some fell, others collapsed, and many became our new enemy. We became the fox in their henhouse. They are just returning the favor."

"I don't need you to wax poetic. Cut the crap. What are they doing?"

"They are trying to strip back the veneer of our society so we have a taste of what they went through. It's a pretty thin veneer. We live in a country of wrinkle cream, $5 coffee, and where people call 911 when Facebook goes down. That's pathetic, calling 911 because you can't get to some stupid webpage. They're peeking behind the veil and spreading sheer terror and uncertainty. What *might* happen is a stronger weapon of terror than what *did* happen. They have the whole country on edge, and it's only going to get worse."

"You've said that before. How do you know it's going to get worse?"

"Because we aren't coming any closer to stopping them. Why would they stop?"

"We need to figure out how to stop them."

"Great! How can we do that? You're looking for a small group of 30 or 40 people out of 330 million. They aren't destroying anything we would consider a high-value target. They attack bridges. You know the numbers. There are too many bridges and tunnels in the U.S. I heard on the news today that there are over 450,000 miles of high-voltage power lines. There are 47,000 shopping centers in the U.S., and about 1000 are enclosed malls. There are 210 natural gas pipelines with 1,400 compressor stations covering over 300,000 miles of pipes. Then you can add in another 185,000 miles of liquid petroleum pipelines."

"What's your point?"

"What's my point? What's my point?! You can't defend everything. The U.S. is over three and a half million square miles. Our whole defense is built around high-value targets. The day after something bad happens on a street corner, an airport, or at a movie theater, everyone starts asking: *What did we miss? Why didn't we anticipate this? How did that person get a gun?* People sound like idiots when they ask that question. Simple, they went out and just bought a frickin' gun. There are more guns in the U.S. than people. What a dumb question...*why didn't someone see this coming? Shouldn't people have noticed the warning signs?* How do you conceivably see warning signs in 330 million people? Well, today, and every day for the last month, we've seen it coming. This is shutting up all the people who sit around asking why we didn't see it coming. They are just proving we can't do anything even when we know it's coming."

McCullum stands up and starts pacing. He pauses at the window and glares out.

"That's what I know." Reardon leans back in his chair. "I know they are going to just keep coming, and we're going to just learn to take it. That's the lesson we taught people in Afghanistan and Iraq – just take it. You have no idea what I saw, the despair, the hopeless feeling these people had. The hopeless feeling I had. It was absolutely unrelenting. Now it's payback time and you won't hear me complain."

McCullum quickly spins with a look of absolute disgust on his face.

"What the hell do you mean complain? You should be pissed. They're destroying your homeland."

"We'll survive this, we always do."

"What the hell is wrong with you?!"

"Nothing, I'm just accepting the inevitable. Sure, we might catch some of them, by accident, but not if they're careful. Let's say we post guards at every bridge and someone every quarter mile along the powerlines and pipelines. That will be millions of people suddenly just sitting around watching nothing, sitting around with their finger up their ass. Even if we do that, they'll just go after something else, warehouses, overpasses, storage tanks, water towers, barns, gas stations, or some 50-year-old chicken coop. The list is endless."

"I don't care if the list is endless. We're going to catch these bastards one way or another."

Reardon is now irritated, he turns in his chair and stands.

"Well, I wish you the best of luck."
"Where the hell are you going?"
"I need a drink."

McCullum starts to walk towards the door and quickly stops realizing there is nothing more he will get from Reardon, knowing there is nothing more *to* get from Reardon.

McCullum turns and starts pacing again. As Reardon leaves people look over to see McCullum pacing and they know to steer clear. McCullum has never been more perplexed and frustrated in his life. Initially, weeks ago, he was excited by this new case, a riddle, intrigue, a chance to show his worth. After Day 30, he realized this put him on the front edge of the most devastating set of attacks in the history of the United States. Now, 42 days after reading the note to Reardon in the middle of God's country, he is nowhere. All he has witnessed is destruction, and all he has felt is frustration and anger. His all-encompassing belief in himself is cracking for the first time in his life. Around Day 30, he was excited because this would make his career and be a pathway to the directorship. After a mere 22 days more, he realizes he is in a nightmare and wishes he had never met Reardon. Everyone above him knows of Reardon's involvement, and this is reflecting on him. But right now, he doesn't care, he just wants it to stop. He heard the truth in much of what Reardon had said. He just can't bring himself to accept it, not now, not ever.

Spencer intercepted Reardon as he left the conference room. They went out for a quick lunch, and she convinced him to come back into the office. A couple hours pass. Spencer and Reardon are alone in the conference room. They are both exhausted and quietly watching the news. Spencer flips off the TV when it goes to break and swivels in her chair to face Reardon.

"There's something I want to tell you."

Reardon stares at her for a moment. "What?"

"I miss you."

"What are you talking about? I see you all the time."

"I miss how things used to be, you know before all this. When we used to spend hours on all those horrible stakeouts."

"You miss those? Long hours, stinky rooms, and nearly rancid takeout food? They were horrible."

"Yeah, they were, but I miss them," she smiles.

"Yeah, I miss them too." Reardon smiles back. "I should also say thanks."

"For what?"

"You know."

"I have no idea what you're talking about." She just smiles, and Reardon lets it drop.

February 27, 2003 – New York

Reardon is quietly watching a monitor while Spencer is stretched on a sofa reading a book. They are half way through their shift, and Spencer is starting to get antsy. Out of the blue, she starts to speak.

"Hey, do you want to hear some statistics I just made up?"

This startles Reardon out of a dull haze, "Huh?"

Spencer quickly pops up to a sitting position. "Do you want to hear some statistics I just made up?"

"Sure, this should be good."

"42% of FBI agents who stare at monitors too long get hairy backs and lose all their teeth by age 45."

"I hope this only applies to men."

"Yeah, I think it does." Her face suddenly lights up. "Oh yeah, I totally forgot, I broke up with Brad last night."

"Now we're onto something interesting – do tell. What was it this time…"

"Oh my gosh, why do you always assume it's something the guy did?"

"Because you are practically perfect in every way Ms. Poppins."

"Ha ha … OK fine. It was him. You won't believe it."

"What?"

"We were eating some hors d'oeuvres at my place, and he dropped one on the floor. He just picked it up and put it in his mouth. He didn't even try to blow it off."

"So! Do you keep your floors clean?"

"Yeah, but it's still disgusting. He has no idea if I ever clean my floors. What's next?"

"Oh my God, you're right. It's anarchy, the whole system is breaking down." Reardon gets a crazed look on his face. "It's practically a gateway crime. It starts off so innocently with an hors d'oeuvre, and then the next thing you know, he's robbing a bank and then murder! It's good you got away from him now."

"Oh, my God, now you're being melodramatic."

"Yeah, I'm being melodramatic. You're the one who dumps guys for the weirdest reasons. Now that I think of it, you are a festival of anger. No, a cauldron of rage. That seems more appropriate. No wonder you are going through guys like I go through socks."

"Go through socks," she laughs. "What the hell does that even mean? I liked where you were going with the rage and anger thing, but then you lost me."

"I don't know. It was the first thing that came to my mind."

"Well, that was probably the worst analogy ever."

"Let me come up with something better."

"Too late, the time has passed - you screwed that up." She waves her hand dismissively. "I was going to give you credit for a good point until that."

"I can do better."

"Oh, my God, *I can do better*. You are such a delicate flower sometimes," Reardon laughs.

They settle in, and a few more hours quietly pass. Spencer is stoically staring at the monitor, and Reardon is lying on the sofa with his arms crossed and eyes shut. Spencer suddenly turns.

"Hey, I know you're not sleeping."

"You sound like you're accusing me of something. Do you think I'm trying to fake you out?"

"No. Whatever … I have a question for you."

"Shoot."

"How do you make it work?"

"Make what work?"

"You and Sara. You guys seem like the happiest couple in the world. How do you make it work?"

Reardon suddenly swings his legs down and sits up. "Uh ohh, this sounds serious."

"I am serious."

"Well first and foremost, we are always honest with each other. Some will tell you to never go to bed mad. That's crap. Sometimes you're just too tired to talk. Total honesty is tough sometimes. For example, she is always complaining about how other people are driving – it drives me nuts. I finally concluded that she is the angriest person I know. When she starts ranting, I remind her that they can't hear her and just tell her she is the angriest person I know. Ironically, she gets mad every time I tell her that, but at least I'm being honest."

"Do you really tell her that?"

"No! I'm not a moron."

Spencer lifts her finger to her mouth and taps it on her lower lip as though pondering the most important question in the world, "I'm not so sure about that."

Calling Reardon a moron becomes a running inside joke for them over the years. It's the type of inside joke that only close partners can share. These are the types of experiences that bring them closer together as great friends.

"Seriously, how do you guys make it work?"

"I'm not kidding. Honesty, it goes a long way. We also talk about what makes us mad. I don't really know how to describe it beyond that. We just love each other and work through things. I guess that's about it. You'll know when you meet the right guy. It'll feel right."

"That's not encouraging advice when most of the guys I meet are too needy."

"Well, just keep looking and don't give up too quickly on these guys."

"Who do you mean when you say *these guys*?"

"Hmm, let me think … how about that guy who didn't tell you your dinner sucked."

About a month ago, Spencer invited a guy over for a third date. She had been set up through a friend of a friend and she really liked the guy. She served dinner and the phone rang. It was her mom, so she said she better take it. She told him to start without her. When she came back, he had started, taken a few bites, and was smiling. As she sat down, he said it was good. Spencer then tried some, realized she added way too much salt, and it was just horrible. She was pissed that the guy lied about liking the food.

"You need to balance honesty with stupidity, just like I don't tell my wife she is the angriest person I know when she's driving."

"Well, it doesn't matter now. I dumped him."

"That's what I mean by giving up too quickly."

"Well aren't you Mr. Smarty Pants when it comes to relationships?"

"Hey, you asked…"

She smiles and says in a mocking voice, "*You asked.*"

"Careful, or I'll start calling you the angriest woman I know." Reardon leans back and lies down again. "I'm going to pretend to sleep for a while if it's OK with you?"

About another hour goes by and they have switched positions. Reardon is staring at the monitor and suddenly turns his chair to face Spencer.

"She's my best friend."

This sudden interruption catches her off guard. "Huh?"

"No one has ever asked me that question before. How we make it work? I've been thinking about it, and I should give you an honest answer. I love her with all my heart, and she's my best friend. I'd rather spend time with her than anyone else in the world."

"God, you really are head over heels in love with her. I just hope I can find the type of love you have with Sara. In fact, you're so cute I could puke. Again, how did you trick a woman as great as Sara into marrying you?"

"It's because I'm charming."

As she lifts her eye brows, "Yeah … that's it … charming. Flaming buttmunch is more like it."

Reardon sneers at her for a moment and then smiles. "Nice! All I can tell you is that when I'm with Sara, well, it's the best feeling in the world. I never want to know what life is like without her."

Spencer is suddenly crestfallen. Reardon now realizes he has given her the equivalent of a punch in the stomach.

"I hope I can find that someday."

"You will. Just wait."

"That's just it, I feel like I've been waiting a long time…" her voice trails off.

"Just keep looking. It'll happen." Reardon knows those are optimistic words, but she is great and deserves a great guy. "But then again, maybe you're just broken inside."

She scowls. "Perhaps, but at least I'm not a moron," and then smirks.

"That's the spirit."

Washington, D.C.

The president's staff has conducted detailed and highly confidential meetings with the governors over the last week. The president has had several intense and adversarial discussions with three governors in particular. The discussions revolve around putting the National Guard under federal authority and discussing the specifics of when control would return to the governors. This may seem like a ridiculous formality considering all that is going on around the country, but they are also painfully aware that there are no suspects. Despite meticulously listening to all chatter from the Russians, Iranians, and everyone else, they have no new information on the attackers.

Many raise an excellent point, what does the president plan to do with the Guard that'll help catch the terrorists? The president's staff has no answer. As requested, the Joint Chiefs of Staff have prepared multiple plans that go so far as recalling over 80% of troops worldwide. This option also raises concern over Russian or North Korean aggression. The problem with all the plans is that they all fall short of providing enough coverage to effectively canvas the entire nation. They discuss focusing the Army in specific areas, hoping to flush out the terrorists. The problem with the plan is that the media will report the troop deployments. The terrorists will just go quiet in those areas and be able to attack elsewhere. This is where it gets sticky.

The president's staff discusses how to suppress all news coverage. Back in the days of FDR, the government had enough pull to control the media during the war and they went along for national security reasons. But now, they have no pull with the media. Even if the media agreed to keep this secret, there would be a million blog posts and Facebook updates. People would be taking selfies with the troops in the background. It is a futile situation. The only option would be for the president to declare martial law and shut down everything including the internet and approve all news stories. This is, of course, impossible and would cripple the economy even further. Killing the patient to cure the disease is simply not an option.

All the governors have agreed to activate some or all of their Guard units to begin searching for explosives nearly everywhere. Units will be assigned to search bridges, overpasses, water towers. Simply put, they are looking for the needle in the haystack, every haystack they can think of. Several states already have their units deployed and are randomly searching the countryside and cities. Within three days Guard units will be activated across the entire nation. The President is satisfied that this is a positive step forward. All the paths forward are riddled with uncertainty. This was the one option everyone felt was reasonable. The question is how much longer should the president attempt to be reasonable in an unreasonable time?

The markets continue to decline. The boards from each major stock exchange hold a highly secretive meeting with the Federal Reserve Committee and decide the only option to stop the decline is to close all the markets for one week. The chairman of the Federal Reserve is initially opposed to the idea, fearing the announcement will have a dramatic ripple effect on the world's economy. He quickly concludes that it is inevitable either way. He agrees and has a meeting with the president late in the evening. The White House will issue a statement at 6 a.m. the following morning announcing the one-week shutdown. This is the first time the markets have ever shut down like this in the history the nation. All the board members are uncertain about the outcome, but letting the stocks all drain down to zero is unimaginable.

Day 53

Reardon awakes to a ringing phone. He rubs his face and looks at the clock before picking it up. It's his super. She's just calling him to remind him his rent is overdue. Reardon apologizes and says he will bring it down later today. This is not uncommon, he is late about half the time. When he and his wife first moved in, she was a real stickler for being on time, but since his wife and little girl died, she has been extremely forgiving. She even refuses to accept any late fees. Reardon sits up and flips on the TV, catching the last five seconds of an ad before James Newburgh comes on with the news of the day.

> Four FedEx loading docks in Clearwater, Florida; Jackson, Michigan; Santa Fe, New Mexico; and Salt Lake City, Utah, sustained damage last night. Four car bombs were detonated damaging the loading docks. The damage was severe at three locations. The fourth only received minimal damage. Police suspect the explosives were not mixed properly, resulting in a car fire and some minor damage to the building. Authorities are examining video tapes from each location. So far, all they are reporting is that a pair of cars was driven up to each loading dock. One person parked the car while the other waited. Then the two assailants at each location fled. The car bombs detonated within one minute. This has been the standard operating procedure for all the bombings. The Seattle warehouse shutdown yesterday is open. All the

doors were torn from their hinges, and repair crews are beginning to replace the doors.

As James speaks, they show a close-up of damaged doors bent in at odd angles. The next shot drops back showing about 15 garage door openings and a heap of door panels stacked at the far left by a front-end loader that was used to push them all to one side after they were pulled from their hinges and thrown out in front of the loading dock area. The next shot cuts to images of trucks pulling in and backing up to the gaping holes that once held numbered doors.

> The repairs are expected to take four weeks, with an estimated cost of over $250,000. The White House announced early this morning that the president will once again address the nation this evening. Up to this point, people are both frustrated and disappointed with the government's inability to find, much less stop, the terrorists. Congress continues to hold hearings that to all involved seem fruitless. The last month has led to a complete paradigm shift in how Congress conducts hearings. Typically, the hearings would start weeks or months after a single attack. However, in this case, the unrelenting attacks are causing tempers to flare and a complete, listless response from both the committee members and the intelligence agencies that are called upon to provide testimony.

Reardon clicks off the television and rolls over in his bed. An hour later he rolls out of bed and walks into the office at just after 11 o'clock. McCullum is just leaving the conference room as Reardon approaches the door.

"Reardon, follow me." McCullum leads Reardon to his office. "Shut the door."

Reardon closes the door as he enters, and they each settle into a chair. McCullum, as usual, forgoes the niceties and gets right to the point.

"They can't track down dick on the list of 227 names you provided. It's getting close to three weeks, and they have found 43 of the people, most of them dead. Most of that info is through unreliable sources."
"That's not a surprise."
"I know, but you gotta give me more."
"Like what?"
"I don't know – something."
"Wow, it's been five years, I doubt I would even recognize the place." Reardon sits quietly for a few moments. "The biggest problem is the

warlords. You aren't going to make any progress without their support. However, they're not going to help unless there's something in it for them." Reardon pauses again, contemplating his next words. "You can't just fly in with a list of names and a pile of cash. That will get us nowhere because they know we are desperate and will just keep asking for more and more cash. It took me months to build a relationship with these guys, and we don't have months. The next best option is working with their lieutenants. A pile of cash and a list of names will work with them, but that's very dangerous for them. Five years ago, I was able to pull that off from time to time because I worked with the lieutenants more than anyone else. Again, it was based on the relationship I had with them. Tell the agents to discreetly contact the lieutenants, use my name, and come with a pile of cash. My name might get'em in the door. Without that, they'll get nowhere. It's the only good option I can think of right now."

"OK, at least that's something to go on."

McCullum contacts the lead agent in Afghanistan and talks to him for over an hour, trying to convince him that his agents need to go deeper and make more direct contact to make progress. He explains Reardon's suggestion, and the agent agrees it is a logical next step. Despite this, the lead agent is hesitant to put his agents in harm's way because the information they have tracked down so far is seemingly meaningless. McCullum senses the agent's trepidation and would likely handle things the same way if roles were reversed. Nevertheless, McCullum needs to close this loop and determine if the people behind the attack are from Reardon's past or if this is just a ruse to keep them distracted.

March 15, 2003 – New York

Reardon and Spencer are above a rundown bar in an even more rundown hotel room that is for rent by the hour. The décor is straight out of the 70s and the entire room reeks of sweat and smoke. Spencer does not even pay attention to the name of these rundown hotels anymore; she just refers to all of them as *The Bedbug Inn*. Spencer refuses to even sit on the edge of the bed. It's obvious the type of clientele they cater to. They have no shortage of suspects to follow, however, most of them are dead ends. But then again, the source of the information they have been using for the last couple months is about as unreliable as it comes. The FBI secretly requisitions records from the New York library system as authorized by Section 215 of the PATRIOT Act. The provision forces libraries and other institutions to turn over all their records without a court order and without needing to specify probable cause. The FBI then churns through the records, looking for suspicious patterns, and identifies possible threats. In other words, people who aren't reading the *right* kind of books. Reardon does not like these sorts of strong-arm tactics, but he's ordered to investigate the names on the list he receives. He has no idea what constitutes *suspicious patterns*. For all he knows, if you check out *The Hunger Games* and *Harry Potter* on consecutive weeks, you make the list. This is their fourth week of watching people on the library list. They have been staring at a man in his mid-fifties for over six hours. This is their third day in a row watching this guy, and the last name on their current list. From what they can tell, all he does is eat, sleep, and watch TV. He has not had a single visitor, a phone call, or read a single book. They are wondering why this guy made the library list.

"Oh, this is such a waste of time. I hate the library list people. Remind me to pawn all these off on the other team next time." Reardon says in a depressing tone.

"I thought they tricked us into taking the list."

"Oh yeah. Crap! How did that happen?"

"Don't know boss," she sighs and shrugs her shoulders. "Well, nothing we can do about it now, so suck it up buttercup."

Another hour passes. Spencer is up, walking back and forth to loosen her legs. Reardon is facing her as he makes a comment.

"What would happen if we just asked all the library list people to call us if they were about to do something stupid or illegal? That would save us a crap load of time." He then takes a sip of his warm flat soda.

Spencer throws up her arms and does a crazy little dance while screaming, "Anarchy, the whole system would break down."

Reardon loses it. It was so unexpected, that he blows soda out his nose and starts coughing. Spencer curls over in laughter and Reardon fights to regain his composure. At that moment, Spencer gets a call from her sister and talks to her for about ten minutes before hanging up.

"Ahh, I'm so frustrated!"

"What's she doin' now?"

"Nothing, that's the problem. She is still trying to *find* herself."

"How's that going?"

"Not well. If she looks any harder, she'll be 50 before she knows what happened."

"How's your mom taking this?"

"Not well."

"Just sit her down and set her straight."

"Yeah, like that will work. I think I need to take a stronger tack. I think the next time I see her," she clenches her fist and swings it down in a low arch, "I'm going to punch that dirty hag in her fun box and tell her to suck it up buttercup."

Reardon bursts out laughing.

"Yeah, I can see you doing that. You're such a rageaholic."

"Rageaholic, not at all. Most dudes don't know that's how sisters resolve their issues. We've been settling things like this since we were five."

Another couple of quiet hours pass. Spencer is dozing off from time to time, and Reardon is staring through the binoculars. It's that time of the night again, and two prostitutes take up their position on the corner. A few moments pass and he suddenly calls to Spencer.

"Oh, quick, come here. You gotta see this!"

Spencer jumps up and races over grabbing the binoculars.

"What?" She looks at the two prostitutes smoking on the corner.

"What?" She looks at Reardon confusedly.

"You missed it."

"What?"

"The one was trying to light the other's cigarette but she dropped her lighter. When she bent over to pick it up I think I saw her blink her one brown eye."

Spencer slaps Reardon on the shoulder while laughing. She hands the binoculars back to him.

"You're so crude!"

"Well, you're laughing, so that makes you just as bad as me." Reardon starts waving the binoculars in the air. "Besides I have no control what comes through these things,"

"Well I guess that's why they have the old saying, *never look a gift whore in the mouth.*"

"I wish all I saw was her mouth."

"You're still disgusting."

"OK, this from the one who's going to punch her sister in the fun box."

"Boys are still grosser."

"Snakes, snails, and puppy dog tails…"

Spencer glares as she plops down on the sofa. The long hours together help forge their friendship, and the ridiculous and crude humor helps them maintain their sanity on the long mind-numbing stakeouts. They just keep trying to one up each other to see who can come up with something more ridiculous or crude than the last.

After another hour, Reardon comes back with an early dinner and a dozen red roses.

"Oh that was nice of you to bring me flowers."

He puts the food down and then pulls out a single rose. "Oh, here you go."

She tilts her head and gives him a foul look with a smirk. "Thanks. That's nice of you."

"I hope Sara doesn't count."

"What's the occasion?"

"No occasion. Just getting my lovely wife some flowers."

"Sometimes you two are so cute I want to slit my wrists. Does she just grab you every time you walk through the door and say *oh you're so dreamy?*" She tilts her head and makes smooching sounds.

"What can I say? I'm a romantic."

"I'm still curious how you found her …"

"You will just need to spend less time on stakeouts and more time in the park."

"I would, but my boss works me too hard."

"I'll talk with him and see what I can do. We just spoke, and he says you should take the rest of the day off. So get out of here."

"What about my dinner?"

"Take it with you and eat it at the park."

"OK! I'm out of here." She instantly grabs her dinner and heads out. "Don't get too bored."

Reardon sits back and smiles. He then tears open the bag and digs into his dinner with delight.

Washington, D.C.

All of Washington is in continuous turmoil. Markets tumble around the globe with the news of the complete shutdown of all U.S. markets. The chairman of the Fed testifies in front of congress as part of an emergency closed door session to discuss what happens if markets continue to fall after the markets re-open. The Fed chair has no good reply. He sums it up with *we'll see*. This is not an encouraging statement. The value of the dollar drops nearly 15%, an unprecedented decline. But then every day is now unprecedented. The global markets rebound a little at the end of the day, which is encouraging, but not encouraging enough to re-open the U.S. markets until the week is up.

Staffers at all the intelligence agencies have been running full tilt for over four weeks. The pace is exhausting. People are working until they literally pass out at their desks. People are being escorted from the building just so they can go home and get some sleep. Many are told to not come back for at least 24 hours. Few listen.

The NSA prides itself on listening to everything, searching for hidden clues, connecting the dots that can't be connected. Right now, they are not only crippled when it comes to connecting the dots, they can't even find any dots to connect. Nothing. All the known terrorist groups won't shut up. They have learned more about their operatives in the last four weeks than they've learned in the last year. However, these aren't the people they are looking for. These are just the people excitedly watching and talking about everything that is going on and reveling in the destruction and chaos. The ones they are looking for are wraiths.

The president is demanding answers. Initially, he met with the heads of each agency three times a day. However, after weeks of frustration, the meetings are now only once per day because the president becomes tired of hearing the same poor answers and seeing the same blank expressionless looks on their faces.

The president has slept on his agreement with the governors and decided it is simply not enough. He must explore his options more comprehensively. He initiates the first serious discussion of actually declaring a nationwide state of emergency and declaring a curfew. However, he already acknowledges that the economic impact would be devastating, and the curfew itself would be unenforceable. How can you put 330 million people under a curfew? While this might be the best of their horrible options, it is simply untenable.

Other options include interviewing every person who has entered the country in the last year. However, based on the pattern of thefts leading up to the attacks, they would need to interview everyone who entered the country over the last three plus years. That assumes the people they are looking for entered the country legally. Even if they limit that to people from Middle Eastern countries, along with, people from Russia and Afghanistan, it makes no sense. The people they really want to interview will be the ones who have simply disappeared. Additionally, a failure to locate someone does not imply they are a terrorist. America is a fluid and free-flowing society with tens of thousands moving every day from city to city. An impossible task.

Others have suggested stopping and searching every car before it enters a tunnel or even a highway. Once again, ridiculous. Putting aside the civil rights issue, an impossible task. The president's staff and cabinet have been going around in circles for well over two weeks. The meetings are now a virtual powder keg of tension exploding repeatedly throughout the long sessions. Discussions keep circling back to closing the borders, shutting down airports, instilling a curfew, checking every car crossing state lines, and random vehicle inspections. One civil rights violation after another. Even if they could justify the inspections, the manpower required is simply out of the question. But then again, do they really have another option?

The President's cabinet is in another long session debating options. The President has been quietly sitting and staring at his notepad while twirling a pencil back and forth in his fingers.

"We need to think differently," the president quietly says.

This comment is enough to quiet the room. All heads turn towards the president.

"Excuse me, Mr. President. What did you say?" asks the secretary of state sitting four chairs down from the president.

"We need to think differently." He pauses and slowly stands. After a few moments, he turns and begins to walk along the edge of the table as heads turn. "We need to think differently. Having National Guard units wander the countryside looking for explosives is not going to catch the bad guys. How do you catch ghosts? How do you track people who have been among us for potentially years without raising any red flags? Who are they and where did they come from?"

These are all rhetorical questions. Everyone sits quietly as the president continues to slowly walk around the table.

"Are these Americans who have been recruited? Or people who entered the country, possibly quite legally?"

Everyone continues to track the President as he circles the table. The problem is that every person at the table feels they have already exhaustively discussed every possible option and most of the impossible options. None even come close to solving the problem. The only hope now is a lucky break. But even then, will that be enough?

Day 57

Reardon awakes with a pounding headache. He slowly rolls over and just lies quietly in bed. After about 15 minutes, he rolls over and sees the clock reading 11:03 a.m. He slowly moves into a sitting position as his legs slide from under the sheets and drop to the floor. He knows he is a long way from standing, and this simple motion has drained him of his strength. He ponders just standing up but decides against it. His head is throbbing, as usual, after another night of drinking. He lowers his head into his awaiting hands. Two minutes of quiet contemplation is enough to encourage him to stand.

Reardon momentarily stumbles before he steadies himself against the wall at the head of his bed. After he regains his composure, he walks to the bathroom and drinks two glasses of water before taking a long look at himself. He realizes he looks like hell and then some. He is starving, and his knee is tight as a snare drum. He decides to start with a hot shower before eating. After 15 minutes of letting the water just run over him, he finally turns off the shower. This is well past the five-minute restriction put in place by the mayor to conserve water. New York still has rough days ahead. At some point they will need to completely shut down the Delaware Aqueduct to repair it, and this will cut off half the water to the city for several weeks. The hot water has done just enough to loosen his knee so that he can get out of the shower without much pain. He dries off and puts on some loose-fitting khakis and a t-shirt.

Reardon enters the kitchen and opens the fridge to find a beer waiting there for him like a long lost lover. He cracks open the can and takes two swigs before reaching for some eggs and English muffins. He quickly realizes the muffins are moldy and drops them in the garbage. A few minutes later, he is sitting at the table with three fried eggs and a second beer.

Tired of the silence, he turns on the TV to get a re-cap of the news and to figure out what further tragedy befell the nation. The irony is that even the newscasters are becoming numb to even reporting the news. They are now like automatons just going through the motion. Their emotion is no greater than if they were reporting the results of a county bake sale. Reardon can tell Alicia is taking this particularly hard. She used to have a glint in her eye and now she looks like the life is drained from her soul. Last week she broke down a couple times, overwhelmed by the stress, but that is gone. Now all Reardon sees is a ghostly expression. Alicia comes back on with more news of *the county bake sale*.

Early this morning a train derailed, plunging into the water after the Sabula Rail Bridge was destroyed in Sabula, Iowa. The bridge is owned by Canadian Pacific. The train was 50 cars long and was carrying grain east towards Pennsylvania.

She continues in her droning listless monotone voice. Over her shoulder appears an aerial shot of train cars in a heap along the river's edge. Emergency crews are milling around their vehicles.

At least 60 trains pass over this bridge on a weekly basis. Authorities are looking for witnesses who may have seen something prior to the explosion. The Manchester, Connecticut, auto parts distributor attacked on Day 54 is beginning repairs after all of its loading docks were also damaged with detcord, just like in Seattle, two days prior. The Carlsbad Desalination Plant and the Encina Power Station in San Diego county attacked on Day 55 are still assessing the damage after bombs destroyed the water intake valves between the desalination plant and power plant. Both are currently shut down and the loss of 50 million gallons of fresh water per day is already impacting the city. The mayor of San Diego is asking everyone to reduce water and power usage. Police have no suspects. Finally, the garbage trucks destroyed yesterday are all considered a complete loss. Each of the four cities is asking for assistance from neighboring cities to ensure that they do not have a garbage crisis on their hands while they order replacement trucks.

She reads the news with no emotion or charisma. How can she? This is just another day of an unrelenting storm, and it's getting pretty old pretty quick. Economists have even given up trying to estimate the economic toll on the economy. They simply say it is costing the country billions of dollars per day.

March 18, 2005 – New York

Reardon and Spencer are returning from another stakeout that was a bust. They sat in an old, dingy, stinking room above a bar for over six hours watching and waiting for a suspected bomb maker to show up at his apartment. A SWAT team is ready to arrest him, but he never shows up. They suspect he was tipped off somehow. Unwilling to wait any longer, they executed a search warrant at 5 p.m. and found nothing but a lamp, some old books, a mattress, and some moldy food in the fridge. They found the newspaper on the sofa from the day before, so it was obvious he had cleared out last night. Reardon is driving Spencer back to her place at just before seven.

"Well, that was a waste of time." Spencer said.

"Yeah, today was a long one, but not the first time we wasted an entire day. At least you got some reading done."

"Yeah, it was a good book, but I had trouble concentrating because of the smell. I feel like my clothes will never be same."

"OK, but this was not nearly as bad as that place over on 80th street a couple years ago. It was above that cigar shop."

"Oh, my God, I had completely forgotten about that place. Yes, that was worse," she laughs. "I think I remember burning those clothes."

Reardon smiles and thinks about how these stakeouts have cemented his friendship with her. This is a good thing because there are many weeks where he spends more time with her than his own wife. Sara has always been understanding of his long hours and never been jealous of all the time he spends with her. The only saving grace has been Sara working full time and working on her graduate degree over the last three and half years. When she finishes her degree in May, and has more free time, things may change. The best part of his week is every Sunday morning when he and Sara sleep in and spend a few hours together before getting on with their day. Spencer admires their relationship. She has plenty of dates but can't seem to find the right guy. Reardon likes to give her a hard time when she hasn't been on a date for a while. He also razzes her when she does have a boyfriend. Reardon is now closer to her than his own sister and has come to love her like a sister. Reardon thinks she feels the same about him but would of course never broach the subject. Reardon knows he shouldn't hassle her because her relationships never last long with the kind of hours she works, but then again, what are brothers for?

Reardon and Spencer swing by the office to submit their report. There are just few other agents still at work. Spencer has pulled up a chair to sit across from Reardon's desk.

"How are things going with you and James?"

"Oh, I decided to break up with him last night."

"And you're just telling me now…"

"Well, I haven't officially done it. I just decided last night. I wasn't going to tell you until it's official. I see him again Friday. I'll do it then."

"Why are you breaking this poor schmuck's heart?"

"Well, first of all, it's only been three weeks. I'm just not really into him that much."

"And…"

"And what?"

"And … there is always an *and* with you."

"I'm embarrassed to tell you."

"Now I *need* to know – spill it sister…"

Spencer blushes a little bit. "It's his mom."

"What? His mom? Did she insist on coming on all the dates so you wouldn't tarnish his reputation?"

"No, she's just," Spencer pauses, "*very* intimidating."

"What is she? Six-four 300 pounds?"

"No, she's only about five-two."

Laughter comes spilling out of Reardon and Spencer blushes more, "Five-two!"

"It's hard to describe. It's just how she stares at me."

"But you're HUGE!" Reardon lifts his arms and starts clawing at the air like a buffoon. "You're like this big giant bear, and she's this cute little bunny."

"Nice! Now I'm huge."

"Seriously, you could reach down and crush her skull, *and* you have a gun." Reardon continues to laugh, and he wipes away a tear just as it starts to run down his cheek.

"I know, it's weird, but she is just so intimidating." She is mildly irritated with his reaction but not surprised. "She looks like a coiled spring who could attack at any moment."

Reardon continues laughing and sputters out, "Are you expecting her to attack you?"

"No! It's just how she looks through me." Spencer pauses for a few moments. "I can't believe you just called me huge!"

"Well, you are…"

"Hmm, nice, well, at least I'm not a moron." She gives an impish smile as she tilts her head to the left and squints at him.

Reardon smiles back, "Touché," and slowly regains his composure. "Oh God, I love your reasons for breaking up with guys."

August 14, 2005 – New York

Those who would give up essential liberty, to purchase a little temporary safety, deserve neither Liberty nor Safety.
Benjamin Franklin

Spencer comes into the apartment with lunch. They have been watching the same store front for two weeks now after getting a tip that the back room is used for clandestine meetings between a group of Ethiopians and Iranians. The rumor revolves around the two groups trying to raise funds more quickly in order to set up training camps. So far, this has been a bust, and they aren't expecting anything today either. Reardon is pulling the plug on this stakeout after today unless something finally happens. He is not holding his breath after the ongoing soap opera of events they've heard over the last two weeks.

"I can officially say I hate this place," Spencer says as she pulls out Reardon's burger and fries. "Here you go."

"Thanks." Spencer pulls out a boxed salad. "Is that what you really like to eat?"

"Yeah."

"Nobody likes to eat salad when they could be eating a hamburger and fries. This is real stakeout food. Want some?"

"Thanks, but I'm happy with what I'm eating. Besides, I don't want to start getting fat like you."

"Whoa! Fat, who says I'm getting fat?"

"You are definitely getting a little chunkier around the middle. I didn't want to say anything, but since you brought it up..."

"How did I bring it up? You're the one who said I was fat."

Spencer waives her hand dismissively. "Details."

"That's just a mean thing to say."

"Mean thing to say," said in a mocking voice, "What are you, a chick?"

This is one of the things he loves about working with her, no holds barred and she gives as good as she gets.

"Anyways, I'm just saying you might want to thin down a little bit for Sara."

"Thanks, I'll tell her you're really concerned."

"No problem, I do what I can."

They continue listening for a few more hours. Reardon steps out for an early dinner and comes back with his standard fare of greasy takeout food for the two of them.

"Hey, what are ya' doing?"
"Just sitting here conjugating verbs."
"Huh?"
"What do you think I'm doing? I'm listening to more calls from the brother-in-law. He is still convinced his wife is sleeping around. Our buddy over there just reminded the guy that he told him his sister was a whore before they got engaged and doesn't have any sympathy for him. If what he says is true, this chick's fun box gets more traffic than the Holland tunnel. This is the worst soap opera ever. If they could change it up a little bit, it might be interesting, but the same conversation day after day is sooooo boring.

They quietly finish their meals and take turns sitting there in quiet contemplation staring out the window. Finally, at four, he calls it.

"Let's get out of here. I'll call and have the equipment picked up in the morning."

The FBI is continuing to take advantage of the "sneak and peek" searches and "roving wiretaps" authorized by the PATRIOT Act. Reardon has never been comfortable using these and feels they will ultimately be ruled unconstitutional. Until then, they're the law of the land and get used extensively. The problem with casting such a wide net is catching a lot of things you don't want. Like a Middle Eastern soap opera in the Bronx.

The paranoia after 9/11 opened law-abiding citizens to many unwarranted invasions of privacy, such as National Security Letters. NSLs allow the FBI to check email, financial, health, and telephone records on millions of people without getting a search warrant. Recipients who receive an NSL are also under a secrecy gag order, which even prohibits them from contacting their attorney.

Most Americans were oblivious to all the intrusions permitted by the PATRIOT Act. The ACLU filed a suit on behalf of someone anonymously in April, 2004, and ultimately, NSLs were declared unconstitutional in November, 2005. But not before the FBI authored well over ten thousand NSLs since the PATRIOT Act was passed in 2001. The FBI has also conducted searches without informing people because of the intentionally vague *delayed notification* clause, which states they can wait a reasonable amount of time if they feel it could impact national security.

The "sneak and peek" search warrants with their *delayed notification* were finally struck down in September, 2007. Reardon always wondered how millions of innocent Americans would feel if they knew their personal records were reviewed by the FBI. As a result, Reardon is starting to feel frustration with the number of false leads they are chasing lately. He feels like they should be getting better at this over time.

Reardon also struggles with the balance between privacy and safety. The FBI has unprecedented access to personal information without needing a search warrant or even just cause. Reardon knows he is having a theoretical argument with incomplete information. He feels the PATRIOT Act is both powerful and dangerous, becoming uncomfortable with the source of the information over time. He definitely does not like the big brother feel of the PATRIOT Act given the fact that it hasn't stopped any big attacks. He knows this is where his argument breaks down. For all he knows, they have stopped forty huge attacks and saved a million American lives over the last four years, but that it is all classified. Therein lies the problem – how can people support something if they honestly have no idea if it is helping or hurting? He also wonders if your rights are violated, and you never find out, do you care? There have simply been too many abuses over the years by the NSA, CIA, and FBI. One thing keeps rolling around in the back of his mind - Quis custodiet ipsos custodies? Who watches the watchers? This weighs on his mind constantly. He has considered having this discussion with Spencer several times but always decides against it. He does not want to jade her too much.

Day 59

Reardon is quietly sitting in the conference room with Spencer in what would normally be a lazy afternoon if the world was not in continuous turmoil. The TV is displaying a list of five new high schools that were attacked today.

Joplin High School, Joplin, Missouri
Grafton High School, Grafton, Massachusetts
Skyline High School, Ann Arbor, Michigan
McKinley High School, Niles, Ohio
Centennial High School, Ankeny, Iowa

A new woman is reporting the news since Alicia is noticeably absent.

Hello, my name is Jennifer Longley. Five new high schools, all less than one year old, were attacked early yesterday. A bomb was placed next to the gas meter going into each building and detonated at approximately 3 a.m. Eastern Standard Time. Each explosion caused significant damage. Fortunately, the attacks were at night so no one was injured. Fire crews contained the flames at each school, however, initial estimates are in the millions. The damage will take months to repair. The worst damage was at Skyline High School where nearly three-quarters of the building burned down and the rest is severely damaged by smoke. The building is considered a complete loss. The damage at the other schools varies. We will provide more details this evening as we learn more.

James takes over and is noticeably exhausted. The images appearing in the upper corner of the screen switch from burned high schools to swimming pools.

Good afternoon, thanks, Jennifer, the five swimming pools damaged in explosions yesterday remain closed today. The explosives were placed near the chlorination and pump units at community swimming pools in Baltimore, Maryland; Greensboro, North Carolina; Birmingham, Alabama; Tupelo, Mississippi; and Conway, Arkansas. The explosions and ensuing fires released large amounts of chlorine gas. Chlorine is a highly toxic and deadly gas. Local authorities evacuated all residents within a one-mile radius of each pool to ensure that residents were safe from the gas cloud released immediately after the explosions. Although the gas is not flammable, it is extremely dangerous. If inhaled, it leads to extreme illness and even death. This attack exposed a vulnerability within each community. They were simply not equipped to quickly deal with this type of chemical release within a highly populated area. The evacuations took hours, and if the explosions had released a highly concentrated gas cloud, hundreds of people would have become sickened. Thankfully, the cloud of gas was limited and dissipated fairly quickly. Only a few dozen people were rushed to hospitals with minor symptoms, and all are expecting a full recovery.

Switching to Boston, authorities report that they have closed the I-90 Ted Williams tunnel until they can figure out if the cracks can be repaired in order to stop the flooding. Traffic around the Logan

International Airport remains a nightmare because I-90 is the highway leading to the airport.

A train also derailed late last night near Billings, Montana. A fifty year old wooden railroad bridge spanning a 20 foot gulch collapsed last night causing a freight train to derail. The bridge collapsed just after the engine passed over the bridge. Twenty-five cars derailed spilling tons of feed grain. The NTSB confirmed that the bridge passed inspection late last year. The crash is currently under investigation. There is no proof this is related to the terrorist attacks at this moment in time.

Sitting here watching this is a mind-numbing activity. knowing there is nothing they can do. It is reminiscent of their long stakeouts over the years where they were simply there to observe and report. If they were lucky, they were able to make a few busts, however, the rewards turned out to be few and far between.

June 14, 2006 – New York

Reardon and Spencer just finished a long day in the office. They spent all day doing paperwork after busting a local wannabe group of home grown terrorists. The group's biggest problem is that they couldn't keep their mouths shut. They were bragging to everyone in their neighborhood about all the weapons they had recently smuggled in from Baltimore. It didn't take long for an undercover agent to get wind of this and set up a bust. After a long day of interviews, they determined the kids were, thankfully, just bored and looking to impress their friends. After Reardon was convinced of this he, turned them over to the NYPD so they could be processed for illegal firearms possession. Reardon offered to give Spencer a ride home. It's only about ten minutes out of his way. As soon as they get in the car, Spencer asks the big question she has been dying to ask all day.

"So, is Sara still pissed at you?"
"Ah, there it is, you just can't let it go."
"Well I don't have time for soap operas, so I have to get it where I can. So..."
"So yes, she's still pissed."
"I can't believe she got pissed at you for a dream."
"I know. Well it's not funny anymore."

Reardon told his wife he had a weird dream and when asked told her about it. It was a simple dream, he was just having dinner with his old high school girlfriend.

"Well you should've never told her."
"It was just dinner! And, oh yeah, just a dream!" Reardon says in a sardonic tone.
"What's it been? Three days now?"
"Four."
"Four!" Spencer laughs uproariously.
"It's not that funny."
"I'm sorry, but yeah it's pretty damn funny. This is all I'm sayin', you're a moron."
Reardon laughs, "Thanks, that makes me feel better already."

They sit quietly for a few moments. Spencer quickly turns with an excited look on her face.

"Oh my God, this might be getting worse than the wedding invitations."
"No, nothing will ever be worse than that."

About six months after Spencer joined Reardon's team, they were on a long stakeout watching the shop of a suspected money man who they believed was funneling money to people in the Middle East. Spencer had just gone through a somewhat bad breakup and was asking how Sara and he always seem so happy. He pointed out it's not always peaches and cream. She asked what's the biggest thing he ever did that got her pissed off. Reardon pointed out they fought, all couples do, but recounted the worst time by far. They were not even married yet. Sara came over and they were going to stuff the envelopes with the wedding invitations. They each had a stack of about 100 and were just sitting there watching TV waiting to seal them at the end. Sara glanced over during a commercial break and noticed that he is not folding the small card in half and not separating the correct two things with the little piece of tissue paper. Reardon explained that the envelopes lay flatter if you don't fold the card. And who cares about the tissue paper? It just gets thrown away anyways. Well, as it turns out, Sara cared a great deal. Reardon said there was no way he was going to re-stuff fifty envelopes. He kept pointing out that no one would care and refused to re-stuff them. Sara became so angry that she stomped out of his apartment and slammed the door. She refused to answer his calls for three days. He finally just went to her apartment and knocked, holding a dozen flowers and fifty re-stuffed envelopes.

"So, are you still sleeping on the sofa?"

"Yeah, and my back is starting to kill me."

"Have you tried apologizing?"

"Yes, that; and flowers, and a card, and more flowers. So far no luck."

"Man, chicks are weird. Tell her she is being irrational. You can even tell her *you* said that."

"I can tell her *I said that*, huh…"

"Yeah, don't tell her I said that. No sense her being mad at me too. Duh!"

"Just wait until you're married."

"I'll never get mad over something like that."

"Ha!" Reardon laughs. "That's just it. She probably isn't mad about this at all; she's just mad that I don't know what she's really mad at."

"Oh yeah, this is one of her *woman tricks*."

"Yeah, it might be."

"You're so full of crap sometimes. Ohhhh it's a *woman trick*."

"I can't wait until you're married."

"At the rate I'm going, I'll be an old spinster."

There's a short pause, awkward for a moment, and Spencer changed the subject. Reardon sensed the awkward moment, which is freakishly unusual for them. However, these have happened more frequently whenever they end up talking about relationships. Reardon let it go for the moment. They spent the next ten minutes discussing their weekend plans before Spencer wished him a good night and got out of the car. She reminded him once again that she was a big girl and can get in just fine. But as always, he waited until she was inside and saw a light go on. As Reardon drove home, he couldn't help but wonder how long it will take for her to find the right guy. He has been tempted to try and set her up except for two problems. One, he doesn't know any eligible guys that would be a good match, and two, Sara jabbed him in the gut when he mentioned it about a year ago saying that it's the stupidest idea he's ever had. She said, "You've got a good thing with Spencer, don't screw it up by trying to be a matchmaker you idiot."

His thoughts quickly turned back to the job. Over the last six months he has been increasingly frustrated by the lack of progress they are making. They are chasing down lead after lead after lead and making no real progress as far as he's concerned. There've been no breaks leading to a complex network of terrorists. But then again, maybe there is no complex network of terrorists. They have made about twenty arrests over the last six months for anything from illegal firearms possession to illegal immigration. But in reality, nothing serious, nothing rising to the level of terrorism or national security. The only thing that keeps him going is knowing that his work is keeping America safe and that there've been no serious attacks in the city since 9/11.

Day 60

Reardon is awake and cooking eggs. Another delicious meal of three fried eggs and beer. He has been up for about fifteen minutes. His only accomplishment so far is a satisfying pee after another long night of drinking. The news is on in the background and he is too dead to the world to pay attention. Reardon sits down to eat at just after 10 and notices the station has gone to its normal daytime programming. It's nice to be able to watch a game show for a while when everything is in chaos. He finishes his eggs, grabs another beer, and becomes instantly enthralled by the show. The contestant picks door #1. The host shows her a goat behind door #3 and then asks if she would like to switch to door #2. She is swaying back and forth as the crowd is yelling. She decides to stick with door #1.

"No, pick door #2. You always want to switch! You have a two-thirds chance of winning if you switch!" He leans back in his chair. "Come on! They should know they wanna switch."

Reardon always gets irritated when he talks to people who think it's a 50/50 chance after one door is revealed. The host is about to do the big reveal and the news cuts to a special news report.

"Ahh! Come on! I wanna see if she wins."

After the flashy News logo spins on the screen and music ends, his favorite newscaster fills the screen.

Good morning, I'm James Newburgh. We have breaking news out of Cincinnati, Ohio. At 10 a.m. local time, just seventeen minutes ago, downtown Cincinnati was plunged into darkness. We don't have any additional details at this moment in time.

"Ugh! Then why are you interrupting? You could have just run a banner across the screen for this!"

Reardon is pissed because for some unknown reason, he really wants to know if the lady won a new car. James drones on for another ten minutes, restating the exact same information, putting his finger to his ear piece multiple times, and pausing on live television. You can see he is praying they feed him some useful bit of information with each reach. Finally, at the end of the ten minutes, he reports they will return to their normal broadcast schedule. Reardon is thinking that is the only new bit of information he has said in the last ten minutes. The gameshow comes back just as the host is signing off and then cuts to the credits. A moment later, an important message comes on for those suffering from chronic intestinal cramping about new drug that may help *and* may cause liver failure.

Reardon decides to shower and head into the office. His head is throbbing as he strips off his clothes to climb into the shower. He pauses for a moment to look at himself in the mirror and realizes that was a mistake. He then lifts his bad leg onto the toilet lid and massages his knee for a moment before reaching down and touching his bullet wound scar on the outside of his calf.

January 17, 2008 – New York

Reardon has had a knot in his gut for over two weeks since taking off time for Christmas. He needs a change and has been contemplating something outrageous. He has a little girl who turns one in just over two weeks, and he is thinking about putting in for a transfer to Afghanistan. This won't come as a shock to Sara since he mentioned an overseas assignment was a necessity for any real career advancement before they got married. Sara definitely won't like this at all. Plus, Sara will hate the idea that he is asking to go to a war zone. However, these are now considered pretty safe assignments, relatively speaking compared to the first couple years after the initial invasion. He decides to talk it over with Sara after they put Charlotte down for the night.

———

Reardon strolls into the office at just after 11:30. The conference room is quiet with Peterson and Spencer watching the TV in seemingly stunned silence as they watch a commercial advertising the latest in kitchen mop technology.

"What've they learned about Cincinnati?"

Spencer is startled for a moment and turns. "Nothing really yet. They don't know what caused the outages. Buildings have lost electricity, water, phone lines, and internet in a fifteen block radius."

"How the heck do they just lose all that and no one knows?"

"Good question."

James comes on and they stop talking to listen to the latest reports.

Police now suspect that explosive charges were set off below ground in the utility tunnels running below the city. Initially, police suspected that a water main break in one of the tunnels caused the power outages. However, they now believe bombs caused the damage because it is spread out over such a wide area. As usual, the police have no immediate clues or suspects.

Utility tunnels and buried pipes run beneath cities like a labyrinth and are the lifeblood of any city. Everything to keep the city alive runs below the streets. Without them, the city curls up and dies. The destruction of these tunnels is a full-on heart attack, and the city now needs quadruple bypass surgery.

Spencer turns to Peterson. "Assuming it's explosives and they used C-4, how much would they need to use?"

"Wow, in an enclosed space like that, not much. A half, even a quarter-pound would do severe damage. It could easily take a month to fix the damage."

Three hours slowly pass as news reports keep coming in. The station resumes its normal programming for most of the time because the trickle of information is simply too slow for continuous coverage. They come on for a quick update at 3:35 reporting that they will have a full update at 4:00. Reardon is blankly watching the TV as Spencer and Peterson quietly work at their computers. Finally, at 4:00, James and Alicia come on and introduce themselves once again. Reardon is thinking, yes, we know who you are. He is momentarily wondering why news people always introduce themselves or get introduced before they speak. It must be some clause in every newscaster's contract. Yes, you get paid crap, but at least we will acknowledge you have a name. James takes over after Alicia introduces herself. Both are listless and speak with hardly any emotion.

Here is what we know so far. Sixty-three buildings have lost electricity completely, and forty-seven buildings are without water. Fifty-nine of those buildings have also lost all telephone and internet. Dozens of other buildings are suffering from partial outages and low water pressure. The fire department continues to rescue people from elevators stuck between floors when the power went out. So far, over 100 people have been rescued from elevators. The fire department expects it to take at least another hour before they can declare the all-clear. The mayor of Cincinnati has ordered the downtown area to be evacuated, fearing secondary explosions or fire that may be caused by severed natural gas lines, exposed wiring, and water. Water from broken pipes has been flooding into underground parking garages. As a result, the city is shutting off water across most of downtown to minimize flooding.

An estimated 65,000 people are now heading out of the city. Approximately 8,000 of the evacuees are downtown residents inside the affected area. The rest commute to downtown for work each day. Police now suspect at least 10 explosive charges were detonated simultaneously. Police are interviewing people and attempting to determine who accessed the utility tunnels through manhole covers and when. City officials have already stated they expect the downtown area to be closed for at least one week while they assess and repair the damage. The city is already making plans to assist the 8,000 downtown residents displaced by the attack.

James reaches to his ear and pauses for a moment. A sudden look of shock and dismay crosses his face.

We have just received a report that Lexington, Kentucky was plunged into darkness approximately ten minutes ago. The initial reports are similar to those from Cincinnati. We can only assume the city was attacked in a similar way.

James continues to speak, however Reardon's attention is drawn to a vibration and pings coming from his front pocket. Removing his phone, he looks down to see three messages on his phone.

"Hello."
"How are you today?"
"I wanted to pass along a little news."

Reardon quickly looks up. "Hey, mute the TV."
"Hold on, I want to hear this," Spencer retorts irritably.
"Mute it, I just got a text."

Spencer quickly turns in shock and Peterson mutes the TV. "From who?"

"An unknown number." Peterson quickly switches screens so he can see the texts and start the trace. "Three texts so far."

Spencer bolts from the room and returns thirty seconds later with McCullum.

"What do they say?" McCullum quickly asks.

Reardon has already responded. "How do you think we are doing?"

A quick reply. "Yes, silly of me to ask." A moment passes. "I wanted to let you know this has been exhausting for us so we have decided to take three days off."

"What's that mean?"

"Just that, three days off, however, we wanted to let you know the attacks will continue as scheduled. I thought I would give you a hint. Think long lines. Bye for now."

McCullum is looking over Peterson's shoulder at his screen. "Another clue! *Long lines!* What are we supposed to do with that?" McCullum asks out loud.

"What kind of lines? Do they mean power lines, lines at the grocery store?" Spencer asks.

Suddenly, Peterson starts speaking out loud, almost absentmindedly. "The DMV has long lines, pretty much any government agency. Amusement parks, where else do people stand in long lines? Then there are power lines, those are long. Oh, and railway lines."

Suddenly Peterson looks up, everyone is staring back at him with a blank look on their faces. It was as though he was having a *Rainman* moment.

Reardon speaks up, "I guess we'll know sometime tomorrow for sure. In the meantime, they must have left timed charges. If we can figure out the clue then we'll have a chance to stop some attacks."

Peterson hesitantly says, "that gives us a head start. If we can figure out what it means."

"Or they are just screwing with us so we go on a wild goose chase," McCullum states flatly.

"Well, they might be, but I don't think we have a choice at this point in time. We have to try and figure out what they're going after," Spencer says.

McCullum asks Peterson to get the hint out to all the field offices, and McCullum calls the director so he can update the president. McCullum is annoyed because he hates passing along useless information. But a clue is a clue, so he feels obligated to pass it along.

Day 47 – 60 Attacks

Day	Attack
47	Destroy natural gas lines, Idaho, Maine, and Georgia
48	Knock out traffic lights in the Meadowlands, New Jersey
49	I-90 tunnel bombings, Boston, Massachusetts
50	High-voltage powerline towers destroyed near nuclear reactors, Kansas, Washington
51	TV transmitter/radio towers destroyed, Cleveland, Ohio; Boise, Idaho; Memphis, Tennessee
52	Loading dock damaged at food distribution center, Seattle, Washington
53	FedEx loading docks damaged in Clearwater, Florida; Jackson, Michigan; Santa Fe, New Mexico; Salt Lake City, Utah
54	Auto parts distributor docks damaged, Manchester, Connecticut
55	Water intake valve destroyed between Carlsbad Desalination Plant and Encina Power Station, San Diego, California
56	Garbage trucks destroyed, Rapid City, Iowa; Butte, Montana; Redding, California; Morgantown, West Virginia
57	Sabula rail bridge destroyed, Sabula, Iowa
58	Pump systems at community swimming pool destroyed, Baltimore, Maryland; Greensboro, North Carolina; Birmingham, Alabama; Tupelo, Mississippi; Conway, Arkansas
59	High schools attacked, Joplin, Missouri; Grafton, Massachusetts; Ann Arbor, Michigan; Niles, Ohio; Ankeny, Iowa
60	Sewers and utility tunnels destroyed, Cincinnati, Ohio; Lexington, Kentucky

Day 61

Reardon arrives at the office just after noon on an unusually cold and blustery day. The office is quiet as Reardon heads into the conference room.

He finds Peterson and Spencer reviewing a map. Peterson is on his laptop and Spencer is standing next to the monitor looking at what Peterson is displaying from his monitor.

"The long lines must be state lines." Spencer comments.

"Which state lines?" Reardon asks.

"We have two reports of small bridges blown up in the middle of nowhere." She pauses and points at the aerial shot of Wayland, Iowa, "this one is on the Iowa-Missouri border. What's weird is there is a highway bridge a hundred yards away. It would have made more sense to blow that one. Much more traffic."

"Maybe that's not their goal."

"Well, what's their goal?"

"I don't know. Again this is small, obscure, and out of the way. That's what they seem to like. Where is the second site?"

"Well this site fits that description to a tee." Peterson switches to an aerial view of the border between Oklahoma and Texas. "This is a small bridge about five miles south of Hollis, Oklahoma. Middle of nowhere. I'd be surprised if more than ten cars a day go over it."

"That's it. Just two."

"That's all we know about so far. If they are picking places this obscure, it might be a few hours before anyone even notices."

McCullum quickly swoops into the conference room. "Peterson, bring up North Sioux City, Nebraska. We just got a call. 30 minutes ago, the bridge leading into Iowa was damaged. The blast was not big enough to take it down, but one of the four lanes is severely damaged. They have shut it down while they inspect it for further bombs. It looks like they screwed up this time. So, what can you tell me?"

Peterson excitedly says, "With this third attack, I think we can confirm the attacks are all on state lines."

"So, what's that mean? All the attacks are going to be on state lines the next two days?" McCullum quickly asks.

"I don't know. One day is hardly a pattern, but I think we should go with that assumption until we have something better."

"This is pretty thin," McCullum states as he paces. "OK, Peterson, get this out to all the field offices. I want them to get word out to all the local police and highway departments. We need to get bomb squads out searching every bridge crossing a state line."

"If all bridges are in obscure places, then most of these places don't have bomb squads."

"Yeah, that just occurred to me. Tell'em to do the best they can. If they find anything, tell them to call the FBI, and we'll get someone there as quickly as we can. Just tell them to not touch anything they find. Who knows what kind of booby traps they've set up?"

A nationwide alert secretly goes out to start inspecting all bridges on state lines. The goal is to avert a panic or have civilians take it upon themselves to start looking for bombs. Within two hours, police and highway crews start inspecting bridges. The secret does not last long. People start snapping photos and posting them to social media sites. It starts a frenzy because no one really knows what's going on. Radio stations pick up the news and report that police are now inspecting bridges, supposedly for bombs. Since authorities have not explained what they are doing people, jump to the conclusion that *all* bridges might have bombs. This causes a nationwide panic across social media, and many people decide to avoid any travel that includes a bridge crossing. The police, highway departments, and 911 across the country get flooded with calls, overwhelming the phone lines in many cases. *#BridgeBombs* quickly becomes the most Tweeted thing in the history of Twitter over a 24-hour period. The paranoia and hysterics starts feeding on itself. Some people who do dare a crossing race across the bridges, some exceeding 90 MPH, hoping they will not be caught in the next explosion. Several accidents occur with people trying to swerve through traffic as fast as they can to get across the bridges. Irrational fear has kicked into overdrive.

The plan to quietly inspect bridges along state borders backfired. Finally, the Governors clear up the confusion at about 5 o'clock. This does little to ease fears. Trucks and cars alike are now stopping short of bridges on state lines and causing massive backups. Tempers flare because some people are willing to risk the crossing but are simply unable to make progress because the roads are blocked.

McCullum talks to the lead agent in Afghanistan again and is frustrated by the progress. In the last week, agents in Afghanistan have tracked down only eight more people on the list. Six are suspected dead. The agents are discovering their ability to make contact is an extreme challenge. Nearly everyone has rebuffed their attempts at contact, fearing retribution from ISIS. So far, only one lieutenant from a small tribal region has expressed any interest in helping. The issue is that this guy likely has no meaningful information. The agents still make contact and a payment, only to quickly discover that the information is out of date and useless. McCullum is trying to balance his need for information from Afghanistan and his more pressing need to stop the attacks. Even if he were given a definitive list on the whereabouts of almost everyone on the list, he would not know what to do about the ones they couldn't track down. They only have photographs for a fraction of the people on the list, and most are only known by name or even a codename. McCullum is tempted to pull the plug on the whole operation but knows they need to press on in the hopes of discovering something useful. McCullum is unaware of all the theories involving the Russians.

Washington, D.C.

The White House has another problem to tackle, this time it is mass hysteria. There is nothing they can do about it. They are still dealing with much larger issues. Accepting a complete paradigm shift is a difficult task for any individual or group. The president and his staff are still thinking in terms of a rule-based system, one of laws, policies, and procedures. How do you fight an enemy with no rules? This is a new world. How do you negotiate with an inferno sweeping across the nation, appearing randomly and disappearing back into the night? What measures are acceptable? Can we break the law to defend law and order? Can we take away civil rights to protect and defend our way of life, one of law and order? How far is too far to stop an invisible enemy?

This is the last straw for the president. He asks the governors to deploy National Guard units and guard as many bridges and overpasses as possible. He knows that there are several problems with this approach. One, he is asking, but the governors are under no obligation to comply. However, he is counting on public pressure to ensure they comply. Two, there are not enough troops to cover all bridges and overpasses in most states. Three, the next series of attacks will likely not impact bridges or overpasses. He addresses the nation, directly outlining his plan in order to put the maximum amount of pressure on the governors to ensure they comply. It will take the governors several days to figure out the logistics and deploy the troops to the bridges and overpasses. The attacks continue to expose the soft underbelly of American society.

The president wants to take on much stricter measures and discusses roadblocks and ID checks with his chief of staff in the Oval Office. It's a difficult conversation. They view it as opening Pandora's Box and speak candidly for well over an hour about how to present this to the American people.

"How do we handle people who refuse the searches and ID checks?" the president asks. "Should they be forcibly searched, detained, or just let them pass through?"
"I don't know right now."

"Well, we better figure it out before we start." The president pauses and just stares at him momentarily, thinking through the logistics. "What if we decide to detain people and just 1% of people refuse the checks? Then we would need to detain over 3 million Americans. Where the hell are we going to suddenly hold that many people who are doing nothing more than exercising their rights?"

This is, of course, an unworkable option. They also know certain people will view this as a takeover and respond with violence leading to shootouts at checkpoints. The violence will be extremely rare, but it will happen. Innocent people will die in the crossfire. How can they justify these risks? But then again, how can they avoid such a risk if it will stop the attacks? This is war, isn't it? Or, at least some new form of war. Ultimately, they decide they need another discussion with the cabinet. In the meantime, another day slips through their fingers, which is another day for the terrorists to control the pace of the attacks. The president has been pacing the entire time as his chief of staff stoically stands near the desk.

"All this crisis does is point out how helpless we are to stop these kinds, or really any kind, of attacks. The people who used to ask 'Why didn't we see this coming?' have finally shut up," the president states flatly.

The president has an epiphany after his own comment, even if you see it coming, you can't stop ghosts. He walks to the sofa and drops into it deflated. His chief of staff quietly walks over and sits across from him. They sit silently just staring at each other. Each one at a loss for words. The president retires to his residence at just after midnight and collapses into bed.

The following day the markets re-opened and the declines are minimal, a pleasant surprise, *only* dropping 2% over the course of the trading session. The relatively small attacks over the last ten days are somehow soothing. Despite that, the markets are only open three hours a day to help stem the tide of losses. People are realizing that panic sales ultimately hurt themselves as much as others.

Day 63

Dow Jones Industrial Average
11,123.94
Total decline: 44.8%
Total loss: $2.33 Trillion

Nasdaq
3,101.36
Total decline: 45.4%
Total loss: $3.86 Trillion

Cincinnati and Louisville are still a disorganized mess. City officials in both cities are now reporting, the damage is extensive, and it will likely take six to nine months to fully repair the damage. They discovered men posing as utility workers not only set off ten bombs in the utility tunnels below each city, they also ran about a mile of detcord in each city as well to maximize the destruction. Downtown residents and workers vaguely remember utility workers accessing the manhole covers approximately six weeks ago. They were feeding black cord off large spools. Witnesses simply assumed they were laying more fiber optic cable and never gave it a second thought. There are no reliable eyewitness accounts because no one remembers any specifics about a work crew from six weeks ago. The descriptions are all over the map with people mixing and matching faces from any number of work crews they have seen during that time. There are traffic cameras at most of the affected intersections, but the images are only stored for a week before they are deleted. The explosions destroyed electric cables, phone lines, fiber optics cables, and gas and water lines running in and near the utility tunnels.

Officials in Cincinnati report *severe damage* in over three miles worth of tunnels as the result of water damage, explosions, or ensuing fires. All the tunnels damaged with detcord will be dug up and replaced. Several underground parking lots are also experiencing varying levels of flooding. The city is pumping out the water with diesel powered pumps because nearly all of downtown is without power. A city worker, speaking on the promise of anonymity, summarized the situation succinctly: *we're* screwed.

In Louisville, the damage is similar with just over two miles of utility tunnels experiencing *severe damage*. Each city has declared a state of emergency and both downtowns are being cordoned off to search for any undetonated explosives and prevent looting.

Cincinnati also announced that the downtown will be closed for at least one month and that the city is scrambling to find temporary housing for almost 8,000 displaced residents. It is expected that at least half will be able to move in with friends and relatives. Louisville has approximately 6,000 displaced residents and has not yet provided any estimates on when it will re-open downtown. Each city will announce a schedule so residents can return to their condos and apartments to retrieve personal belongings. Both cities have completely shut off water, electricity, and gas to large sections of downtown to prevent fires and further damage.

City workers are already digging up large sections of road in each city. This is a devastating attack on each city with over 60,000 displaced workers in Cincinnati and 65,000 displaced workers in Louisville. The Louisville Convention center also announced that it will shut down indefinitely until the city is able to restore water and electricity. They have already cancelled all six conventions over the next two months, costing the city an estimated $100 million from lost revenue. Hundreds of cities across the country are now frantically searching their underground sewers and utility tunnels, costing cities millions of dollars in overtime.

Minneapolis and St. Paul are coming to terms with their new reality – the great divide. Truly a tale of two cities. The process of removing debris from the rivers is still in progress at several bridge locations. State officials are slowly becoming more organized and doing a better job of providing food, water, medication, and gasoline. The attorney general of Minnesota announced several indictments against businesses for price gouging, similar to those after hurricanes Katrina and Sandy, for gas, food, and other supplies. The initial chaos is slowing; however, the ongoing disruption is still absolute for many people. The governor has been working with state and federal officials, outlining plans for when they can rebuild the bridges. The current goal is to start with rebuilding the Interstate Highway 94 and 35W bridges. Construction will start within two weeks and is expected to last approximately eight to ten months. Construction on all the other bridges will start within the next three months. It will be well over a year before all the bridges are rebuilt, and the economic impact will last for years to come.

The entire New York office is drained after two solid days of keeping in contact with the other offices to track the progress of the bridge inspections. To add insult to injury, just getting in and out of the office is an ongoing nightmare. The Holland and Lincoln tunnels remain closed, leading to ongoing chaos for all New Yorkers. The mayor stated a week ago that the tunnels will remain closed indefinitely. The ongoing news out of Cincinnati and Louisville is also taking its toll. McCullum's staff has convened in the evening, Reardon and Spencer sitting near the front. After two full days of ongoing panic and bridge inspections, they found four ticking bombs but they still missed two. One bomb had a timer set to explode on Day 62 and three had timers set to explode on Day 63. The two that exploded were for Day 62. To calm fears police were posting hastily made *all-clear* signs on bridges after they were inspected.

McCullum calls the meeting to order as he enters the room. "Good job everyone! We stopped four bombings. This is a good step towards stopping these bastards. We just need to keep up the hard work. It's late, I want everyone to go home and get a good night's sleep."

Everyone gets up to leave. McCullum already indicated earlier in the day that Reardon, Spencer, and Peterson should stay. McCullum walks over and closes the door once everyone else leaves.

"Shit!" Everyone is suddenly caught off guard by McCullum's change in tone. "Look at what they did; they had us by the balls dancing around like puppets for the last two days. This is a whole new level of screwed up across the country, people afraid to drive anywhere. This is panic on top of panic on top of panic. They wanted us to find the bombs under the bridges. They put big flashing LED clock displays on them so we'd have to be blind to miss them. The bridges in Lil' Old Backwater U.S.A. are inconsequential – they don't give a damn about the four bridges we saved. They are savoring the control they have. And look, we still don't know thing-one about what's going to happen tomorrow. We are no closer to solving this problem. They are just dickin' us around. These attacks were purely psychological."

Mentally McCullum is second guessing himself with the insane notion that in hindsight they should have said nothing and let the four piss-ant bridges just explode. This train of thought shakes him to his core because he doesn't think he would have ever considered it before if circumstances were different. But they are different. The world has been turned on its side. Just before the meeting, McCullum was watching a news report on the frantic searches now going on under every city.

In a calmer tone, McCullum asks, "Did you see the story on the new underground searches in every city?"
"Yeah, we saw that," Spencer quietly responds.
"They've got us on a goddamn Easter egg hunt looking under every manhole cover and bridge. Except instead of an egg, you might find a ticking time bomb waiting to explode. How did we never get wind of anything like this coming our way? How many other bombs do they have just sitting around waiting to screw us over?"

Everyone quietly just sits knowing there is no response to those questions. They have been asking themselves the same thing every day since Day 20.

There is a knock at the door, and McCullum waves in a young agent.

"Sir, this just came in." She hands the sheet of paper to McCullum, turns, and leaves the room.

McCullum walks over to the window and reads the sheet of paper. After two minutes, he turns waving the sheet of paper in his hand, "This is Day 8." That catches their attention. "The derailment a few days ago."

"How do they know?"

"The investigators were able to get down under the cars and found one of the support posts was cut through about 90% at an angle. It was only a matter of time before the weight and vibration caused the wood to splinter and collapse. They found the post was spray painted with NRFBOI and a date. The date is Day 8. They were surprised the post held together as long as it did."

"Wait!" Peterson blurts out, "Old wood. That was the clue."

Everyone turns in surprise to look at Peterson.

January 20, 2008 – New York

Reardon has been in bed for about ten minutes as Sara comes in and lies down next to him after refusing to touch him for the last two days. It would be too much to say she has warmed up to the idea of him going to Afghanistan, but she gives him the go ahead. She hates it, but she knows how frustrated he has been the last year and how important his job is to him. The last time they actually stopped something, and it was not really even a *thing* yet, was in 2006. Reardon's team helped identify the Hudson River bomb plot back in July, 2006, when it was in the "talking phase". It was well publicized and got quite a bit of coverage for two days and quickly faded. After that, Reardon's team got back to chasing down one dead end after another. Reardon looks into Sara's eyes and gives her a big hug and a kiss. He knew that would not be easy, but now he thinks he will have an equally big challenge when he tells Spencer. He has been thinking it through and plans to put in Spencer's name to take over as team lead. She has been his close confidant for nearly five and a half years. He knows she can handle the job and is ready for the promotion more than anyone he has ever worked with in his career.

February 3, 2008 – New York

Reardon's daughter, Charlotte, is celebrating her one-year birthday and they have invited a small group of friends over to celebrate, including Spencer. Reardon relishes being a father and spends every possible moment with her.

Since she was born, he also makes it a point to get her out of the house whenever possible to give Sara some quiet time. He took Charlotte to the park for the two hours leading up to the party so Sara could get things organized with her mom's help. It's a delightful party and they get the obligatory photos of Charlotte smearing cake and icing all over her face and highchair. Everyone laughs when she burps after guzzling down half a bottle of milk with her cake. As people are slowly leaving, Reardon finds himself alone in the kitchen with Spencer. He figures now is as good a time as ever.

"Laura, I have something to tell you."

She quickly switches from glaring at the baby in the living room with an exuberant smile on her face and puts out a pouty lip as she turns to Reardon.

"Why so serious?" But she knows this is serious because he never calls her Laura.

"I don't know how to say this." Spencer's face suddenly turns ashen. "I decided to put in for a transfer to Afghanistan."

"What? Why?" She is shocked.

"I think you know I've been pretty frustrated over the last six months."

"Yeah, I know, but Afghanistan, that's a *big* change."

"I know it's pretty drastic, but I feel like it's something I need to do."

"How is Sara taking it?

"Not well, but she is coming to terms with it."

"Oh, my God! I'm never going to get a good night's sleep while you are over there."

"I'll be fine."

"Everyone says that."

"Well I mean it."

"Everyone says that too."

Sara was just showing out the last guests. Spencer suddenly takes two steps towards Reardon and hugs him. Reardon is taken aback. This is the first time they have ever hugged. Reardon slowly puts his arms around her, and they just stand there a few moments. Just then, Sara walks in.

"Oh, I'm guessing you've told her?"

Spencer quickly pulls back from Reardon.

"Sorry about that."

"It's OK. I would have done that, but I was too pissed at him. I didn't hug him for two days. I couldn't bring myself to hug him until I knew he believed he was doing the right thing."

"So you are OK with this?"

"No, not at all, but I know how important it is to him."

The three of them sit at the kitchen table and discuss it for about another twenty minutes. Spencer wants to know all the details, but he doesn't have any. He still hasn't put in for the transfer yet. He wanted a little more time to come to peace with his decision before he did that. Until then, Spencer needs to keep this to herself. He also explained that he planned to put her in for team lead. She was deeply moved by that. They walked her to the door and Spencer wraps her arms around both of them pulling them in for a crushing three-way hug then turns and walks out the door.

"That was weird, I didn't know she was a hugger." Sara says with a smile.

"Neither did I. I guess I dropped a pretty big bombshell on her."

Washington, D.C.

The President is fed up and orders roadblocks. He has to do something to try and catch the terrorists. So far nothing is working. They can't find a single piece of electronic chatter pointing to the terrorists. These are the perfect sleeper cells. As far as leaving any clues, they are doing their job and staying below the radar. The president addresses the nation and explains why he is ordering the roadblocks. He says they will initially be randomly located and explains that they are only looking to root out the terrorists. He asks that the public please comply with the checkpoints. If anyone is caught with other illegal contraband, they will be permitted to continue through the checkpoint without anything being confiscated. Social media goes crazy over the proposal. People are openly mocking the president. The moment the president signs off, the news anchors and pundits begin to discuss his proposal. Initially, the feedback is in favor of the checkpoints. However, within an hour of his speech, various news sources begin considering the legality of what he has just ordered. There is no strong conclusion. However, most suspect this is not legal.

Technically, the president is asking the governors to order the roadblocks and work with his team to identify specific locations and work out the logistics. Subsequently, the governors do not feel they are legally authorized to order roadblocks. Questions abound around letting people through checkpoints with illegal contraband, such as cocaine and stolen weapons. They see how this can work, but someone asks how the police should react if they find a dead body in someone's car. What if they stop people engaged in human trafficking? Are they really expecting the police or National Guard to just turn a blind eye? The president's plan is quickly turned into a joke and viewed as totally ridiculous. Needless to say, the president has put his fate in the hands of the governors. Many respond immediately and others drag their feet while they confer with their staff. The ACLU files a lawsuit stating the president has no legal basis for what he is doing and that the searches will violate people's fourth amendment rights.

Within two hours, just 40 miles north of Washington, D.C., the governor of Maryland hastily sets up multiple roadblocks along several highways. Police set up a roadblock along Highway 270, just north of Rockville. The highway backs up quickly and officers are trying to get people through the roadblock as quickly as possible. The line of cars is slowly moving forward. The terrorists are about to be stopped and questioned at this unexpected roadblock. They are heading towards East Liverpool, West Virginia, where they are scheduled to carry out the Day 69 attack. The officers are doing a quick visual inspection of each car and asking the driver a quick question or two. This is more of a psychological screening. They are looking for anyone who seems nervous or jumpy for no apparent reason. Two men are fifth in line, then fourth…

"Do you think we'll get inspected?" asks the passenger, whispering and refusing to look at the driver.

Several cars are quickly waved through and then suddenly a car in the left lane is signaled to pull over to the shoulder. A couple cars are on the shoulder of the road. People are asked to pop their hoods and trunks for a quick inspection. Everyone who is pulled over is back on the road within 30 seconds.

"Shut up and just stay cool," says the driver.

They are suddenly at the head of the line. The officer twirls his finger to indicate the driver should roll down his window.

"Good afternoon sir. How are you today?"
"Um, I'm fine. Thanks." His friend continues to awkwardly stare forward.
The officer bends down to get a closer look at the passenger. "How are you today?"

"Fine," the man says quickly and jerks his head towards the front window again. This is exactly the sort of behavior they are looking for.

"Sir, I'm going to need you to pull over to the side."

"Is there a problem officer?"

"No, just standard protocol. Please pull over."

The passenger starts to squirm in his seat. His hand slips off the edge of his seat while he is adjusting. The officer quickly lifts his hand and places it on his revolver. The men look at each other.

"Sir, I need you to put your hands where I can see them." The officer lifts his arm and that draws the attention of other officers who were moments ago casually standing by. "Sir, please pull over now, behind that car."

They comply and the officers walk next to the car as it slowly moves forward. "Please turn off the car, pop your hood, and get out. Put your keys on the hood of the car and step to the front of your car. The passenger is now extremely jumpy, fumbling to open the door. The officers are on high alert. The two men are patted down when they reach the front of the car. Nothing. One officer lifts the hood to find nothing out of the ordinary. The first officer takes the keys and walks towards the trunk.

"No, no, no," whispers the passenger to his friend.

"Shut up!" he replies with a whispered intensity.

The passenger starts to fidget which makes the officers nervous. The officer reaches over and turns the key. The passenger is now nervously bouncing up and down.

"We are so screwed!" said again in a whispered voice.

The officer opens the trunk and his initial shock turns to relief. The trunk is full of marijuana. The officer breaks the tension stepping to the side.

"OK, everyone relax, it's just a little reefer." Turning to another officer, "Steve, help me get all this out."

Suddenly the driver speaks up. "Hey, we get to keep it! I heard we get to keep it. We're not terrorists!"

In the meantime, four cars later, the three terrorists, acting jovial and relaxed calmly answer the officer's questions and are waved on. They had nothing to worry about, their car is clean. They hid the pipe bombs they are about to use eight weeks ago. They are located in an electric utility box located on the backside of an abandoned store along a country road two miles from where they plan to attack. The terrorists anticipated roadblocks and couldn't afford to get caught with anything incriminating. The country is littered with secret stashes of vehicles, drones, fertilizer, and explosives, all planted before Day 20.

The Governor of New Mexico is also on the forefront of deploying police and troops to perform random inspections. There are thirty-four inspection sites by the next morning. At just after 10 o'clock a shootout begins on a rural highway leading into Albuquerque. One officer and three drug smugglers are killed. Two National Guard troops are also injured during the shootout. The smugglers were driving a large white truck carrying 200 pounds of cocaine and a half-ton of marijuana. The smugglers either didn't hear the president or didn't believe they would get a free pass on the drugs. The president is briefed an hour later. The drug dealers came around a bend in the highway and were caught off guard by the police roadblock. They attempted to turn around and began firing as police approached the truck. The president's initial thought is *heaven help us*! By the end of the day, another dozen incidents have already occurred resulting in three additional deaths.

Day 68

Reardon is sitting at home enjoying a weekend ball game. He hasn't moved from the sofa for over an hour. He wants another beer, but he is simply too comfortable to get up. The tide has changed, however, because his need to go to the bathroom now overrides his comfort. After returning from the bathroom, he grabs a tall glass, two cold beers, and a bottle of whiskey. He pours a beer into the glass and tops it off with whiskey. The Yankees are playing the Red Sox on a windy day up in Boston. They have just started the fifth inning when the game is interrupted with a breaking news story. A person he has never seen before suddenly comes onto the screen.

Hello, I'm Jose Sanchez and I'm coming to you with breaking news from Milwaukee, Wisconsin. Approximately twenty-five minutes ago, a bomb detonated over the Milwaukee Brewer's stadium. The game was in the top of the third inning when a drone flew in over the pitcher's mound at an altitude of about 100 feet and exploded. The sound was deafening.

The TV cuts to the game as a cameraman starts to focus on the drone. It hovers for a few seconds, and then a concussive boom accompanies a brilliant flash of light. Players on the infield are nearly knocked down by the force of the explosion

> The explosion was completely unexpected and started a stampede. Initial reports indicate hundreds of people were injured as they were pushed down and stepped on as people were attempting to evacuate as quickly as possible fearing additional bombs. The stadium announcer attempted to instill order, however it was too late, as pandemonium instantly ensued. We will provide additional updates as they come in. We will now return you to your normally scheduled program.

The TV cuts back to the game in Boston, and the field is clear. People are leaving the stadium. The announcer is telling everyone that the commissioner of baseball has ordered the immediate suspension of all games. A total of 12 games in progress have been stopped, and three others planned for the evening will also be postponed to a future date. Reardon is stymied by the news. This is getting so bizarre and out of control. It is clear the attackers did their homework well and planned out everything to the letter.

Reardon is quietly sitting, staring at the screen as the newscaster discusses how this is unprecedented. Nothing like this has ever happened in the history of baseball. The closest equivalent is when all NFL games were cancelled the Sunday after 9/11. Reardon hears his phone ping and reaches for it. A short simple message is displayed from an unknown number.

> "Hint: lines and planes for the next five days."
> Reardon quickly replies, "What does that mean?"

That is the end of the conversation. No one ever replies. Twenty minutes later, Peterson sends Reardon a text:
"Traced it – no luck – informed McCullum."

Reardon doesn't bother doing anything other than finishing his second beer topped off with more whiskey. He wiles away the afternoon in a drunken haze. He finally orders some Chinese food so he can add to his collection of soy sauce stained boxes strewn about his apartment. In the meantime, McCullum and Peterson are putting out a nationwide alert. Airports descend into near anarchy over the next few days. The TSA pulls in every available screener to ensure nothing slips past. The lines balloon at every airport. Waiting lines are pushing three to four hours at every large airport.

Police are closely monitoring every car picking up or dropping off people. There are hundreds of police officers scanning the skies around airports looking for drones. They are armed with shotguns and ordered to shoot down any drones. The tension is palpable around every airport – near anarchy would be a better description. Fearing the worst, thousands of people are cancelling their flights every hour.

Foreign countries are re-issuing travel advisories for any travel to the U.S., and many foreign carriers are simply cancelling flights outright. In two days alone, over 2000 foreign flights are cancelled. The team couldn't decide if the hints made things better or worse. There was something to the old saying *ignorance is bliss*. It's like knowing a big asteroid is going to hit the earth in a week and destroy all life. If there's nothing you can do about it, do you really want to know? Having the hints means there is something they can do, something they *should* do. But the clues do not really lead them to a solution; all they really do is cause panic. The hint about planes was almost worse than the actual attacks because *everyone* feels vulnerable, whether you plan to fly or not, because you might know someone who is flying. There is almost a perverse feeling after an attack. It happened. Now you know for sure if you are a victim or not. In cities around the country, people feel almost a perverse relief after their city is attacked because it feels like *our turn is over*, but who's next? The relief a city feels after a mild attack is almost palpable while perverse at the same time. No one wants an attack, but it is now so routine that it almost feels inevitable at this point in time. The terrorists can now instill fear with a single text if we take the bait and react. But then again, how can we not take the bait if it means we might save even a single life?

January 23, 2012 – New York

It has been two weeks since Reardon's wife and beautiful young girl died. Reardon, through some miracle, makes it into the office and arrives at Dr. Miller's office on time for his appointment. It is 10 in the morning and he is already drunk. He walks into the waiting room and immediately walks into Dr. Miller's office. She is initially surprised by the intrusion but quickly notices he is staggering slightly and slurring his words. He appears to be wearing his clothes from the night before. Either that or he crumpled up his suit and used it as a pillow. She stands immediately.

"Sorry to barge in Doc. I didn't want to be late."
"It's perfectly fine, please come in and sit down."

Reardon immediately staggers over to the sofa and sits down. This is not the first time an agent has come into her office drunk.

"Noah, are you all right?"
"No, I'm not alright! How could anything be all right? Everyone I love is dead!"
"How much have you had to drink?"
"About this much…" as Reardon extends his arms wide.
"Do you want to talk right now or just lie down?"
"I'm here Doc, sorry, Liz, let's talk."
"OK, go ahead."

Suddenly, Reardon starts sobbing uncontrollably. For the next 25 minutes he talks about all the innocent lives that were lost as a result of his actions. He can see their faces in his dreams. They speak to him. He talks about watching the two little girls get blown to oblivion while he watched. He discusses how he should be dead, how he should have been in the hooch with his friends and died with them. His wife and little girl dying is his punishment. Dr. Miller explains how none of that is his fault, how he was doing his job. His wife and girl dying are a horrible tragedy but not a punishment. He just couldn't shake the idea that this is his punishment. On one hand, this was a breakthrough. He opened up to her. But it was not what Dr. Miller was looking for. She finds these types of emotional releases usually set people back and allow too much to come flowing out at one time. However, once it happens, she deals with it.

This was the last time Reardon visited Dr. Miller for over four months. He simply can't deal with the idea of discussing his family's death ever again. This was the moment when his career, and more importantly his life, began to spiral out of control. Within weeks, he was removed from the counter terrorism unit and put on stakeout jobs for low-level mafia. Spencer had to call in every favor she had collected over the last five years to keep Reardon working in the office. The combination of her efforts, his promise to keep his drinking in check, and his outstanding service record keep him on the job. His drinking had become the new norm. He morphed from the brilliant agent who recruited her all those years ago into a functioning alcoholic living on the edge of collapse. Spencer initially kept a close eye on him. Within a few weeks, he was able to put up a good façade that tricked Spencer into thinking things were getting better. The reality was that he was getting better at covering for himself. As time went on, they drifted apart. Spencer was always there, but she was simply too busy to babysit Reardon in any meaningful way. He appreciated her efforts but wanted her to let him go. Dr. Miller finally reached out to Reardon after four months had passed, and he agreed to start seeing her again.

Washington, D.C.

All the governors have complied with the president's request for roadblocks to some degree. In some states, there are hundreds of roadblocks all over the state. Some are in remote rural areas and others lead into big cities. One thing is perfectly clear, there are simply not enough National Guard troops and police to effectively set up enough roadblocks everywhere. In many locations, the checks are only performed from sun up to sun down. In other places, the inspections are random. Some governors set up a few token roadblocks to show they are trying something. Nearly all governors state the inspections are voluntary; most citizens comply. Even then, there are some hotly worded debates at the roadblocks. No one has died at a roadblock since the initial day, but tensions run high. Not what the president was expecting. The other unintended consequence is that militia groups are now starting to set up their own roadblocks in isolated areas – this is quickly spiraling out of control. Many fear this is the first stage of a government takeover. Some conspiracy nuts even believe the government is behind the reign of terror as a ruse to justify their actions. Police attempt to shut down these private roadblocks. Gun fights break out with several militia groups. Two officers and three militia members are killed in Michigan's Upper Peninsula. The other gun fights end quickly with several wounded, and the militias quickly withdraw back into their compounds. After three days, the president considers removing all roadblocks because they are not helping and to assuage fears of a government takeover. Traffic has become a nightmare, and they have not caught a single terrorist. Many of his staff who argued against the roadblocks now argue against removing them, fearing it will make the President look weak. He can't win. Damned if he does, and damned if he doesn't. Two days later, the president retracts his order and asks to remove all roadblocks.

Day 73

After five days of frantic screening and searching the first actual airplane attack occurs. All airports have been in complete disarray since the hint was passed out to local and federal authorities. All airports were braced for an attack. However, the attack was not what they were expecting. The Day 71 attack was at aviation museums. They blew up old planes on display outside museums. The museums were located in Arizona, Delaware, North Dakota, Rhode Island, and Utah. The attacks on Day 69 and 70 involved telephone lines and gas lines in remote areas. The Day 72 attack involved four theaters in Tennessee, New Mexico, New Hampshire, and Oregon at 11 p.m. local time. The team is just getting the morning news as they all sit around the conference room table. Spencer, Reardon, and Peterson are waiting for McCullum at just after 10:00. McCullum wants to have another group discussion to see if they have come up with anything else for the hints *lines and planes*. Peterson just got in the reports on the theaters about thirty minutes ago. Spencer, Reardon, and Peterson were surprised they did not get a new hint since they switched from lines and planes to theaters.

"Were these movie theaters?" Spencer asks.
"No, all live performance," Peterson replies.

McCullum walks in after a two-hour meeting with the director. McCullum just got chewed out because his team has not been providing any more information leading to the disruption of the terrorist's plans. He tries to explain the only reason they disrupted the attacks is because they wanted us to find the bombs for Day 62 and 63. The director did not care.

"Still no attacks for Day 72?" McCullum asks.
"Actually, we just got a report. There were four attacks on theaters," Peterson quickly corrects.
"Criminy! Now we can't even go to the movies."
"Live performance actually, not movie theaters."
"Oh, OK. Did we get a new hint?"
"No," Reardon responds. "Nothing new."
"OK, with this switch to theaters, can we turn down the hysteria we created at the airports?"
"That seems like a reasonable assumption at this point in time," Spencer adds. "They didn't do anything that affected the airports besides create another level of panic."
McCullum walks to the window and then says in a disgusted tone, "They're taunting us with every text. They know we can't trace'em. It's like trying to wrap our arms around the fog."

With this sudden switch to theaters, McCullum's meeting now seems meaningless. They are back to grasping at straws without a clue. An agent walks into the conference room telling him the director would like to speak to him. McCullum immediately goes to his office for the call. Spencer flips on the TV to catch the end of the news. They are just covering what has happened over the last several days. Peterson continues to click away on his computer as Reardon turns his attention to the TV. After a few minutes, the news anchors sign off. A daily game show comes on to fill the day after a quick commercial break trying to sell our kids more delicious candy.

"This is really pissing me off," Spencer comments as Reardon suddenly turns his head. "Why no clue this time?"

"Don't know. It is certainly keeping us off guard. We're screwed when we have a clue because it creates chaos and screwed when we don't because everything is a target."

"They certainly screwed with us in the airports. Have you seen the lines at the airports on the news?"

"Yeah, it's a nightmare. They said lines at JFK were over four hours yesterday. In Atlanta, nearly 20% of people missed their flights because they couldn't get through security, even though they warned people to get there three hours early. People were missing flights all over the country."

"Yeah, I saw there was a mass brawl at LAX. Forty people got into a fight after some pushing. The police arrested 27 people."

The game show is suddenly interrupted, and the sudden change of pace draws all their attention to the TV. James Newburgh's face is ashen.

We have just received reports from Louisville, Kentucky, and Memphis, Tennessee. Highway overpasses along Interstate Highway 69 and Highway 841 in Louisville have just been destroyed by suicide bombers. These explosions disrupt traffic into and out of the UPS hub at Louisville International Airport. There were three additional explosions outside the FedEx processing center near the airport in Memphis, Tennessee. Emergency crews are at the scene looking for any victims. We will return you to your normal programming and return again when we have additional information.

The game show returns.

"Holy cow! What's that mean? Are the airports shut down?" Spencer asks.

Peterson is immediately typing away on his computer looking up information on the airports. Ten minutes later, McCullum comes swooping into the conference room.

"Peterson, what does this mean?"

Peterson looks up and starts to explain. "Worldport is located in Louisville. It's the largest hub in the world for UPS. It can handle up to

416,000 packages per hour. 130 aircraft fly in and out every day. It's one of the largest buildings in the world. The outside of the building is 7.2 miles long."

"Is the building damaged?" McCullum interrupts.

"No, just the highways."

"Then what the hell's the point?"

Reardon asks, "How many people work there?"

"About 20,000 work for UPS in the Louisville area. I can't find how many work in the building."

"OK, let's say half work there. 10,000 people who can't get to work," Reardon adds.

Peterson quickly brings up an aerial view of the airport. "Yes, wow! The main entrance for the airport to the north is unaffected. But the employee entrance to the south is now nearly completely blocked off. The entrances to the Ford assembly plant are now also cut off. They just shut down UPS and Ford."

"How about Memphis?" McCullum asks.

Peterson now zooms in to look at the overpasses destroyed near the FedEx facility. "Same thing. This is their largest processing facility, handling about 1.5 million packages and 140 flights per day. They have about 7000 employees at that facility." Peterson zooms out to see an aerial view of the entire airport.

"Why go after these?" Spencer asks.

Silence hangs in the air.

Reardon's head hangs low and he mumbles to himself, "Holy cow, they just crippled the internet."

"What?" Spencer asks.

"Simple," Reardon replies as his head snaps up, "six car bombs just shut down any company on the internet that ships packages. They just shutdown Amazon, eBay, Zappos, you name it. They can't ship packages. This is far more devastating then what they did with the overpasses by all the airports. The packages are going to start piling up all over the country."

McCullum turns to Peterson. "How many packages going through these places are from internet orders?"

Peterson clicks around for about a minute as they quietly watch him typing along. "According to UPS, about 45% of their packages are internet orders. In fact, a lot of companies located near Worldport just so they could get their shipments out faster."

"Un-frickin-believable!" McCullum adds.

McCullum walks from the conference room. Peterson is continuing to type along on his computer.

Spencer is pacing and pauses by the window. "I don't get it."

"Don't get what?" Reardon asks.

"Why were they attacking lines and planes for three days, then switch to theaters, and back to planes today? They said the hint was for five days. Why didn't they attack UPS, FedEx, and then give us a hint about the theaters?"

Reardon leans back and thinks for a moment while staring at the ceiling. "Why live theaters. There must be something special about why they chose them."

"It's probably just as random as anything else they choose."

"Lines, lines, … wait! Actors deliver lines. You only get that at live theater."

"That's a stretch."

"A hint's a hint. They aren't giving us a detailed plan for each attack. Look at Ford too."

"Why Ford?"

"They shut down the Ford assembly *line*. Blowing the overpasses gets them lines and planes at the same time in Louisville. This must have been what they were building up to. The theaters were just another clever ploy to throw us off guard."

"All the clues have been accurate up to this point." Peterson suddenly interjects.

"Yeah but…" Spencer suddenly stops talking realizing she has nothing insightful to say.

Two hours later, they are eating lunch in the conference room. The TV station has continued its normal daytime programming for most of the morning. At one o'clock, the afternoon news comes on with an update.

Hello, I'm James Newburgh. We want to provide you with the latest update on the attacks near the UPS and FedEx sorting facilities in Louisville and Memphis. Authorities have confirmed 8 people died in the explosions near the UPS facility, with 14 injured. There were 12 people killed and an additional 9 injured near the FedEx facility. Authorities have confirmed that these six brazen daytime attacks were all committed by suicide bombers. Both facilities run nearly continuously. The current daytime workers at UPS, Ford, and FedEx have been informed of the situation. Nearly 20,000 workers at the three facilities are impacted by the explosions. Workers will need to use side roads when leaving work and will encounter horrendous traffic backups as they enter the highways. Commuters are already encountering huge delays on all the highways near each airport. The mayor of each city has declared a state of emergency. The governors have issued orders to deploy National Guard units to guard overpasses and bridges around Louisville and Memphis. The TSA is on high alert and fears another round of attacks similar to those on Day 30 when overpasses near eleven major airports were destroyed. UPS and FedEx are already attempting to figure out the best way to get employees in and out of the buildings. Experts are already predicting that they will need to shut down the facilities for the night and redirect all incoming flights because they will not be able to get enough workers in the buildings to operate properly. If they close the buildings, this will have a ripple effect around the world. These two facilities handle over 3 million packages a day from over 220 countries. Nearly 1.4 million packages are internet orders. This will have a crippling impact on Amazon, eBay, and other large internet companies until these facilities are operating at full capacity.

Spencer mutes the TV and turns to Peterson.

"Do you think they will need to close the buildings?" Spencer says to Peterson.

"Yeah, I don't see how they will have a choice." Peterson shows a highway map of Louisville on the monitor. It's all red. "The roads are all backed up in nearly all directions." He then flips to a map of Memphis. "By the time everyone leaves work later today, it will be a bigger mess. Anyone trying to get to work later today will be stuck in traffic for hours. There are only a few small side roads people can take to get into UPS and FedEx. They depend on the highways. It will be next to impossible to get people in at all, much less on time."

McCullum walks back into the conference room. "What have we learned?"

Spencer provides McCullum with a recap of how Reardon figured out the lines and planes hints explaining how all the attacks fit the hints. McCullum is not amused but is happy that Reardon is engaged. Peterson then explains some of the ramifications he would expect to kick in over the next few days. UPS and FedEx took weeks to recover after the Day 30 attacks because so many of their cargo flights were delayed or cancelled. But they were able to adapt. This attack is a knife to the heart. There is no way to adapt. Each company has invested billions in these sorting facilities, and without them, they simply can't function effectively. They will figure out something, but it will be a nightmare like no other. Each company has a couple dozen flights expecting to land within the next four hours. Each plane will need to be manually unloaded and the packages removed from the packing crates. Each 747 carries 258,000 pounds of cargo. At the UPS facility, packages are unloaded onto 155 miles of conveyor belts that sort them so they can be loaded onto a truck or the next plane. It's an amazing site to behold, however without workers to load and unload the planes, it is all for naught.

"It will likely take about a week to put up temporary overpasses and a few weeks to return to normal. In the meantime, it will be a complete mess. The impact on the economy will be immeasurable. Our economy now revolves around all these packages being sent and received every day. This is crippling."

"Dammit! Why didn't we see this coming? I am getting tired of asking that question. We don't see it even when they give us a hint." McCullum turns to stare out the window. "They've had us pissing around at the airports checking and rechecking every bag twice. In the meantime, they are blowing up power lines, old planes, and theaters. Now it's more overpasses and shutting down a couple sorting facilities. I never thought I would give a damn about a couple buildings that sort mail."

Everyone just sits quietly as McCullum turns and stares at them. Everyone is speechless.

Over the next several days packages start to pile up by the millions. Amazon and eBay remove estimated delivery dates from their websites. Orders backup at Zappos, Dell, and all other online retailers. The post offices become inundated. The demand for shipping does not decline. Lines at post offices circle the block in some locations as tempers flare. The Postal Service is simply not equipped to handle an extra couple million packages per day.

May 3, 2012 – New York

Reardon is sitting at his desk collecting a few sheets of paper and tucking them into a drawer.

"So, when were you going to tell me?"
Reardon is jarred by Spencer's sudden appearance. "Huh?"
"When were you going to tell me?"
"Tell you what?"
"That you finally requested some time off." This was an uneasy conversation for Spencer. She has been trying to remain upbeat whenever

she sees him. But, the dull look of pain behind Reardon's eyes is still as raw as the day after his wife and girl died nearly four months ago. "McCullum mentioned you are going to Europe. That's great."

Reardon's voice is expressionless. "Yeah, I'm going to Greece. I figure seeing the cradle of humanity might do me some good."

From the day after his family died, McCullum tried to get him to take some time off, but he said he had nowhere else to go. McCullum was relieved and surprised when he asked for some time off. He didn't care what changed his mind since he just wanted to see Reardon get out of the office for a while.

"When do you leave?"
"In about two weeks."
Spencer finds herself standing there awkwardly. A feeling she never used to have before he left for Afghanistan. She misses the instant connection they had all those years ago. That great sense of him being the older brother she never had growing up. "Well, OK, I'm sure I'll see you before you go." She misses their close comradery.
"Yeah, OK."

Reardon just looks down listless and exhausted. Spencer walks away and hopes he will be a changed man when he returns.

She discovers the trip did change him, but for the worse. Spencer is shocked to find out Reardon's drinking problem has escalated. She figures going overseas must have caused a rush of emotion to bring back all his bad memories. She tries to talk to him about it, but gets nowhere. She decides to start covering for his drinking wherever possible and helping out when she can. Reardon doesn't need any help and closes her out whenever she tries to get close. They remain cordial and talk from time to time but nothing like the good old days. Reardon is a humorless and broken man.

Day 77

Dow Jones Industrial Average
8,569.51
Total decline: 57.5%
Total loss: $2.98 Trillion

Nasdaq
2,314.24
Total decline: 59.3%
Total loss: $5.03 Trillion

McCullum is sitting in the conference room with his usual suspects. Peterson is typing busily away on his computer as Spencer and Reardon watch the noontime news.

UPS and FedEx continue to struggle because employees are still having trouble getting into their sorting facilities. Packages are backing up at an incredible rate. UPS has ordered all UPS stores to simply hold packages onsite while they try to drain down the backlog at the sorting center. FedEx continues to experience the same difficulties. They have started to bus in employees from remote parking locations to reduce traffic congestion. UPS and FedEx are each running at about 40% capacity.

The UPS and FedEx facilities aren't designed to run at 40% capacity with less than half of the employees being able to get in on time. The facilities, which teeter on the edge of chaos under normal circumstances, are now a madhouse. Packages that used to take hours to sort now sit for days in some situations. Planes sit for hours waiting to get unloaded. UPS and FedEx order all their stores to stop accepting packages at close-of-business. Each company is hemorrhaging money, and millions of packages are now delayed. Amazon, Zappos, Dell, and many other online retailers suspend orders in many cases while they attempt to deal with their inability to ship their products. This costs each company millions per day. Six destroyed overpasses outside two sorting facilities have pushed the economy a little closer to the brink of collapse. The newscaster continues.

The gas stations blown up in remote locations on Day 74 are a complete loss, and police have no suspects. The eight grain silos damaged throughout the Midwest on Day 75 are still closed for repairs. The Day 76 attacks on six high voltage transmission lines out west have also cut off electricity to large sections of several states. These powerlines had been under close observation for over three weeks. Police now suspect that the explosive devices were buried near the base up to several months ago. Hidden explosive devices have become standard operating procedure for the terrorists. State and local officials are now proactively searching more and more locations. The problem is that there are nearly an infinite number of places to search and not enough trained personnel to search for explosives. Authorities want to emphasize that civilians should not under any circumstances look for explosive devices. If they do encounter anything resembling a bomb, they should immediately evacuate the area and call 911.

The warnings do not work. Wannabe heroes start looking in every nook and cranny hoping to find a bomb so they can report it to authorities. 911 gets flooded with calls. Most supposed bombs turn out to be trash or old oil cans. People start digging holes around nearly everything that could be a target in their mind. Cities put out emergency warnings to simply stop digging. Several people across the country nearly die after electrocuting themselves when digging around electric utility boxes. Others start removing manhole covers hoping to find more bombs beneath large cities. Two people suffocate to death in a sewer when entering a pocket of methane gas. City officials are at a loss as to what to do next. Guarding every manhole cover is simply not a priority, but dealing with idiots is becoming an increasing concern.

McCullum walks into the conference room visibly agitated and stops next to the window for a few moments before turning to face the table. He just got done watching the news covering the attacks on roadside attractions across the country.

"We have guards at every stinking thing you can imagine. Does that work? No, so now they burn a big ball of twine! What are they up to? It's almost like they want to lull us into a sense of complacency with a big ball of twine and Barney the dinosaur after taking out UPS and FedEx," McCullum says while fuming.

"Two balls of twine actually," Peterson interrupts.

"Huh?"

"They burned the *two* Largest Balls of Twine. One's in Kansas and the other one's in Minnesota."

"What the hell does that mean? How can you have two largest balls?"

"Turns out it's more complicated than you might think."

"What the hell is so complicated about it? You're either the biggest ball or you're not. Oh my God, why am I even talking about this? Fine, the two biggest balls," emphasizing the *s* in particular, as he continues ranting, "and Barney the dinosaur." He pauses for a moment trying to think of the next attraction. "What other attractions did they blow up today?"

"Ah...", Peterson quickly picks up a sheet of paper. "The World's Largest Beagle in Idaho, Carhenge in Nebraska..."

"What the hell is Carhenge?"

"It's like Stonehenge but with cars."

McCullum is shaking his head in disbelief, "Go on..."

"The World's Largest Basket in Ohio. The World's Largest Wind Chime in Illinois. The World's Largest Fork in Missouri. And Foamhenge in Virginia."

"Let me guess, like Stonehenge but with foam?" Spencer interjects before McCullum has a chance to react.

Washington, D.C.

The stock markets are in free fall again four days after the attacks on FedEx and UPS. Big drops every single day and the markets closing early every single day. The markets were open for 12 minutes today on the east coast, and the rest of the markets never opened. Every single company that ships packages is impacted. In other words, every company that is part of the modern world. The inundation of packages into U.S. post offices is unrelenting. The postmaster general orders the Post Offices to stop accepting packages until they can deal with the flood from the last four days. The president's cabinet and staff are simply speechless. He held a three-hour meeting today with his cabinet and dismissed them after 20 minutes because everyone was listless. He would have gotten a better response from a dozen post-op patients just waking up from surgery. A comment from any of them coming out of their hazy stupor would have been more insightful than anything he heard from his cabinet today.

November 15, 2010 – Afghanistan

Reardon and Abdul are driving back from a meeting with another informant. The informant gave them a heads up that an insurgent is returning from Pakistan in just a few days. They were pursuing this insurgent closely up to about six months ago when he just disappeared. They figured he was either killed or escaped into Pakistan. Now they know. U.S. officials have been frustrated with Pakistan over the last few years because they are reluctant to bend to our will and blindly pursue insurgents escaping into Pakistan. We are on a diplomatic tightrope. Publicly we want a strong independent and democratic Pakistan, and privately we want a puppet nation that will blindly support us. An additional sticking point is U.S. special forces operating within Pakistani borders. Officially, the U.S. has stopped these unauthorized incursions so the Pakistani government can show its resolve and maintain support among its people. The U.S. agrees this is also important for the stability of the region. In the meantime, special forces ratchet back its presence but continue to secretly operate across the border, and the Pakistani government officially looks the other way. The most famous incursion into Pakistan is in its planning stages and is kept completely secret from Pakistani officials. The suspected hideout of Osama bin Laden in Abbottabad, Pakistan, is currently under 24-hour surveillance.

Six months from now, SEAL Team Six quietly crosses the border and kills bin Laden.

Abdul and Reardon have been spending a lot of time discussing world history since World War I and how the Middle East has increased in strategic importance over the last 100 years. Reardon and Abdul would use their evenings to read up on this and discuss it during their long days. It simply gave them something to do with their evenings. They learned the tipping point came when Churchill ordered the conversion of the British fleet to diesel. After that, all western powers became obsessed with the Middle East and feverishly spread out after World War II to combat communism at every turn. The British, French, and Americans increased their presence in Southeast Asia, Africa, and the Middle East as part of a continuous chess match with the Soviets. Human rights atrocities were consistently ignored in the name of democratic ideals. Reardon explained that the U.S. and British would blindly support any horrible psychotic egomaniacal dictator who would align himself with the U.S. and decry the communist scourge while brutally suppressing his own people.

Their conversation floats all over the map before they finally end up discussing the embarrassment of Fidel Castro, and then they move on to discuss human atrocities.

"We really screwed the pooch with Castro. We supported him, helped him get in power, and then, oops, found out he was a commie when it was too late. I guess we forgot to ask," Reardon jokingly states. "We had no vested interest in fighting in Vietnam, Korea, or Central America. It was just the fight against communism. Hell, we would have supported Stalin if he convinced us he was a progressive looking to support democracy around the world."

"I don't understand how this happens."

"Which part?"

"Why you support tyrants."

"I don't really get it either. In reality, the CIA was, and likely still is, simply out of control. I spent a lot of time researching this last night. The worst examples of this were Saddam Hussein in Iraq and Idi Amin in Uganda. We supported the dictators. The best estimates are that Hussein killed up to a half million people and that Amin killed anywhere from 100,000 to 500,000. Each was guilty of torture, ethnic cleansing, and other horrific human rights abuses. *But* they were against communism, so that is ultimately all that mattered. Amin was a prime example of our blind stupidity. We provided Amin with weapons and bombs. The CIA was even helping with military operations. In the meantime, he slowly switched and aligned himself with the Soviets once that was to his advantage."

"You make your CIA sound crazy."

"They might be. Last night I was reading and found out the OSS, CIA, and NSA have all done horrible things. The CIA's MKUltra program conducted illegal experiments on Americans. The CIA brought cocaine into our own country to support the Contras in Central America. Although, we weren't the first to do this. The British used money from opium sales to help control China in the 1800s. The CIA has rigged elections or assassinated democratically elected foreign leaders when it's convenient. The list goes on and on. One of my favorites is Operation Paperclip. In it, we brought Nazis to the U.S. who committed horrible crimes against humanity. Our secret agencies even created fake IDs and bios on people and lied to President Truman so Truman would approve because he said we would not take in any war criminals."

"Why don't Americans stop this?"

"Simple. For the most part, we don't know what they're doing. We find out decades later, and this is just the stuff we know about. We even do stuff to ourselves. In the 1940s and 1950s, we dropped chemical agents over U.S. cities and even Canada to see what would happen. The government exposed people to deadly levels of radiation, experimented on kids and the disabled. In Operation Top Hat, we exposed our own people to nerve agents. That finally came out in 1975. We do horrible things."

"I don't understand America."

"It's really quite easy. Follow the money. It's about greed and serving the self-interests of the rich and the powerful."

"That's very pessimistic."

"I don't think so. Just look at our history. It's not that other countries don't do the exact same thing. It's just that we claim to be this shining beacon of freedom, hope, and democracy. That's simply not true. Don't get me wrong, I love America. It's just that we do a lot of stupid and horrible things in the name of freedom and democracy."

"Well then, why Afghanistan? I understand the Middle East. You want oil. But here our only export is opium, and you don't want that."

"Well now, we think you are also exporting terrorists, and we definitely care about that. Again, money, power, and control. I'm sorry to say Afghanistan has no strategic importance. In the 80s we were just fighting against the Russians. Today we're fighting against the terrorists. The fact that we are doing it in Afghanistan is incidental. We could just as easily be fighting in Iceland or Timbuktu. No natural resources to protect. If the Middle East didn't have oil, it would also likely be ignored."

Day 61 – 80 Attacks

Day	Attack
61	Small road bridges between states bombed, Iowa-Missouri border; Oklahoma-Texas border; Iowa-Nebraska border
62	Two small road bridges between states bombed, Montana-Idaho; New Hampshire-Vermont; one bomb found and deactivated
63	Three bombs discovered under small road bridges and all deactivated
64	Railroad bridges on state lines bombed, Eads Bridge, Missouri-Illinois; Rulo Rail Bridge, Nebraska-Missouri; St. Joseph Swing Bridge, Missouri-Kansas
65	Bridges destroyed, Bloomington Viaduct, Maryland-Virginia; Point Pleasant Rail Bridge, Ohio-West Virginia; Oliver Bridge, Minnesota-Wisconsin
66	Power lines destroyed along county lines, Idaho, Nevada, Illinois, Indiana
67	Power lines destroyed along county lines, Georgia, Florida, Utah, Arizona
68	Explosion over Brewers baseball game, Milwaukee, Wisconsin
69	Telephone poles destroyed with pipe bombs Valentine, Nebraska; New Castle, Wyoming; East Liverpool, West Virginia; Connellsville, Pennsylvania
70	Natural gas lines cut, Franklin, Tennessee; Wichita Falls, Texas; Reno, Nevada
71	Planes destroyed at air museums Pima Air and Space Museum, Tucson AZ Delaware Aviation Museum, Georgetown DE Fargo Air Museum, Fargo ND Quonset Air Museum, New Kingston RI Western Sky Aviation Warbird Museum, St. George UT
72	Theaters destroyed Shakespeare Theatre, Ashland, Oregon Palace Theatre, Manchester, New Hampshire Light Hall Theatre, Silver City, New Mexico Tennessee Theatre, Knoxville Tennessee
73	Overpasses near UPS and FedEx processing centers destroyed: Louisville International Airport

		Memphis Tennessee International Airport

74		15 gas stations destroyed in rural areas
		    Along Interstate Highway 94 – between Fargo and Bismarck, ND
		    Along Interstate Highway 40 – between Flagstaff and Kingman AZ
		    Along Interstate Highway 94 – between Bozeman and Billings, Montana

75		10 doors on grain silos in Nebraska destroyed
76		High voltage powerline towers destroyed near Albany, New York; Tulsa, Oklahoma; Grand Junction, Colorado; Provo Utah. Over 100,000 lose power

77		Roadside attractions
		    Largest balls of twine, Kansas and Minnesota
		    Cabazon Dinosaurs, California
		    Largest Beagle, Idaho
		    Carhenge, Nebraska
		    Largest Basket, Ohio
		    Largest Wind Chime, Illinois
		    Largest Fork, Missouri
		    Foamhenge, Virginia

78		Car bomb destroys furniture factory, Lexington, South Carolina

79		Inflatable domes destroyed by drones with explosives
		    Carrier Dome, Syracuse University, New York
		    Bennett Indoor Athletic Complex, Toms River, New Jersey

80		Drones with explosives blow holes in Santa Barbara convention center first day of ComicCon – convention cancelled

Day 81

Reardon, McCullum, Spencer, and Peterson are in the conference room examining security footage of today's attack. They are all sitting at the table with Peterson displaying his screen on the large TV. They are watching footage of drones flying into ten open air malls in southern cities at 2 p.m. EST. Each drone is carrying a small amount of C-4, and each one detonates after flying into a store. Chaos instantly breaks out as people near the explosions frantically flee and help the injured get out of the stores. Within minutes, the screaming and panic has spread throughout the entire mall as people flood into the parking lots. Only a few people are killed. Dozens are injured. And hundreds are scared to death. They are closely reviewing the security footage and notice something interesting.

"Look at that," Spencer quickly notices something weird.

"What?" Peterson asks while sitting at his computer.

She points at the screen. "There that…"

McCullum leans forward staring at the TV on the wall. "What?"

"Rewind five seconds and then pause just before the explosion." They sit there idly for a few moments as Peterson replays and then pauses. "See that? The drone veers away from the people at the last moment. That's a group of eight people. Why didn't it drop into them and then explode?"

"Maybe the guy turned the wrong way," Peterson responds.

"I don't think so. There were hardly any deaths. I think that was on purpose."

"Why?" McCullum asks. This question keeps coming back to McCullum day after day. Why aren't they killing more people with these attacks? "This is just enough to scare the hell out of a few hundred people. The mall gets evacuated, and the news spreads across the country, scaring more people into staying away from the malls or any public location."

Reardon suddenly leans forward in his chair and stands up. "Like I've said a dozen times. The goal is disruption. They don't have to kill us. In fact, survivors are better."

"How so?" Spencer asks.

"Survivors are much better at spreading fear and panic. The more survivors, the more people to spread the word. Look," he says as he points to the muted TV. "They have been interviewing them all morning. They are planting the seed of doubt into everyone who is listening – maybe not consciously, but it's there. People five states away will now skip a trip to the mall or grocery store out of the *what-if* fear kicking in. People become desensitized to dead bodies, but it's hard to ignore someone screaming and crying in your face. They know exactly what they're doing."

"When did you become an all-knowing psychiatrist? It's like you don't even care about all this."

"I care. I care more than you could possibly know." Reardon's eyes are empty and his voice is cold and unemotional, but he is speaking from the heart. "Seeing this and doing this destroyed my life. I have nothing. This job took everything from me. Look at me. I'm a washed-up alcoholic who can't sleep through the night unless I'm plastered – the only way I can make the nightmares go away. So, don't say I don't care! I've just come to accept the inevitable! I also know there is nothing we can do to stop them. We have no idea what they plan to attack or when. Everything is a target."

McCullum shouts, "Well I'm not taking this lying down!"

Reardon's voice calms, "Well I'm not sure you have a choice."

McCullum slaps his hand on the table as he stands up and turns to face the window.

With a sad and sympathetic tone, Reardon continues. "For heaven's sake," he says while shaking his head and drops his arms. He is distraught. "People now live stream shootings on Facebook. We're not even surprised by this anymore. But a person spreading fear face to face – that makes an impact. They know what they're doing. Technology now drives our lives, and we are numb when we see the carnage. It all started with the Vietnam War. They stopped trying to glamorize war. Vietnam was blood and guts. Cameras changed the way we fight wars. The horror of footage from Vietnam had a huge impact on the American psyche. Fast forward to 1990 and our first invasion of Iraq. It was like watching stuff blow up in a video game. They even said Hussein got more reliable information from CNN than his own generals. How crazy is that? The war made Wolf Blitzer and General Schwarzkopf celebrities. We were fascinated by the smart bombs and bunker busters. We made war cool. Then 9/11 hit, and war got ugly again. Our leaders lied to us about Weapons of Mass Destruction, and we invaded Iraq again. Now we need to deal with IEDs, suicide bombers, and Afghani soldiers turning their guns and killing American soldiers standing right next to them. This is ugly, horrible, and out of control. Look at our country. We spy on our own allies, and they, of course, spy on us. It's the dirty little secret of all the intelligence agencies. Look at Snowden blowing the whistle on the NSA. Look at our government – it's a joke. I remember a Gallup poll from a few months ago, before all this started happening; only 9% of people have confidence in congress. I don't know how many people have confidence in the president, but I bet it's a hell of a lot lower than it was three months ago. I care, there's just nothing I can do about it any more than I can keep congress from being a joke. Congress is completely dysfunctional. They spend more time posturing and fund raising to keep themselves in office than anything else. Anyone willing to talk of compromise is considered a radical and will likely get booted from Congress in the next election. Those are the people we want to keep." Reardon suddenly stands. "You can say a lot of things about me, but don't say I don't give a damn!"

McCullum starts to pace in disgust. He knows Reardon is 100% right because even after 81 days, they still have nothing. Not a single piece of hard evidence.

McCullum turns, "I'm sorry." A rare admission for McCullum. "What you are saying is spot on, but I still can't accept it. We need to find a way. How the hell are we supposed to catch these guys? They have to screw up sometime."

In a calmer voice, Reardon begins to speak. "This is just how I felt in Afghanistan. Helpless. We couldn't do anything to stop the mortar attacks or IEDs. I felt like we were playing whack-a-mole with a hydra. On the days we got lucky, we cut off a head only to discover two new heads popped up a month later. That was the great lie, that we were somehow in control and winning. There is no winning – only *not* losing. These are the lessons we learned back in the Revolutionary War. Fight a guerrilla war and don't lose. We forgot that lesson in Vietnam, and it cost us. The Russians re-learned the lesson in Afghanistan during the 80s, and we're re-learning it now in Iraq and Afghanistan."

Silence hangs in the air. It is suddenly so quiet you can hear people breathing as they soak in the conversation. Reardon is momentarily at peace in this instant of clarity.

In the back of Reardon's mind, while they talk, he is replaying a news report he saw in the morning. They discussed a new phenomenon that has started over the last two weeks. It's no surprise that the number of visits to public locations has dropped off dramatically and that our economy continues to crumble. However, the new oddity is that within an hour of an attack hitting the news, people flood out of their homes to grocery stores, gas stations, and other public places to quickly live their life. Roads and parking lots surge to life for a few brief hours each day. This results from their sense of relief for the day that they are safe. They can quickly get on with life, do what they need to do, and then hunker down at home waiting for tomorrow's attack. In the name of public safety, cities are cancelling parades, festivals, carnivals, concerts, and anything else that draws a crowd. The ripple effect continues with both subtle and devastating results. Others are more pragmatic and simply get on with their life figuring *the hell with it I'm not going to let the bastards win.* Even these people have the *what-if* scenarios running through their head whether they like to admit it or not. In a mere 60 days, a small group of terrorists has gotten into the heads of 330 million people and affected the entire world.

The efforts to track down people in Afghanistan has completely stalled. They found six more people over the last three weeks, and four of them are believed dead. One group conspicuously missing from the list is a group of liaisons that worked closely with the Americans for years. This includes the liaison officers that worked within the American compounds. The agents are suspecting that they were quickly tracked down and murdered after the American withdrawal. McCullum suspects something different and calls Reardon into his office.

"We are having trouble finding most of the people on your list. So far the agents have only found 57 out of the 227 on your list." McCullum leans back in his chair. "What bugs me is that they haven't found any living liaison officers."

"Why does that bother you?" Reardon asks.

"They can't be that good at hiding."

"I bet a lot of them are dead and the rest are in fear of their life. Under those circumstances, I'd be pretty good at hiding too."

"Maybe, but I want to know more about them."

"What do you want to know?"

"How were they recruited?"

"Well, one of the biggest fears we had was basically double agents. So we focused our efforts on two groups. Those with some long-standing ties to the U.S. or unfortunately," Reardon nods his head slightly, "the Taliban killed some or all of their family. In many cases, they found us, and we vetted them."

"So would you say they were all loyal to America?"

"No, loyal is not necessarily the right word. They did all love America, or, more accurately, the idea of America. I'd say they were all unified. Unified in their hatred of the Taliban. That was the consistent thread that ran through our relationships with them. We paid special attention to this and did not really trust anyone who didn't fall into these categories."

"Did you ever suspect dual allegiance or them turning on the U.S.?"

"No, not with the people we worked with. Although, I can't speak for all the liaisons."

"What's your gut tell you about who's doing this? Could the liaisons have turned, and they are the ones conducting these attacks?"

"I can't see them turning against us. What they did was for a love of their country and the hope that the U.S. would make things better. Besides, how would so many people sneak into the U.S. unnoticed?"

"That's just it, we aren't looking for our friends, we've been looking for our enemy."

"Well I can promise you, there is no way they turned on the U.S. They had too much hatred of the Taliban. If any of them are still alive, I bet they are still willing to help the U.S."

McCullum stares at Reardon for a moment while his comments soak in, and then he stands and faces the window for a few moments.

"OK, that's all for now…"

December 21, 2010 – Afghanistan

The mood of the team has taken a distinct turn for the worse. President Obama is getting pressured to pull troops and turn over control to local authorities as soon as possible. This comes at a time when the Taliban is experiencing a resurgence in areas and taking back ground as soon as the allied forces pull back. This show of strength also increases their ability to recruit more fighters and encourages more attacks on U.S. troops. Everyone in camp realizes that this is a losing battle. More and more of their informants are disappearing into the background, blending into villages so they are not immediately killed if their identity as an informant is ever revealed. Everyone at camp is on edge as momentum swings towards the Taliban. They are also coming up on the one year anniversary of the suicide bomber attack at Camp Chapman where seven CIA officers and contractors were killed by a highly trusted informant permitted into the camp without being searched. Ever since that incident, everyone is extremely cautious with informants. Taliban fighters are once again operating within five miles of the camp. An Apache helicopter thwarted an attempted mortar attack two weeks ago, killing a group of fighters as they approached camp. Every meeting with informants is now teeming with stress because they don't know which ones may have turned or are getting blackmailed.

Reardon and his team are getting pressured more and more to get intel that can counteract or deflect the Taliban insurgency. It isn't working. The information from informants is harder to come by and less reliable because they quickly realize that the Taliban has two new tactics. The first is misinformation, and the second is moving more quickly from location to location. Reardon's teams are either going on wild goose chases following the misinformation or arriving a couple days late at Taliban hideouts. Additionally, Reardon can sense that they are running out of time before the camp gets closed. He can sense this because they are starting to ask him weird questions about how many files he has stored on site and about morale. In his three years, they have never asked about morale. In the meantime, Reardon wants to finish with a few more wins. Abdul and Reardon received information that Mohammad Ismir was staying in a hut about one mile outside a small village just a three hour drive from their base. The informant was the eldest son of a tribal leader. While the son hates the presence of the Americans, he has come to loathe the Taliban more deeply since the death of his youngest brother at the hands of the Taliban in an ambush two months earlier. Ismir is a lieutenant of the Taliban leader and moved into the area to begin recruiting and killing those he is unable to convince. High-altitude planes have been surveying the area for four days and have been unable to identify the target despite the ongoing activity in the area. The person believed to be Ismir has been doing a good job of staying under cover, going to the point of even using an umbrella when moving in the open. They are to the point of needing a visual before calling in an airstrike. Abdul and Reardon have climbed all morning and taken a position on a high bluff to oversee the operation. They are overlooking a small farm with a single large hut. They take turns lying on their stomach and sitting behind a small outcropping to hide themselves. A special forces unit is using a long-range camera with facial recognition software and is stationed where they can observe the front entrance. Everyone has been in place since 6 a.m. and patiently waiting. They want to strike Ismir, his men, and the hut all at one time to knock out another hiding place.

"Team lead, we have movement," states the commander of the special ops unit.

"Please specify," Reardon asks.

"The front door has just opened and someone has stepped out for a smoke."

They are both now anxiously lying on their stomachs. Reardon and Abdul can't see this because the person is under the awning, and they are too high up.

"Can you ID?"

"ID in progress. Hold." A few moments pass. "ID confirmed, Mohammad Ismir."

"Roger. Initiate airstrike. Confirm." Reardon commands.

"Confirmed. Calling it in now."

Two fighter jets have been continually circling at 20,000 feet since 6 a.m. and get the call.

"Team lead. The package is on its way. Two minutes out. Over."

With that, Abdul and Reardon pull their binoculars close to their eyes and wait. Four days of patient observation has come to this. The two minutes stretch out into what seems like an hour. Reardon's heart is palpitating and his hands are sweating.

"Missiles away," comes over the com link.

At this point, he knows the missiles are less than 10 seconds away. His heart rate increases. Seven, six, five, ... Just then two small girls come running out from under the awning, and Reardon can't believe his eyes. He reaches to activate his com.

"Abort! Abort!"

It's too late. The missiles smash into the hut, creating a gigantic fireball. Reardon screams and rolls onto his back.

"NOOOOOO!!!! NO!!!!" Reardon stands up and removes his binoculars from around his neck and throws them onto the ground. "Noooo!!!" Tears start to run down his face.

Abdul just continues to stare through his binoculars, transfixed by the fireball. A few moments later, he rolls over to see Reardon in tears as he slumps down. This is his fault. He decided to get greedy and try to make this a trifecta. He could have easily waited for them to drive away from the hut and killed their caravan. But he got greedy. He wanted Ismir, his men, and the hut all in one fell swoop. How did they miss this? They had been watching the hut for four days, and they never saw any sign of children.

"I'm sorry my friend," was all Abdul could say.

Abdul knew the pressure was getting to Reardon. The Taliban has been mounting a relentless and growing resurgence ever since troop levels were dropped in their area. A true test of the theory that nature abhors a vacuum. After hiking down to their vehicle, Abdul drove Reardon back to the camp with their escort following closely. Reardon slowly regained his composure.

"How did we miss that Abdul? We've been watching the hut for four days."
"I don't know. It's unfortunate. However, you did everything you could do."
"No, I didn't. I got greedy. I wanted it all in one strike. We could have raided the hut."
"And risked lives. Why? We did it the right way, just like with all the others."
"We should've done it better…" his voice trails off.

Reardon is simply disgusted with himself. The remainder of the drive is done in silence. Reardon just blankly stares out the side window as mile after mile of dusty barren road passes into memory. Two weeks later, Reardon is informed that he has been awarded the FBI Medal for

Meritorious Achievement. This is really for the culmination of his outstanding work over the last two years. However, the citation officially states this incident as the reason for the award. Earning the award is like a dagger to his heart. The feelings of guilt flooded back as an assistant director pins the medal on his chest during a small ceremony just outside their hooch. There is a round of applause to celebrate this tremendous achievement. Reardon nods in appreciation. Thirty minutes later, Reardon is back in his room, balling, taking in convulsive gasps of breath. This is the worst day of his life – earning an award for killing small children.

May 30, 2012 – New York

Reardon is standing in a long hallway. Reardon paces back and forth in the hall for nearly ten minutes before finally stepping through Dr. Miller's door. It's his first visit to Dr. Miller's office in four months. He sits down and picks up a magazine. Within moments her door opens. Reardon is thinking, "How does she do that?"

"Noah, please come in."
"Thanks Doc, I mean Liz." Reardon walks in and sits down in the chair his head is hanging low. "First of all, I wanted to apologize."
"It's really OK. The worst thing in the world just happened to you. I'm so sorry."
"No, It's not OK. I should apologize."
"OK." She is willing to accept an apology if it will make him feel better.
Reardon lifts his head and looks at her. "I'm sorry."
"I accept your apology. Let's put it behind us and move on. OK?"
"Yeah."
"I won't bother asking you how you're doing. I think we both know the answer to that."
"Yeah, horrible. Big surprise."

Reardon and Dr. Miller spend the next hour discussing how things have been going and spend a considerable amount of time discussing his drinking. Dr. Miller is careful to just listen and not judge. Alcohol and drug problems occur with agents at a much higher rate than most people would suspect. The job is agonizingly stressful on agents. She wishes all agents who had an issue would seek help, but she knows most keep it a secret. Dr. Miller is genuinely concerned for Reardon. It is rare to work with an agent who has been through so much. PTSD *or* the loss of a family member is difficult enough to deal with alone, but both? Dr. Miller is impressed that

Reardon is holding it together as well as he is. They finally get around to discussing his time in Greece.

"Did you find any relief in being away for a while?"

"It was good to get away, but it was not a relief. If anything, being out of the country caused a lot of memories to rush back."

"How so?"

"It's hard to describe. Being back in such a different place reminded me of Afghanistan, I guess."

"How do you feel now that you are home?"

"OK, I guess. I just feel like it triggered a lot of emotions."

Dr. Miller glances up and sees the clock. "Well we are nearly out of time for this week. Would you like to come back next week?"

"That might be too much too soon. Can we do this once a month for a while?"

"I would prefer every week, but once per month is OK until you are more comfortable talking."

"Yeah, once per month."

"OK, then I will see you next month." Dr. Miller stands and walks him to the door. "I hope you start to feel better."

Day 89

Reardon is sitting in the conference room vacantly staring at Spencer's list. He is trying to assimilate the breadth and expanse of the list. It's mind-numbing at this point in time. Anything is a target. Reardon is both shocked and in awe of the planning that went into these attacks. He is dumbstruck by the consistency and by their ability to elude detection. It's mindboggling. Not that they can do it, but that it is so easy and hasn't been done before. A small group of attackers has embarrassed the entire U.S. government and made the intelligence agencies look like they were not only asleep at the wheel, but it is now glaringly obvious that they can't even find their own car.

Day 80 – 89 Attacks

Day	Attack
80	Comicon - Santa Barbara Convention Center, California
	Indianapolis Colts Stadium, Indiana
81	Bombing in 10 open air malls

82	Signs destroyed at the entrances of National Parks
	Hot Springs National Park, Arkansas
	Acadia, Maine
	Cuyahoga Valley, Ohio
	Great Smoky Mountains, North Carolina
	Mammoth Cave, Kentucky
83	Powerlines destroyed leading to Las Vegas, Nevada
84	National Historic Landmarks
	O.K. Corral, Tombstone, Arizona
	Fort Ruby, White Pine County, Nevada
	Kit Carson House, Taos, New Mexico
	Chief Joseph Gravesite, Wallowa, Oregon
	Fort D.A. Russell, Cheyanne, Wyoming
85	Museum entrances destroyed
	Dali Museum, St. Petersburg, Florida
	North Dakota Heritage Center & State Museum
	Art Museum of the University of Memphis, Tennessee
	Ford Museum, Detroit, Michigan
	Beavertail Lighthouse, Jamestown, Rhode Island
86	Indianapolis 500 racetrack section destroyed by car bomb, Indianapolis, Indiana
87	Propane tank exchanges outside 8 gas stations and hardware stores destroyed
88	College building entrances – main building on campus destroyed by drones
	University of Oregon
	University of Vermont
	University of Rhode Island
	University of Oklahoma
89	

Reardon is quietly staring at the last spot on her list – Day 89. Everyone is wondering what Spencer will fill in for today. People stopped wondering if Spencer would need to add another row weeks and weeks ago. She is now so confident that she adds them ten at a time. Tomorrow her list will include rows for Days 90-99. As far as everyone is concerned, there is no end in sight. Everyone's expectations of a quick resolution died at a different point in time. Some knew this would be all over on Day 35 and had that dream quickly destroyed. Others were convinced this would end by Day 50. Everyone's hope was dashed by Day 60. Most agents still put on a good façade, especially McCullum, but Reardon can see it in his eyes. He can see it in everyone's eyes. He saw the look in Afghanistan too many times and can't mistake it for anything else. He looks around the room, and it's plain on the face of every agent at the table. McCullum finally walks into the room; his mere presence is enough to instantly quiesce the room.

"Peterson, anything yet?"
"No, sir."
"OK. So, it's Day 89," McCullum pauses. "Well," he pauses again. "So," another awkward pause. "Peterson, what have we got on the attacks over the last several days?"
"Nothing really. More drones and more explosions. All the security footage has been examined, and we've got nothing. They are still removing debris from the underpass that destroyed a section of the Indianapolis Speedway. They have recovered the body of the suicide bomber, well pieces they believe are the suicide bomber. The group of kids smoking pot outside the hardware store in Somerset, Wisconsin, are all recovering. Luckily, they were on the side away from the propane tanks, but the wall falling on them still did serious damage. Two will be in the ICU for at least a week, but they are expected to make a full recovery. All the museums from Day 85 are…"
Peterson is cut off mid-sentence. "Look!" Spencer suddenly says as she interrupts Peterson. She points to the muted TV.
"Unmute the TV," McCullum quickly adds.

The spinning breaking news logo finally stops, and the camera settles on the mid-morning newscaster who has been filling in more frequently.

Hello, my name is Jeffery Bullock. We have breaking news out of St. Louis. The St. Louis arch has just collapsed. Reports indicate an explosion detonated near the top of the arch. We have no additional details at this moment in time. We will return when we have additional information.

The breaking news ends as quickly as it began. "Peterson, call the St. Louis field office immediately and find out what you can." Peterson bolts up with his computer and immediately leaves the room. Spencer's computer screen is still displaying on the other TV. She immediately googles *St. Louis Arch*, and people are already posting photos of the collapsed arch as it lies in a crumpled heap. The room is instantly crestfallen.

News reports continue to flow in throughout the morning. Peterson is sitting in the conference room along with Spencer and Reardon. They have been idly watching the newscast and eating a lunch that Spencer brought back for both of them. Peterson gets a call on his cell phone, and he lazily answers.

Within ten seconds of taking the call, he is noticeably excited. He puts his phone on speaker and places the phone on the table.

"Get McCullum," Peterson quickly says.

"Why?" Spencer asks.

"One of the burn phones has been activated, and we think we've got something."

"OK," Spencer rushes down to get McCullum, and he returns within twenty seconds.

"What have we got?" Asks McCullum.

The FBI has been patiently monitoring all the numbers on Peterson's list of burn phones. A couple times a week one of the phones is turned on, used, and turned off. Sometimes the phone is used for a quick text and other times a quick call. The FBI closely scrutinizes every call and text message looking for clues. Except for texts that came into Reardon's phone, nearly every call has been boring and mundane. On rare occasion, it is a couple of people negotiating a drug deal. Something with this phone has piqued their interest.

"I think we've got something, Miller. Go ahead," says Peterson.

The voice of agent Miller from Washington, D.C. emanates from the phone. "We've got text messages that might be referring to an attack."

"Be more specific," prompts McCullum.

"I just sent the text messages to Peterson along with the numbers and locations. The text message is from a burn phone near Madison, South Dakota. The message is to another phone in Barre, Vermont. This one isn't on our list. The message says 'there are guards near the equipment so we are going to wait until nightfall'. The reply was 'OK'. The phones were turned off, and we lost the signals."

"OK, thanks. Let us know if you get anything else," says Peterson.

"Will do. Bye."

"Yes! Peterson, tell me about Madison, South Dakota," says McCullum.

Peterson instantly goes to Google. "Let's see..." Peterson is scanning down through the city's Wikipedia page. "Population of about 7000 ... two radio stations ... and they've won a bunch of state gymnastics tournaments. Wow 16 in a row!"

"I don't give a crap about that. What else? They mentioned guards and equipment," McCullum asks.

"Well, that's about it. I will need some time to look into it."

"Spencer, I want you to look into Barre, Vermont. Come and get me as soon as you find something. I'm going to get agents on the way to both of these places."

McCullum leaves the room and makes several quick calls, including a call to the director of the FBI. The director quickly calls the president's chief of staff who informs the president of the situation. McCullum is now coordinating with the FBI in South Dakota and Vermont. The director has made it clear that all information should flow through McCullum. McCullum's heart is racing. He is already trying to figure out the best way to get agents in place without spooking anyone and letting them disappear into the mist. After thirty minutes on the phone, he is impatient and returns to the conference room.

"Peterson, what have you got?"

"Well, I didn't find anything interesting on the web. But I did call the chief of police in Madison, and I think I might have it. I asked him if they have any equipment in town that would be under guard. I didn't explain why I was calling, just that it was important for him to help." Peterson grabs the HDMI cord for the TV on the wall and is suddenly displaying a map. "He then told me about the Dakota pipeline. See that red line? It runs about 15 miles southwest of Madison. You've seen it in the news. They've been having a lot of protests, and they have started guarding the equipment as a precaution. I think this is what they are talking about in the text message."

"Good!"

"It could be anyone of several sites along where they're digging."

"I have agents on the way, and they are contacting the state police. Spencer, what have you got?"

"Nothing much. The metropolitan area has about 60,000 people, just your standard quiet Vermont city from what I can tell. We don't have much to go on. I called the police as well and told them we are trying to track down someone using a burn phone. I didn't give him any other details. The chief asked what we had, and I told him all we know is a single text message was sent from someone at 12:14 near the city square. Again, without a face we haven't got much to go on. I asked him if they have any surveillance cameras on the square, and he said no. He's going to get anything he can from ATM cameras, see if any shop owners have any cameras around the square, and call me back."

"Hmm. That's not much to go on. Keep me informed."

McCullum retires to his office and calls the police chief in Madison. He wants to know the exact location of where all the equipment is stored. After a twenty minute talk with the police chief, he hangs up. The equipment is stored at five different locations along the pipeline. This is a manageable number of sites. His next call is to the director. They speak for fifteen minutes. They discuss two options and can't immediately decide the best course of action. Option one is to immediately set up roadblocks around the city in Vermont and rain down on the city, trying to identify the texter. This could be Reardon's good friend, and if they get him, it could mean an end to the whole thing. However, there are about 60,000 people in the area. How are they supposed to pick out the one person they are looking for? If they choose option one, then the terrorist might be able to get a message to the attackers in South Dakota, and they will just disappear into the night. Option two is to focus on South Dakota. They now know the time and place of an attack ahead of time. If they can catch a group in the act, then they will have the terrorists for sure. Finally, they choose option two, figuring the texter in Vermont headed out of the city within minutes so the trail will run cold. They still plan to collect all video surveillance from the city, so they can hopefully put a face to the main attacker.

It's five o'clock, and the entire focus of top government officials revolves around Madison, South Dakota. There are two drones in the air above Madison, and satellites with infrared cameras are now focused on each equipment storage site. There are several planes circling at a 200 mile radius. The planes contain special ops forces from around the country. There are SEALs, Delta Force, and Rangers all ready to drop down from the sky at a moment's notice. The president is watching from the situation room in the White House. They have no idea when the actual attack will occur, so they plan for a long night. They expect the attack to occur by midnight because it appears that this attack is scheduled for today. Everyone is on edge.

As part of his briefing, McCullum learns that the president authorized drone flights on Day 31 after the jet fuel pipelines in Missouri and Georgia were damaged. There have been at least 150 Predator drones in the air at any one time, nearly the complete arsenal of Predator drones. The problem with the drones is that they do not know what to look for. Once again, it is just too much data. All the images were fed to the Army's central command center for processing. Once there, they were randomly scanned. They found plenty of interesting stuff, but nothing that brought them any closer to catching any terrorists. This is the first time the drones have a specific mission.

McCullum walks into the conference room. Spencer and Peterson are frantically typing away. Reardon is continuing to watch the news coverage.

There is, of course, no news of what is happening in South Dakota. This mission is occurring with the same level of secrecy as when Navy SEALs crossed the Pakistani border heading in to kill bin Laden.

"Peterson, have we got the satellite feed yet?" McCullum asks.

"No, it'll be coming up soon."

"OK, good." McCullum has not mentioned what is going on to anyone else in the office, fearing it will leak out. "Call me when it's up."

McCullum leaves the room to Spencer, Peterson, and Reardon.

"I told you we would get a lucky break," turning to Reardon.

"Yes, this is a good thing." Reardon seems a little caught off guard by her comment. "Let's just hope this works."

The nervousness in the room is now palpable as all three of them anxiously sit and wait. The waiting is the worst part. Spencer looks at her watch.

"Dang, this is going to be a long night. We might be sitting here seven hours before anything happens. But it'll be worth it if we catch these guys."

"Yeah. We should order some dinner in. Just like the good old days. Maybe a few greasy burgers and fries," Reardon says with a subdued look on his face.

"Yeah, that's a great idea. Let me make a call." Spencer is suddenly excited. This might be the spark that helps pull him out of his funk and get him fully engaged in the case. "I'll call Mickey's. You always loved their burgers."

"If I remember correctly, you always hated them."

"I don't even care. I'd eat anything right now."

Spencer makes the call, and 45 minutes later, they are sitting around the table eating. They devour their food.

"Oh my gosh, I didn't know I was that hungry. I forgot these are such a gut bomb. I think I'm going to be sick," adds Spencer.

"Your tolerance has just dropped over the years. These are still as good as ever," Reardon comments.

Reardon looks happier than Spencer has seen him in a long while. Who knew a burger could do so much? Another two hours tick by as they watch the news on one monitor. McCullum has been in and out of the conference rooms several times asking about the status of things. Peterson has the live feeds from the drones and the satellites. So far, nothing. Another hour passes and the sun is finally going down. They have not informed the guards at any of the five sites about what is going on. They don't want anything to appear out of the ordinary. Based on what they have heard, the guards are really just there as window dressing. The guards are even given permission to sleep in their cars overnight. That explains why the terrorists want to wait for nightfall. The guards are just there as a precaution against vandalism as the number of protests against the pipeline is gaining momentum.

Another hour and a half slowly ticks by, and Reardon returns to the conference room. He really wanted a drink, so he slipped into the locker room and downed two beers and a small bottle of whiskey that he keeps in his locker for emergency purposes. He feels better after the drinks, comes into the conference room, careful to eat some food left at the end of the table and makes it a point to stay away from Spencer for a while so she won't smell the alcohol on his breath.

It's just past midnight eastern time. Peterson has connected a speaker to his computer so he can hear the comms. They are expecting the attack by midnight central time, which is now less than an hour. McCullum comes back into the room.

"Anything yet?" Asks McCullum.

"No sir. There is a lot of chatter on the line, but nothing yet," says Peterson. The sound is at a low volume, so really only Peterson can hear it.

"Damn! I hope they didn't do anything to spook them. I told the chief of police to pretend like I never called and to play it cool." McCullum also called off the state police. McCullum paces for a few seconds, and then sits down in his chair and watches the news.

About five minutes pass. Suddenly Peterson hears what he has been waiting for.

"We have movement," comes a voice over Peterson's speaker. "We have a car about a half mile west of the northern-most site. The car just stopped, and three men just got out of the car."

Peterson is now displaying a live infrared satellite image on the second TV in the conference room.

"Drop the Delta and SEAL teams."

Those are the two planes closest to the north site when the call comes in. The planes make quick turns and begin a rapid descent.

"What's the time to drop?" Comes another voice over the speaker.

"Five minutes."

McCullum is now pacing as the five minutes slowly tick away. In the meantime, satellite images show three men heading toward the north site with three backpacks, and two of them are also caring bags. They are moving slowly. The bags must have some weight to them.

"We've got these little pricks. There is no way they're getting out of this alive," McCullum finally says.

There is no one close on the ground. Since they had no idea where the terrorists would come from, they could not chance them seeing anyone preparing for an attack. For all they knew, the terrorists had dinner at the local cafe and would become suspicious if they suddenly saw a bunch of police cars and National Guard standing around. Everything will drop from the sky.

"The SEALs are away. Delta drops in 30 seconds."

The SEALs are dropped just a few hundred yards from the terrorist's car. They will quickly inspect the car, disable it, and then pursue the terrorists. Delta Force drops just a few hundred yards north of the site. There is only a sliver of a moon, so they are dropped unnoticed. The three terrorists continue to slowly approach the vehicles. A minute later, they are on the edge of the site. There are nine vehicles parked at this location. The guard's car is parked a couple hundred yards away along the service road leading up to the site. The car is dark, the guard obviously sleeping. Everyone in the conference room can see the three men fan out. Each man pauses next to a vehicle for a moment. They can see each man fiddling with a bag and then they move to another vehicle. The terrorist's car is empty, and the SEALs are quickly closing the gap. They are now four hundred yards from the edge of the site and stop to take up their position. Delta Force has taken up a position just a hundred yards from the site. They have their guns at the ready and the three men in their cross hairs.

"Alpha group ready," comes the signal from the Delta Force leader. "We have eyes on three."

Fifteen seconds later, "Gold team ready, we are in position."

The soldiers have orders to take them alive, if possible. They will not approach, fearing the terrorists will all kill themselves. Their orders are to let them plant all the explosives and capture them as they are returning to their car. As soon as the men leave the site, Delta Force will mirror them just to the north. They don't want to fall in behind them in case there is a gun fight, fearing they might accidentally start shooting the SEALs.

McCullum is intensely pacing back and forth like a caged tiger. Spencer is now standing within inches of the TV watching the action. The satellite has panned out, so they can now see all the men on the ground. The three men in the site have completed their work and have regrouped for the walk back to the car. The SEALs are now lying in wait.

"Here we go," says Spencer.

McCullum stops pacing and approaches the TV. Reardon is now also up. Peterson continues to stoically sit in front of his computer. Spencer is starting to shiver with anticipation. The gap between the terrorists and the SEALs is less than 50 yards. The three men appear completely oblivious to the fact that they are walking into a group of men that will kill them without hesitation. The SEALs are being given orders to slowly move left, so the men will walk into the heart of the 12-man team. The SEALs are belly down in foot high grass. The men are 15 yards away ... ten yards away.

"I can't take this." Spencer turns her head for a moment, and then turns back, mesmerized by the glowing images on the screen.

The SEALs are in a semi-circle, perfectly positioned. Five yards ... the men now enter the semi-circle. In a flash twelve men pop up, converge on the three unsuspecting men, and are suddenly down on the ground. The Delta Force team comes running in for support. By the time they arrive, the three men have been searched and their hands are secured behind their backs.

"We have three. All alive, no injuries," reports the Gold leader.

There is a sudden cheer over the intercom and McCullum pumps his fist. Spencer turns and gives Reardon a big hug. He is slow to lift his arms, caught off guard by the sudden hug. Spencer's face is glowing as she pulls back.

"I told you we'd catch a break," Spencer says excitedly.

"Yes, I guess we did," Reardon says with little enthusiasm. He doesn't want to remind her that this is only one of many terrorist groups roaming the country.

"Yes! We finally have a few of these bastards," proclaims McCullum.

"Choppers are 15 minutes out," comes a voice over the intercom.

McCullum finally sits down and leans back with a huge smile on his face. Reardon and Spencer follow his lead. They continue to listen to the comms. They hear the SEALs preparing the terrorists for transport as the choppers land, and all the soldiers are loaded on board. The last thing they hear is *choppers away*. The main radio operator signs off, and the feed to Peterson's computer goes blank. All they can assume is that these guys are going to an undisclosed location and may never be heard from again.

"OK, there's nothing else we can do tonight. Everyone, go home and get some sleep." McCullum leaves the room.

"Oh, my God! I can't believe we got these guys," Spencer says while looking at Reardon. He still looks sullen. He needs a drink.

"Yes, this is good news. I'm just tired. I'm going to take off."

"Let me give you a ride."

"No, it's OK, I'll catch a cab."

"I won't take no for an answer."

"Fine." Reardon just isn't in the mood for a discussion.

Twenty minutes later Reardon is walking up his steps. Spencer dutifully waits to make sure he gets in and sees a light before she drives off. The first thing Reardon does is crack open a beer. He finishes that off and has a shot of whiskey before falling into bed.

Day 90

The next morning, Reardon comes into the office at just after 11 o'clock. So far, the arrest of the three terrorists remains a closely guarded secret. They don't want to tip their hand before they have a chance to debrief the captured terrorists. So far, the four of them are the only ones in the office that know about the capture last night. It's all Spencer can do to contain her excitement. Reardon is quietly sitting and watching the news. They are still waiting for any news of today's attack. If they are lucky, today's attack was going to be carried out by the guys they just caught. Moments later, McCullum walks in and slams the door.

"You won't believe it!"

"What?" asks Spencer. McCullum is clearly irate.

"We got the wrong guys!"

"What do you mean the wrong guys?"

"These are some nut ball eco-terrorists."

"What do you mean? We caught them red handed."

"I just got off the phone with the director. These guys cracked after 10 minutes of interrogation. They were texting their leader who lives in Vermont with their change of plans. The FBI in Vermont just picked him up this morning. They are members of the Earth Liberation Freedom Society or some idiot name like that. They were using all the attacks as cover for this attack. When they searched the guy's house in Vermont, they found plans for five more attacks over the next couple of weeks. They figured this would be the perfect cover."

"Well, that explains why the attacks were against two different kinds of targets," interjects Reardon.

"What?"

"So far, all the attacks are related each day, planes, factories, overpasses, whatever."

"Yeah," McCullum says not caring at this moment. McCullum paces for a few moments. "This puts us back to square one. We've got nothing!"

McCullum walks out of the conference room. Everyone is crestfallen. They really thought they had something. This would be the thread that unravels their whole plan. Instead, nothing.

Washington, D.C.

The president is notified in the middle of the night as soon as the interrogators discover the truth. He was in bed but wasn't able to sleep. This is the most disappointing piece of news he has ever received. After the sudden elation of the capture, only to find out hours later, it was all for naught.

In the meantime, the search continues. Word of the capture quickly spreads among the top leaders of the intelligence agencies along with the news that it's the wrong guys. As a result, the NSA and CIA continue to relentlessly look for a link between the Russians and their spies in Afghanistan. They are meticulously combing through their records from four to six years ago, and the trail has gone cold. At that time, our agencies paid little attention to the Russians. They learn some interesting and utterly useless information. At this point, it is ancient history as far as the spy business is concerned. They can't find any link between the liaison officers at Reardon's camp and the Russians. The lack of evidence is not proof that no link exists. The president is provided a full report. He is still deflated from last night and is frustrated that this report provides no conclusive link between Reardon and the Russians – or any group for that matter. The president continues to obsess over a single word: *Who?*

The president is coming close to cracking under the pressure. News finally leaks out that copycat attackers were caught last night in South Dakota, and the news agencies go crazy for about two hours recounting the story. However, people quickly lose interest because it is not the *real* terrorists.

To add insult to injury, the president is getting hammered in the media with calls to stabilize the financial markets. What can he realistically do? The S&P, Dow, NYSE, and Nasdaq continue to operate on limited hours doing everything they can do to keep the markets from collapsing. Thousands of stocks that were trading above $10 a share are now penny stocks. The president is thinking back to the catastrophe in April, 2013, when hackers broke into the Associated Press newsfeed and put out a bogus report that the White House was bombed and the President was injured. That single report caused the Dow to drop 145 points in two minutes, and the S&P lost over $136 billion in the same period. In hindsight, that was easy to deal with. The markets rebounded within an hour, and life moved on. Now it is one unrelenting hellish day after another. The market cap of the Dow has plummeted 65% from $5.2 trillion to just over $1.8 trillion over the last three months. Nasdaq has dropped 67% from $8.5 trillion to just above $2.7 trillion. The NYSE has tanked as well, dropping from $16.6 trillion to $3.4 trillion. An entire generation of people has lost nearly all their retirement savings in only three months. The losses far exceed all stock market crashes combined and make the Great Depression look like a distant ripple on hot asphalt. The unemployment rate is expected to reach 15% in the next month. No amount of emergency bailout money can stem the tide.

Day 99

Dow Jones Industrial Average
7,079.29
Total decline: 64.9%
Total loss: $3.37 Trillion

Nasdaq
1,857.46
Total decline: 67.3%
Total loss: $5.72 Trillion

Reardon once again finds himself staring at Spencer's list on the monitor. He scarcely believes nine days have passed except for the pile of cans and bottles strewn about his floor as he walked out of his place this morning. This is not unusual; however, his landlady came in and cleaned his place up about eight days ago. This was a first. He has been practically living at the office but still been finding the time to drink himself to sleep. Spencer is blankly staring at the list on her screen and tapping her finger on the base of her computer. It is a surprisingly quiet morning. It started off with a quiet cab ride to the office. The roads only have about half the normal traffic for a weekday. It's almost eerie, but this is not unusual based on what Reardon has seen going on across the nation. People continue to wait for news of the attack and then rush out to live their lives. Obviously, most people are still going into work but with the shocking impact on the economy, many stores and other businesses are telling people to stay home. Everyone is wondering if the attackers have something big planned for Day 100. The tone in the office is best described as catatonic. For over a week, it's almost like everyone is stoned on acid and blindly staring at their monitor waiting for the screen to begin morphing into a serpent or a disturbing clown head. McCullum has sequestered himself in his office for the last five days. Peterson is occasionally seen dashing in or out of his office.

Spencer and Reardon have been just hanging out in the conference room all day for over a week. It reminds him of their long days on the stakeouts. They are not accomplishing anything meaningful, but they both find comfort in their time together. They spend most of the day just watching daytime television and talking about what else they could possibly find to attack. They throw out a couple dozen ideas every day, and they're always wrong. Spencer came closest to a guess when she said they have not blown up any bridges for a while, and then yesterday, another bridge was blown up. Reardon gave her credit for that. It's a morose game, but it's all they have to keep themselves busy. All the fun they used to experience on their stakeouts is long gone because these people are slowly destroying America one day at a time. The time they're spending together now is the equivalent of comfort food. It's just something they both need to feel good. Good is not even the right word, just to make them feel like they can survive the day. They are quietly awaiting news on the Day 99 attack. At just after 4 o'clock they get the news, drones with explosives blew holes in the roofs of two chicken processing plants. People can now get on with their day. They can quickly go shopping and run errands before they once again go into hiding and wait for the next day's attack.

Day 90 – 99 Attacks

Day	Attack
90	H and D on Hollywood sign destroyed, California
91	Fermentation tanks destroyed in 9 micro-breweries Milwaukee, WI Omaha, Nebraska Boulder, CO
92	Kentucky Derby, Preakness, and Belmont race tracks damaged
93	Front door of The Alamo destroyed, San Antonio, Texas
94	Front entrances to bowling alleys and movie theaters destroyed Stillwater, Oklahoma Pueblo, Colorado Duluth, Minnesota Conway, Arkansas Montpelier, Vermont Waterbury, Connecticut
95	Crane cab destroyed at shipyards Copper Harbor, Michigan Portland, Maine Wilmington, NC
96	Front doors of large home improvement stores destroyed Norfolk, Virginia Cincinnati, Ohio Plano, Texas Tucson, Arizona
97	Jim Beam rack house blown up destroying 2000 barrels of Bourbon, Clermont, Kentucky
98	Highway 20 bridge leading to Whidbey Island Naval station destroyed, Oak Harbor, Washington
99	Chicken processing plant explosions, Albertville, Alabama; Luverne, Minnesota

Day 100

For people like me, who have blocked out a chunk of
their past, you wonder - if you open that door, if you
walk into that room of your memories, what will happen?
Will it destroy you or will it make you stronger?
Tim Daly

The morning sun comes through a slit in the curtains and hits Reardon in the face. The gleaming light is just enough to wake him. He reflexively stretches and then rubs his hands on his face to shake off the night. Reardon rolls over and slowly gets out of bed. He managed to control his drinking to a certain degree last night, so he is waking up with only a mild throbbing headache. He looks at the clock. 8:34. He slowly saunters into the living room for the TV. As he flips it on the newscaster is discussing the weather for the day and is reminding people that the water restrictions are still in place. The city is still working out plans on when to shut down the Delaware Aqueduct to assess the damage. Repairs to the Catskill Aqueduct continue to take longer than expected as debris is still making its way down towards the pumps. The good news is that the city is optimistic that the water supply will return to 100% within the week. That is, of course, until they need to shut down the Delaware Aqueduct, cutting the city's water supply in half while they make repairs. Other than that, it looks like it will be another beautiful day in New York City. They take a short commercial break as a celebrity actress shows how her new line of makeup helps you have flawless, wrinkle-free skin.

> Good morning, and welcome back, I'm Alicia Washburn. So far, this morning we have no reports of any attacks on what is Day 100. Police are on high alert fearing a particularly big attack may occur on this one-hundredth day.

Reardon rolls his eyes at this comment. How could police be on *higher* alert? The country has already been on *highest* alert for months. What's next *super-duper highest alert*? This reminds him of Star Trek when Capt. Kirk would want to push the engines to 110%. He always thought *how can you push them past 100%*? Reardon takes the time to retrieve a six-pack of beer from the fridge.

With pleas from the President, clergy people, and civic leaders, attacks on Muslims have subsided. However, they remain a concern. The President continues to remind people that none of the attacks have been linked to the Middle East or people of Middle Eastern descent.

At this moment, Reardon's phone buzzes. He is not paying that close attention and misses the buzz because he's cracking open a can of beer at that exact moment. Then another buzz catches his attention.

"Good morning," the second buzz asks. "How are you today?"

Reardon quickly picks up his phone and sees that it is once again from an unknown number. He knows Peterson is already tracking this, so there is no reason to call it in.

"I'm fine, you dickhead!"
"Such language. Is this how friends speak?"
"You're no friend of mine."
"Perhaps we can change all that. I would like to meet today."

Reardon sits back reeling from such a comment. There is no way this guy is going to just meet with him, not without a cost. However, Reardon wants to keep the conversation going. Just then, another text comes in from Spencer.

"Keep him texting."
"OK," he quickly replies.

Returning to the original thread.

"Yes, I would like to meet. When and where?"
"I will contact you later. Bye for now."

Fifteen seconds later, the phone rings.

"Crap! I tried to keep him on longer."
"It doesn't matter. The signal was coming from a phone in Nevada, but it was a number from our list. That means someone turned on the phone, sent the text, and shut it off. The phone is on the outskirts of Phoenix and only picked up by a single tower. We can't triangulate a position. By the time we track it down, he'll be long gone."
"Did the text come directly from that phone?"
"I don't know yet. I will need some time," Peterson replies.

"Give me that phone," McCullum barks. "How long before you can get in here?"

"Ah, give me an hour."

"I'd say be here in 30 minutes, but that won't matter. Just get in here."

Reardon senses an urgency about today and doesn't want to miss a chance to meet this guy if he's being serious. He quickly showers and gets into the office 40 minutes later. As he walks into the conference room, he can feel the palpable tension.

"Reardon, get up here."

The table is covered with a bullet proof vest and two cases of high tech gear. Peterson is quietly working on his computer, and Spencer and McCullum are standing next to a tech.

"How do we plan to handle this if they're serious?" Spencer asks.

"I'm not getting my hopes up. Why would they just open themselves up like this? We still don't have anything on them after 100 days. This would be like just turning themselves in at the local police department," McCullum speculates.

Reardon sits down and leans back. This is the most sober he has been in three months.

"Reardon, if this son of a bitch is really willing to meet, are you up for this?"

"We're not really going to let him meet this guy, are we?" Spencer asks.

"Hell yes, I want this meeting," McCullum replies.

"Yeah, I'm ready for this."

"What if it's a trap?"

"What if it's not? What if he really just wants to turn himself in?" McCullum asks.

"You don't believe that. They're up to something," Spencer states.

"Yes, and we are going to figure out what that is."

"Send me instead," Spencer pleads.

Reardon stares at McCullum with steely cold eyes, "I need to see this through. I need to see if this is really Abdul."

"So now you think Abdul is alive?"

"I don't know what to think anymore. All I know is that this needs to end." Reardon stares at the table. "Did we figure out if the text came directly from the phone?"

"Yeah, we did. Someone was just texting back and forth what you and the other texter were typing. This number was also on our list. However, it was also shut off as soon as the texts stopped."

"Where did the texts originate?"

"In a rural area about 75 miles due west of here. Outside Bridgewater, New Jersey. Agents are on the way, but we don't expect to find anything there either."

"OK. So, he's close."

"Yeah."

McCullum retreats to his office for a call. Spencer and Reardon banter back and forth for a few minutes while Peterson is clicking away on his computer. Suddenly Reardon's phone dings. He pulls the phone from his pocket.

"Another unknown number."

"What's it say?" Spencer asks.

"I would like to meet at 2:30 if that is OK?"

"Yes, just tell me where?" Reardon replies.

Peterson is already tracing the text messages. McCullum walks back in at that moment and sees Reardon staring at his phone.

"Be in Morristown, New Jersey at 2:30. See you there. Have your phone with you. Good day."

"The signal just went dead." Peterson turns. "It was in the Seattle area and on the move. Another person re-texting for your friend."

"*Good day.* It's like he just set up a time for some tea and crumpets. Peterson, get up a map, where is that?"

A few moments later, Peterson has a map on the monitor.

"Here's Morristown. It's about a 90 minute drive from here. It's about 30 miles north of Bridgewater. Looks like he'll be heading north."

McCullum starts to pace. He does not even care about tracking the phones anymore. He just wants to see this play out – he wants to get this guy - today.

"Peterson, that doesn't give us much time, and I don't want to screw this up. Call down and get the mobile comm van on the road now. Have them set up about two miles outside of town." McCullum stands and stares out the window for a moment. "Spencer, call the Jersey office and tell them we're coming. Give them all the details. Tell them I want three choppers in the air, each one carrying a tactical assault team. I'm going to call the director." McCullum turns to the tech. "Get him wired up."

McCullum, Spencer, and Peterson all leave as the tech approaches Reardon. Thirty minutes later McCullum finishes a call with the director and the head of the Jersey field office. The director makes it clear that McCullum is in charge and that the Jersey office is there to assist in every conceivable way. He says it in such a way that there will be no hesitation with any form of help. The Jersey Highway Patrol is now also on alert and will take up positions around Morristown in marked and unmarked cars. At just after 1:15, Reardon is in a chopper with McCullum, Spencer, and Peterson to meet up with the comm van near Morristown. The chopper lands in a field just, outside town. They immediately transfer to the comm van. Ten minutes later a car arrives for Reardon to use for his meeting. The three surveillance choppers are already in the air circling. McCullum has a direct feed to their cameras and begins asking for a status. All report nothing out of the ordinary, but then again, it's not like they will see a big blinking neon sign saying *meet here*. All they can do is wait.

"I don't like this. There is no way this guy is just going to have you meet on the corner of Elm Street and Main."

"That's probably why he made sure Reardon has his phone," Spencer comments.

"Peterson how much time?"

"43 minutes."

Spencer and Reardon are standing at the back of the comm van. Twenty minutes pass. They are both making casual conversation.

"So, how is Roger?"

"Oh, he broke that off with me a month ago. You know, the hours."

"Sorry, I should have asked sooner."

"Not your fault. A lot's been goin' on. I simply never had any time to see him. He said he understood, but at this rate, I might never have time for him."

"It still sucks."

"Yeah ... next time ... besides it saved me the trouble of breaking up with him."

"What was it this time?"

"I hadn't figured that out yet. He seemed like a really normal guy. But if I could guess, maybe his toes were too hairy or his fifth cousin twice removed is a xenophobe. Don't worry, I would've found something. I always do."

They stand quietly for a few more moments. Suddenly Reardon's phone buzzes.

"Start heading north on 287."
McCullum's head pops out of the van. "Reardon, get going."

Reardon and Spencer walk over to the car and turn to face each other.

"Noah, you don't need to do this. It might be a trap."
"I need to do this. I need to do anything I can to stop this. I feel responsible. I told Abdul how to do all this."
"So, do you finally believe it's Abdul?"
"Abdul or someone he recruited to do all this. This is all just out of hand and needs to stop. The world needs to be a better place."
"Noah … this is not your fault." Spencer starts to tear up. "Noah…" She does not know what else to say. "So …"
"So …"
"Be careful." Spencer gives Reardon a rib crushing hug.
"Laura, it'll be OK. I know what I'm doing." He pauses for a moment and pulls back to meet her eyes. "My failures don't bother me. Regret is what haunts me in the night. I need to do this."

Spencer pulls back and stands in front of him. She has a tear running down each cheek. Reardon lifts up his finger and brushes away each tear. He then steps bac, opens the door, and is about to slide into the car.

"It'll be OK. You were the best partner I ever had…"

Reardon slides into the car and starts the engine. McCullum has been watching from the doorway of the comm truck.

"Spencer, let's go!"

They do a final comm check with Reardon just before he drives away. There is a second car for Peterson to use. A minute later, Reardon is in the car and driving. Peterson is following in the chase car, and McCullum and Spencer are riding in the comm van following a couple miles behind.

Five minutes later, another text comes in from a different number.

"Take off-ramp 147 and wait on the ramp. Text me when you are there."

Reardon arrives at the off-ramp at 2:17. He texts that he is there and waits. Peterson and the comm van stop a mile short of the off-ramp. McCullum calls the three choppers asking if they see any cars parked within a half mile of the off-ramp. They report over a dozen cars. Most are sitting in the parking lot of a small restaurant right next to the off-ramp. McCullum has confirmation that the state police are ready to close all the northbound entrance ramps at his command and shut down the highway at a moment's notice. McCullum is staring at his watch. Spencer is nervously swaying back and forth. Minutes seem like hours.

"I just got a text from another number. It's telling me to start driving."
"OK, start driving," McCullum orders.

As soon as Reardon starts to drive, McCullum orders the comm van to park at the off-ramp near the small restaurant, and Peterson pulls in just behind the comm van. There are hundreds of cars on the highway traveling in each direction. McCullum is on edge. This is just what he feared. This is a worst-case scenario. They have no real control of the scene because the *scene* is now hurtling down the highway at 60 MPH. They have no idea who they are looking for, and there are too many civilians in the mix. After three agonizing minutes, McCullum orders Peterson to get on the highway and stay back at least two miles.

Another text comes in. "Let me know the next mile marker you pass."

Reardon travels about a half mile before he sees mile marker 161 and texts that back. McCullum is frantically watching all three monitors in the van, each chopper showing a slightly different angle. Cars traveling at all speeds. One car tucks in behind Reardon for a quarter mile. McCullum is about to call in the police but then it pulls out and passes him moments later. He is finally thinking *calm down* I just need to let this play out.

"Where are you now?"
"163"
"Stop at 164 and get out."
Reardon speaks up, "I'm stopping at mile marker 164."

McCullum orders one of the choppers to fly ahead and get eyes on the mile marker. Within a minute Reardon slows and stops at 164. He steps out of the car and leans against the trunk of the car. Less than 45 seconds later, another car slows and pulls up in front of Reardon's car. McCullum is now bursting with anticipation. Is this really the guy, or some poor schmuck pulling over to help Reardon, or is this all just a ruse? The car is a grey 4-door sedan with slightly tinted windows. Reardon sees the driver wearing a baseball cap and dark glasses. Reardon talks so they can hear him in the command center.

"I can't ID the driver, male, ball cap, dark glasses, beard. I'm going to approach the car."

Spencer is anxiously watching the three monitors. Reardon walks up next to the car on the passenger side and waits a moment. The sound of cars whizzing by at 70 MPH overshadows the slight hum of the window lowering. Reardon leans down and looks in through the window. They have no low angle shot of the driver. The three helicopters now have tight shots of Reardon and the car sitting before him. The driver removes his glasses and looks at Reardon.

"Say nothing. Leave your gun and any listening devices on the ground, and then get in the car."

A moment later Reardon places his left hand flat on the roof as he stands up. McCullum is mumbling to himself.

"Yes," McCullum pumps his fist.

McCullum's excitement is now palpable. Reardon and McCullum worked out a signal, if Reardon has never seen the driver before he would put both hands on top of the car. If the person was someone he knew from his time in Afghanistan, he would put his right hand on the car. And if it is that son of a bitch Abdul, he would put his left hand on the car.

"Yes, we've got this bastard! There is no way he is going to get out of this," McCullum says excitedly.

McCullum orders the three choppers to maintain a visual on the car at all times. At the same time, Reardon is removing his sidearm and ear piece with a wire running to the transmitter unit, just as they had planned. After slowly placing them on the ground, he opens the door and sits down. The dropped ear piece is a ruse to distract the driver from the transmitter in Reardon's front suit pocket. A moment later, the car starts to drive away. McCullum immediately starts barking orders into his comm.

"Peterson, can you hear me?"

"Yes, sir."

"Go get Reardon's gun immediately and call back when you've got it. The rest of you cars – GO!"

Peterson has been maintaining the two mile gap. When Reardon pulled over so did Peterson. They figured whoever was coming to pick up Reardon would see the car, but who cares at this point in time. Peterson speeds down the highway towards Reardon's car. McCullum now turns his attention to the monitors in front of him. McCullum is watching the live feed from the three choppers. Reardon hears the first words coming from the car.

"Hello my good…"

There is a scratching noise and then the mic goes dead.

"What the hell just happened?" McCullum barks at the tech running the sound system and monitors.

"I don't know, the line just went dead," replies the tech with strained fear in his voice.

"Dammit! Stupid worthless mics! Get it back!"

"I'm trying."

"Could he have a jammer in the car?"

"Possibly."

"Well, get it back!" McCullum is livid that they lost audio.

Spencer and McCullum are now anxiously watching the three monitors as the car hurdles down the highway. Calls are coming in from three unmarked pursuit cars that took off the moment McCullum roared "GO!" The cars are racing down the highway at over 90 miles per hour closing the gap with Reardon. Two minutes have passed, and still no audio. McCullum orders the pursuit cars to stay back at least a quarter mile after they have closed the gap. He wants to see where this will go. He wants Abdul alive and doesn't want to pressure him. Police units are shutting down all the on ramps so they can control the flow of traffic and reduce the chances of innocent people getting hurt if this turns into a fire fight. Another minute passes, and the car is moving along like it's on a nice leisurely Sunday drive out in the country. Another minute passes, but this one seems like an hour is slowly ticking by. Spencer anxiously watches and is wringing her hands together as her stress level builds. In an instant, the car transforms into a blinding flash of light on all three monitors. The explosion startles everyone. Spencer's face is aghast with horror as she opens her mouth wide, covers her mouth with both hands, and instantly starts crying.

McCullum is also in stunned disbelief. The flaming car rolls across two lanes of traffic into the center ditch and abruptly rolls to a stop. A few moments pass before McCullum is jerked back to reality.

"All units close in. Shut down the highway," McCullum instinctively orders without thinking. "Get a fire truck and ambulance on the scene immediately." He turns to the driver of the comm truck, "Let's get going!"

The explosion rocked the highway, causing three cars to swerve wildly. Luckily none of the cars were close enough to suffer any severe damage. The drivers were simply shaken up and came to a stop out of sheer instinct, not yet comprehending what just occurred. McCullum knows Reardon is dead and sending in the ambulance for this is a waste – he needs a hearse. Spencer is continuing to weep. McCullum steps closer to Spencer and puts his arm around her. She leans into his shoulder and continues to cry.

Epilog

It is not until we have lost everything that
we are free to do anything.
Chuck Palahniuk

Five minutes earlier.

Reardon gets in the car and closes the door.

"Hello my good…"

Reardon turns to Abdul with his finger to his lips to keep Abdul from saying anything more. Reardon reaches into his front suit pocket and pulls out a stamp size transmitter and cracks it in half.

"OK, we're free to talk." Reardon says.
"Hello my good friend it is done. How are you?"
"I'm fine given the circumstances. Are you still sure you want to do this?"
"Yes."
"The irony is I will die a terrorist and you will die a hero."
"There is no hero in this, only a lesson, a lesson that will hopefully not be soon forgotten. Are the others ready to continue the work?"
"Yes, they will start on schedule. Are you ready?"
"Yes." Reardon lifts up a small black box with a switch. "What's the timer set for?"
"Two minutes."
"Thank you for doing this." He flips the switch.
"Anything for you, my good friend."

Reardon then reaches into his inside jacket pocket and pulls out his FBI medal for Meritorious Achievement and just stares at it. Abdul glances over and sees the medal in his hand but says nothing. Abdul knows the guilt Reardon feels for earning this award. He remembers going to Reardon's room after the award ceremony all those years ago and hearing Reardon weep uncontrollably. This is when he knew Reardon was a good man and would do anything for him. For the next two minutes, Reardon and Abdul drive in silence until the car transforms into a brilliant glowing flash of light on four wheels hurtling down the highway at 60 MPH.

Two hours later, the FBI extracts a fireproof metal box from the trunk and pries it open. The letter reads:

Dear Mr. President,

> I have done what I have done to teach the American public and its Government a lesson. The United States government has been interfering with the lives of people around the world to pursue its own self-interests and greed for over 100 years. Now it is time for the world to push back and the American people to take responsibility for the actions of their government. It is time to stop the government from interfering around the world and look inward, to protect and save the American people.

> I lost my wife and child because of war and decided to commit my life to ending terrorism in the only way I knew how, through terrorism. Violence appears to be the only language you understand. I am truly sorry for each death. That was unintentional. However, the government uses the more innocuous, collateral damage to describe the death of innocents. The American public must understand death is death. There are no innocent bystanders. If the U.S. Government does not curtail its oversees activities, then the reign of terror will continue in the fall. You must issue a statement within the next sixty days apologizing for America's destructive policies and outlining a new path for future conduct around the world.

> The longer you pursue your intrusive policies around the world, the longer you will need to defend yourself against terrorism. You've been fighting against the world since World War II. Ask yourself how it is working.

> We are already here and awaiting the announcement. If you choose to ignore this warning, the attacks will commence in 60 days. The choice is yours, so choose wisely.

No one realizes the note was actually written by Reardon. He sent it to Abdul over nine months ago through the U.S. mail. They secretly communicated through the mail for the first 12 months after Abdul arrived in the United States. This is the last letter he sent to Abdul before he went deep undercover to execute Reardon's plan. The president receives a copy of the letter and discusses it with his staff. Of course, they do not plan to ever apologize or change because the United States does not negotiate with terrorists. The president knows how to react to terrorists trying to destroy the country, but how should the president react when the terrorists are trying to save the country? What the president does not realize is that he is actually negotiating with patriots, with people who love the American dream and are willing to die *for* America in order to save it.

January 9, 2012 – New York

Reardon awakes to a phone call at 2:28 a.m. and the caller introduces herself as Julie Benson with the New York highway patrol. Instinctively Reardon rolls his feet off the edge of the bed and sits up in a haze.

"Is this Mr. Noah Reardon?"

Reardon is still half asleep trying to register the call and attempting to understand her words.

"Huh? What? Who is this?"
"This is Julie Benson with the New York highway patrol. Am I speaking with Mr. Noah Reardon?
"Ah yes."
"I have some terrible news, your wife and child were killed about two hours ago."
"What? No, you must have the wrong person. They were staying with her mother last night. I spoke to them just last night."
"No, sir, I'm afraid they were killed by a drunk driver on Highway 9, just north of Crontonville. The driver was heading northbound in the southbound lane and hit them head-on. I'm sorry for your loss."
"No, you must have the wrong person. They were staying with her mother."

At that moment, he flashed to the drunken conversation he had with Sara just hours before, the despair in his voice, the crying. He remembered she was scared. He talked about how he wanted the pain to end and if she is OK with that. He then realized she must have decided to come home early to be with him, fearing he might do something stupid, something unimaginable. The officer continued speaking, but Reardon placed the handset back on the receiver. Tears start to run down his face as he stood and stumbled into the bathroom. His knee nearly failed him twice, and he reached for something to balance himself. In this shocking, indescribable moment Reardon stood in front of the bathroom mirror and wiped the tears from his eyes. Looking up, now for the first time he understood the look in the disheveled hopeless faces of the Afghanis, the ones he knew had lost family, had lost everything.

For the first time in that moment he realized Abdul was right. He could never understand true despair, but he does now. He knew he could no longer sit idly by and watch more lives lost. In one brilliant, and simultaneously horrendous moment, an idea crystallized in his mind. The idea was more horrible than he could have imagined just moments ago, and yet at the same time, it is now perfectly reasonable in his moment of despair. He saw a path forward in his mind, the only path to vindicate himself for what he had done and to provide some semblance of meaning for his life. His body was enveloped within an all-encompassing force, and in that moment of clarity, a sudden chill passed through his body and then a wave of heat. His knuckles turned white from gripping the edges of the sink so tightly in grief. He realized how all those parents in Afghanistan felt when they discovered their family dead. That they would fight, and who they would fight against, depended on who did the killing. At that moment, he knew he would reach out to his good friend and hatch this plot to teach Americans a lesson about destruction and the shocking loss that can only come from true fear. Fear beyond a single event, viewing every stranger as a potential threat, and knowing the actions of your government are what pushed people to the edge, to lash out in the only way they could. Destruction was the only way to rebirth. He was able to justify this because he would have rules. He would do it the right way with minimal casualties. His is a lesson, not a death sentence.

February 9, 2011 – Afghanistan

Reardon and Abdul are heading back to the compound after a long day on the road. The trip was a bust, four hours of driving for nothing. As they get closer to the compound, Reardon begins a serious conversation, one he has been hesitant to bring up.

"There is something I want to talk to you about."
"Yes, what is it?"
"You know how we are losing ground here as we withdraw troops."
"Yes."
"Well, I'm starting to get some strange questions from my superiors that give me the impression our camp will get closed down soon. Maybe not the whole camp right away, but I think they plan to pull out the FBI agents. They feel like we've done enough out here, and it's time to concentrate our efforts around Kabul."
"That is not surprising, for I agree."
"You don't seem too surprised or upset."

"We both knew this was temporary. This is the history of Afghanistan. Conquering legions come in and then are slowly beaten back. It's been like this since the time of Genghis Khan. Guerrilla warfare is a hopeless endeavor to overcome."

"What will you do when we leave?"

"The only thing I can do, go into hiding. There's a price on all of our heads."

"I can try to get you a ticket to America."

"Thank you my friend, but my home is here."

"But you'll die here."

"We all must die sometime, this is nothing to fear."

"Yes, but things are going to hell fast."

Reardon is surprised that they are back at the compound so quickly. He now realizes he should've started the conversation thirty minutes earlier. He slows his vehicle about a quarter mile from the gate and stops, waving the escort Humvee up. It is just past eight.

"Hey, you guys go on ahead, we are in the middle of a conversation."
"OK."

The Humvee continues to the gate as Reardon and Abdul sit in the idling car.

"I'm not kidding. The shit is about to hit the fan."

"Yes, I know, but fleeing to America will not solve my problems. My home is here."

Reardon happens to be looking at the four soldiers as they get out of the Humvee and are passing in front of the hooch on the way to their barracks. In an instant, the night sky is transformed into a giant fireball. The four soldiers are gone in an instant. The fireball reaches 50 feet into the air. The guard and his tiny hut at the front gate are flattened. Flying debris covers the compound.

"OH MY GOD!!!" Reardon exclaims.

Reardon and Abdul are in stunned silence. A couple dozen soldiers come rushing up from the rear of the camp with guns in hand. There is nothing they can do. There are clearly no survivors.

"You need to get out of here," Reardon states as he quickly looks at Abdul.

Abdul is still in stunned silence. Reardon reaches over and shakes Abdul to bring him back to the moment.

"You need to get out of here. Now!"
"What do you want me to do?"
"Just get out and run. I will tell them you died in the explosion. That will give you a head start and hopefully keep you off the Taliban's hit list if they think you're dead."
"No, I must go in to see if any survived."
"Look, you can see from here. They're all gone."
"But I must go in."
"No, just go!"

Abdul sits and ponders Reardon's request, still stunned from the explosion.

"Hurry, you must just go. Here take this. Contact me when you are safe, you know my number."

Reardon hands Abdul the bags from the back. Abdul reaches forward and pulls Reardon into an embrace across the seat.

"Thank you for all you tried to do here, my good friend."
"No, thank you. Now go!"

Abdul slips out the side of the car and disappears into the night. Reardon starts to well up as a tear runs down his cheek. He puts the car into drive and pulls up next to the flaming guard hut. He can see the guard is dead, pieces of flying shrapnel cut into his neck and torso. The hut is on fire, and the compound is in chaos. Reardon reports that Abdul stayed at camp that day because he was not feeling well and died in the explosion. All the witnesses to his lie had just been vaporized, and no one questioned his report. Why would they?

May 19, 2012 – Greece

Reardon is walking down a small dusty back alley between two buildings that open to a quiet square. He crosses the square to enter another alley that opens into a tiny square. He is well off the beaten path, and there are no tourists in sight. He walks over to a small table at a café in a quiet corner. Abdul is there waiting for him. Abdul stands, and they embrace.

"Hello, brother," Reardon says, and they release and sit.

"It is good to see you once again, brother."

This is the first time they have met face to face since Reardon left Afghanistan. They don't even discuss the bombing at the hooch. Abdul spent the next year trying to figure out who did the bombing. He quietly asked around trying to figure out who planted the bomb. He had to be careful to never reveal his own identity or let anyone know he worked for the Americans, knowing it would be an instant death sentence. He would keep Reardon up to date on his progress. They finally concluded it was likely a liaison officer, possibly the one who worked with Josh. However, that is still pure speculation because they have no proof. The truth died that night in the hooch.

They start with casual conversation, each discussing what has transpired in their lives over the last three months. Reardon slowly turns the conversation towards his plan. Reardon begins to explain his idea, and Abdul just sits there becoming increasingly uncomfortable. Reardon makes it clear that this is the only way America will learn its lesson. Reardon finally pauses and looks deeply into Abdul's eyes.

"This is insane," Abdul plainly states.

"Perhaps an insane act is the only thing that we can do in this world to help make things normal once again. I can think of nothing else." Reardon pauses. "I have nothing left," Reardon adds with deep despair in his voice.

"I also have nothing left, but is this the path you must choose? Is this how you plan to honor your daughter and wife?"

"I have to do something meaningful with the time I have left."

Abdul argues, "This is absurd. Despite all the terrorists' propaganda and railing against the United States, it is not the people who should suffer. It is your government that does the damage. The people are just pawns."

"Yes, but the pawns elect the government, and they will never just change. They need a catalyst that will cause a revolt."

"It's still not fair to the American people."

"Is what we did fair to your people? Nearly all of them were innocent bystanders."

"Doing this will not bring any of them back."

"This is true. I'm looking forward trying to save countless lives. The U.S.'s policy of sticking its nose into where it doesn't belong will never stop until we feel the pain."

"What you say might be true, but we both know killing to save lives is an endless fate."

"Our goal is not death; our goal is a lesson. A deeply needed and long overdue lesson."

"Don't kid yourself, people will die. Collateral damage, as you say is certain."

"Yes, it is certain, but it's not the goal. That's why this is different, why it will work."

"The death of your wife and child is what's driving this insanity my good friend. I now see despair, true despair, you now understand it."

Reardon slams down his fist. The waitress looks up from a distance staring for a moment before returning to her work.

"I just can't go on like this! I have nothing left, they were everything to me. Now, I want to do something with the time I have left, something meaningful."

Reardon continues to argue and debate Abdul for another thirty minutes. Finally, Reardon pauses for a moment and stares deeply into Abdul's eyes.

"Afghanistan took away my humanity, and the death of my family took away my life. I want to do something meaningful with the time I have left."

Reardon went to Afghanistan to save lives. Over time, he started to feel like he was the terrorist. It was easy to justify that the things he was doing were things he had to do. But that was not the reality. It was something he chose to do on behalf of the U.S. government. One man's terrorist is another man's hero. This was the one thing he could never straighten out in his mind. This is ultimately *the* secret that haunted him in his dreams. Was he a hero or terrorist ... possibly both? So rather than wonder anymore, he decided to become a terrorist on behalf of his government in order to help save America in the only meaningful way he could. He learned that violence never provides the answer, but he decides to use violence in order to make his point. The ultimate contradiction. It was the same cold, calculating math he used in Afghanistan. Is he willing to sacrifice a few hundred for 330 million? His all-consuming thought was *they made me a terrorist, so I will embrace what I have become.*

Abdul leans back in his chair, never breaking his gaze with Reardon, as he contemplates this last comment for several moments.

"I will do this for you, but only because I love America and what it stands for, but not for what it does. It will be hard to watch. How will you deal with it?"

"I'll figure that out. You leave that up to me. Even if I beg you to stop, you must keep going. Do you promise me that?"

"OK."

"No, you need to promise. Keep going even if I beg you to stop."

"Yes, I promise. I will contact people that will help with the planning. There are still many of us loyal to America and may help if I make the same impassioned speech you're making now. We'll need dozens of people and years of planning to do it successfully. It will also be easy to recruit radicals to do much of the dirty work. They will be blind to the real purpose of what they are doing."

"Take your time and just let me know when it starts."

"This is an insane and fruitless endeavor. However, I will do this for you."

Reardon and Abdul spend the next hour talking about the logistics of the plan. Reardon provides him with pages of hand written notes outlining various ideas and potential targets. Reardon outlines the first 30 days in great detail. They never discuss specific targets after Day 30 because Reardon does not want to know too much. At the conclusion of their detailed discussion, Reardon stands, prompting Abdul to stand, and they hug.

"This is the last we will speak until it begins."

"As it should be. Good luck brother, and I will see you in the end."

These are two broken souls attempting to make amends for the wrongs they have done.

As Reardon departs, he looks over his shoulder one last time as he sees Abdul turn a corner. Reardon only hopes this can work. He sees no other alternative that will force the politicians to reign in the intelligence agencies and force a hard look at America's policies around the world. Through his perverted world view, this makes sense, in fact it is the only path forward. He has convinced himself that sometimes you need to destroy what you love in order to save it. This meeting is the catalyst that fuels his drive to drink himself into oblivion each day as he awaits the attacks.

Abdul returns home and sets about recruiting former liaisons who, like him, have lost everything. These are Afghanis who are loyal to the ideals America represents, people willing to lay down their life for America. People who know America has lost its way and want to see America return to its greatness and that of being a great protector. As with Abdul, this was the only reason they would help. A perverse form of logic for a perverse world.

One week later...

Spencer is still reeling from the loss of her close friend and mentor. Her place is a mess, and she has been letting the mail pile up for several days. At last, she decides it's time to clean up. As she is cleaning the table, she starts to pile up her mail and tosses junk mail and flyers into her recycle bin. A letter catches her eye. The return address in the upper corner is a single hand written word *Reardon*. She immediately tears into the envelope, pulls out the letter, and begins to read it. She is half-way down the page when she starts to cry.

To my dear sweet Laura,

I don't know how to say this, so I will just say it. In case you have not yet suspected, I am responsible for all that has happened. Abdul and I started planning this over four years ago when I took my trip to Greece. Let me explain why I did what I did. I don't ever expect you to forgive me, but I wanted you to know. I know this is a heavy burden, and you can do as you wish with this letter. My country made me into a terrorist. It happened so slowly over those three years that I did not notice until the end. When those two little girls died, I knew my evolution into a terrorist was complete. Abdul and I are trying to make this better now so future generations do not need to suffer in the future. Perhaps this is a fruitless task, but it was the only thing I could think to do. Since the government ultimately created a terrorist, I felt it was only right to use my new skills to fight against the government in an attempt to stop their reign of terror that has been going on around the world for decades.

My family was everything to me. After I lost my family, I was lost. I chose this path as my road home to them. I don't expect you to ever understand. All I can hope is that you will one day understand and forgive me.

Your friend forever.

Love,
Noah

After completing the letter, she walks into her bathroom, tears the letter into small pieces, and then flushes them down the toilet. A secret she will take to her grave.

Author's Note

I hope you enjoyed reading *100 Days of Terror*.

If you enjoyed this book please…
   …write a great review on Amazon.com and GoodReads so
      the book can start to get noticed – this is really important
   …email/text/Facebook your friends and recommend the book
   …talk to people about it face to face
   …recommend it for your book club

Thanks!

Above all else, this is a story about a man. This is a story about a man broken by war and the loss of his family. A man whose life falls apart in the worst way possible, one piece at a time. His life is full of hope and slowly spirals out of control. He's looking for redemption and meaning but instead follows a path of destruction. In his mind, he has chosen a path to redemption, an unconventional and perverse form of redemption. A man trying to save his country through what he has learned speaking the only language he believes will be heard. He also knows deep down that lessons are soon forgotten.

One man's patriot is another man's terrorist…

Book Club Questions

<u>Warning – Spoiler Alert</u>

Who is your favorite character?

Does Reardon or Abdul have a more realistic world view? How does their world view change over time? What are the key factors that change their point of view?

Did you think Abdul was alive and behind the attacks?

How do you feel about Reardon sending the letter to Spencer confessing to what he did? Should she have turned in the letter to the FBI?

Did you expect Reardon to sober up and turn back into a super-agent?

Did you notice that Reardon confesses several times throughout the book? Pages 55, 141, 158, and, 250.

After initially denying any knowledge of what is happening. Did you also notice that Reardon never lies after Day 30 - instead he withholds the truth?

Did you have any sympathy for Reardon when he said this?
Afghanistan took away my humanity, and the death of my family took away my life. I want to do something meaningful with the time I have left.

What ultimately drove Reardon to do what he did?

Did you suspect Reardon was behind the attacks?

Do you feel Reardon is still a good man at his core?

Is there anything to justify Reardon's actions?

Do you think he believed that he is really trying to do a good thing?

Do you feel the terrorists could evade detection for 100 days? Consider they never attack the same place twice and we have zero idea who is behind the attacks. How do you find 30 or 40 people in 330 million who simply blend in? They could be casually eating at the booth next to you in a restaurant on any given day.

What do you think about how the relationship between Spencer and Reardon changes over the years?

Do you think Spencer would continue to help Reardon and stay loyal?

Do you think Spencer would quietly get Reardon from the drunk tank and just take him home? Is she enabling Reardon?

Were you expecting McCullum to keep his word to Reardon?

How do you think the president would handle these attacks?

Would a nationwide state of emergency be effective?

What else could the government do to catch the terrorists?

Your civil rights ... how far is too far?

Those who would give up essential liberty, to purchase a little temporary safety, deserve neither Liberty nor Safety.
Benjamin Franklin

Is Franklin's comment still relevant today or from a naïve and antiquated past?

How do you define safety and security?

The most important question: Do you trust the government?

How do you feel about National Security Letters (P. 179)?

Would you be willing to have your car stopped at roadblocks and inspected?

Would you be comfortable with the police or military searching your house during a state of emergency?

If the government ordered everyone to temporarily turn in all firearms would you comply?

How many rights are you willing to give up for a perceived sense of safety?

Do you consider your civil rights conditional?

Conditional civil rights – is it a sliding scale:
    If 1 attack – give up 10% of your rights
    If 2 attacks – give up 20% of your rights
    If 10 attacks – give up 80% of your rights

Which rights are you willing to give up first?

If you give up your rights, how do you ensure they come back? Too many countries have entered a state of emergency and never relinquish power until there is a violent uprising.

Consider these scenarios:

There have been no terrorist attacks for over 6 months. You are taking a day trip with your family and driving about 50 miles. Halfway there you are forced to stop because of a roadblock on the highway.

Scenario 1: Two police officers are stopping cars asking people to pop their trunks. You ask why? They say it's a *National Security Issue.* Do you pop your trunk or argue they need a search warrant?

Scenario 2: There are ten heavily armed police with automatic weapons, riot gear, and large intimidating military style vehicles. They demand to search your car. You ask why? They say it's a *National Security Issue.* Do you pop your trunk or argue they need a search warrant?

You're just trying to get from Point A to Point B to have a fun day with your family. How much are you willing to argue? You figure you've done nothing wrong, so you just pop your trunk and quickly move on with your day. You figure, *what's the harm?*

How do you know they are telling the truth?

You figure you have nothing to hide so why not?

I think most people would just say *yes.*

Two weeks later, you are at the grocery store in the parking lot and police in riot gear pop out of large vehicles. Same question – do you let them search your car?

Two weeks later, you are at home, and police in riot gear pop out of large vehicles. Same question – do you let them search your house?

At what point do you start saying *no*?

Now consider the scenario in this book – continuous attacks – do your answers above change or stay the same?

How would you ensure your rights are restored?

Do you think a nationwide state of emergency that includes door to door searches would be effective?

Would you be in favor of a more expansive PATRIOT Act to protect America while further undermining your privacy?

29882945R00150

Made in the USA
Columbia, SC
07 November 2018